DEATH ON THE HAUTE ROUTE

A LENNY SAXON THRILLER

By

Ken Scott

Fortis
Publishing Services

First Edition 2022 Fortis Publishing

ISBN: 978-1-913822-31-6

Fortis Publishing
Kemp House
160 City Road
London
EC1V 2NX

Author's Note

This is my first work of fiction in nearly ten years, but I have been busy on other projects. I have authored, co-authored or ghostwritten nearly forty books, I am a book coach and a literary agent.

Further information at **www.kenscottbooks.com** and follow me on Twitter, @kentheghost

When writing fiction, I like to develop my characters along the lines of real people and I make no apologies in dropping a few non-fictional names in this book and a couple of my real-life heroes too. I am sure they won't mind and may even enjoy their fifteen minutes of fame.

In this novel I have used real places, the actual names of hotels, cafes and campsites but I only say nice things about them so no need to consult your lawyers.

A lot of the action takes place around Zermatt and the police stations of that town and other Swiss Cop Shops too. The police characters mentioned are purely a figment of my imagination and bear no resemblance to any man or woman who has ever worn a Swiss police uniform. Any coincidence is unintentional.

I coincidently started work on my first Lenny Saxon novel at the same time as I was helping an adventurer with her book. She went missing while hiking the French Spanish Pyrenees. As each day passed with no sign of her, along with countless others, I imagined the different scenarios where she would turn up safe and sound and give a logical explanation as to her prolonged absence.

Sadly, there was no happy outcome to that story and her body was found more than six months after her disappearance, believed to be the result of an accidental fall. My own cousin Pauline, suffered a similar fate on Great Gable, in the English Lake District some forty years prior.

During the completion of this book, the two hill walking adventurers were always in my thoughts.

Acknowledgements

Once again, thank you to the wonderful team at Fortis Publishing, including Tom, Kate, Mark, Hannah and Reinette, but especially to my wonderful editor, Joan Elliott. Thank you to my readers for their constructive feedback and pointers on how the plot could be improved. I have taken (most of) your comments on board.

Thank you to Lee Child and his character Jack Reacher. It would be remiss of me not to give that fabulous fictional character a mention and pretend that he did not influence this book. It never started out like that, but half way through the first draft I found myself thinking more and more along the lines of 'What would Jack have done now?'

Once again, I acknowledge life's adventurers. The world would be a dull place without you.

Finally, to Military Personnel everywhere, and especially to the Royal Marines, who I have been fortunate to work with in the past and more recently.

Thanks to Mike Byrne who gave me a great insight into Bootneck life.

Dedication

To those who set out on an adventure and never returned.

Prologue

Kate loved the mountains. She loved everything about them: the scenery, the vastness, the smells, the sounds, the birds, and the wildlife, but above all, she loved the solitude. They'd been taking more and more solitary hikes these last few months. James claimed to like the solitude too, and they'd meet up after a few days, sometimes a week or two. They'd rest and then walk together again. What was the saying? *Absence makes the heart grow fonder.* At least, that was what James said every time they met up.

Kate convinced herself that she had the best of both worlds. She was a wanderer and had the security of a strong relationship, a man who adored her, a comfortable home; albeit one on wheels.

This parting was a little different. She never liked heading for the mountains after a disagreement. There seemed to be a lot more of them these days.

It wasn't anything too dramatic. James wanted to talk when she returned. They'd been on the road for two years. They weren't getting any younger, he'd said.

She knew what that meant.

James wasn't doing any hiking this time, or at least only a few kilometres at a time. He was having a week to rest up, let his old joints recover, he had joked. He'd sleep overnight in the car park at Chamonix and then take the motorhome over to their agreed rendezvous point at a campsite a few kilometres from Zermatt. A week, Kate had said, although he thought a week was a little ambitious for the distance Kate was hoping to cover. She'd need to be walking twenty to twenty-five miles a day; with potential winter weather just around the corner and the extreme elevation, she was pushing her limits.

It was a little over a hundred miles by road. James planned to drive over the Swiss border and spend a few days mooching around in Riddes, a small village high in the mountains. He'd done a little research and there were a couple of places where he could park up and be left alone. There was a popular cable car ride to a place called Iserable. Who knows, he might splash out a few euros and give it a go.

He could enjoy the mountains that way too.

He wasn't as obsessed as Kate, who believed that if a mountain hadn't been physically conquered, then it wasn't worth even mentioning.

From there he'd take a slow run over to Sion and Sierre, spend a couple of days in St Niklaus and eventually head to the campsite.

He would have plenty of time to plan what he was going to say. She wouldn't like it, that was for sure, but she'd come to terms with it, eventually.

He'd even thought about hiking up to meet her on the last leg of her journey.

Then again, second thoughts.

Perhaps not.

She'd be tired, possibly cold and wet and definitely hungry. She never packed enough food to eat. No, maybe that was a bad idea. Dropping the bombshell, he was about to drop halfway up a mountain. No, anything could happen. He'd wait in the car park for her as they'd arranged. He'd let her rest up, maybe even book them a double room in a decent hotel in Zermatt. A pleasant restaurant, a good evening over a few beers with an expensive bottle of wine. He'd push the boat out. That was a far more sensible idea.

The Haute Route was a spectacular and demanding summer hike. Doing it at the end of the summer season, when heavy snow was a real possibility high up, was what some people would call foolhardy. It was a strenuous, high-level traverse in the French, Swiss Alps, but the weather forecast was good, the first of the winter snow not forecast until early November. There'd be a few snow flurries and snow on the top, that was for sure and she knew that, but it all added to the adventure and her North Face insulated waterproof jacket and pants could handle anything that nature could throw at her.

Her planned route would traverse ten mountain summits, the highest of which would reach nearly 10,000 ft. The only downside of autumn hiking high in the Alps was that nearly all the mountain huts and refuges would be closed to the public. That made little sense. The autumn and the winter, that's when hikers needed shelter the most. It didn't worry her too much; she had pitched her tent in the worst of conditions and got a good night's sleep most of the time. In a howling gale or a whiteout blizzard, a brick built or wooden refuge was always a welcome stay over, where it was sometimes possible to get a hot shower and a night on a soft mattress.

She had forgotten all about the argument just as soon as she'd made her way from Argentiere village.

She walked through a lush, green, alpine valley surrounded by grass covered meadows, the last few flowers of the year sporadically dotted around. She looked up ahead at her beloved world of glaciers and towering, snow-capped peaks.

She couldn't help herself as a smile pulled across her face.

It was where she was meant to be and at that precise moment she felt like the luckiest girl in the world.

By the time she had clocked up her first hour, the familiar light sheen of sweat covered her brow. She didn't hang around. That was part of the challenge and she set herself little mileage goals, before her first stop, before lunch, before she called it a day.

As she climbed, she studied the light clouds carefully and noted that there was snow on the higher paths. Her experience told her they could be icy and dangerous, but hoped she wouldn't have to pull on her crampons too early. She didn't mind walking in crampons, but after a few hours, they took their toll on the muscles and the joints. They caused a different walking gait altogether.

She knew that those first two or three days would be tough as her body acclimatised, as it got used to less oxygen in the air. She took her first break after two hours as she crested the Col du Chardonnet.

She took a little water, a banana and an energy gel to boost her sugar levels, but after just five minutes' rest she could already feel the cold creeping in. She checked the App on her phone, the little red line monitored her progress and told her it was another 5 hours, 47 minutes walking and climbing time to her planned evening's rest stop at Envers des Dorées.

There was a bivouac shelter there and, if it was open, she'd spend the night there. If not, she'd pitch her lightweight Alpine tent behind the solid structure and shelter from the inevitable wind at nearly 9,000 ft altitude.

She had her trusty Norwegian sleeping bag and was looking forward to curling up after a little food and drifting off to sleep. She stood, lifted her rucksack and hauled it onto her back, her crampons and an ice axe strapped to the outside.

There wasn't an awful lot inside her rucksack other than the tent and sleeping bag. She always travelled light, a little food, plenty of water, her stove to make hot food and tea and a change of clothes.

She checked the forecast again. She was quite obsessive about that. She took a selfie and posted it on her Facebook page with a location. She hated Facebook. People posting photographs of what they had eaten for breakfast, their espresso coffees in Starbucks, or their healthy grilled fish salad in Marks & Spencer's food court.

But it was all about safety for her, something she always promised to do when going solo.

She pressed 'post' and zipped up her phone in her breast pocket. It probably wouldn't post straight away; the mountains were notoriously bad for reception, but it would pick up a signal eventually and 'ping' into cyberspace, appearing on Facebook just a few seconds later.

After another couple of stops, a two-hour torrential rainstorm, a ridiculous amount of ascent, and an hour of technical climbing, she eventually made it. She had hiked for 8 hours and 17 minutes and was exhausted.

The wooden structure, not much bigger than a standard garden shed, looked closed at first, the door locked. But from previous experience, she knew that a key to open it wouldn't be far away. She was right. She found it under a large flat stone around the back of the bivouac.

It was empty. The mattresses were laid out on six wooden bunks and there was a pine table in the middle of the hut. She smiled to herself. It was the feel-good factor and while she loved her tent, she also loved the space the hut gave her and the guarantee that her sleeping quarters wouldn't be blown away during the middle of the night, something that had happened to her just once, but it was still one time too many. The abject misery of that night would always live with her.

She dropped her rucksack onto the floor and quickly located her primus stove. Within ten minutes she was enjoying a hot cup of tea and preparing her evening meal. Mushroom risotto in creamy sauce, straight from the packet. Just add boiling water and stir for two minutes.

It was one of the best weeks she had ever spent in the mountains. That in itself told her something she perhaps had to face up to.

Her route took her over the Grande Lui, around the Swiss Three Cols and into the village of La Fouly where she treated herself to a four-cheese pizza and a small beer.

Sheer indulgence but good carbs and even though she waited an hour for her food to settle, she regretted the first mile on the climb towards Val Ferret after La Sielo.

Day four was a long, long day, up through the Great St Bernard Pass and over Mont Vélan. Another selfie at the top and a night in the tent a few hundred metres below the summit with the flap left open so that she could gaze at the blanket of stars above her. It never ceased to amaze her. Billions of them twinkling like little pulses of light. She counted over twenty shooting stars before exhaustion eventually took over and she could no longer fight her eyelids.

She had ticked them off her mental list in her head. The iconic sites of the Alps. Grand Combin, Plateau du Couloir, the Glacier du Mont Durand and the Otemma. Before she knew it, she was preparing for the last couple of days via the Cols de l'Evêque, du Mont Brulé, and the Col de Valpelline, the long drag into Zermatt.

It had been a week of being at one with nature, with the vastness of the Alps and at times a battle with whatever weather nature had thrown at her. But she'd made it to the refuge at Europahütte and tomorrow was her final day in the mountains, a relatively easy descent into Zermatt to meet up with James.

A fleeting moment of… what? She wasn't sure.

She sat outside the refuge on a small canvas camping stool and looked up into the sky. A tear. She wiped it away and scolded herself.

Don't be so stupid.

But now she knew what it was she was feeling. Quite simply, she didn't want her adventure to end. This is where she belonged.

They'd been on the road for two years, but it felt like it was yesterday when they'd set off on their first long distance footpath, the Pennine Way, back home in England.

Once again, she was the only one there in the refuge. That was exactly the way she liked it. She enjoyed her own company. A book, the mountains and the sky. She needed nothing else. She loved being alone.

Only she wasn't alone.

He had tracked her for many kilometres, keeping his distance as he picked out her movements with his powerful binoculars. He was waiting for the perfect opportunity and time was running away from him.

Just as it was getting dark, there was a knock at the refuge door.

'Shit,' she muttered to herself.

She opened the door. A tall blond man who introduced himself as Hans. He was looking for a home for the night too. He never carried a tent, he explained, always hiked from refuge to refuge.

Kate told him she had just brewed some tea and asked did he want some. Hans nodded eagerly, dropped his rucksack on the floor and almost collapsed onto the bunk.

Fifteen minutes later, there was another knock on the door.

Kate grumbled to herself, 'I didn't sign up to hike bloody Piccadilly Circus.'

This time a German man. From Dusseldorf.

Chapter 1

Lenny Saxon was the wrong side of forty and had gained three stones since his wife's death. After nearly thirty years in the Royal Marines and enough money in his pocket without having to work another day in his life, what else was there to do but to take off late afternoon and venture around the pubs of Newcastle, catching up with a few old friends?

He'd never lost a street fight or a bar brawl. He put that down to his Bootneck training, his love of boxing and mixed martial arts, but even as the argument developed, he realised he wasn't feeling as confident as he usually did. He stared down at the bottom of his t-shirt, the small gap between the belt of his jeans and the beer gut that now appeared to be fighting to be seen.

What a bloody mess, he thought to himself.

From the man who had completed an Iron Man challenge as recently as five years ago, he wondered if he could even catch a bus these days. He wouldn't know. It had been at least six months since he pulled a pair of trainers onto his feet.

Newcastle had always been a macho city, some would say quite violent and there was always the wanna be gangsters hanging around.

It had all started out so innocuous. Saxon had been drinking for some hours and was a little unsteady on his feet. He remembered some good advice from a colour sergeant many moons ago.

'Never fight when you are pissed.'

There was a good reason war zones and battle grounds were dry. Colour Sergeant Dave Caswell could drink like the rest of them, but only in the mess when they'd been stood down, or at a local pub when they were off duty. The Royal Marines got themselves into more scrapes than the next man. People saw them as the 'elite' and there was always a mob ready to throw down a challenge.

Saxon had a nose for it. He sensed when it was going to kick off and whatever he was drinking and wherever he was, he'd switch to the water and, as sure as eggs were eggs, within the hour the ruck would begin.

His nose was twitching again. It was one bouncer. He had suggested that Saxon had perhaps had his fill.

'I'm fine,' he'd replied.

'You don't look fine to me, fat boy,' the bouncer had replied.

Saxon had told him he'd finish his beer and then be off. That seemed to placate him and it had seemed fine until a group of younger lads had trooped into the pub. They knew the bouncer. Man hugs. All the rage these days. Everybody was everybody's best friend.

Saxon had noticed a couple of glances, one lad in particular, with a punk haircut, who kept staring over to where he sat. Insecure. Had to be the centre of attention. A finger pointed, then a raucous bout of laughter. Him. They were laughing at him.

It was time to go.

He drained the dregs from his glass and then stood. Unsteady on his feet, perspiration on his brow. The toilet. He needed to pee.

He was standing at the urinal when they came in. Just two of them, the youngster with the punk haircut, no more than 20, 21 years old. Two brave lads. He couldn't help himself.

'Hey fat twat,' Punk said. 'My mate says you should be leaving. You've had enough.'

Saxon didn't even turn round. 'Who's your mate?'

'Johnny on the door.'

'Well, tell your mate I'm on my way, son. I'm just taking a last leak and then I'll be gone.'

That really should have been it. Punk should have walked away. Saxon had been asked to leave, and he'd complied politely. Didn't offer one word of protest.

'And don't fucking come back,' Punk said.

Saxon zipped up. Took a deep breath and turned. He gauged the situation quickly. They stood prepared. The boy on the left puffed out his chest. His mate stood with clenched fists and they blocked the doorway. Battle stations.

Punk snarled. He bared his teeth, wolf like.

'Get the fuck out and if I ever see you in here again, I'll take you outside and give you a good hiding.'

Saxon let out a little laugh. 'And where are you going to get ten men from?'

Punk frowned. 'What are you on about?'

'The ten men,' Saxon repeated. 'Where are you going to get ten men from, because I've counted your mates and there isn't enough of you to tell me when and where I can take a drink or a piss.'

Saxon's confidence caught him off guard a little. He turned to his mate, thrust a thumb over his shoulder.

'Get Bob and Kev. Let's teach this twat a lesson.'

Saxon let out a long sigh as Punk's mate made a hasty exit.

'Big mistake kid,' he said as he stepped forward and before the aggressor could even open his mouth, he struck him in the throat with a knife hand strike. It was effective, as the boy slid to the floor, gasping for breath.

Saxon leaned over and whispered in the boy's ear, 'I fight dirty. I should have warned you.'

He heard the other attackers rushing towards the toilet doors. Two doors, he'd already noticed. An interior and an exterior, a narrow four foot gap between the two. He opened the interior door wide open and stood behind it. As the three men reached the exterior door, they opened it and piled through in a heap. Mistake number two.

Saxon timed it perfectly as he slammed the corner of the door hard into the lead man's head and it split open like a melon. The noise of his scream had taken his mates by surprise but also alerted the bouncers. More footsteps, another surge of adrenaline as Saxon powered a fist into the second man's nose and, as he fell onto the cold tiles, the last man tripped over him and sprawled onto the floor. Saxon kicked him hard on the side of the head. Lights out.

Three bouncers were next into the small, confined space, but Saxon was drained and cornered. He'd never felt like this before. Now he knew why boxers trained the way they did, running up to a big fight.

Three ugly gorillas, no necks and steroids, built like brick shithouses. He laid the first one out with a left uppercut but was too slow to react as one of his colleagues wrapped his massive arms around him in a bear hug. Saxon didn't have the strength to break the hold as the remaining bouncer launched a dozen punches into his face in a frenzied attack. Saxon felt his knees buckle as he slid to the floor. That had never happened before.

So unfit, so out of condition. And now other voices as the punk and his friends recovered from their injuries, keen to join in the affray.

The attack lasted a full six minutes before one bouncer called an ambulance. They dragged Saxon out through a side door and left him in the alley. The doormen didn't want any trouble associated with their drinking establishment and would casually mention to the police and the ambulance men when they arrived that they had simply found the stranger and had no idea what had happened to him. The doormen had sent Punk and his mates packing; their injuries were evidence that a disturbance had taken place on the premises.

Saxon was aware of blue flashing lights, the taste of blood in his mouth but could see nothing out of his eyes, they were closed to the world.

He spent three days in hospital before discharging himself against the doctor's advice. The hospital had inserted 57 stitches in head and facial wounds, he had a fractured cheekbone, three broken ribs and two broken fingers and a dislocated thumb. The hospital said that the retina in his right eye had become detached and he would need surgery, he'd need complete rest and wouldn't be able to drive for at least six weeks.

He was given the doctor's all clear two months after the attack. He'd spent the time wisely attempting to re-evaluate his life. He'd only ventured into Newcastle city centre once and cut down on the booze drastically. The one time he'd been in Newcastle, he'd been on duty, in the field, on a reconnaissance mission, and he'd gathered most of the intelligence he needed. He'd require another one or two visits before he was ready, and the pub across the road offered the perfect vantage point. With a baseball cap and glasses, sitting in the outside smoker's quarter, he'd noted most of what he needed to know. It had been a Friday when Punk and his thug mates had showed up and he guessed that their little rendezvous was a regular weekly event.

He'd be patient.

He wondered if he could possibly build himself up to full fitness, to his old fighting weight and if he could, this time he'd be sober and he'd be the one to spring the surprise.

Chapter 2

It was during another recce that he'd walked through the town centre and onto Grainger Street. He hovered by the shop window. It brought back distant memories.

And thoughts of the future.

The bike on display was Ridgeback Panorama, cable disc brakes, full Shimano drive, mudguards and a pannier rack. The ad read, *The Perfect Tourer*.

There were worse ways to spend a day out he figured.

He walked in and old Tom was still behind the counter.

'Jesus, it must be thirty years,' he whispered to himself. 'The old boy must be well in his eighties.'

Saxon had been taken to the bike shop when he was around eleven or twelve. His dad had bought him his first Raleigh Racer and Tom went through every nut and bolt on the bike, told them how cycling was the greatest sport on earth, even claimed to have completed a couple of *Tours* himself.

'Can I help you, son?' Tom asked.

Saxon nodded. 'Possibly. I'm looking at the bike you've got on display in the window, the Ridgeback Panorama.'

'Beautiful machine,' Tom said enthusiastically.

'A bit expensive?'

'You get what you pay for, son. I'll do you a little discount though if you're serious.'

Before Saxon could reply, Tom was into his sales mode. 'What do you want it for anyway? It might not be the right bike for you. It's a sturdy touring bike, made for a hundred miles a day with a shed load of kit hanging off it.'

'A hundred miles a day?' Saxon gulped. 'I hadn't really thought about the distance, reckon I'd start with about ten.'

Old Tom burst out laughing. 'I guess you haven't been on a bike since you were a young lad, have you, son?'

'Nailed it,' Saxon grinned. 'In fact, my last bike I bought was from you; from this very shop.'

'As a teenager?'

'Preteenager, I was eleven or twelve.'

Old Tom couldn't stop laughing, said how bad the bike must have been if it had taken thirty years to consider another one.

Tom took him through to the workshop in the back. He clicked an electric kettle on. 'Cup of tea, son?'

'Please.'

‘So tell me what you want out of a bike and I can point you in the right direction.’

Saxon surprised himself as he spoke without even thinking about it. He explained that he wanted to get fit, first and foremost, but wasn’t discounting some long-distance stuff.

‘You married?’ Tom asked.

Saxon shook his head.

‘Family?’

‘No. Parents are both dead, just a sister in America. She moved there twenty years back. We keep in touch now and again.’

Tom handed him a cup of tea. ‘Sugar?’

Saxon shook his head.

‘What about work?’

‘Not at the moment. I left the Marines a couple of years back and was looking forward to some quality time with the wife.’

‘And?’

‘The Big C took her.’

‘I’m sorry to hear that.’

‘Life’s a bitch, but I got a generous death in service benefit from her company and I have an army pension. The life assurance paid off the mortgage.’ He took a sip from the teacup. ‘That’s been half the problem Tom. I’ve plenty of income and don’t need to work. I’m spending most days in the pub.’

Tom listened.

‘I need to do something, otherwise I’ll end up drinking myself to death.’

‘Well…’ Tom started. ‘Nothing will bring your good lady back, but apart from that, I’d say you are in a very fortunate position.’

‘How come?’

‘Because you’re free, that’s why. You’ve no ties, no millstone around your neck. That bike in the window could be perfect for you. Buy a tent and see the world.’

‘A tent!’

‘For sure.’

‘The World.’

‘Why not?’

‘On a bike?’

‘That’s the best way to do it.’

‘But it sounds like too much hard work.’

‘Not once you find your fitness level.’

Tom stood. Drained his cup and placed it onto a dirty but neat work bench. ‘Let’s show you the bike. First things first.’

Saxon got up and followed him into the main body of the shop. There were three or four assistants, two young men, clearly bike mechanics, loitered over what looked like a badly broken race bike, two buckled wheels and a broken front fork. They were discussing the cost of putting it back together.

Tom pointed at it. ‘Now that’s what you call expensive son, a real race bike, five and a half grand’s worth.’

‘You’re kidding,’ Saxon said. ‘You could buy a half decent motorbike for that.’

‘Aye, you could lad. But you’ll still be a fat bastard in six months’ time.’

Saxon’s mouth fell open. *The cheeky old bugger.*

‘Now, are you in a car?’

‘No,’ Saxon replied.

Old Tom called over to the two mechanics. ‘Could you stop what you’re doing lads and get me the Ridgeback out of the window? Put a pair of flat pedals on it and take the pannier frames off.’

The youngest one stood, ‘Righto Tom.’

Tom pointed at Saxon. ‘This lad here is taking it out on loan for a few days.’

Saxon held up his hands. ‘Whoa Tom, I didn’t say anything about that. I was just looking.’

‘Take the bike for a few days, lad. You won’t regret it.’

‘But… but…’

‘If your arse doesn’t like it, just bring it back. No harm done. At least you’ll have saved the price of your bus fare.’

Before Saxon could object further, the young mechanic had a tape measure out, and he was told to hold the metal strip into his groin. Saxon was almost lifted bodily onto the seat while they made minor adjustments to the handlebar stem and the seat. In a little under fifteen minutes, Tom had thrown him a helmet, and he was in the street cycling along Market Street, Northumberland Road and out towards Jesmond.

It was an incredible experience. The fact that it was a nice sunny day helped. The bike was sensational. He couldn't believe it glided along effortlessly, it felt so light, but he was more than aware he hadn't encountered any sort of gradient and as he approached Jesmond Dene and Armstrong Bridge, he gauged he had probably descended more than he had ascended.

The real test would be the uphill sections.

He'd watched the Tour de France on TV on many occasions, watched how men had been broken on some of those famous climbs. He laughed to himself. Twenty minutes in on a bike and he was already thinking about the Tour.

He pushed along onto Armstrong Bridge, a lattice girder bridge presented to the citizens of Newcastle by Sir William George Armstrong in the late 1800s and now closed to traffic. Just short of a kilometre in length with a 25-foot carriageway and beautiful views over the tops of the trees of Jesmond Dene, Heaton Park and Paddy Freemans. It was Saxon's adventure playground as a child and a teenager.

He stopped halfway. He was a little out of breath, but aware of something happening deep inside. Chemicals. Feel-good chemicals coursing through his body. Dopamine, oxytocin, serotonin, endorphins. Whatever the hell they were, they'd been redundant for longer than he could recall. He was bathed in a light, sweaty sheen. Even the stickiness felt good.

Wrong clothes. He had on a heavy pair of jeans and a sweatshirt. How good would it feel with a pair of shorts and a t-shirt and, of course, a bottle of water in the empty bottle holder on the frame?

He calculated he'd cycled for about three miles and planned his first expedition. He could cycle down into Armstrong and Heaton Park, back into Jesmond Dene, past the Dene waterfalls and up into Paddy Freemans. He'd swing a left out of the park, past the Freeman Hospital, cut through Castle Farm Road, a stiff climb up Matthew Bank and then home. About ten miles give or take, a good first blow out after so long away from a gym, a run, a swim, in fact, any form of exercise at all.

The first few miles were idyllic Saxon playing with the gears and getting used to them as he cycled past Pet's Corner and the Fisherman's Lodge restaurant. It had been so many years since he'd been in that particular oasis of urban tranquillity, he'd forgotten just how beautiful and peaceful it was, and had already made his mind up to return the following day to see Tom and make the purchase.

It was the Paddy Freeman hill that changed his mind.

No more than a kilometre, but with a ridiculous heart bursting gradient. He almost fell off the bike halfway up, despite being in the lowest gear possible. The endorphins had gone and were replaced with a side-splitting stitch and a struggle to force enough oxygen into his blood stream and sufficient air into his lungs. He pushed the bike the last few hundred yards and collapsed on a park bench at the top.

He rested for ten minutes before setting off again, ashamed of how he'd let his body go since he'd left the military.

Thankfully, he faced a relatively flat stretch and a steep downhill along Castle Farm Road. His breathing returned to normal. He hopped off the bike, pushed and walked the last stretch up Matthew Bank, genuinely scared of falling off the bike into the heavy rush hour traffic. On a flat stretch, he started to cycle again. By the time he opened the gate and turned into the driveway of his house, he was dripping with sweat, his legs were trembling and he was on the verge of collapse. He dragged the bike into the garage and if it hadn't been for the fact it didn't belong to him, would have happily thrown it into a corner, never to see the light of day again.

But a strange thing happened as he sat nursing a beer watching late night TV. He realised that he was beginning to feel good again. Sure, his joints ached a little and his muscles were tighter than a bandsman's snare drum, but it was as he eased himself from the sofa and walked through to the kitchen that he had a strange sensation. At first, he couldn't quite pinpoint what it was. And then it came to him.

That was it. Yes… it was almost as if he was walking on air.

He reached into the fridge for another beer. Hell, even the beer tasted better.

As he gripped the tin with his left hand and levered the ring pull up with his right forefinger, he had a change of mind. He placed the beer back in the fridge and walked up the stairs to his bedroom.

During the course of the night, someone had clearly beaten him with a baseball bat. At least that's what it felt like, a similar feeling to the day after the beating in the pub. There was only one cure.

He spent three hours in the spa. Sauna, ice bath, swim, sauna, ice bath, swim, sauna, ice bath, swim.

He walked out into the Newcastle sunshine like a new man and despite the urge to drop into the nearest pub for a beer or two; he walked into the local supermarket and bought the ingredients to make a spicy but healthy vegetable pasta bake.

It had been a while since he'd spent so much time in the kitchen. There wasn't really any point in cooking for one. A microwave ding surprise was quicker and far more convenient.

But he surprised himself again.

He'd forgotten how relaxing it was spending an evening in the kitchen, with a half-bottle of Rioja and his favourite tunes on Spotify.

A half bottle was good. Not a full bottle with a large Talisker or two to round the evening off.

Little by little, poco y poco as the Spanish would say.

Chapter 3

The alarm woke him at 7 am.

He rubbed the sleep from his eyes and threw his legs over the bed, praying to a god he didn't believe in that his legs wouldn't say no.

He stood.

Stretched.

And then started to walk.

A big grin pulled across his face. A little stiff, no more than that, and it wasn't going to stop him. By the time he made it into the shower, his stiffness had even eased a little. He took a shower. Three minutes hot, three minutes cold. Repeat.

He stepped out of the cubicle, ready to take on the world.

Saxon had planned the route carefully. He didn't enjoy cycling in the city; the idea was to get out of there as quickly as he could.

It was a forty-four-mile route, perhaps a little ambitious, but with all day to do it and plenty of café stops on route, he'd do it. It might kill him, but he'd take his time and complete it no matter what.

He cycled out of Jesmond, through Gosforth and towards Newcastle Airport. The traffic began to thin out as he approached Ponteland on the A696. He had his first coffee stop at a café clearly popular with the cycling set and only just managed to find a seat.

Always the observer, he studied the men and women, the girls and boys on their bikes. Smiles.

He set off towards Belsay. It was mostly uphill, not a steep gradient but constant and after three or four miles, it began to take its toll, his calf muscles cramping up for a while. He persevered. He wasn't going to quit and had pledged that he wouldn't stop until he reached the village itself.

He had hit the fifteen-mile mark and took on plenty of water as he sat on a bench right outside the local Post Office in the middle of the village. He ate a banana, taking in the peacefulness of the pretty village, and enjoyed the sound of the birdsong.

The feel-good factor was back as he climbed onto the bike, determined that he wasn't going to beat himself up. He was aware that younger, more experienced, fitter and thinner cyclists were passing him by the score, but that wasn't going to bother him in the slightest. A few that passed him somehow sensed where he was in his life and gave him a few shouts of encouragement. Cyclists that passed him in the opposite direction gave a little wave or raised a hand. Some just nodded, a camaraderie that somehow made him feel a part of something.

He turned left onto the B6309 and headed for Ingoe and Matfen. There were a few uphill stretches, but nothing compared with the long drag into Belsay. He felt good as he passed the halfway marker, knowing that wild horses wouldn't stop him now.

He passed close to the Matfen golf course, took a brief break and watched a four-ball teeing off from a hole adjacent to the side of the road.

He snacked again, a snickers bar and a carton of orange juice, and winced as he threw his leg over the frame of the bike. A little stiffness was setting in. It was bound to happen as he headed for his lunch spot at Heddon on the Wall. Thirty-three miles in.

Lunch was burger and chips in a beer garden at the back of a local pub. He even allowed himself two halves of beer, convincing himself that it was all about the vitamin intake and then a much needed thirty-minute doze on the grass in the early summer sunshine.

The last ten miles were tough. He wasn't going to deny it, but it wasn't over tough and didn't come anywhere near to the mind-bending physical endurance experiences he'd been put through during Royal Marine basic training. He kept convincing himself that a gentle cycle was a piece of piss, that Old Tom's suggestion of a hundred miles a day was easily achievable.

In time.

He followed the river Tyne for a while, through Newburn and Lemington, before turning northwards towards Fenham and the Town Moor. It was a glorious summer day as he cut through the huge Newcastle Park on a cycle path. He hadn't been this way for twenty years. He marvelled at how peaceful it was, just him and a handful of dog walkers, a few cows, and a vast expanse of greenery as far as the eye could see.

His body felt great as he lifted it from the bike when he arrived home late afternoon.

He certainly felt better than when he'd climbed aboard several hours before.

He'd been out of the house for nearly seven hours. The Google Map bicycle app suggested he should have been on the road for 3 hours 55 minutes, but he'd exceeded that by nearly an hour. That wasn't going to lose him any sleep. He felt ecstatic as he pushed the bike into the garage and walked upstairs to the shower room.

The endorphins were back, coursing through his body like there was no tomorrow.

This was it.

This was exactly what he needed to get his life back on track. It's exactly what Angie would have wanted.

Chapter 4

Sunday was a rest day, and he needed it. He had pushed himself a little too hard. He hadn't exercised for months and then had thrown himself into a five-hour stretch. Crazy, but nevertheless satisfying all the same. He was entitled to feel a little stiff.

Sunday, a day of recovery, and then see how he felt on Monday morning. Sunday… half a dozen pints of Guinness and a Sunday roast at one pub on Osborne Road. The old routine, a few hours at home, watch one of the big games on TV and then a meeting with the lads in the pub at night, another six pints and then home to sleep it off.

Not this Sunday.

Another trip to the hotel spa. Sauna, ice bath, swim, sauna, ice bath, swim, sauna, ice bath, swim.

To the supermarket on Acorn Road, a small chicken, cherry tomatoes and some greenery. A chicken salad lunch. Unheard of.

And on the way home, a mobile call to one of his mates.

‘I won’t be out today, Frank. Let the lads know. I’ve something on, got a little planning for a trip I’m looking into. No problem, Frank… yeah, next week for sure.’

On Monday morning, he cycled back to Grainger Street. He was there for 8.30 am. Unsurprisingly, it was Old Tom who arrived five minutes later to open the shop for 9 am.

Saxon wondered about teasing the old man for a minute, telling him he didn’t want the bike but Tom was a shrewd one and he knew that he knew.

‘You like it, eh?’

‘Incredible Tom. I’ve found a new lease of life.’

Tom pressed a button on a key fob and the roller shutter doors rolled opened. He unlocked a series of deadbolts, then disabled an alarm. They walked into the shop.

Tom talked him through the additional extras if he intended on going down the touring route. Everything Tom suggested, Saxon nodded in agreement and as the mechanics drifted in just before 9 am, they proceeded to fit a back rack and front and back panniers.

‘You can carry as much as you want on this little lady,’ Tom explained, ‘but be warned, pack it well and travel light. You’re ex-military, so I would hazard a guess that you’ll be planning a few camping expeditions.’

‘You’d be right, Tom.’

'Then get yourself around to the Outdoor Store in the Bigg Market and spend a few hundred quid on some good gear. You'll need a good tent and sleeping bag, a wee stove and some decent Gortex waterproofs. But then…'

Tom seemed to backtrack.

'What is it?' asked Saxon.

'You're a Bootneck, son, you don't need an old bugger like me to tell you how to survive outdoors.'

Saxon smiled.

'I bet you've been through some shit under canvas, haven't you?'

Saxon nodded. 'Minus forty in the north of Norway. We were in tents for the best part of a month.'

'And the other extreme?'

'In the desert in Iraq.'

'How hot?'

'You don't want to know. We were there for six months, and it was so hot you couldn't sleep. At the end of the tour, we were all exhausted. It was a record heatwave that year. It hit a hundred and twenty-five degrees one day.'

Tom let out a long whistle. 'That's bad.'

'It was worse than being cold. Give me Norway or the North Pole. I'd rather freeze my bollocks off than sweat them off every time.'

Tom was laughing. 'Like I say, son, you don't need me.'

The mechanics put the final touches on the bike while Tom guided him to the back of the shop. Tom threw in some extras, the front and back panniers and a double water bottle holder, a pump and a small tool kit.

Tom clicked on the kettle. 'So, what are you going to do first?'

'I need to get fit,' Saxon said. 'That's the goal for the first month. I was looking up all the long-distance cycle routes in the UK and I like the sound of the North Coast 500.'

'Aye, lad, in Scotland.'

'That's right. Around the Scottish Highlands, starting and ending in Inverness. I'll take the bike up on the train and it will throw me into the deep end as far as hills are concerned.'

'It will make you or break you and you're an ex-Bootneck, so you won't break easily.'

'That's the idea. If I do that and actually survive it and enjoy the experience, then I'll know.'

Tom frowned. 'Know what lad? I'm not with you.'

'I'll know,' Saxon said. 'I'll know if I'm cut out for something really serious.'

'Like what?'

'Like taking off around the world.'

Saxon expected a different reaction. He expected shock, thought that Old Tom might tell him to take it easy, he'd never suggested anything like that. After all, he'd only cycled forty-four miles a couple of days back. How could forty-four miles turn into a round the world trip?

Tom handed him his cup of tea and nodded. 'I knew,' he said. 'I knew as soon as you set foot in the shop.'

Saxon bought a bike lock and cycled down to the Outdoor Store in the Bigg Market. He locked the bike onto a lamppost and walked into the shop.

And so, £472 later, he walked out, packed his new gear into the panniers and strapped it onto the back rack. He was ready and raring to go.

Saxon spent just a couple of days making the arrangements for the North Coast 500. He packed his bike several times and made minor adjustments. He wasn't too worried about the weight of his kit, just over twenty-five kilos. It was part of the training after all, and he was more than happy that he had covered all eventualities. He had somewhere to sleep, something to cook with and something to hunt with. A little living off the land kit, as his old RSM used to say. He had a decent knife and a catapult. Along with his breathable waterproof gear, he was confident that he would be comfortable, and once he built up his fitness, there would be no better way to see the sights that nature had to offer.

His North Coast 500 route turned out to be more than seven hundred miles. He took detours, cycled ten and twenty miles extra each day to find the campsites that were tucked away by the side of a loch, or wild camped a few hundred feet up a Munro. That was when he was at his happiest, just him and his positive thoughts, thoughts of the future. There was nothing he could do about the past.

He had packed his tablet and had downloaded a few books.

That was all he needed, his tent, a book and the stars.

After a couple of weeks away, he was in a good place mentally. Physically, he had shed at least five or six kilos. After he returned to Inverness, he treated himself to a hotel for the night. The rain was coming down in torrents and he did not intend to be a martyr to the cause. He also allowed himself a half bottle of white Rioja with his evening meal, the first drop of alcohol that had passed his lips for two weeks. He wasn't going to skip alcohol forever; he enjoyed the taste too much. No. But he was definitely going to redress the situation and get out of the habit of drinking every day.

The following morning before breakfast, he swam a hundred lengths in the hotel pool, enjoyed a sauna and then a full English breakfast. He surprised himself by booking another night. Why not?

The next day he set out for Inverness train station on his bike, saw a signpost for Pitlochry, ninety-two miles away and decided to keep on pedalling.

He cycled the three hundred and two miles back to Newcastle in three days. He had the bug. There was no greater feeling in the world.

He slept nearly twelve hours and awoke refreshed and surprisingly agile. There wasn't a hint of pain or stiffness anywhere in his body, and just for a change, he ambled out for a gentle ten-mile jog through Jesmond Dene and Heaton Park.

There was an estate and rental agent a mile from his house, and despite being hot and sweaty, he called in.

A middle-aged woman, name badge *Sandra,* greeted him with a smile and a disapproving look, but despite his appearance and probably a hint of an unpleasant odour, asked him to take a seat.

Saxon explained his situation. He was looking to rent out his property long term. He gave the details.

'We would expect an income of around twelve or thirteen hundred a month, sir. Agent's fee is fifteen percent. We take care of everything and inspect the property each month, even have an in-house gardener.'

Saxon nearly fell off his seat.

'That much?'

'Yes, sir.'

'Great,' he said. 'What happens next?'

'We come to see the property and as long as it's tidy and well kept, would expect a renter within a week or two. It's a very popular location, perfect for the professional and his or her family.'

'And the contract?'

‘Twelve months at a time, a clause to renew each year if both parties are happy to continue the agreement.’

Sandra came round to visit later that afternoon, and Saxon could see that she was pleasantly surprised at the décor and the general condition of the property. Saxon had kept it well maintained. They signed an agreement immediately. As she was about to leave, Saxon handed her a spare set of keys. ‘There you go. I’m heading off next week, so just let me know what happens.’

‘You’re going so quick?’

‘Yes.’

‘What is it, a new job?

Saxon shook his head. ‘No.’

He felt like he should give an explanation, but in reality he didn’t know where he was going or what he was going to do.

She frowned, tilted her head to one side. She waited for the details too.

‘I plan to see a bit of the world.’

‘Nice,’ she said. ‘Lucky you.’

‘I have a little unfinished business to tie up and then I’ll be gone.’

Sandra shook his hand, and he gave her his email and telephone number. It was all so very easy.

Chapter 5

It was a few days before he left. A Friday.

He'd spent no more than an hour in the smoker's quarter. He ordered a coffee and a bottle of sparkling water, stood and casually walked over to the bar. As he neared the two bouncers on the door, he pulled his baseball cap down over his eyes. One of them grunted. He walked through the door unrecognised. Saxon was disappointed there were only two on duty. What had happened to the third man?

The bar was fairly quiet. It was early afternoon, a few postmen who had clocked off early and a couple of suits who had forgotten to go back after the lunch hour.

Punk and his mates arrived just after 4 pm. Saxon pulled his baseball cap down a little further and took stock. Same three.

It was another half an hour before Punk decided to visit the toilet. On his own. Nobody else had been in there for ten minutes.

Saxon gave him thirty seconds and followed him in. He stood behind him while he finished peeing.

‘Remember me?’ Saxon said as the man zipped up and turned around. ‘I’m your worst fucking nightmare.’

As he opened his mouth to speak, Saxon swung a right uppercut into his chin. His head snapped back, and he slid to the floor in a daze. His right ankle rested over his left leg. Saxon stamped hard on it and heard a crack. The man screamed out in pain and Saxon leaned over him. ‘You put me out of action for six weeks. An eye for an eye.’

Saxon walked slowly towards the door. He listened. He wasn’t sure if they had heard the scream at the front of the pub. Two double doors. Possibly not. He opened the first door and listened for footsteps. Silence.

He opened the exterior doors, looked around and then took up a position at an empty table, the nearest table to the toilets. He’d wait. Only a matter of time.

And sure enough, after five minutes, his two mates trooped over towards the toilet door, keen to investigate why Punk hadn’t returned. As the first body reached out a hand to open the door, Saxon stuck out a leg and swept it backwards. It had the desired effect, and he crashed headfirst into the wooden doorpost. Before his mate had even realised what had happened, Saxon unleashed a flurry of punches into his head and face. As he lost control of his legs and fell to his knees, Saxon aimed a heavy kick under his chin and his head snapped back. He was in the land of blackness. There was a scream somewhere in the pub. A girl. Saxon knew that the two bouncers wouldn't be far behind.

The man who had hit the doorpost was dazed but slowly rising to his feet. Saxon finished him off with a left hook then a right hook to the chin, the latter fracturing his jaw bone.

He looked to his right and saw the two bouncers sprinting towards him.

'Hello lads, it's me again,' Saxon called out as they were just yards from him. 'I'm a bit fitter today and not pissed, so you might have a fight on your hands.'

A spark of recognition. A pause in proceedings. They stopped where they were, not so confident now.

The handful of people who were in the pub were running out the door, wanting no part in the action.

Saxon took a step forward.

He had already selected his chair, a heavy wooden barstool, well put together, nice craftsmanship, a leather seat embedded with stainless steel studs. He sat down on it, wrapped his right hand around the top end of the leg. He waited for them to make the next move. He liked to counterattack. It was always his favourite tactic in the ring, wait for the first punch and then be quick enough to deflect disarm and then attack.

The two bouncers looked at each other telepathically. They had done this before, and Saxon noticed a slight nod from No Neck. They were going to rush him together. And they did. No Neck cried out something indecipherable, and they surged forward, hands out in front of them. Saxon was on his feet quicker than they could make the short distance between them and in the same movement lifted the stool and swung it hard in a wide arc, timing it perfectly as it smashed into the head of No Neck. The wood splintered and cracked, and the chair disintegrated on impact. There was no scream, No Neck was out for the count before he even hit the ground. His bouncer buddy froze on the spot. It was a big mistake and Saxon covered the void that separated them, head butting him not once but twice. As the man instinctively put his hands up to protect his face, Saxon crashed his boot in between the man's legs. As his hands slid down to his balls and he fell forward, Saxon executed a perfect uppercut into his face.

The two bouncers were sprawled out on the floor. It was all over.

There was a little sign of life from No Neck. He was groaning, his eyelids opened slowly, and he started mouthing obscenities.

'We'll track you down, you cunt. We'll catch you and we'll fucking kill you.'

Saxon let out a long, deep sigh. 'Ahh, a man with a little spirit. I do like that.'

He lifted the broken chair from the ground and separated the square cross section of wood that held the four legs in position. He bent down and pulled one of No Neck's legs through the square as he lifted the other leg to rest over the top of the frame. No Neck tried to struggle, but Saxon gripped the leg in place without too much effort.

'Now then, No Neck,' he said, 'you're going to tell me where the other twat is, otherwise I'm going to break your shin bone in two and you'll be on crutches for six months.'

The man was begging, 'No mate, please no, don't, I'll tell you anything.'

'Then tell me and you won't be hopping out of here. There were three of you monkeys when you battered the fuck out of me in the alley, where's your mate working now, the one who's not here?'

'Big Phil,' the man flustered. 'He works at the Black Garter now.'

'What days?'

'I don't know.

'Wrong answer my friend.' Saxon picked up a chair leg, flipped it so that he held the thinnest part in his hand.

'Please mate, no. The weekends I think.'

'Good. That wasn't too difficult was it.'

The man on the floor seemed to relax for a second. He was breathing hard.

More obscenities, a threat that he would be strung up from a lamppost within a month. Saxon brought the heavy chair leg straight down on the thinnest part of his tibia, two inches above his ankle, and it snapped like a dry twig in a forest.

It was the following evening when he decided to take a taxi into town. It was early, but already a small queue was forming outside the Black Garter. Saxon sat in the bar opposite, by the window, drinking coffee.

Big Phil was there. Dressed in a smart black overcoat, white shirt, black jeans. He looked anxious. Word had obviously got back to him and he was smoking cigarettes like they were going out of fashion.

Saxon ordered another coffee. This was going to be difficult. He tried to work it out but the queue never let up in the hour and a half he sat at the window. Phil never left the door. There were four on the door. Saxon sensed there were others just inside the pub. They were all on high alert. No doubt about it.

Saxon stood. Walked towards the crowded bar and, after a few minutes, caught the young barmaid's eye. 'A bottle of Peroni please.'

She returned. 'Five pounds fifty, please.'

Saxon handed over a ten-pound note and told her to keep the change. She smiled.

His place in the window had been taken, but that was okay. He stood amidst the crowds and drained half the bottle. Looked around carefully. He spotted the student standing with his girlfriend. A student, too, stood out a mile. Always short of money. He took another mouthful of beer and walked over.

‘I wonder if you could be so kind as to do me a small favour.’

He was polite. Smiled at the girlfriend and then back to the young boy. The boy nodded, a little unsure. Saxon handed him a piece of paper and a twenty-pound note. ‘There’s a bouncer over there,’ he pointed, ‘at the Black Garter, a big ugly bastard with short cropped ginger hair and a goatee. You can’t miss him. Just deliver this note to him.’

‘That’s it?’ the boy replied.

‘That’s all,’ Saxon said.

‘He won’t beat me up?’

‘I doubt it.’

‘And I get twenty quid?’

‘Yes.’

The boy looked at the twenty-pound note in his fist. Two or three rounds of drinks. Big money for a student. ‘I’ll take the chance,’ he said. ‘I’m a fast runner.’ He grinned.

The boy and Saxon left the bar together, and Saxon walked slowly in the opposite direction. He stood on the corner and watched to make sure the job was completed. The boy handed the note to Big Phil, who looked puzzled. He read it.

The strongest of all warriors is patience.

A look of confusion pulled across the bouncer’s face. Then the penny dropped. He grabbed the student’s collar, who pointed over the road towards the bar Saxon had been in, and the bouncers sprinted over the road.

Saxon couldn't help but smile to himself as he watched the show. *Plan B,* he thought, *always have a Plan B*.

Two minutes later, the bouncers piled back into the street, looking in all directions. Saxon walked over to the taxi rank and climbed into a cab. 'Jesmond please,' he said.

Chapter 6

Old Tom had suggested he made it onto the continent as soon as he could and head south. The late summer weather had been good, but autumn and winter were just around the corner and cycling in the rain and snow was not something he had planned to do a lot of. It was the same as camping. He loved the feeling of being in his own personal canvas cocoon when the rain was hammering down, but putting a tent up in torrential rain was not something he wanted to do. If the weather was bad, he'd find a hotel or a B&B close by. Even the Air B&B apartments were dotted all over the place these days.

So he'd decided on the ferry from Hull and a cycle through a relatively flat Holland, through Belgium and head for Luxembourg, a place he'd always wanted to visit. From there, who knows? He'd see how he felt when he got there.

He cycled down to York, a distance of ninety miles, and pitched up on the Naburn Lock campsite on the south side of the city.

It was the start of his adventure. The following morning, weather permitting, a forty-mile trip to the docks in Hull and a ferry to Rotterdam. A night in Rotterdam to see the sights? Perhaps.

The docks at Rotterdam and the heavy city traffic put paid to any thoughts of a stay over. Instead, he cycled out towards the city limits and headed due south.

There was a lot to be said for flat cycling. Within less than five hours, he had cycled right through Holland and had crossed into Belgium before nightfall. He cycled for another hour and found a small camp sight not far from Turnhout, in the Flemish province of Antwerp.

After he'd pitched his tent and dropped his luggage inside, he took the front wheel off the bike and loaded and locked it together into the porch part of the tent. The two man Hoolie tent was a nice set up, spacious inside and even had room for the bike if you removed the front wheel.

He eased his rucksack onto his back and took a stroll into town.

It was a pleasant evening and he stretched his legs along the river, doubling back on himself, stopping at the local café where he allowed himself a couple of beers.

He'd wanted to change his whole relationship with alcohol. His wake up moment was when he was getting his head kicked in, in that back alley in Newcastle. If he hadn't been so pissed, who knows…

it might never have ended up there. He swore a few days later, in the hospital, that he would never hit the drunk stage again.

Not ever.

He made a few ground rules. He'd allow himself a beer or two or a glass of wine after significant exercise, figuring out that the exercise would cancel out and take care of the liquid sugar he was pouring into his body.

This was one of those days.

Six hours on a bike was a kind of reward, and furthermore, he was in Belgium, a country that boasted that they brewed some of the finest beers in the world. Who was he to argue?

He was eating better too. He wanted to look after himself. What was the point of cycling to the point of exhaustion and rewarding your body with shit? He picked up the standard fayre Belgian café menu. Pizza's, burgers. No thanks.

But then another section with a selection of pastas. Good carbs. Perfect cycling food and so he ordered a smoked salmon carbonara and a bottle of Perrier water. He laughed to himself. What would his old Bootneck buddies say if they could see him now.

It was as he strolled back to the campsite when the phone call came in. Unusual. His old RSM.

He answered. 'Sergeant Major, what can I do you for?'

'You can cut that shit out Sax, you're on Civvy Street now.'

‘But you’re not, Sergeant Major.’

‘But you are Sax, so it’s Neil from now on.’

Regimental Sergeant Major Blacklock had been part of Saxon’s life for the last twenty years and, unlike him, had signed on to take his service up to retirement. He had progressed through the ranks of the Royal Marine Military Police and now headed up a department that was all rather secretive. Saxon had last seen Neil Blacklock at an MP reunion less than a year ago and the entire section of old boys had got wasted toasting the health of a fallen comrade.

‘To what do I owe this pleasure, Neil?’ Saxon asked.

His old RSM made a little small talk and asked what Saxon was up to and where he was.

‘You wouldn’t believe me if I told you.’

‘Try me, Sax.’

‘Well, I am in Belgium at the moment on a long-distance cycling holiday.’

‘Fantastic, not working then?’

‘Don’t need to, not since—’

‘I know Sax, since Angie, that must have been hard.’

Saxon wanted to tell him how hard it had been, how he’d sank into the depths of despair and had even contemplated calling it a day. In reality, he had never spoken to a soul, not even to his sister. Men didn’t. Not men like him. There’d been counsellors offered, but he’d always preferred the company of his mates and a collection of beer glasses.

‘The thing is Sax…’ The RSM’s voice brought him back from his thoughts. ‘One of our lot has gone missing, disappeared off the face of the earth.’

‘One of our lot?’

‘Yes, an ex Bootneck, she’s only been out a couple of years. She was trekking in the Alps, due to finish her hike and drop into Zermatt to meet her boyfriend.’

‘She?’

‘Yes, Kate Henshaw.’

A shiver ran the length of Saxon’s spine. ‘I knew Kate.’

‘I know you did. You served with her in Bosnia.’

‘I did. A great girl, she always loved the mountains, didn’t she?’

Blacklock filled Saxon in with a few of the details. Saxon asked the obvious question. He hadn’t seen her for a few years, what did her disappearance have to do with him?

‘You were always my top investigator Sax, once you got your teeth into a case, you were like a dog with a bone. Sherlock Holmes would have been proud of some of those cases you worked on.’

Saxon had finished his time in the military, investigating friendly fire incidents, a couple of suspicious suicides and missing soldiers, thought to be potential AWOL cases. He had also investigated what turned out to be two murders by a Royal Marine, who, if he hadn’t been caught, was well on the way to fulfilling his ambition of becoming a serial killer.

That was the past. History.

'But I'm not in the military now. I'm a civilian on a long adventure.'

Saxon heard a deep sigh.

Then Blacklock spoke. 'She's been missing for two weeks now and we don't think the Swiss police are treating it seriously. They are more or less saying that she's slipped and fallen to her death, that her body will be stumbled upon eventually, that the Alps are a big place.'

'That makes sense, I suppose,' said Saxon. He paused momentarily before, 'there's a but isn't there?'

'Yes. There's a but, Sax. Her boyfriend said she was an expert climber and an experienced hiker and that she never took risks. The area where she went missing was high up, but the conditions were excellent. He says there's no way she's had an accident.'

'But they've looked for her, there have been searches?'

'Yes, three days after she went missing, they sent up the Police Mountain Rescue. They claimed to have searched the area with a fine-toothed comb for more than a week. They didn't find anything, not a trace of her. If someone falls, they nearly always drop a walking pole or a glove, perhaps a hat or sunglasses. They found nothing.'

'Mobile phone?'

‘Never been found either. Her boyfriend said that both their phones were fitted with trackers. The phone fixes onto the nearest transmission mast even when it’s switched off. As the location of each mast is fixed, the phone’s location can be measured by power levels and the antenna patterns of the mobile phone. Her boyfriend, and incidentally the police too, are in agreement on that point, and based on the available data, the system should have been able to determine where the phone was to within twenty or thirty metres.’

‘And?’

‘Not a sausage, Sax, absolutely nothing.’

‘That doesn’t make sense.’

‘That’s what the boyfriend said. Incidentally, it was the boyfriend who contacted us, he said that we were his last hope of finding her. The poor bugger thought we could rustle up a complete team of MPs at the drop of a hat. I had to explain that it doesn’t quite work like that and at the time of her disappearance, she was a civvy anyway.’

‘And of course it’s not in the UK.’

‘Exactly. There’s nothing we can do from an official standpoint; we could only get involved if the Swiss Police asked for help and that’s not going to happen. We were… err I was… wondering if you could take a look.’

‘I’m retired, Neil, and anyway, I’d have no authority. How could I possibly head up an investigation? The Swiss Police would run me out of town. I'd end up getting locked up. You know how much I hate the average civvy cop.'

Blacklock hadn't forgotten about Saxon's epic run-in with the Greek police, how he'd put half a dozen of them in hospital and had to flee the country in a stolen boat. It had almost created a diplomatic incident, and he was informed in no uncertain terms that if he ever entered the country again, he'd be jailed for at least ten years. 'Don't remind me about it. We still laugh about that incident from time to time.'

'It was no laughing matter mate, I've still got those scars.'

'And so have the Greek cops.' Blacklock roared with laughter. It took him some time to compose himself. 'We'll fly you into Switzerland Sax, cover all your expenses, of course.'

'No Neil, the answer's no. I really need to be doing what I'm doing.'

'Just tell me you'll consider it.'

'The answer's no mate.'

'I'll call you in the morning.'

'The answer will be the same.'

Saxon pressed *end* and cut his old RSM off. He was a little annoyed. He'd been stress free for over a month. He was feeling good about himself and delighted with his overall fitness, his transformation from a fat slob to someone who looked half respectable when he removed his shirt. Why had the

RSM even called him and where the fuck was Zermatt anyway? It was miles away.

It was 850 kilometres according to Google Maps, or 536 miles. The elevation was ridiculous as the line on the map got nearer to Zermatt and he wondered why he was even looking at it.

He'd planned to do the big climbs, not just yet. He wanted to build up his muscles slowly, over weeks and months, and he certainly wasn't going to abandon his bike and jump on a plane.

Back in the sanctity of his canvas paradise, the night was warm enough to leave the flap of the tent open. He manoeuvred his body and his head so that he had a good view of the stars. Surprisingly, he fell asleep quickly, even though his head was filled with memories of Kate. That cheeky smile, that determined personality. She took no shit from anyone. In the killing grounds of Bosnia and, in particular, Srebrenica, she was a pillar of strength and someone he admired and looked up to. And she was cautious. Ultra-cautious.

Their section had almost walked into an ambush. It was only Kate who had stopped them. Something wasn't right, she'd said. It was too quiet. Market day, normally a hive of activity, but that day no one. The market wasn't happening for some reason and they were ready to walk right through where it was supposed to take place.

A few of the lads had cracked jokes about shopping and girls, and yet for some reason they'd listened to her.

The American patrol hadn't.

They walked on.

Their platoon leader wasn't ready to alter their plans on the hunch of a stupid chick. His exact words.

The Staff Sergeant lost his life along with six of his men when a huge land mine was detonated electronically at the exact point where his platoon stood, right at the entrance of the market that never was.

No risk Kate. That's what they had nicknamed her. But never to her face.

Chapter 7

Saxon reached for his phone. The display read 06.45 and the early morning rays of the sun were clawing at his wet tent. Perfect. He'd take a little breakfast, let his tent dry out, and then pack it away. Nothing worse than packing up a soaking wet tent, especially in the rain. He wandered back to the café he'd eaten in the evening before and ordered some scrambled eggs and a pot of coffee. He sent a text to his old RSM. It was simple and to the point.

Cycling to Zermatt. Will take a week. Speak then.

Keep me posted with any developments.

He couldn't be fairer than that.

Two minutes later, Blacklock sent him a thumbs up emoji. Nothing else. No thank you, nothing.

As he cycled out of the campsite just after 10 am, he hoped that Kate would have somehow been found by the time he made it to Zermatt. Perhaps she'd had a change of heart, a different route perhaps, and maybe a problem with her mobile phone so that she wasn't able to contact anyone. He doubted it somehow.

Two weeks.

That was far too long.

If she had planned to change her end destination, she wouldn't have waited a fortnight before she'd wandered into civilisation to tell someone, especially if she had lost her mobile phone.

No. Something had happened to Kate. Of that, he was fairly sure, though he didn't know what. An accident appeared to be the most likely, a fall down a ravine or into an ice crevice. That could also explain why her mobile tracker hadn't been picked up. Some of those mountain crevices across glaciers were thousands of feet deep. Even an antenna fairly close by wouldn't have picked up a signal. Then there was the other possibility. She'd been taken against her will.

He texted Blacklock later that day, asked him to send him details of everything that he knew. Blacklock didn't answer with words. Just another thumbs up emoji and pages and pages of documentation.

Saxon had set his target on a place called Eupen, ninety miles away on the edge of a natural park called Haules Fagnes Eifel. Natural Parks were generally dotted with campsites and hotels. If he couldn't find one, he'd camp wild.

Natural Parks were perfect wild camping territory, even though it was against most local laws. That was never going to stop him. He'd always find a pitch away from the beaten track, preferably on high ground, and set up at dusk. He'd be away before first light, making sure that there was no trace of him ever having been there. Nobody would ever stop him sleeping wherever he lay his bed.

He rolled up outside a camp site just three miles from the village. Quite an impressive set up with a small but obviously popular brasserie. He booked in and looked through the window of the brasserie. A group of youngsters were eating and sharing some wine, a few middle-aged couples doing the same.

He pitched his tent and secured his bike, showered, washed his cycling clothes in the bottom of the shower with shampoo, on *stamping feet cycle*.

It worked a treat. He wrung them out as tightly as he could and hung them over his tent, catching the last of the early evening rays. The forecast for the next morning was good. He'd string the damp clothing on top of the bike. It might not look Tour de France, but a couple of hours and they'd be bone dry and fresh as a daisy. Who needed washing machines and tumble driers? It was his personal effort in reducing his carbon footprint.

As he sat in the brasserie after dinner trying to get into one of the books he'd downloaded, he found himself thinking more and more about the documentation Blacklock had sent over. After another thirty minutes of putting wasted effort into the book, he realised that this story and the plot weren't sinking in.

He picked up his mobile phone and sent the documentation to his tablet. Far easier to read on that device.

Where to start?

A couple of pictures of Kate, a recent one in Civvy Street, a pair of blue jeans and a white t-shirt, the background of a mountain and a big smile. Another one, this time as he remembered her in full combats, her luscious blond hair tucked up into the famous green beret.

Saxon had been a part of the recruit cadre that Kate had been on, and she was as tough as they came. She failed the battle fitness test in week five. She was devastated. Saxon wasn't surprised, he only scraped through by the skin of his teeth himself and 25% of the recruits failed. It was regarded as the toughest of its kind anywhere in the world, designed to make or break the recruit both mentally and physically.

Their paths separated after that; Saxon was assigned to his unit, but he'd heard that Kate hadn't packed it in. She had been given another chance, re-joined a new cadre and started all over again. This time, she had been more prepared and knew what to expect. She was one of the first females to have ever qualified as a Royal Marine Commando.

Saxon read through the officers' reports, the sergeant who ran both recruit cadres and the RSM who had overseen her basic training. Nobody had a bad word to say about her and words like ''professional'' ''meticulous'' ''alertness'' and phrases like ‘‘attention to detail’’ a ‘‘team player’’ jumped out from the pages. The more he read, the more he sided with Neil Blacklock’s view that it was highly unlikely she’d met with an accident, especially in such favourable weather conditions.

Chapter 8

It was destination Luxembourg. The forecast had been spot on and Saxon wandered into the brasserie for a light breakfast, allowing his tent and clothes another hour to dry out in Mother Nature's drier.

He wasn't feeling so good as he cycled up the short hill that would take him into Eupen. After the first mile, his joints were stiff, and he was panting hard.

He'd read up a lot about relatively inexperienced long-distance cyclists hitting walls after too many days in the saddle. He'd read up about rest days and regular food intake. He was sticking rigidly to his calorie and carb intake, eating healthily and hydrating regularly.

He thought nothing of it and concentrated on getting the first twenty miles in. After that, he would be fine.

Saxon pulled into the first camp site he came across, just inside the Luxembourg border at a place called Weiswampach. He was thirty miles short of his target for the day and it was still early afternoon, with plenty of light on offer. He didn't care. This was what his planned adventure was all about. Stop when your body tells you to stop. Stay a few days in a place if it looks nice or if the weather is good and you fancy a few days with a good book.

He cursed his old RSM. He didn't want to go to Zermatt. He didn't want a schedule, and he didn't want to work. Why hadn't he just told him point blank?

The campsite was barely a site. There was a freshly painted notice that read Camping, but clearly just a local farmer trying to supplement his income. Two small tents, a mobile camper van, and an old VW were in a small grass field. There was a small unisex toilet block with two toilets and one shower cubicle.

The farmer relieved him of €20 for the night and said something in French which Saxon didn't comprehend. The farmer pointed up the road and, with his hands imitating a knife and fork moving towards his mouth, indicated that it was possible to get some food in the village.

Saxon stripped and walked into the shower. There was no hot water. It was freezing. That's what the farmer was trying to explain.

Saxon didn't mind. He remembered the cold showers from his training days and there was something invigorating about a cold shower once you got over that initial first shock. He used to have a cold shower every day but had lost the habit in recent years. He held the shower head over his back and then moved it down to his midriff, the kidneys. The internal organs kicked into action. Back up to the chest and twenty or thirty seconds around the heart and the liver. His body was beginning to respond, to come alive, burning and tingling and the initial shock of the ice-cold water was now completely forgotten. He started to shiver gently but it was a pleasant sensation.

The joints now. He took the shower head to his elbows, his knees and finally gave his tired feet and ankles a full minute of the cold treatment. The cold water was telling the brain that it was under attack and the blood was pumping hard around the arteries of the body.

He stepped out of the cubicle like a new man with a big smile on his face.

He'd walk into the village and take a look, see if he could get a coffee, perhaps find somewhere to eat later in the evening.

There was nowhere open in the village, apart from a garage shop where Saxon was able to buy a baguette, water, a tin of beans and a type of sausage shaped dried salami. *Oh well*, he thought, *it's about time I did a little cooking.*

He bought some chocolate and refrained from buying an expensive litre bottle of beer. At 12 euros, it was well seen he was in Luxembourg. He'd have one of his dry nights that were becoming more and more par for the course.

As he wandered back into the farmer's field, he looked up above the hills. A smattering of clouds cast their shadows over the area, and he was aware that a slight breeze had picked up. There was a storm brewing. He'd be cooking in the tent for sure.

Once again, he had forgotten about the simple pleasures of life and that he didn't mind his own company one little bit.

The rain had started to fall about an hour after he'd made it back to his tent. But he had everything he needed. He had gas and a stove and sliced the salami into the small pan along with a clove of garlic. The oil from the salami and the tomato juice from the beans created a wonderful infusion, and he added the remaining beans after a few minutes. He removed the pan a little later and replaced it with the camping kettle.

Within five minutes, he sat at the front of the tent with a hot cup of coffee and his makeshift new recipe of salami and beans. It tasted great as he mopped up the juices with the bread and finished off with a few squares of chocolate.

The rain was falling hard now and it was getting cold. He unwrapped his sleeping bag, slipped his legs in and picked up the tablet.

The book or Kate Henshaw?

He opted to study the case of his ex-comrade.

Blacklock had received a copy of the police report and had sent it over. There was also a detailed map of the route Kate Henshaw planned to take, supplied by her boyfriend James.

James had been questioned at length by the Swiss police. Apparently, they were satisfied with the mobile phone tracking records he had supplied and at the time of her reported disappearance, he'd been nowhere near the mountain. Once he had reported her missing, he'd booked into one of the campsites just outside Zermatt so that he could be easily reached. The camp site staff confirmed he had only left briefly and his presence could be verified by several members of staff and management.

A photograph that Kate had uploaded to Facebook also confirmed that on the last day she'd been seen, she had taken a selfie. It was a photograph of her on the final mountain she'd set out to climb. The summit point of the Col de Valpelline was clearly visible in the background. Police had confirmed, by studying the shadows on the mountain that they coincided with the timings relating to the Facebook posting.

And again, according to her boyfriend, she was planning a final evening in a refuge high on the hill with a steady descent the next morning for a reunion in Zermatt.

Just before he turned in for the evening, Saxon logged into the Internet and downloaded several hiking guides and route maps of the Haute Route including every refuge along the way.

Chapter 9

He cursed his former RSM again. It was 6 am and not yet light, but he was packed up and ready to go. A man on a mission, a mission to get to Zermatt. He wheeled the loaded bike quietly out of the farmer's field and onto the E421.

He had an early start with an ambitious target for the day, 150 miles to Sarrebourg in France on the edge of the Vosges Forest. He'd even booked a hotel for the night, so whatever the weather he'd battle through it, knowing that a warm bed, a shower and a decent meal awaited him at the end of the day.

He made the hotel, arriving just before 8 pm, but it wasn't the finest day he'd ever had on a bike.

He'd planned an overlong day because the Google Map had said there was more descent than elevation. He'd encountered a few steep hills in the middle and towards the end of the route and congratulated himself that he'd planned it all well.

What he hadn't planned was the torrential driving rain and sometimes gale force head winds on some stretches of the road after Saarbrucken. He'd made up great time until that point, 109 miles, and it had just been after lunchtime. But those last forty miles had been a nightmare. At one point, he'd barely been hitting six miles an hour, and the rain had found its way into every nook and crevice. He was wet through and cold, his limbs aching, his fingers almost frozen to the handlebars.

It was Blacklock's fault.

This is exactly what Saxon hadn't planned to do. He didn't mind cycling in an occasional shower, but not in heavy rain hour after hour.

And yet, as he checked into the hotel and the receptionist explained they had a drying room for his camping gear and his bike, he was beginning to cheer up.

'Would you like to eat in the restaurant, sir?' the young receptionist asked in perfect English.

'Yes, for sure.'

'The restaurant closes in an hour, so I'd suggest you order now. That way, we can guarantee some food for you.' She took a look at him and smiled. 'My guess is that you'll be spending a fair while in a hot bath.'

Saxon knew he looked like crap and was well aware that he was dripping water all over the hotel lobby.

'I'm sorry about this, it's just—'

'Don't worry, sir, we are used to rain in these parts. The porter will help you with the bike. The drying room is in the basement.'

‘Thank you so much.’

Saxon was stepping out of his waterproofs when the porter appeared and within a short time the bike was safely locked up in the basement, his tent, sleeping bag and wet clothes hung over a metal frame next to an industrial sized radiator.

He spent the best part of forty minutes in the hot bath, changed and made it down to the restaurant with five minutes to spare.

They brought his steak to him almost immediately, perfectly cooked, just how he liked it, with a large portion of French fries, vegetables, and fresh bread. Red wine complimented steak; that was a given, and he pigged out on three large glasses. He ended his meal with a local cheese and biscuits and when he had finished, found it very difficult to lift himself from the table. It was as if his body was rebelling, shouting out, ‘No!’

He took the lift to his room, had no desire to use the stairs and once he was in bed, had every intention of reading through more reports that Blacklock had sent over.

He was asleep as soon as his head hit the pillow and the tablet slipped onto the carpeted floor with a dull thud.

It was after 8 am when he woke up. He had slept right through.

He logged into Google Maps.

‘No way am I going that sort of distance again,’ he mumbled to himself.

It was 300 miles to Zermatt, and he was well on schedule. He wouldn't beat himself up. If he got there in three days, that would be fine. Four was okay, too. The real climbing started once he hit Switzerland.

Old habits die hard. He wanted to take full advantage of the bed-and-breakfast arrangement he'd paid for. He'd eaten too much; his stomach was bloated, and he knew he'd have to wait a little while until the food digested, but that didn't stop him raiding the buffet area before he left. It was all rather casual. He was an expert after all, and he strolled up to the counter on the pretence of a final coffee. When no one was looking, he stuffed his pockets with biscuits, individual wrapped cheeses, slices of cake and sachets of honey. Perfect on the bike food. He sat down at the table and sipped on his coffee.

The waitress approached him. 'Are you finished, sir?'

'Yes thanks.'

She lifted his plate from the table.

'Is it okay if I help myself to a couple of pieces of fruit before I leave?'

'Of course, help yourself.' She smiled.

Saxon walked over. Helped himself to three bananas, an apple and an orange and a handful of grapes.

He settled his account at reception and took the lift to the basement.

The rain had disappeared. The sky was a brilliant blue with just a few wispy clouds in the sky and he pledged yet again that he would never cycle in the wind and rain again. Didn't need to, he told himself.

He remembered he had met a young Spanish hiker in the southern mountains of Spain some years back. It was a beautiful hot day and the mountains were spectacular but it was forecast rain the next day. He asked her what it was like walking in the rain in the mountains of Spain.

'I don't walk in the rain,' she'd said. 'I don't need to. The sun will be shining again in a day or two.'

By late afternoon, he'd managed a very slow seventy miles and called it a day. He was on the quiet D1004 road approaching Wasselonne and decided that whatever came first, hotel, motel or campsite, that would be his base for the evening.

He was directed to a campsite at the next crossroads. It pointed down a rather poorly maintained rough track, but it read, *1 kilometre*. His bike tyres would cope with that.

Over the years, he'd always been impressed with the French campsites, and this one was no different.

Chapter 10

Two days later, he saw the first sign for Zermatt. Fifty-two kilometres. It was a temptation to keep going, but more of a temptation to call it a day. He'd checked the elevation and the fifty-two kilometres was another 1,000 metres of climbing. Too much after the previous day's introduction to the Swiss Alps and 1,500 metres of climbing. He checked into a small roadside hotel outside the village of Ferden. The hotel was situated in between two huge mountains capped with snow. Google told him they were Hogleifa and Chistehorn at 3,275 metres and 2,785 metres, respectively. They were mind blowingly spectacular and a great backdrop from his bedroom window. Hogleifa, in particular, dominated the skyline.

He was in real high hill country, and he loved it. He knew exactly the pull that the mountains had on certain individuals and hoped harder than he had hoped for in a long time that Kate's cold, lonely body wasn't up there somewhere where the animals would have a field day.

It was a long, 15-kilometre downhill stretch to start the day. Exactly what he needed after the previous couple of days. The terrain was relatively flat until around twenty kilometres from Zermatt and then the climbing started and it was relentless.

It was late morning, and he knew he had all day to get there, so he just kept plodding along and just after lunch eventually made it to the iconic skiing and climbing town 1,600 metres up, nestled underneath the famous pyramid-shaped Matterhorn peak.

He texted Blacklock from the main street, Bahnhofstrasse, outside a coffee shop, enjoying the early autumn rays of the sun.

His message was a simple one.

Arrived. Any news?

Neil Blacklock called him thirty seconds later. 'I thought it better to call. I'm not one of those keyboard warriors, much prefer an old-fashioned conversation.'

'Me too, mate. How's it going?'

'So, so. You made it then?'

'Yes.'

'On two bloody wheels, I'm impressed. Are you sure you didn't hop on a train?'

'Never even thought about the possibility.'

They chit chatted for several minutes and then Saxon asked the question.

'She's still missing then?'

'Not a single sighting, no clues, no body, nothing.'

'It doesn't make sense.'

‘And the police don’t seem interested. I called them again on Monday morning. They are pleasant enough, but I get the impression they think I’m a pest now. I spoke to the desk sergeant. They wouldn’t even put me through to one of the detectives, kept telling me they were all busy.’

Saxon listened as Blacklock filled him in on a few more details. He said that the weather was forecast to turn. They were expecting the first snow of the season in the next few days. Saxon looked up at the peak of the Matterhorn. Nature had dusted the lower slopes with a covering of snow, but the peak was white, not a patch of rock to be seen. He supposed it was like that for most of the year. Even in the height of summer, the snow and ice would still hang in there like a stubborn child refusing to let go. By all accounts, Kate hadn’t intended to scale the Matterhorn. She’d done it twice before and it wasn’t the sort of place to climb alone. Her boyfriend had said that she knew her limits, and that rang true with Kate as far as he could recall. It was all about the risk factor, knowing when to stick and when to twist. Kate had always been a shrewd player.

‘It’s looking rather bleak, to be honest,’ Blacklock said. ‘It’s coming up for three weeks now and if the weather turns, you can bet your bottom dollar that the police will shelve the case and put it down to an accident.’

‘They’ve said as much?’

‘Yes, more or less, they said last week that if she had fallen and had been injured… even if she’d had food and shelter with her, it was impossible to survive once the temperature drops below freezing.’

‘And what’s the temperature up there now?’

‘The last peak she was photographed on, the Col de Valpelline is a balmy eleven degrees at the moment, but at night it drops to well below freezing, it’s forecast to be as cold as minus eight tonight.’

‘Ouch.’

‘Exactly. Even if she had fallen and say, broken a leg or an arm and even managed to crawl into her sleeping bag, she wouldn’t have survived more than a few days.’

‘She had a tent with her though, didn’t she?’

‘Yes. She had all the gear to survive up there but only had the bare minimum by way of supplies. She travelled light, only ever carried two days’ food at the most. Even if by some minor miracle she managed to put a tent up, in those temperatures, my guess is that she’d have starved to death by now.’

‘So you want me to look for a corpse. Is that what you’re saying?’

Blacklock let out a long sigh. ‘… it looks that way, Sax. Her boyfriend and her family want answers. Closure. I don’t think we will be able to give them the answers that they are looking for, but even if we find a body, then at least we’ll know.’

Saxon was a positive man. Always had been. But he was getting nothing. He was working over every eventuality that would mean she was still alive. An accident, a broken ankle, a fall, or even attacked by wild animals. The police had claimed they'd covered the area. Found nothing.

They should have found something. Anything. 'What if she's not up there?' he asked.

'How do you mean, Sax?'

'I mean foul play. What if she has been taken against her will, taken somewhere else?'

'You mean kidnapped?'

'Or murdered.'

'It's possible. We're not ruling anything out. That's why we've asked you to look into it. Strangely enough, that's what her boyfriend said. The poor bastard is convinced that someone has taken her. He says there's no way she would ever have had an accident. He said she doesn't like heights.'

'What the fuck, Neil? She was a climber.'

'Not so much a climber as a hiker. He said she would never stray too near the edge of a cliff or a sheer drop, said she was terrified, that he used to tease her about it.'

'I get it. So that's why he is ruling out an accident.'

'Yes. They plotted the route she would have taken, right from back where she started. They avoided the danger areas, said Kate was happy to hike five or six kilometres more out of the way if it meant avoiding anywhere that posed any sort of a risk.'

Saxon was making notes all the while he spoke to his former RSM. He typed them into the document section of his tablet.

They spoke for more than an hour. Blacklock told him that he had booked him into a boutique hotel in the city centre. 'I'll text you the address after this call. It's called the Backstage, there's an open bill behind reception. We'll cover your expenses and you can stay there as long as you want. I really appreciate this, Sax.'

'I'll hang around for a week or so,' he said. 'I'll go and see the cops and then take a hike up to where she was last seen. I might even spend a night in the last refuge she was in.'

'Good idea. Her boyfriend said that they loved to spend nights in those refuges high up on the mountain. I've sent you all the details. Oh, and by the way, I believe the boyfriend is still in the area. Try to catch up with him. I've sent you his mobile number.'

They said their goodbyes. Saxon paid his bill and walked towards his bike as his phone pinged and the text with the hotel address came through. He put the location into Google Maps.

A 5-minute cycle ride.

Chapter 11

James Bonnier was indeed still in the area. He was staying in his motorhome at Camping Attermenzen, in a place just outside Randa, nine kilometres from Zermatt.

Saxon had telephoned him after he had checked into the hotel and agreed to cycle out to Randa the next morning. Zermatt city centre was a combustion engine car free zone, James had explained. The cars Saxon had seen around town had all been electric, so unfortunately, there was no way James could get there in his old diesel motor home. He said he could walk, but Saxon explained he had two-wheel transport of his own and didn't mind in the slightest. It looked a lovely run out, just a few kilometres away along the side of a golf course.

He set off just after he had a leisurely breakfast in the hotel.

The camp site was set in a long valley, nestled between the hills. As he pulled into the site and hopped off his bike, he thought for a minute about relocating from his Zermatt hotel. It was a stunning location. There were half a dozen camper vans, and the same amount of caravans scattered sporadically around what was probably no more than three acres of well-kept grassland. It was clearly the end of the season and he counted ten tents, placed here, there and everywhere. That was part of the attraction of the site. The owner clearly not the type of person for uniformity or structure. It was definitely a pitch where you like type of affair.

He pushed his bike along the narrow tarmac track towards the wooden lodge. After he laid it against the outside fence, locked it up and walked in, he saw a reception area with a small café. He ordered a coffee and sat by a window offering incredible views of the snow-capped mountains as far as the eye could see.

James Bonnier walked into the lodge ten minutes later. Saxon hadn't seen a photograph of James, but he knew. He looked into the eyes of a broken and tortured man, looking far older than his thirty-seven years.

Saxon pressed record on his voice recorder app. Slipped it into his small rucksack and laid it on the table.

James Bonnier looked around. Saxon was the only body in the café and as their eyes met, he smiled. Saxon stood, gave a little wave and they greeted each other with a handshake.

Not the sort of physical specimen Saxon was expecting, not the sort of boyfriend he would have thought Kate would have taken up with. Kate was slim but strong, very attractive and stood taller than the average woman at five ten.

Bonnier was at least two inches smaller and looked, well… a bit of a weakling if Saxon was being honest with himself.

'I'm so pleased you're here,' Bonnier said. 'I can't thank you enough.' He sat at the table and attracted the attention of the man behind the counter. 'The usual,' he shouted over in English.

A minute or two later, a large beer glass was placed on the table.

'I know, it's a bit early for a beer,' Bonnier said, 'but I must confess I'm slipping into the habit of drinking most days now. This is a nightmare I would never have dreamed of.'

Saxon nodded.

Let him do the talking.

Saxon was very much of the opinion that an accident had happened. That was the logical explanation despite Kate's cautious attitude, but the fact that there had been no body recovered, the case was very much still open.

'Rule nothing out,' Blacklock had said.

Bonnier looked like shit. He drained half the glass in his first drink, then wiped the froth from his lips.

He smiled. 'Don't worry, I've got it under control now, a couple of large beers at lunchtime and then nothing until this evening. I make sure I get something decent to eat and the beers in the evening knock me out. It's the only way I can sleep. A couple of weeks back, I was drinking like two Irish navvies.'

'It must be tough,' Saxon said. 'How long have you guys been together?'

'Ever since she got out of the Marines, about five years. We've been on the road now for two years.'

Let him finish.

'It was Kate's idea, but I was glad to go along with it. After the Marines, she'd settled into a decent job and made good money, but Kate was never going to last very long in an office environment. She was itching to get away, missed the excitement, missed the outdoor lifestyle.' Bonnier took another sip from the glass. 'You must know what it's like, Mr Saxon.'

'Please, call me Lenny. And yes, I do. It's hard to adjust to civilian life for some.'

'Well… I had some savings and, of course, Kate got a good payout from the Marines, so we invested in that beautiful machine over there.' Bonnier pointed out of the window. 'The one by the trees, the Adventurer, with the two bikes on the back.' He paused for a second, realised he'd been caught out, and started to apologise. 'I'm sorry, Lenny, I really should have cycled into Zermatt to meet up with you, but the truth is those bikes have never been unlocked since Kate disappeared. I haven't got the heart to take her bike down, knowing that she might never use it again. She loved that bike. She was a real hardcore cyclist, thought nothing of heading out for the day and cycling a hundred miles.'

‘Don’t worry about it, it’s no problem, really.’

‘Two years ago, we were ready and took The Bus, as we call it, over the channel from Dover. We spend a month just being lazy and then started to plan. In Europe, we wanted to hike all the long-distance trails. We started with the Camino de Santiago in Spain, drove the bus to a campsite on the west coast of Spain and then took a train five hundred kilometres away into the Basque Country of France. Simple, we would walk back to The Bus. We didn’t know what to expect, but within just a few days, we knew we had made the right decision. We had the clothes we stood up in, a backpack each, and a tent. The weather was pleasant. We hiked it in June and I can honestly say we enjoyed every second, even the shitty days when we ended up hungry in a wet forest in the middle of nowhere. Kate loved the high ground, her favourite times were high in the Pyrenees. She came alive in the mountains; it was where she was born to be and she said she never wanted it to end.’

Saxon sat back in his chair. Bonnier talked, told him about their adventures in Norway, Sweden, on the Nordkalottruta Finland. He told him about the long-distance trails in Bulgaria and Iceland, the Grande Travesta in Italy.

‘We even travelled to Slovenia, on the Slovenian Mountain Hiking Trail.’

He finished his beer. Signalled to the waiter. ‘A beer Lenny?’

'No thanks mate, bit early for me. Just another coffee for now.'

The waiter appeared at the table. This time Bonnier spoke in perfect French. The waiter walked away.

'And then we did the Tour of Mont Blanc and then the Haute Route. Those two adventures made Kate's mind up that the high hills were really what rocked her boat.'

'And yours?' Saxon questioned.

'I loved them too, but just not as much as Kate. We had some differences of opinion over the last six months. Kate wanted to go to America, she wanted to climb higher and longer. Me… I wasn't so sure. I said The Bus would cost a fortune to ship over to the States. We'd been two years out and I knew the money wasn't going to last forever. Plus…'

'Yes...'

'Well, there was a bit of me that thought two years was just about enough. I'd suggested another few years back on the treadmill of the corporate world, to see how we felt. It made sense. We could build up the finances again. We were both great savers, never needed much to live on. But Kate was one of life's sulkers and she had long spells where she gave me the silent treatment and every time I asked her what was wrong, she shook her head and said nothing. One evening, she handed me a piece of paper. She'd contacted a motorhome company, said that they'd offered €15,000 for our Bus. I smiled, thought she had eventually come around to my way of thinking.'

'There's a but?'

'Yes, there's a but… In the same breath, she said she wanted to fly to America and walk the Appalachian Trail.'

'The what?'

'The Appalachian Trail. It extends between Springer Mountain in Georgia and Mount Katahdin in Maine. Two thousand, two hundred fucking miles of it, the longest hiking trail in the world, passing through fourteen different states.' Another mouthful of beer. 'I hit the roof, mate. She hadn't listened to a word I'd said.'

'So you argued.'

Bonnier looked over the glass suspiciously at him. 'Hah, Mr Saxon, you sound like those Zermatt policemen.'

'I'm sorry, James, I'm not going to lie. They've asked me to investigate Kate's disappearance, and that's exactly what I'm going to do.'

'You suspect foul play?'

'I'm ruling nothing out.'

Bonnier nodded, took another drink from his fresh beer. 'I'm glad to hear it. And I realise that if something has happened to her, then I'm a suspect.'

'Not in my eyes. My boss told me that the police are happy with your whereabouts, your phone tracking, and your alibi before and after her reported disappearance.'

'They are?'

'Yes.'

'They could have fooled me. They were a pack of bastards during the interviews.'

'And there are accusations on social media.'

'Yes, the trolls, the keyboard warriors. That lot are unbelievable; you wouldn't believe some of the things they've said.'

'I do. I've read every word on your Facebook page.'

'Yes?'

'And I've studied Kate's page too. You've left it up there live. Why?'

Bonnier ran his fingers through his hair. Another mouthful of beer. 'I don't know, Lenny. Of course, I have the passwords. I could close it down, I suppose; I'm getting tired of the insincere messages of support from people who didn't even know her. Would you believe, between us, we are getting twenty or thirty friend requests a day?'

'No way.'

'Yes. It seems everyone loves a tragedy. But the reality is that I need to keep her memory alive. I need to keep posting her photos, begging and pleading with everybody to look out for her. They criticised the McCanns when that little girl went missing. I was one of them too. But now I know why they hogged the media spotlight. They did it to keep their little girl's name out there.'

Saxon cleared his throat. ‘You believe she’s still alive, James?’

Bonnier leaned forward on the table. As he spoke, Saxon could smell the stale beer on his breath. Never the nicest of smells.

‘I do, Lenny. Her presence is around. I feel she is still with us and that’s why I need to keep going. I’ll talk to the press, to the police, to anyone if it means a line or two in a newspaper or a website.’

Saxon reached into his rucksack. He pulled out the papers and spread them onto the table. ‘This is the route that she proposed to take. You sent it over to my old RSM.’

Bonnier pulled the papers towards him. Looked at them. ‘Yes.’

‘And how accurate would you say that was? Are you sure she stuck to this exact route?’

‘Yes and no, that route was the route we’d both planned together, but we always used to throw in an odd rest day, where we’d cheat a little and jump on a bus if we felt we needed the rest.’

‘I see.’

‘Yes, and there were plenty places where you could drop down into a valley, take a little time out in a hotel and some transport to the next day’s starting point.’

‘And she may have done that?’

‘Possibly… ’ Bonnier hesitated for a second.

‘What is it?’ Saxon asked.

‘Well… it was normally me who encouraged the chicken out days, the days where I knew that there was a hotel vacancy and I would put it to her. She’d always say no at first because she hated cheating. I’d work on her for a while, tease her about warm beds and showers and a swimming pool and steak and wine and after a few hours she’d always give in.’

Bonnier was grinning. He pulled the route towards him again. Studied it some more. ‘But Kate being Kate, and unless there was any really bad weather, she would have soldiered on.’

‘Been committed to walking the whole route?’

‘Pretty much so. It all ties up with her Facebook diary. Facebook is great for that.’

Saxon knew. He’d spent more than twenty hours on Facebook, studying every picture and every entry on Kate’s page. He’d gone back two years on her Timeline. And Bonnier’s too.

And then Bonnier came up with something strange.

‘They should have investigated me more, Lenny.’

‘In what way?’

‘Well. The phone tracking is all very well and good, but it only tracks the phone, not the person. If I’d been wanting to do Kate any harm for some reason and I didn’t want to tracked via my phone, then I could easily have hiked up the mountain and left the phone in The Bus.’

‘Agreed, but there were people who confirmed you were here for at least a few days before and after her disappearance, when that last photo was uploaded onto Facebook.'

Bonnier held up his index finger. 'One person, mate, that fellow over there serving my beer. He's the manager, come cleaner, come janitor, come odd job man. He sleeps here too, Pierre his name is, and he's here twenty-four hours a day. The police came to interview him and of course he vouched for me. They asked him if there was any CCTV footage which could verify that I was here.'

'And?

'Pierre had said yes, but it would take him a day or two to locate the exact tapes. He'd condense it and said to the police that they could call by and collect it. That would pretty much clear my name. Pierre called them two days later and said it was ready.'

Bonnier placed his elbows on the table and sighed.

'And?'

'And…' Bonnier said. 'The tapes are still here. They've never bothered their arses.'

'Fuck no.'

'Fuck yes,' Bonnier said. 'For all they know, I could have been in cahoots with Pierre. We both could have been lying through our teeth.'

Not good, thought Saxon. *Not good at all.*

As Bonnier went to the toilet, Saxon pressed end on the voice recording. He had everything he needed.

When Bonnier returned, Saxon had one final question. 'So how did you get from wanting to walk the Appalachian Trail to Switzerland?'

‘It was a compromise, as easy as that. The Haute Route was always her favourite. I managed to convince her we would give the Haute Route one more blast and then return to the UK.’

‘And she agreed?’

‘Yes, albeit reluctantly, and she wanted to do it solo.’

‘And you were okay with that?’

‘Yes, she often took off solo. I was ready for a rest. It suited me just fine.’

That night, Saxon compiled twelve pages of A4 notes from James Bonnier’s recording. He spent another two hours transferring them onto the word file in his tablet.

Chapter 12

He awoke with a start.

The same dream again, the missing girl. Angie had been dead for nearly two years now, but she would not leave him. It wasn't a pleasant dream, some would call it a nightmare, but however unpleasant it was, at least he'd seen her beautiful face again, not the face he had been left with, the face eaten away by cancer. No more than a skeleton, something akin to a Belsen victim.

He walked naked into the shower room and stared at himself in the mirror. Let out a deep sigh.

The missing. Lucky is the spouse who dies first, who never has to know what survivors endure.

But Angie wasn't lucky because she had been tortured, especially in those last few months. Those last couple of years had been a blur and he could never thank Blacklock enough for pulling him out of active service and to possible postings around the world and giving him a desk job where he could work from home most of the time.

It allowed him to spend more time with Angie because they both knew that their time together was coming to an end.

But there were times that he wished he had been away on a totally different continent, in the deserts of Iraq or the jungles of Belize. It was hard to watch the woman you love slip away into another dimension, sheer torture the day when he knew that she'd given up the fight.

Blacklock's newly created department, which Saxon headed, was a simple one. Find the missing men who had disappeared off the radar for one reason or another.

He found a lot of them on the street. They showed him what it meant to hit the bottom, a bottom where they couldn't get any lower. The homeless boys had lost everything, but Saxon told them that because they'd hit rock bottom, there was only one direction they could go.

Dave Valentine was the first.

Valentine was a great soldier and an even greater drinker. Tales of his twenty-pint nights were legendary. Mess hall booze was cheap and there was always a buddy to stand him a drink. A great character and well loved and respected. He had missed an annual reunion of retired Bootlegs two years running and one of his old comrades had tried to find him without success.

He reported in to Blacklock, and Saxon took the case.

Valentine hadn't been hard to find. Saxon found him in a shop doorway in Leeds on a wet Wednesday night in December. Bizarrely, he was wrapped up in his old army issue sleeping bag. Valentine was a Yorkshireman, born and bred in Sheffield and Saxon knew he wouldn't have run too far. He'd made some enquiries, discovered that he had withdrawn some cash nearby. The rest was just old-fashioned detective work and shoe leather.

'Can I buy you some dinner, Bootleg?' Saxon had asked.

Valentine was suspicious at first, and no wonder. There was a warrant out for his arrest after an altercation in a Sheffield pub where Valentine had gone a little too far and put two bouncers in hospital.

Who's buying?'

'Captain Saxon, Forty Commando.'

Valentine let out a short grunt. 'Come to nick me, have you?'

'Not at all, didn't you hear me? I've come to buy you a hot dinner. It looks like you could do with one.'

They sat in a KFC restaurant on Otley Road and Valentine ate like he hadn't eaten for a week. He was remarkably well presented, given that he had lived on the streets for several months. He was clean shaven, his hair cut short, but his skin had a deathly yellowish pallor.

'You don't look so good,' Saxon said.

Valentine shook his head and answered with a mouthful of chicken. 'You'd look shit if you had to sleep in a shop doorway in minus temperatures.'

'So where did it all go wrong?' Saxon slipped a file onto the table. 'I have your service record here. It's exemplary. If I was back in the mix, you're exactly the type of man I'd want fighting in my unit.'

'Yeah well, that's history. Those days are gone.'

'The demon drink?'

Valentine nodded. 'I guess so.'

Saxon pointed to the file. 'You could drink with the best, but you were always in control. You abstained completely for three months every year, never drank in a war zone, on a mission or even when on exercise.'

'That's true.'

'So why now? Now that you've retired, you have a decent pension. You should be out on the golf course, in the gym, walking the Yorkshire Dales.'

Valentine told Saxon what was to become a familiar story, one that he'd hear time and time again over the next couple of years.

'The Army did everything for me for thirty years. They housed me, fed me, clothed me, there was never a day that I had to worry myself about organising anything other than my personal kit.'

Valentine's record said that he had never married. There was no known family, just a sister in London who had done pretty well for herself. She was a top defence barrister, one of the highest paid in the capital.

'But we've seen some shit, haven't we? You know yourself, sir, war isn't pretty and Libya was about as bad as it got. Our patrol came under attack from friendly fire, the Americans, who had targeted what we thought was a rebel camp in the desert. Someone got the comms wrong because we were staking that camp out too and when they hit it, we were only 200 yards away.' Valentine picked up another piece of chicken, stuffed it into his mouth and chewed. 'One of their missiles hit a fuel dump, and it went up like a bonfire night display.'

Valentine rolled up his sleeve. His arm was scarred from the wrist to the elbow. It looked like candle wax.

'I was one of the lucky ones. Three of my mates were cooked like this fried chicken and didn't make it. I sat with one of them for twenty minutes before he eventually gave his last breath.' Valentine sniffed. 'I can still remember that smell of charred skin and bones. It will never leave me… not ever.'

More chewing. 'And then from living a lifestyle like that, we're dumped into Civvy Street, and it's a street I barely recognise.'

Valentine took Saxon through the entire process. How he'd started drinking more in an attempt to blot out the demons who visited him on a daily basis. He explained the anxiety attacks, his fear of crowds, and how paying an electric bill at the local post office was a big ordeal.

More drink.

'I'd led a team through the darkness of an Arctic Winter for three months, but a visit to a bank was a step too far. Can you imagine that?'

Valentine was embarrassed, ashamed of himself… a failure. His self-esteem had been shot to pieces, and it brought Saxon to the verge of tears. How could this happen? How could the MOD, the government and the politicians allow this to happen?

'We'll get you help.'

'Save your breath, Captain. I've tried that. They aren't fucking interested because we've served out our useful means. I've fought their scraps and their wars, done their dirty work for thirty years, they couldn't give a fuck.'

'What sort of help would you need?'

Valentine stopped chewing. 'Stop kidding yourself, Captain. I'm too far gone. I'm a lost cause. I've got fuck all left to get back on the rung of any ladder ever assembled.'

'No one is a lost cause, least of all you. You are respected, there're a lot of pals looking out for you and there's the ex-servicemen's charities too. We'll get you the help you need.'

Valentine leaned back in his seat and let out a sigh. 'You are serious aren't you?'

'I am.'

'Okay, well, first and foremost I need to be checked into one of those fancy rehab clinics, you know the sort I mean. They charge about two grand a week and it's a six-week course.' He laughed out loud. 'That's just for starters, because I'm not going to get clean on these mean streets. I don't think there's any government body or charity in the country who will help me out with that sort of cash.'

'That's a good start. You've recognised you have a problem.'

'But no way to fix it. And even if I did, then I need a job to keep me out of mischief and to get a job you need a permanent address and to get a flat or a house you generally need a job or at least at reference from your previous landlord which ain't gonna happen because the fucka had me evicted and I still owe him the best part of five grand. It's a catch twenty-two, Captain. It's a road with no junctions or turn offs, a long road which only leads to one place.'

Saxon knew exactly where that place was.

Suicide rates in ex-military personnel were unacceptable. But it wasn't true, there was help available. Valentine just didn't know where to look. Or perhaps he didn't want to.

Saxon cleared his throat. 'Sit up straight when you are talking to a superior officer.'

Valentine jerked into life. 'Yes, sir.'

'Listen soldier, I've had enough of this feeling sorry for yourself shit. What kind of Commando are you anyway? Because quite frankly, the Commandos under my command aren't quitters.'

'No, sir.'

'You didn't quit your basic training, did you?'

'No, sir.'

'Or any mission you were ever sent on?'

'No, sir.'

Saxon stood. He leaned over the table. Valentine's stale breath was putrid, but he moved in even closer. 'So you ain't quitting life, soldier, is that clear?'

'Yes, sir.'

'Right. Pick up your kit and follow me.'

'Sir.'

Saxon walked with Valentine northwards along Otley Road. They stopped outside the Parkway Hotel. 'Okay, let's get you checked in. You'll never sleep on the streets again. That's a promise.'

Chapter 13

A visit to the Zermatt police was a good place to start. That initial approach was all important though, Blacklock had already indicated that they were tired of outside interference.

He had downloaded just about every online news article about Kate Henshaw's disappearance. In several Swiss reports, they'd quoted from a Zermatt police spokesperson, a Detective Oscar Nuessle.

He'd see if he was around. Put on his best smile. He had his opening few lines prepared and well-rehearsed.

A young man, early thirties, dressed in civilian clothes, sat at the reception desk just inside the police station. A roughhewn wooden block, four inches long, sat on his desk. It read *Eggen Fassnacht.*

'Do you speak English?' Saxon asked politely.

'Yes I do, sir, most Swiss people do.'

A little dig at the average Brit.

'Yes, I must apologise,' Saxon said. 'I speak Russian and Spanish, a little Mandarin, but I'm afraid French and German passed me by.'

Not so smug looking now.

'I wonder if Detective Oscar Nuessle is around?'

'Do you have an appointment?' He smiled.

'No, but I'm happy to make one. I'm in town a few days. I'm happy to come back.'

'And what's it in connection with?'

'Kate Henshaw.'

Fassnacht's face changed in an instant. The smile was gone, and a frown replaced it. 'The missing English girl?'

'Yes. I worked with her some years back. We were very close. She was very special to me.'

'And your name?'

'Lenny Saxon.'

The young man nodded. Pointed to the other side of the room. 'If you'd just take a seat over there, monsieur, please. I'll give him a call.'

Saxon waited an hour before the young man came out from behind his desk and wandered over casually. 'Detective Nuessle is very busy. He said that it might be better to come back another day.'

The brush off.

Saxon had studied him intently. Fassnacht had never left his desk and while he had spoken a few times on the telephone, the calls had all been incoming. Not once had he heard his name mentioned in any of the calls.

'It's okay, tell him I'll wait.'

And he did. He wasn't going anywhere.

After another ten minutes, Fassnacht picked up the phone and dialled three numbers. When the call was answered, he spoke in German and while Saxon missed most of the conversation, just an odd word here and there, he heard the word Henshaw and then as clear as day, Herr Saxon.

Ten minutes later, a door opened on the far side of the office and a tall, gangly, but fit looking middle-aged man strode purposely over towards him, extending a hand out to greet him. 'Monsieur Saxon, I am Detective Oscar Nuessle. How can I be of assistance?'

Saxon stood and shook the man's hand. He had a tired look, short, cropped hair going thin on top. He had sharp, rodent like features, a deep red, bulbous nose. Drinks too much. No pride in his appearance. His shirt needed a good iron, his suit needed to see a dry cleaner. Divorced. No interest in the opposite sex. Two or three years of a hellish marriage. Probably henpecked.

'I'm here about Kate Henshaw. I served with her in the military.'

'Ahh.. another commando.'

'Yes, the Royal Marines, we trained together, and our units were together in Northern Ireland and Bosnia. We were very close, remained friends long after we left the service.'

A little white lie wouldn't go amiss. The truth was he hadn't set eyes on Kate for over six or seven years.

'It's very sad. I'm so sorry.'

Detective Oscar Nuessle had put on his best sorrowful look. 'But we don't hold out much hope of finding your friend alive.'

'I know. I read your last report in the newspaper. Have you called off the searches?' Saxon asked bluntly.

The detective hesitated. Saxon knew he didn't want to commit himself. 'We have police mountain rescue teams in the Alps most days, and Air Zermatt are always in the air. The helicopters, in particular, have combed the area where your friend was last seen. A couple of hikers remembered her drinking tea outside of the refuge early morning. Her boyfriend heard nothing from her after that, no social media posts or phone calls.'

Saxon decided it was time to up the ante, to let the detective know how serious he was about finding the missing hiker. He pulled out his tablet, referred to his notes. 'Kate's last night that we know of, was spent in a refuge hut.'

'That's correct.'

'The Europahüttc.'

'Yes.'

'And have you spoken to anyone else who stayed that night in the refuge?'

'I'm afraid, monsieur, that is police business, part of the official investigation. Those details are confidential. If you have flown all the way from England to question how we are conducting the search, then I'm afraid you have wasted your time and I must ask you to leave.'

Saxon jumped straight into a charm offensive. He explained that he wasn't questioning the investigation at all and that he was on a long-distance cycling adventure and just happened to be cycling through Zermatt.

'It was Kate's family who asked me to call into the police station. They wanted me to convey their thanks and their gratitude to all the police and rescuers involved in the search.'

It seemed to work. The detective mellowed a little.

'There are guest books at most of the refuges,' he said, 'but generally they don't give an awful lot away. The guests leave a comment here and there and there's a section to write their name and where they are from. There were only three entries in the book that evening. One was from your friend, another by a Hans from Norway and the last was from someone called Tomas Bauknecht who didn't even bother to say where he was from. We have placed information in the local newspapers trying to trace Hans and Tomas, but no one has come forward.'

'Yes… it's a mystery,' Saxon said. 'Her family are baffled.'

Confusion on the policeman's face now.

'A mystery?' the detective said. 'Why would her disappearance be a mystery? The high Alps are a very dangerous place.'

‘But Kate was one of life’s cautious people. She would never have taken any risks.’

The detective shrugged his shoulders. Said nothing.

Saxon continued. ‘I knew her well. I don’t think she’d have had an accident.’

‘Let me assure you, monsieur, I know the mountains better than most, almost certainly better than you, and all the signs point to exactly that. The area she was last seen is a place well known by Air Zermatt.’

The detective frowned. Let out a short sigh, turned around, and started walking. ‘Follow me,’ he called out over his shoulder. ‘I want to show you something.’

He walked back out the door he had entered from and led Saxon down a long, gloomy corridor to an open doorway. Saxon fiddled with his phone and slipped it into his breast pocket.

They walked through to what was clearly Detective Oscar Nuessle’s office.

It was basic, quite small, with a huge map of the Alps that filled the entire back wall behind his desk. He stood beside the map with his back towards Saxon. He lifted his arm and started to speak as his finger brushed the map. ‘There are over four hundred mountains in Switzerland, Monsieur Saxon. More than a hundred are over three thousand metres high. Anyone climbing above that is taking a risk because if a climber has an accident above three thousand metres and isn't found within a couple of days, he or she generally dies.'

He walked around his desk and sat down. 'We call it the dead zone.'

He beckoned Saxon to sit. 'I too know the Haute Route well. At least once a year, I like to walk it. I take the train to Chamonix and walk back.' He let out a little laugh. 'Hah, unfortunately as the years go by, the duration of my little pilgrimage gets longer and longer. It's an age thing, monsieur.'

'Not at all,' said Saxon. 'That's still impressive. It looks like a tough trip.'

'Thank you. But nonetheless, every year throws up something new. Every year, there are times when I wonder what the hell I am doing. I have had several near escapes myself. I slipped from one of the ladder climbs a few years ago. Dropped three or four rungs but luckily managed to kick out against the rock and land on one of the steel platforms. I thought my time was up, Monsieur Saxon. I lay on that platform for some time and prayed like I had never prayed before. We lost a lot of people in the Swiss Alps last year, many of them on the Haute Route. In one month alone, there were six deaths and the Air Zermatt helicopter rescued at least the same number again. Many of those hikers and climbers were cautious people too.'

'So you don't think anything untoward may have happened to her?'

'In what way?'

‘Taken against her will.’

‘You mean kidnapped?’

Saxon nodded.

‘That’s a little dramatic, but yes, it’s a possibility, of course. Everything is possible, and that thought did cross our minds, but only fleetingly. My team are all in agreement that she has met with an accident. If she’d been taken, I’m sure she would have put up a struggle and something would have been left behind.’

‘Like blood?’

‘Yes, blood, or hair, skin, a glove, perhaps a piece of clothing or a walking pole.’

‘But nothing was found?’

‘Nothing, Monsieur Saxon. We even took the dogs up there. They found nothing either and believe me, they’re not called bloodhounds for nothing. If Miss Henshaw had had any sort of altercation up there, they would have locked on to it.’

The policeman moved a few papers around his desk, replaced his pen in a glass jar full of desk top junk. ‘I realise your concerns and I understand that you want to cxplorc all anglcs, but believe me, Monsieur Saxon, we really did conduct a thorough investigation. We dusted that refuge for fingerprints and ran them through the computer. Nothing of note, no murderers or rapists, no bank robbers, not even anybody with an outstanding speeding fine. You see, most of the people who have a love for the mountains and the outdoor life are law abiding citizens.’

‘And the other refuges,’ Saxon asked, ‘what about them?’

‘What others?’

‘The others on her route.’

Saxon produced Bonnier’s detailed route from his rucksack and placed it on the desk.

The policeman frowned. He let out a long sigh. ‘Monsieur Saxon, do you know how many refuges and bivouacs are on the Haute Route?’

Saxon shook his head.

‘Clearly not,’ the policeman said. ‘Off the top of my head there are manned stations at Les Dix, Les Vignettes, Bertol, Chanrion, Mont Fort, Valsorey and Schonbiel and then are the huts, or bivouacs as we call them, lone huts and prefab buildings, unmanned and only accessible on foot. There are dozens of them all over the place. And then there are the campsites and we believe she wild camped too.’ He stood. Paced slowly around to the side of the desk.

‘We spoke to her boyfriend at length and he can’t tell us exactly where she stayed each night she was on the route, so we have no way of knowing for sure. But let me ask you a question. Why would we send men on a hundred-mile hike to check up on a guest book for a campsite or a refuge where she left unharmed?’

‘I know but…’

‘But nothing, monsieur, it would be… how do you say, a wild goose chase and, rightly or wrongly, we concentrated our search on the twenty-seven kilometres of the route she planned to take from the Europahütte to Zermatt.'

'I understand, detective,' Saxon said, biting his tongue.

'We simply haven't got the resources to go and check for fingerprints and look at the guest books of all the places she may or may not have stayed, looking for someone who may have stayed there too, who may have wished to cause her harm. But even if we did, in all likelihood we wouldn't be able to track them down anyway.'

'Because they don't give their names and addresses.'

'Yes. How can we possibly locate Hans from Norway, for example? There are probably twenty thousand men in Norway called Hans.'

Saxon needed to keep the policeman onside. Perhaps there would be more questions at a later date.

That was for sure.

He wondered if he should bring up Bonnier. Best to leave it for another time.

He stood. 'Thank you so much for your help. I won't take any more of your time.'

The policeman walked towards him, proffered a hand. 'I understand your concern, Monsieur Saxon. I am ex-military too. But we have no evidence to suggest she was harmed or taken against her will.'

Saxon shook his hand. 'Thank you, detective, I really appreciate your time. As long as there is no body, her family will continue to live in hope.'

The detective raised an eyebrow. ‘No, there isn’t a body, but that isn’t unusual in the mountains. Every year, the mountains throw up different skeletons of mountaineers who disappeared years ago. They are lost in avalanches mostly, but some found in crevices, snow holes, or in forests in a remote part of the Alps where nobody ventures.’

‘I see.’

‘Do you know how many hikers and climbers die in the Alps on an annual basis?’

‘No.’

‘Take a guess.’

‘Twenty, twenty’-five.’ Saxon offered.

The policeman let out a mocking laugh. ‘Monsieur Saxon, on Grand Combin, on the Haute Route, there were ten known fatalities last year and at least another six persons unaccounted for, who, just like your young lady friend, vanished without a trace. Miss Henshaw’s disappearance is not unusual. Far from it. It’s just what happens here. Ten thousand people a year attempt to climb Grand Combin, so accidents and fatalities are to be expected.’

The policeman walked across the room and reached for the door handle. He pulled it open. ‘The Matterhorn and Grand Combin account for most of the deaths, but as you know, Miss Henshaw scaled at least six or seven testing peaks that we know of and while the weather wasn’t too bad, perhaps her luck just ran out. The surface area of the Alps in Switzerland is forty-one thousand square kilometres and we have well, nearly a hundred people who die here every year.'

'And the Haute Route?'

The detective twirled a pen between his fingers. 'Errr… I'm not sure of the exact numbers, but certainly more than twenty, I'd think.'

The figures were mind blowing.

Saxon gave the policeman a slip of paper with his email and mobile telephone number. He didn't do business cards.

'If anything crops up, I'd appreciate if you'd give me a call.'

'I will Monsieur.'

'I think I will probably take a walk up there.'

A look of shock. 'Really, monsieur. To the refuge?'

'Yes, I told her family I would.'

The detective appeared angry. 'So you don't think we have done our job correctly?'

Saxon thought quickly. 'No, no, that's not what I meant. If she's met with an accident, I want to leave some sort of memorial.'

'Like what?'

'Oh… I don't know… perhaps something in the guest book, a framed photograph of Kate for the refuge, you know, that sort of thing.'

The policeman didn't look so convinced.

They shook hands again. 'Thanks for all your help,' Saxon said.

Saxon had concluded that a lot of people went missing or were killed every year in the Alps. He'd also concluded that the Zermatt police, and Detective Nuessle in particular, weren't too concerned and that their investigation had been pretty shoddy. They had no real intention of devoting any more manpower to the search, happy to write it off as an accident. Case closed. Bonnier and his CCTV tape were examples.

'You need to be careful, Monsieur Saxon. The first snow of the year is only days away and as soon as it arrives, there is little point carrying out more searches. A huge white blanket will be thrown over everything. There will be nothing to see, nothing to find, and some parts of the route are treacherous. The Haute Route is very much a summer route, in my opinion.'

'I understand.'

The policeman was trying to talk him out of it.

The detective appeared to pause for a moment, as if he'd thought of something. 'There's a video on YouTube, by a man from Zermatt called Heinz Frei. He's a recognised expert on the Haute Route, but even he won't hike the route in the winter. You'll find it very interesting. Heinz spends most of the summer on the Haute Route and in winter he heads to Australia.'

'Nice life style.'

The detective laughed. 'Yes, he's a bit of a playboy from a very wealthy family. They own at least half a dozen hotels here in Zermatt, many others in Europe and several in America. They have Heinz as a non-working director. He spends his life in the mountains he loves.'

'In Australia too.'

'Yes. He walks a long-distance walking trail in the Australian Alps.'

'And a regular on the Haute Route?'

'Yes.'

'And spends most of the summer up there?'

'Yes.'

It seemed like an obvious question to ask.

So Saxon did. 'Do you know if he was up there when Kate disappeared?'

The policeman's eyes rolled towards the ceiling.

'I mean, would he have come forward if he had been in the area?' Saxon asked.

'Yes. He's a local. He would have seen all the reports, the Zermatt TV news, that sort of thing. I think he would have contacted us if he had seen her.'

'But you haven't contacted him directly?'

'No.'

'And you mentioned he goes to Australia for the winter. Might he have already left? Might he not have seen anything? Might he not even know there's a girl missing?'

The detective didn't answer the rapid-fire questions. Instead, he walked towards the office door. Opened it.

'I don't like your tone, Monsieur Saxon. To be frank, your questions offend me. I feel as if I am sitting in front of some sort of police disciplinary hearing, being accused of neglecting my duties.'

'But they're just questions. The family want answers. Surely if there's a man who spends half his life in the mountains where Kate disappeared, then at least you should speak to him?'

'Goodbye, monsieur, I'm really very busy.'

Saxon decided not to push it. 'Of course, you must be up to your eyes in work.'

He held out a hand and they shook again.

'See you around, detective.'

The policeman grunted, turned around, and looked back at the map.

Saxon walked out along the corridor, past the desk clerk, and called out goodbye. Fassnacht never even looked up from his desk.

Saxon walked outside, pulled up his shirt collar. It had turned cold. He headed back to the hotel.

Something wasn't quite right.

The detective appeared in a state of rage as he walked along the corridor less than a minute later. He opened the door into the main reception and glared at the clerk.

'Why do you bother me with these fucking people?'

The young man didn't know where to look. He flushed with embarrassment.

'Fucking time wasters, don't they know we have better things to do?'

'I'm sorry, sir, I did try, I—'

‘The fucking newspapers, the girl’s boyfriend and now this fucking clown.’

‘I’m sorry, sir, I tried to ignore him but he was quite persistent; I got the impression he would have hung around all day.’

Nuessle reconsidered. Thought he was perhaps a little unfair on his friend. He walked over and leaned on the reception counter with his elbows. ‘I’m sorry, Eggen, it’s not your fault.’

He ran his fingers through his hair and sighed. He tried his best, but sometimes things were just beyond his control.

Chapter 14

Saxon mooched around Zermatt for the rest of the day. He sat at the window tables in various cafés with a view to the street and he people watched.

One of his favourite pass times.

He had his notepad and his phone. He connected the earphones to the phone. Pressed play and picked up the pen.

He drank two more coffees and made several pages of notes.

And he was frustrated. Heinz Frei. Why the hell hadn't they spoken to him? He checked out the Zermatt directories on the web. No telephone numbers for Frei, but listed as having a residence at several addresses. A playboy, Nuessle had said, possibly a suite in each of his father's hotels. But no other info.

There were a few online articles but when Saxon clinked on the link, the information read either *link expired*, or *this information is no longer available.*

A few Facebook pages in the name of Heinz Frei, and Twitter pages too, but none listed in Zermatt and none resembling a lean man who spent most of his life walking mountains.

He located the number on his phone, *Flying Pig,* pressed call.

'Flying Pig. How are you, my friend?'

'Bootneck, how are you?'

'Good man. I'm on a case.'

'The only time you ever call me.'

'Can't argue with you on that.'

Saxon explained the situation, told the Flying Pig where he was.

The Flying Pig was a hacker, one of the best on the planet, and he wasn't cheap, but he could generally dig up shit on anyone. He didn't use that terminology, of course. He preferred the term researcher.

'Busy?' Saxon asked.

'Ish.'

'I need some research on someone. There are a few links that come up on Google, but they have expired. Why would that be?'

'A number of reasons. Legal perhaps, the originator could have pulled them for a number of reasons or it may be as simple as the website no longer exists.'

'If I send you the links, can you get me the articles?'

'Is the Pope a Catholic?'

'Great. And get me anything you can on the bloke. Dig as much shit as you can. I'll send everything over in the next hour or two.'

‘Give me a few days.’

Saxon left the café as a fine sleet began to fall. He pulled up the hood on his jacket and looked up at the Matterhorn. It was fading rapidly in the gloom of the night. Iconic. Imposing. Dangerous.

More than 500 people had died there since records began.

Was Kate really up there somewhere?

The next morning, Saxon wanted to clear his head and pulled his bike up from the basement. He’d plotted a small route, a couple of hours in the mountains. A run back out to Randa and beyond, through St Niklaus to Stalden, twenty-three kilometres out and the same distance back again. 650 metres of descent to Stalden and then a tough climb all the way back up into Zermatt.

The city of Zermatt was a cyclist’s dream and a nightmare at the same time. At 1,600 metres above sea level, the hardest part of a Zermatt cyclist’s day would always be at the end. That was the reason Saxon didn’t see many cyclists in town.

He cycled out past the golf course, through Randa and James’s campsite. James’s motorhome was in the same spot. It hadn’t moved, the two bicycles still attached and chained to the back rack. It was still quite early. The curtains in the front window were still drawn. James was fast asleep. A late night, perhaps?

Saxon pushed on and almost freewheeled all the way into Stalden save for a few small uphill drags.

The town was located between the Matter and Saas valley. Stunningly picturesque at the foot of the enormous Dom Mountain.

Saxon laid his bike against a slate wall outside a café and wondered if it was warm enough to sit outside at one of the two small tables situated on a stone terrace. The terrace was surrounded on three sides by Alpine window boxes full of red geraniums.

It was getting cooler now despite the fact he had dropped so many metres. He looked once again at the monumental view of the snow-capped Dom and just couldn't bring himself to sit inside. He opened up the pannier on his bike and pulled out a light fleece. Another layer. He unzipped his jacket and took it off. He slipped the fleece underneath and put his jacket on top. He'd be fine for the duration of a couple of coffees and some sweet Swiss pastries.

He'd need the sugar boost for the return journey.

The sun made an appearance from behind the Dom. Soon after, the waitress brought the pastries and the coffee and once again, Saxon half wished he wasn't working on a case and that there weren't so many thoughts flying around his head. Around two in the morning, during his research on the Alps and missing people, he'd finally convinced himself that it was unlikely that Kate had met with an accident.

He'd been sitting outside the café for an hour when the sun disappeared behind a dirty black cloud and the temperature dropped ten degrees within five minutes. He picked up his coffee and headed inside.

It was time. He picked up his mobile and called Blacklock.

He shared the statistics relating to missing people and accidents in the Alps. He'd double checked the figures for fatalities in the Swiss Alps that the policeman had shared with him.

'Something isn't right, Neil.'

'No?'

'I spent most of yesterday evening checking out the fatalities and the missing persons and broke them down into specific regions. I concentrated on what the policeman called the dead zone, mountains more than three thousand metres high.'

'Go on.'

'Well, something doesn't add up. Two things to be specific. Firstly, for some reason, the death rate in the Swiss Alps appears slightly higher than in France and in Italy, around 15% higher over the last ten years. Prior to that, the deaths on mountains over three thousand metres in Italy, France and Switzerland were more or less the same.'

'More visitors,' Blacklock interrupted. 'As simple as that, Switzerland has worked hard on the tourism figures in recent years. There are more people visiting the Swiss mountains.'

'That may be the case,' Saxon said, 'but I was going on the ratio of visitors and besides, there's a more glaring discrepancy.'

'Which is?

'The sex of the dead people. Only one in ten of the dead in France and Italy are female.

'Makes sense, more men mountaineers than female.'

'Obviously. But do you want to take a guess at the ratio in Switzerland?'

'Over the last ten years?'

'Yes.'

'Tell me.'

'One in seven.'

There was a long silence as the figure sank in.

'Well, I agree, that doesn't make any sense at all?'

'I know Neil; I really don't know, but something doesn't add up. I can get that more people are visiting the mountains of Switzerland and therefore, by the law of averages, more people are dying. I get all that, but the male, female ratio just doesn't sit right.'

Neil Blacklock found it hard to comprehend what he'd just been told. 'And the figures are correct?'

'Yes, I've checked them out on three different databases.'

'So… what are you saying?'

Saxon didn't know what he was saying, but he had written the exact figures on a small notepad in front of him. He'd transfer the information to his tablet later.

Deaths on the mountains in general were on the increase. He'd found an article from an Alpine Climbing Group expressing concern that there should be some sort of a minimum level of competency for anything over 2,000 metres, some sort of a qualification. Good idea. But that would be almost impossible to police and it was all about tourism. Why would the authorities impose anything that would restrict visitor numbers?

'And I met with James Bonnier too,' Saxon said.

'Yeah. What did you think?'

'I'm not sure. The poor kid is in a bad way, drinking way too much and yet there were a few things which didn't make sense to me.'

'Like what?'

'I need to meet with him again, and the police, I'll go and see the police again and I'll push an initial report together after that. You'll need to let me know at that point whether you want me to carry on.'

Saxon could hear the frustration in Blacklock's voice. He knew the dog had got his teeth into the bone.

Chapter 15

The Swiss Police worked the standard three shift rota.

Six till two, two till ten, and a skeleton night shift. Saxon knew that if he positioned himself in the café opposite the police station shortly before two, he'd catch Detective Nuessle either going to work or leaving.

Nuessle was on the late shift. Saxon spotted him walking along the street fifteen minutes before 2 pm. He handed the waitress a 20 Franc note and didn't bother waiting for the change as he sprinted across the street and caught up with Nuessle just as he walked into the main reception area.

There were a lot of policemen in there. Logical, some just finishing, others just starting their working day.

'Detective Nuessle,' Saxon called out. The policeman turned. 'I wonder if I could have a word?'

Nuessle stopped. Looked at his watch. 'Not really, monsieur, I start work soon. I'm really quite busy and

I need to catch up with one of my policemen before he heads off home.'

'I understand,' Saxon said. 'It will just take five minutes.'

The policeman shook his head. 'No, sir, I haven't got the time. I'm busy.'

'It's important.'

'Not as important as my working day.'

Eggen Fassnacht was also on duty behind the reception desk. He had looked up and wanted to get involved somehow. He'd stepped out behind the desk and was confronting Saxon now. 'Monsieur, I really must ask you to leave. This is a busy police station. You shouldn't be here.'

Saxon called out to Nuessle who was about to disappear behind the door that led to his office. 'That's fine. I can always go to the newspapers with what I've found.'

That seemed to work.

Nuessle stopped dead in his tracks.

A few of the policemen stopped what they were doing, more than interested in what Saxon was saying. Fassnacht moved closer.

'I just need a few moments, detective.' Saxon smiled his best smile.

Nuessle turned, walked back towards Saxon. 'This better be good.' He raised his voice. 'This better be bloody good.'

'Oh, it's good,' Saxon said. 'I believe you have a hunter on the Haute Route, a man who is hunting young girls and killing them.'

There was a stunned silence. Saxon glanced around the room. Every policeman was looking at him.

He felt a hand on his arm. It gripped him hard. Fassnacht.

Saxon looked at him. 'Big mistake,' he said in a whisper. 'Now remove your hand or I'll snap your wrist like a stick.'

Fassnacht's hand fell away as he turned a ghostly white.

Saxon was sitting in Nuessle's familiar office within a minute. He wasted no time presenting the facts, laying out the details on a piece of A4 paper.

'It was the ratio of male to female deaths in Switzerland that threw up some discrepancies.' He pointed to the top of the sheet of A4. 'Here, look, this is the ratio of male to female deaths in the Pyrenees, the French and Italian Alps, the Scottish Highlands and even in Sweden and Norway. I've even looked at accident rates in America and the Himalayas. Female deaths in all of these mountain ranges account for around one in ten, which fits in perfectly with what the National Association of European Hikers state, that around one in ten of all hikers and climbers are female.'

The policeman sat in silence.

‘But not Switzerland. Your figures detective don’t correspond with the norm. Your figures are around one in seven, and do you want to know why?’

‘Shock me, Monsieur Saxon.’

‘Because of the Haute Route, that’s why.’

The policeman stiffened up. Leaned forward on the desk.

‘Take away the statistics for the Haute Route and Switzerland’s ratio climbs back to one in ten.’

Nuessle picked up a pen and twirled it between his fingers.

Saxon waited. He still held another ace up his sleeve.

Eventually, the policeman spoke. ‘I can’t explain it, monsieur. I’ll admit it’s quite unusual, but could it be that the Haute Route simply attracts more girls? Perhaps the Swiss Tourist Department advertises in female outdoor centres and gyms around Europe. Advertising is very clever these days.’

‘The same thought crossed my mind, detective. But then I did a little more research. I checked out the female deaths in the Pyrenees, the French and Italian Alps, Scotland, Sweden, and Norway, as well as America and the Himalayas. I studied only the female deaths, and I came to yet another interesting conclusion.’

The policeman steepled his hands, raised an eyebrow as Saxon continued.

‘Of all the female deaths, there were very few of them who met with an accident while going solo. It appears very few girls go solo, for the simple reason that they are less reckless than we men.'

'I can understand that.'

'Right. It's more of a risk going solo. We all know that. Break an ankle or a leg when you're with a companion or a group and someone goes for help. If you're on your own and there's no mobile phone reception, unless someone trips over you, you're pretty much fucked.'

The policeman laughed. 'Well, I wouldn't quite put it like that, but I take your point.'

'Look,' Saxon said. He pointed to the bottom of the page, to the figures. 'That number represents the total number of females killed or missing over the last decade while climbing or hiking in the eight countries I've mentioned.'

A huge female body count.

'But less than 5% of those deaths were girls who were going it alone.'

The policeman was aware of a sickening feeling building in the pit of his stomach. Bile was slowly creeping into his throat. 'Go on, monsieur.'

Saxon turned the piece of A4 paper over. More figures. More scribbles. 'Here detective, here are your total deaths on the Haute Route over the last ten years.'

His finger rested underneath the figure.

207

‘And here.’ His finger moved to the side. ‘The total number of girls who have been killed or whose bodies have never been found.’

28

‘So, if we were to apply the 5% solo female statistic to that number, we’d expect to have no more than a couple of girls who met with their death while going it alone. Correct?’

‘Yes,’ the policeman answered. ‘I can do the maths. Between one and two, three at the most.’

Saxon leaned back in his seat. ‘So do you want to take a guess how many solo girls have died or gone missing on the Haute Route over the last decade?’

‘Monsieur Saxon, I’m a policeman, I’m not in the habit of guessing. Go ahead, tell me.’

Saxon picked up his pen. Wrote on the bottom of the sheet in big black numbers.

17

‘Good God no!’ said the policeman. ‘That’s impossible.’

Chapter 16

It was a totally different man that Saxon sat opposite. His whole demeanour had changed, like a switch had been flicked.

He was angry at first, perspiration stood out on his brow as he sparred with Saxon. 'I can't fucking explain it, but nor am I going to start jumping to conclusions either.'

'Seventeen female deaths while going solo, detective.'

'There's a logical explanation.'

'Then tell me what it is?'

'I don't know, but it could be anything. Perhaps it's because the Haute Route is so busy, perhaps the solo climbers don't feel so vulnerable.'

'Fourteen or fifteen bodies too many, detective. You may have a hunter on the Haute Route, a hunter who targets lone females.'

'Rubbish.'

'You need to address this, detective; you need to open up an investigation.'

‘Don’t tell me how to do my job, I’ll do nothing of the sort. There’s a logical explanation. Someone has made a mistake with the data.’

Saxon reached into his rucksack. Pulled out his notepad. He started to speak. ‘*Kate Henshaw, Wilma Oetting, Jayne Hess and Patricia Oostag* disappeared while hiking the Haute Route, bodies never found.’

He turned the page. ‘They recovered the dead bodies of *Selena Garcia, Hejsa Gruber, Antoinette da Silva, Nadene Hanses, Emica Chan, Morgan Murphy, Shonda Johansson, Bridget Smith, Nicholle Palmer, Susan Muller, Chloe Korhonnon, Tierce Peeters and Taiya de Jong.*’

He tore out a sheet from the notebook and pushed it over the desk. ‘Here are the dates.’

Nuessle pushed it straight back. ‘I don’t bloody well need that. We have police computers. I have all the information.’

‘Then you’ll be doing something about it then. That’s good. I’ve given you the facts, something your department should have picked up years ago, but they haven’t.’

The policeman took a deep breath, wiped the perspiration from his brow with a handkerchief. ‘It’s not possible, it’s just not possible,’ he repeated.

‘What’s not possible?’

‘A murderer. You’re telling me we have a killer here in Switzerland?’

‘I’m saying that it’s a very real possibility and, furthermore, I don’t believe Kate Henshaw met with an accident. You would have found something.’

‘But serial killers, that’s an American disease.’

‘Then you have a poor memory detective, what about Werner Ferrari, Erich Hauert and the Sadist of Romont? All of them were Swiss serial killers.’

‘Yes, of course. I remember now, but…’

The policeman stood up and paced the room, not sure what his next move should be.

‘I’m here to help, Detective Nuessle,’ Saxon said. ‘You are burying your head in the sand if you are going to ignore this.’

‘I’m not going to ignore it,’ he snapped. ‘We’ll double check all of the figures.’

More pacing.

‘You still think it boils down to some messed up statistics, someone inputting the wrong data?’

The policeman walked over to his desk, flipped a cigarette out from a packet, and lit it. He took a long drag and blew a plume of smoke high into the air. ‘I am not saying anything, just that I don’t know for sure and we’ll need to check things out.’

Saxon had delivered his message; he knew now that at least the police were going to look seriously at what he had said. ‘I may be totally wrong, detective, and I hope I am. I sincerely hope that the deaths can be easily explained, but you need to be sure, because if more girls go missing and the press get a hold of this, there will be nowhere to hide.’

The policeman glared at him. ‘Monsieur, I don’t respond to threats, and believe me, I don’t intend to hide either.’

Saxon nodded. ‘I’m glad to hear it.’ A pause. ‘There’s one thing we can look at which will tell us for sure whether these girls met with accidents or whether they were killed.’

‘Go on,’ the policemen said.

‘I’m assuming the women’s bodies were photographed?’

‘Of course they were. That’s standard procedure, their bodies and the surrounding area. As a rule, we take at least a dozen photos.’

‘Then that’s where you need to start. That’s where the clues will be. A crime scene can give—’

‘Crime scene! Crime scene,’ he repeated. ‘Who said anything about crime scenes? These girls met with accidents. That’s what the coroner has reported and until anyone comes up with anything that convinces me otherwise, then that won’t change.’

‘I understand, but if there is a killer on the loose, he’ll have made mistakes and those mistakes may be found in the photographs.’

The policeman went to speak again. Saxon held up a hand.

‘Hear me out.’

The policeman let out a long, deliberate sigh.

‘As far back as 1912, an eminent forensic scientist, Edmund Lockart made a claim that most serial killers will not only leave something at a crime scene, but they often take things away.'

'Yes, I know that. They take trophies.'

'That's right. So, I think we should take another look at the photographs.'

'The policeman raised an eyebrow. "We?" You have no authority in this police station or this country.'

'But a fresh pair of eyes might—'

The policeman was already on his way to the door. He opened it. 'Goodbye, Monsieur Saxon. Thank you for all your help. We'll take it from here.'

'Just let me take a look at the photographs.'

'Goodbye.'

The detective accompanied Saxon out into the reception area. Most of the previous shift had disappeared, but a handful of policemen still hovered around, chatting with colleagues, studying their shift pattern, looking at what time their first coffee break was.

Nuessle walked Saxon right to the front door and even held it open as he watched Saxon disappear down the street.

He walked back to Fassnacht's desk. Leaned over, placed two elbows on the veneer top. 'You wouldn't believe that one. Claims we might have a murderer on the Haute Route, targeting lone females.'

Fassnacht's jaw fell open.

'Wants to help with the enquiry, wants the photos of all the girls who met with accidents. He claims there'll be clues that will point to a serial killer.' Nuessle stretched up towards the ceiling. Arched his back and Fassnacht heard a loud crack. 'Fucking clues. Sherlock fucking Holmes that one.'

Nuessle wrestled another cigarette into his mouth. 'Eggen, when you have five minutes, could you come into my office? I need a few things checked over.'

'Certainly, sir, I've a quick phone call to make and then I'll be right there.'

Chapter 17

Saxon had made up his mind. He would hike up to the Europahütte. He started to copy more information, found a detailed route guide on Amazon, and downloaded it onto his devices.

He'd always been a mountain man and knew what it meant to be prepared for all eventualities. Weather was key.

He logged into a weather app provided by the Swiss Tourist Office. There were also web cams placed at various locations on the mountains. He made a note. Would it be possible to view a tape of the webcams from the time Kate went missing? If he had been a policeman on an official enquiry – possibly. For him – unlikely.

But it was worth a try. He'd call into the tourist office.

The Europahütte was a refuge situated on the mountain at over 3000 metres.

According to the weather app, at 2,000 metres the temperature was three degrees above freezing with little or no snow covering. At 3,000 metres it was a different story altogether, between ten centimetres snow cover and six below freezing.

There was a ski and mountain shop not far from the hotel. His bank account was about to take a big hit.

The sales assistant, a young girl whose name tag read Claire, clearly knew what she was talking about. At first, she asked where he was heading and what he needed. He handed her a list, and he noticed a flash of a smile as she made a mental note of her potential commission for the day. She started with footwear. She said he needed winter insulated boots with a minimum of 400 grams of insulation.

'The weather will turn in the next few days,' she said. 'There's a lot of snow forecast.'

'I know,' Saxon replied. 'I checked it out.'

She asked his size, wandered through to the back of the shop and returned a few minutes later with four boxes.

He tried on all four pairs and she advised him not to choose based on price. 'They are new boots and you must choose based on comfort, on how they feel. It's as simple as that.'

She'd given him three branded pairs of boots and another which was shop brand. She smiled proudly as he announced that he preferred the shop's own make.

'Excellent choice, monsieur,' she announced. 'Swiss made in a factory less than ten kilometres from here. Unfortunately for you, also the most expensive.' She grinned.

She was clearly going to enjoy her morning.

'How much?' Saxon asked.

'Two hundred and fifty-five Swiss Francs.'

A mental calculation. *Just over 200 British pounds. Ouch.*

He bought a Berghaus insulated parka jacket, two pairs of socks and a hat, as well as some waterproof and windproof pants and a forty-five litre backpack. As he walked around the shop in his new footwear, Claire asked him for his list. She took it from him and returned ten minutes later with a small basket full of kit.

'These are my recommendations for your compass, whistle, binoculars, first aid kit, snow glasses, gloves, high energy snacks and lightweight avalanche shovel. Most of them are our own brand. They won't let you down.'

'I'm in your hands,' Saxon said.

She smiled.

'And would you recommend crampons and an ice axe?'

'Absolutely. You can never be too sure. You probably won't need them at this time of year, but you might encounter a little ice higher up. We hire crampons and ice axes. I'm happy to waive the charge, so you'll save yourself a few hundred francs. Just bring them back when you are finished with them.'

She wrapped everything up for him and handed him the ice axe and the crampons. The total bill was 1,360 Swiss Francs.

'Just over a thousand British pounds,' she announced with a big smile, as if reading his mind.'

'But worth every penny?'

'Absolutely, monsieur. You can't put a price on safety.'

As he walked out of the shop, a light drizzle began to fall.

Suddenly, he was looking forward to the adventure.

It had been some time since he'd been in the mountains.

Back in the room of his hotel, he was trying his backpack out for space. His Hoolie tent and his sleeping bag took up most of the bottom half of the pack, his extra layers came next and then his gas stove, pan, water bottles, first aid kit, and shovel. He lifted the pack onto his shoulders. Around twenty-five kilos, he guessed, perhaps a little more, but there was more than enough space for five or six days' supplies. He wrapped the crampons and ice axe in thick plastic and slipped them into a side-pocket. His knife and catapult went in the other. He had no plans to live off the land, no plans to be up there more than a night or two, but you could never be cautious enough.

Be prepared for any old shit was something that had been drilled into him for twenty years as a

Commando. Poor preparation prompts piss poor performance.

That night he found the short, twenty-two minute video of Heinz Frei and the Haute Route. He watched it six times.

There was a reason the policeman had recommended he watch it. Frei said on more than one occasion that the Haute Route was a summer hike and should not be attempted during the months from October to April. The wiry, stick thin man in his late thirties with a thin goatee beard thrust a finger at the camera at one point. 'Be responsible,' he said. 'It's not just your life at stake.'

Clear and concise advice.

Later that afternoon he wandered into town again, to the supermarket where he bought a bag of rice and some pasta, a dozen packets of dried soup and two boxes of cereal bars. He purchased an assortment of dried fruit, chocolate and nuts, some carrots, oatmeal, coffee, powdered milk, a small block of cheese, and a selection of preserved meats. Finally, he bought a single bulb of garlic. Worth the extra weight.

He was almost ready.

He made sure that his phone and his tablet were on charge for the rest of the evening and also charged up his high-capacity power pack charger, powerful enough to fast charge his iPhone and tablet up to five times.

The Google walking app had suggested it was a 6.35 hour climb to Europahütte. He'd take much longer than that and he was up and out of the hotel at 6.15 am. He strode out purposely for the first couple of hours, figuring that if Kate had met with an accident, it would be unlikely that she had met her fate at lower level.

After that he slowed down to a steady pace.

It certainly wasn't a moderate hike, and he was surprised just how technical it was in some places. Climbing. No other way to describe it. He remembered a very serious Heinz Frei in the video, in a distinctive red snood and fly away, jet black hair, telling his viewers and followers that it was anything but a Sunday afternoon stroll.

He couldn't agree more as he encountered his second climb using chains that had been secured to the rock face with metal bolts. The chains were there for no other reason than to hold on to, to stop you plunging more than 1,000 feet to your death. It was only about a 20 feet section, but as he got halfway across, he couldn't help taking a quick look down. An almost vertical drop onto the rocks below.

He pulled himself gingerly across the cold steel chain. It was probably time to consider putting his gloves on. He checked his phone. The temperature read -1.

When he was sure that his footing was secure and there was no chance of falling, he pulled his backpack onto the ground and located his binoculars.

He spent a full five minutes scouring the valley floor below. Looking back at the chains and the sheer drop, it was not beyond the realm of impossibility that a simple slip could be fatal.

But he discounted it.

At the bottom of the valley, it was fairly barren, a huge rock field. Kate had been wearing a red walking fleece. Her body would have been easily spotted down there.

He walked on. It was another few kilometres before he encountered the first ladders. 60 or 70 feet of metal ladders bolted to the rock face with a platform halfway up.

He remembered her boyfriend's words. *She wasn't good with heights.*

He rested on the platform, halfway up the climb. He sat down. Took out his water bottle and drank half a pint. He had some nuts, and dried fruit. He spent ten minutes taking in the sensational views out and over the iconic Matterhorn. Out came the binoculars again.

This was an insane place for someone who didn't like heights. Could it be that she panicked or simply slipped to her death on a section like this? He'd read that there were as many as half a dozen ladder climbs and a couple of sections with D rings hammered into rock.

He was beginning to side with the detective's theory that an accident was the more likely cause of Kate's disappearance and someone had messed up the stats on input.

He'd walked just short of twenty kilometres when the scenery changed. A slight covering at first, the grey rock and the grass visible in between the patches of snow, but gradually as he climbed higher, the white blanket that the detective had described began to hide everything.

He made it to the refuge at 5 pm.

It had been a long, hard climb, and he was ready to call it a day.

He had seen the photos of the refuge on the internet. There were even half a dozen videos on YouTube. He had always taken his research and preparation seriously.

The hut was empty, unsurprisingly, but it was unlocked. A simple slide bolt allowed the visitor access to the shelter. He couldn't help but smile as he looked around. A small wood stove in the centre of the octagonal structure and a generous supply of wood with a box of firelighters.

The fire would be his first task. He was beginning to feel the cold already. He had envisaged a quick dinner and then crawling into a sleeping bag to keep warm, but the fire was a real bonus. Saxon loved a real fire. It was a man thing and despite the temperature reading -4 outside, the small hut was like a sauna within twenty minutes.

He cooked up some rice and carrots and a couple of ounces of cured meat and chopped two cloves of garlic into the mixture. He took the pan from the stove and laid it on the table to rest. He searched around the small hut and found a dozen tins of beers in a cupboard that a warden had left behind. There was an honesty box on top of the cupboard and a notice where the warden asked for a contribution to the upkeep of the refuge and a few francs more if you took a beer.

Saxon slipped twenty francs into the slot of the wooden piggy bank. Money well spent. What a bonus.

He almost forgot why he was up there as he finished his evening meal and opened up another tin of beer. He lay back on one of the bunks and let out a long, satisfying groan. It was getting a little too hot in the hut, and he walked over and opened the door. A rush of freezing cold air hit him like a sledge hammer, but after a few minutes, the hot air from inside and the cold air from outside cancelled each other out, bringing the temperature down to a pleasant level. He slipped his jacket back on and sat on a stool by the door. He couldn't recall the last time he had felt so content as he watched a stunning sunset over the mountains.

He sat at the back door of the cabin for an hour or more, but eventually the temperature dropped even further and he had to retreat inside. He threw another log on the fire and his eyes fell on the visitor book.

Detective Nuessle had been right. Three entries. Hans from Norway, Tomas Bauknecht who'd had *a schönen abend,* a beautiful evening and finally an entry from Kate from England. Her comment read:

'Give me the sky and the stars and I want for nothing else.'

Chapter 18

It was a group of walkers knocking on the refuge door that woke him up. The guided walkers were well equipped and had set off early morning from the next valley. The guide leader apologised and had only wanted to show his clients the inside of the famous refuge, but wondered if there was any possibility of a hot drink. The weather had changed, a dull overcast day with flakes of snow in the air and the temperature had plunged dramatically.

Saxon played the perfect host and invited the group in.

The bottom of the wood stove was still glowing red from the night before, and he sparked it into life again with another couple of logs. Within ten minutes, the hot plate was red hot. He filled a pan and brewed up some fresh coffee.

The group were all Swiss apart from a lone Brit, a young female student from Bristol called Marnie. He thought about warning her not to go it alone, but as he got talking to the group and Marnie in particular, he ascertained that she wasn't the type to head off solo. She'd be safe enough.

The guide was an experienced hillwalker and climber from Zermatt, a middle aged man called Gert. Gert said that it was his last walking group of the season and he would have a few weeks' rest at home with the family before picking up his ski poles and spending the winter as a ski instructor. Another Haute Route summer only man.

Saxon picked his brains a little, about the black spots on the Haute Route. Gert told him categorically that it was one of the safest high altitude walks in the world, that if someone came to meet with an accident, it was generally, their own stupid fault.

'It's about assessing the risk factors,' Gert explained. 'Yes, there are places where you can fall, the ladder climbs, for example. I would never attempt them when they are iced up. The glaciers too, always with an ice axe and crampons. Walking across a glacier without the right equipment is suicide. There have been people caught out in blizzards and in avalanches too, but as long as you listen to the avalanche reports and the weather forecasts and wear the right clothing, you should be fine.' Gert swept a hand in a circle. 'And if the weather does turn unexpectedly, you can generally sit it out in one of these places as long as you have a little food.'

Saxon liked Gert and his group. He decided to tell Gert about Kate, that he was up there to have a look where she was last seen.

‘I suspect she met with an accident but her body has never been found.’

‘And where was she last seen?’

‘Here,’ Saxon said. ‘She posted a photo online more than a month back and has never been seen since.’

Gert was surprised when Saxon explained that she had been heading for Zermatt and that the weather had been good. Saxon gave Gert the exact date and he checked via an app on his phone what the weather had been like that day. ‘Clear blue skies and sunny, no snow or ice on the ground. That’s very surprising,’ he said.

Gert said that of course there were a few places where she could have met with an accident but he was fairly sure that if the police had carried out a thorough search, her body would have been found. ‘They found no equipment either?’

‘Nothing.’

Gert shook his head. ‘Unlikely,’ he said, almost bloody impossible.’

‘But bodies do go missing?’ Saxon asked.

‘Yes, of course they do, but that’s rare, and it’s normally in an avalanche.’ Gert held up a finger. ‘Just a minute,’ he said, as he pulled out his phone. He had located a website which detailed all of the known avalanches in the area. Gert was shaking his head. ‘The mountains were very stable during the time she disappeared.’

The mystery deepens, thought Saxon.

‘She hasn’t been lost in an avalanche, that’s for sure,’ Gert said. ‘And as for snow holes and crevices, well, unless she took a different route back to Zermatt altogether, then that’s an impossibility. The high route via the Europahütte is a bit tricky, the terrain is constantly moving and is prone to rockfall, so it can be quite dangerous. But again, we are only talking broken legs and ankles and even if she had cracked her skull on a fall, her body would certainly have been seen. There would have been plenty of hikers around at that time of year.’

‘And even if she hadn’t been seen and had died after a fall, the police should have discovered the body.’

‘Yes,’ Gert replied. ‘If the police had been doing their jobs right, then yes.’

Therein lies the problem.

Gert stood. ‘Well, it’s time we were getting going. We have a lot of kilometres to cover today. And you, my friend, where are you heading today?’

Saxon had only just made his mind up. ‘I’m heading for Chamonix.’

‘Is that wise?’ Gert asked. ‘The weather this time of years can change very suddenly and the snow and the ice and—’

‘I know, but I am well prepared and I’m going to stick to the low ground wherever possible, cut out the high passes.’

‘A wise move.’

‘And I have a tent as an emergency but I intend to stay over in the shelters and the refuges.’

‘And plenty food?’

‘Yes.’

‘Okay, I wish you luck, and don’t forget, you can drop down to a lot of towns and villages if the weather gets really bad. There’s no shame in spending a couple of nights in a warm hotel.’

‘Don’t worry,’ Saxon said. ‘I’m no martyr. The older we get, the less appealing a cold night in a tent is.’

They shook hands. Gert slapped him on the shoulder.

Saxon said goodbye to the group after they had finished their last of their coffee. He made a series of notes on what Gert had said, tidied the refuge up, washed the cups, and left it exactly how he had found it. Despite the weather closing in, more persistent snow falling, he had decided to retrace Kate’s footsteps, to the refuge James believed she had stayed at two nights before she went missing, the Cabane de Moiry.

Chapter 19

It had been a couple of years since Saxon had completed any serious mountain work and he felt the pain in his legs from the day before. The fifteen kilometres he had planned to walk turned into a twenty-one kilometre trek as he lost the trail so many times. Even though he had taken the lower route, parts of the trail were still dusted in snow and the red and white way markers were often hidden.

Nevertheless, he made it to the cabane in good time, well before darkness crept in over the mountain.

The Cabane de Moiry took Saxon completely by surprise. He knew the building was a permanent structure made of stone but was very much expecting basic accommodation similar to that of the Europahütte. The young couple, who introduced themselves as Paul and Suzy explained that they ran the cabane, cooked, cleaned and maintained it, said that he would likely be one of the last visitors of the season and that they were returning to civilization in their town of Grimentz, the following weekend. Paul said they'd had a long, hard summer; they were both looking forward to it.

He caught Suzy looking at him just a little longer than was necessary. A smile. Then it was gone. Suzy was attractive in a plain sort of way: a natural look, fine delicate features, no make up, perhaps twenty-eight or twenty-nine, blond hair tied up in a ponytail and a yoga body. Yes, definitely yoga. She walked like she was floating on air.

They both led Saxon through to his accommodation for the night, a spacious and well-planned room with half a dozen bunks with mattresses, spotlessly clean bedding and thick duvets.

'Are you doing the Haute Route?' she asked.

'That's the plan.'

'Lucky you, it's been ten years since I last did it, with some of my uni friends. We had a great time. I must do it again soon.'

'Well, you can't,' Paul said.

They looked at each other. Some telepathy, a glare, and then Paul spoke. 'She's always talking about heading off on her own, but I've told her that's just irresponsible. It's not safe for a girl on her own.'

'Sexist pig,' she replied with a forced smile.

'Only looking after you, darling,' Paul said.

Suzy ruffled one of the duvets, gave the pillow a shake, 'You'll be in here on your own tonight, monsieur.'

She explained that there were just another couple of guests booked into the other rooms. The accommodation area was clearly a bolt on modern extension to the original 1920s stone building. It was a modern glass addition offering sensational views of the Moiry Glacier.

'It's stunning,' Saxon said.

'It gets a little boring at times,' Suzy said. She walked towards the window and looked out. 'I know, it's spectacular, but sometimes you walk out in the mornings and don't even notice it.'

'Speak for yourself,' said Paul. 'I love it, I could stay here all year round.'

'He's a mountain man,' said Suzy. 'He sometimes takes off on his own and leaves me for two or three days at a time.'

'Only when we're quiet,' Paul said. 'But yes, it's true, it's like a drug. I book in and feed all of these bloody hikers and they tell me what a great time they're having in the hills and sometimes I get the urge and there's nothing I can do about it. I just have to get out of here and walk.' He turned and ambled slowly out of the room, 'See you later,' he shouted, as he walked down the corridor.

Suzy smiled again, introduced the evening menu. 'We have a traditional Swiss Bündner Gerstensuppe, followed by some oven baked chicken with vegetables and some fruit to finish off. The cost is 60 Swiss Francs and includes wine.'

A little expensive but, hey, what a view.

'That sounds great. What time do you want me?'

‘What time do I want you?’ A wicked grin. No doubt about it, this girl was flirting with him.

‘For dinner,’ Saxon said.

‘Ah yes,’ Suzy looked at her watch, ‘About an hour, Mr Saxon.’

‘Call me Sax.’

‘We eat on the terrace. It’s just about bearable at the moment but you will need a warm jacket and gloves. Most guests want to eat out there for the views, but if it gets too cold, we can always move inside.’

‘Fantastic, the terrace will be great.’

As Saxon walked out onto the terrace, Paul ladled him a glass of hot gluhwein. It was chilly on the terrace and he welcomed the feel of the hot glass in his hands. As the hot liquid trickled down his throat, he was centrally heated from the inside too.

What an incredible place to stay.

‘We are used to the cold,’ Paul said. ‘The gluhwein helps though.’ He grinned.

There were five place settings and within a short while, the other two guests, a young Canadian couple, sat at the table. The man, a small Maple Leaf crest on his lapel. Not married, no wedding rings and a recent courtship for sure. Holding hands under the table, sitting close. In love, plenty to say to each other and clearly enjoying each other’s company. Saxon took it all in.

Suzy and Paul were in situ too, enjoying a generous bowl of Gerstensuppe and fresh baked bread. Not close, the total opposite to the Canadians. A distance apart, looking for conversation with anyone but themselves. Friction. Tension.

At the end of the first course, Paul wheeled out a portable stone log burner and placed it at the end of the table.

'This will take the chill away,' he said.

When the chicken and vegetables arrived, Saxon had changed his mind. The dinner was worth every penny as he watched a multi coloured sky as the sun dropped behind a mountain in the distant south and for a while, forgot all about the reason he was there. He was another tourist, a hill walker, enjoying nature at its finest.

Saxon brought up the missing girl as Suzy brought out a large bowl of fruit and placed it in the centre of the table.

'Yes, she stayed with us. What a crying shame. She seemed a lovely girl, quiet but nevertheless a lovely girl.'

Quiet, thought Saxon. *Are we talking about the same girl?*

'She sat where you're sitting, Lenny, in that exact same seat. She had a little wine but turned in early.'

'Yes, and she left at first light,' Paul said. 'We didn't even see her for breakfast.'

Saxon sat for a while, thinking. The Canadian couple drifted away. They'd had a long day.

'Did you know her?' Paul asked.

‘I did,’ said Saxon. ‘We were in the military together. Her family have asked me to look into her disappearance. The fact that there was no body found gives them a little hope to cling to.’

Paul leaned back in his seat. He poured himself another gluhwein and topped up Suzy’s glass. ‘Mountains are dangerous. People don’t realise how dangerous.’ He looked at Suzy. ‘These mountains, for example,’ he swept his hand round in a half circle, ‘can hang onto bodies for years. Sometimes they are never found at all.’

‘So I believe,’ Saxon said.

‘You don’t suspect foul play, do you?’ Paul said.

Suddenly, Suzy’s eyes lit up as she sprang forward in her seat. ‘A mystery. Wow!’

‘A mystery for sure,’ Saxon said. ‘No body, no clothing, no blood, no equipment. It looks like she disappeared into thin air.’

‘And the police,’ Suzy said. ‘What do they think?’

‘Well…’ Saxon said, wondering how much he should disclose. ‘To be honest, I haven’t been over impressed with the Zermatt police. I don’t think they have been very thorough.’

‘No?’

Saxon shook his head. ‘The night Kate was here, were there many guests staying?’

Paul and Suzy looked at each other. Remained silent.

‘But you have a guest book?’

‘Yes, of course,’ Suzy said.

Paul was a little more hesitant. 'But not all guests sign it.'

Saxon turned to Paul. 'I realise that, but you keep a register of guests?'

'Yes, of course.'

'Then you'll know then.'

The vibes weren't good. For some reason, Paul didn't want to divulge the information. He tried to change the subject. Saxon persevered.

'So you'd have a register of all the names of the guests who sleep here.'

'Of course.'

'Could I take a look?'

'That information is confidential.'

Suzy interjected, 'it's not that confidential. It's no big deal if we tell him who stayed over that night.'

'That would be great,' Saxon said. 'I'm trying to get a hold of anyone who may have seen her the day she left here, possibly walked with her on the same route for a few hours.'

Suzy jumped to her feet and said something to her boyfriend in Romansh. He glared at her and she disappeared into the building. She reappeared ten minutes later with a sheet of A4 paper. 'I've photocopied this. These were the people who stayed that night, quite a few.'

Saxon took the list and studied it.

Paul stood. 'It's time for bed for me. He closed the door and the air vent to the log burner. A subtle hint. The red glow subsided almost immediately. 'It's been a long day, monsieur, and we are up at first light preparing breakfast.' He looked at Suzy. 'Are you coming?'

She held up her glass. 'I'll just finish this.'

Another steely glare and then he was gone.

Saxon's eyes followed him as he disappeared into the darkness.

'Miserable bastard,' Suzy whispered under her breath before breaking out into a laugh. 'Honestly, he needs to chill out sometimes.'

Definitely not the sweetest relationship, Saxon thought.

Saxon held out his glass and Suzy poured him another wine.

'It can't be easy,' Saxon said.

'What can't?'

'Running after people's arses for months on end. Not a lot of privacy, I'd guess. He seems uptight. Perhaps he's ready for that little break.'

'Hah! Suzy exclaimed. 'Don't let him kid you. He'd spend his life up here if they'd let him. Like I said, he takes off whenever the mood gets him, generally after some teenage blond bimbo who has stayed over.'

'What?'

'Oh, he thinks I'm stupid, but I've seen the pattern, I've seen the way he looks at them and I'm convinced he's fucked one or two of them here. I've woken up a couple of times and he's been gone. He comes back and I pretend to be sleeping. He thinks he's a real clever bastard.'

'You don't confront him?'

'No. What's the point? If that's what he thinks of me, then what can I do about it? He isn't going to change. Then they leave the next morning and after breakfast he announces he needs a break in the mountains and before I can say anything he has his boots and his backpack out and he's away chasing after them.'

'Oh… I'm sorry,' Saxon said as a shiver rippled down his spine.

'Don't be. When we get back down into Grimentz, he's history. It's my flat we share, and I already had the locks changed a month back.'

Saxon couldn't help but smile. Suzy topped up the two glasses. Moved a little closer.

'Tell me about that night with Kate. You say she was quiet.'

'Yes, like a little mouse, it was clear she didn't want to be a part of it. As you can see by the list, we had quite a crowd in that night. Everyone took dinner and there were four German men who made a bit of a hole in our beer supplies. Around 10 pm one of them produced a small speaker and connected it to his mobile phone. He started blasting out 80s disco music and Kate made her excuses and went to bed.'

Saxon shook his head. 'Very strange. She was always the life and soul of any party. It just doesn't sound like her at all.'

‘It was terrible when we read the papers about the missing girl and realised she had stayed with us.’ Suzy took another mouthful of wine. She drew her coat collar up to her chin. It was getting cold. ‘Did you know her well, intimately I mean? Was she your girlfriend at any point?’

‘No, not at all. We were in the same unit at one stage, relationships were strictly frowned upon.’

‘I see.’

‘Don’t get me wrong, she was very attractive, but we always kept everything on a professional footing.’

‘Very sensible, Monsieur Saxon.’ She raised her glass. ‘Here’s to keeping everything professional.’

Saxon raised his glass and as it was halfway to his mouth, Suzy leaned over, stopped the glass and kissed him gently on the lips. The kiss lingered. Saxon responded. Suzy slipped her tongue between his teeth and he felt the familiar swelling in his trousers. It had been a long time.

They sneaked through the ancient stone building and into the modern accommodation area like courting teenagers giggling and whispering, one or two glasses too many. Suzy placed a finger over her lips and stopped at a closed door. ‘Paul’s bedroom,’ she whispered. She held him back just long enough to hear a gentle low snoring emanating from the room. She pointed up the corridor. ‘Go.’

Saxon had no intention of objecting.

Suzy stayed until the early hours of the morning as they made love several times, convincing him that her boyfriend, only a matter of a few feet away, was out for the count until his alarm sounded at 5.45 am.

Nevertheless, Saxon persuaded her to go shortly before 4 am. He needed at least a few hours of sleep.

Saxon listened carefully as the soft footsteps plodded down the corridor. He heard a slight creak from the wooden door as it opened and then closed again. He gave it fifteen minutes. He dressed. Picked up his phone and switched on the built-in flashlight. He opened the door and crept barefoot along the wooden floor towards the office area.

Chapter 20

It was the rattle of dishes that woke him. It was just before seven and he'd felt better. The combination of one or two wines and no more than two hours' sleep had turned him into a walking zombie. God knows what sort of state Suzy was in, helping Paul prepare the breakfasts and the packed lunches for the other guests. Oh well, not the busiest of times. She'd cope.

After a cold shower and a shave, he made his way gingerly through the building and onto the terrace. Suzy's beautiful lithe body was on display in a lycra all in one. She was bare footed on a yoga mat in the downward dog position on the wooden platform of the terrace. *A little cold for that*, was Saxon's initial thoughts.

The Canadian couple were tucking into what looked like bowls of muesli. Their back packs were by their table, jackets on ready to leave as soon as the breakfast ritual was complete. Paul was nowhere to be seen… probably in the kitchen. Saxon moved to the edge of the terrace. Suzy flipped over into the

Sphinx position, arched her back and let out a long purposeful, deep breath.

Their eyes met. 'How you feeling?' she whispered with a grin.

Saxon stretched up to the sky, 'Like I could benefit from something like that. My body feels like it's been trampled on by a herd of donkeys.'

'You can join me anytime you want.' She winked.

Suzy stood, grabbed a towel and wiped the perspiration from her lower back and her forehead. 'Breakfast?' she asked.

'Please.'

'What would you like?'

'Whatever's going, some eggs if possible, a little toast and coffee.'

'Coming right up.' She squeezed his backside secretly as she slipped past him and disappeared.

It hadn't been a dream after all. It had really happened.

In a hugely embarrassing and awkward moment, Paul and Suzy waved off the Canadians and joined him at the table with a pot of coffee and the breakfast he had requested.

'Sleep well?' Paul asked.

'Err… not as well as I normally do.'

'And why was that?'

Did he know?

'Not sure, probably a little quiet out here if that makes any sense. I'm used to the noise of the city. Perhaps I've too much on my mind.'

‘You two put an awful lot of gluhwein away,’ Paul said. ‘Load of bloody empty bottles I had to move.’ He looked at Suzy and scowled. ‘I’m surprised you made it safely back to the bedroom.’

‘Well I did,’ she said, ‘and look at me, nearly two hours yoga this morning so I couldn’t have been that bad.’

Suzy didn’t wait for any approval. Instead, she asked Saxon what time he was leaving and where he was heading.

‘Chamonix possibly. Though I’m not one hundred percent sure. I want to check out a few of the refuges she may have stayed in, and—’

‘You really think something has happened to her, don’t you?’ Suzy interrupted. ‘Like she has been kidnapped or something.’

Before Saxon could think of a suitable answer, Paul had shot her down.

‘Don’t be stupid, you idiot.’

Harsh.

Paul continued. ‘She was hiking and climbing in the mountains. She’s had an accident; any fool can see that.’

He was on his feet, tutting and cursing under his breath. He collected the dishes and stomped away from the table.

‘I’m sorry,’ Suzy said. ‘He’s not normally like that.’

Saxon held up a hand. ‘Don’t apologise for him. He’s his own man, but something is getting to him.’

Saxon leaned forward. 'He either knows about last night or—'

Suzy shuffled a little closer. 'Mmm… last night… I wish you were hanging around a bit longer.'

The back of her hand brushed his leg. Saxon felt chemicals stirring deep within as he remembered the throes of passion from the night before, made all the more exciting because of the danger involved in getting caught. 'No, I'd like to, but I have to get going.'

She looked a little disappointed. 'But perhaps… we could meet up again?'

Saxon stalled. It wasn't what he wanted to hear. He had no time or inclination for any sort of relationship.

'After I've—'

He remembered what she'd said about ending it with Paul.

She didn't finish her sentence, instead she collected a few plates and disappeared into the cabane. She reappeared and handed him something. 'The guest book. You were looking for it yesterday.'

'Yes.'

'It would be nice if you could sign it.'

'I will.'

He took the book from her. It was open at today's page. He skipped back a page or two. No entries from the Canadians. Why?

He signed it, placed a comment in the comment box.

A thoroughly enjoyable stay, stunning location.

'And your phone number too,' Suzy grinned as she handed him the pen back.

'Of course.'

Against his better judgement, he jotted down the number. He flicked back to the previous month. He found Kate's entry.

My mountains are waiting. I won't let them down.

Me and my mountains, that's all.

'It's a bit of a strange comment, don't you think?' Suzy said. 'I remember reading it after she left.'

Saxon nodded. 'I was thinking the same thing.'

'It's as if—'

'What Suzy? Tell me what you are thinking.'

'Well… it's like something is on her mind, like she is writing for herself, like she is convincing herself that she is doing the right thing. Those last two words, *that's all.*

Like that's all she needs. In a way, it's quite inspirational and determined and yet I remember her that night. She was anything but determined. She looked nervous, frightened even.'

'Frightened?'

'Well, perhaps not frightened, but like something was bothering her.'

Saxon made a mental note. Very similar to the message at the Europahütte.

He felt ready to share some more information with Suzy, but just as he was about to talk, Paul appeared back on the terrace. He tapped Suzy heavily on the shoulder. 'I'm not paid to do your work as well.'

Suzy let out a sigh, picked up the coffeepot. 'I must get on. We have a lot of things to do to secure the cabane for the winter.'

Saxon eased himself from the table. 'Me too. I need to get going.'

'Where are you heading today?' Paul asked.

'Les Haudères,' I hope. 'It's about sixteen k, but if it's anything like yesterday, I'm bound to get lost.'

Paul looked serious. 'Like I said last night, it's easy to get lost up here, to stray from the paths and then… well, if the mist or low cloud comes in, anything can happen. The mist comes in, you get disorientated and wander towards a sheer drop.' He stared at Saxon, in a whisper, 'That's what probably happened to your friend.'

A face like the prophet of doom.

'I'm sorry, monsieur, but that's the reality of it. Her broken body will be found one of these days and then her family can grieve properly.'

'Paul!' Suzy said. 'Be a little tactful.'

'I'm sorry Suzy,' he turned to Saxon, 'but you have to face facts. She's had an accident. There's no way would she survive in this hostile environment. I feel, Monsieur Saxon, you are on one of those wild English goose chases.'

Chapter 21

Saxon was following the shoreline of the beautiful Lac de Moiry when his mobile rang. *Unknown number.*

'Hello.'

'It's Suzy.'

He didn't know why, but he smiled. 'Hey, what are you up to? I thought you were busy.'

'Where are you?'

'Lac de Moiry.'

'Beautiful, I know it well. Look, I'm an hour behind you if you could hang around. Do you mind if I join you for a day or two?'

Momentarily taken by surprise, Saxon stalled. 'Do you think that's a good idea? I mean, Paul, what will he say? I thought you were both busy?'

'I've walked out on him; it was the last straw.'

'What happened?'

'I'll explain when I get to you. If you let me, that is?'

What could he say?

It was a fine day; the sun was almost directly overhead and warm enough to sit out. He walked down to the shore of the lake and bent down. He put his hand in the water. It was like ice. What did he expect? The lake filled directly from the glacier. He laid his rucksack down and opened it, reached for the towel, and started to strip naked.

He managed twelve minutes in the icy cold water before he started to shiver, but the burning sensation as he walked out of the water was exhilarating. He towelled off and dressed. He lifted out his stove and boiled up a kettle of water, made some tea. He sat and took in the stunning mountain views, sipping on the hot liquid as his temperature gradually returned to normal and the shivering subsided.

He'd had worse days.

Saxon spotted the familiar tiny figure cresting the hill from the far side of the lake. She shouted and waved. Saxon stood up and waved back. He refilled the kettle, relit the camping stove and dropped a couple of coffee sachets into the water.

He welcomed Suzy to his little personal paradise with a cup of sweet coffee, and she sat down beside him.

She was quiet at first. Almost reluctant to tell him what had happened, but eventually blurted it out. 'He heard us.'

'Fuck.'

'Yes, apparently I'm a little noisy when I climax.'

'I hadn't noticed.'

‘As soon as you left, he confronted me. Said I was lower than the dogs on the street. I threw it back at him. I knew who he’d been fucking over the last six months, at least three that I could recall. I even remembered their names. Girls called Joan, Shonda, and a Scottish girl called Aggie. I said—’

‘Whoa,’ Saxon interrupted. ‘Did you say Shonda?’

‘Yes, the first month we were there he was all over her, a Scandinavian girl I think, Norwegian or Finnish.’

‘But definitely called Shonda?’

‘Yes.’

Saxon shook his head slightly. He took her hand.

‘What is it, Sax? What’s wrong? You look like you’ve just seen a ghost.’

‘Shonda,’ he said. ‘That was one of the girls who met with an accident this year. They found her body at the bottom of one of the ladder climbs. It’s an unusual name.’

He reached for his tablet and switched it on. ‘Do you remember her surname?’

‘No, I don’t. Scandinavian sounding, I think. But no.’

Saxon located the document. Scrolled down the page. Found her. ‘Was it Johannsen?’

‘Yes,’ she said immediately, ‘that was it. Shonda Johannsen, she stayed with us in the first few weeks of the season. My God, I never realised she had died.’

It wasn’t difficult to establish that the Norwegian girl who had been killed on the 14,000 feet, Dent

Blanche Mountain, at a notorious accident black spot, had been the same girl who had spent an evening in Cabane de Moiry.

'Lenny, tell me what's going on. Please.'

'It's a long story,' he said, 'but I think you should know, and more importantly, I want you to tell me everything you know about Paul.'

They sat down on Saxon's inflatable bed mattress and he told her the details of all the girls who had died on the mountain in recent years and the fact that most of them had been hiking on their own. 'Was Shonda Johannsen on her own?' he asked.

Suzy nodded silently.

He explained the lack of interest and activity from the Zermatt police, how he'd asked for the accident scene photographs of each girl, but how the detective had flatly refused.

'If I could see those photos, there may have been a clue or two, something that proved it wasn't an accident.'

'How come?'

'Well, I've studied the profile and actions of serial killers over the years. The mindset of a serial killer fascinates me greatly. I was lucky enough to spend some time with one of the FBI's top profilers in the States.'

Suzy stiffened up in shock. 'Stop! Stop right now. You're not telling me there's a serial killer up here, are you?'

'No. Not yet anyway, that's not what I'm saying. I'm investigating Kate's disappearance and I'm keeping an open mind. But—' he hesitated.

'Yes.'

'But there are some inconsistencies that need explained to me.'

'What sort of inconsistencies?'

'Well, what if I told you that there have been more girls killed on the Haute Route than any other long distance walking trail on the planet?'

It was Suzy's turn to turn a pasty shade of pale. 'I feel sick,' she said.

'And there's another thing.'

'What?'

'He turned the tablet to face her. He started to scroll down the page. 'These are the dates of the girls who have died.' He pointed to the screen. 'Here, look, Kate Henshaw was the last one to go missing, but then, just a few months before that, Shonda Johansson's body was found. And look, here, ten years back, just one dead girl in a sixteen-month period, Taiya de Jong. And then, fourteen months later, we have another girl, young Tierce Peeters. But then, the next girl is found ten months later.'

Suzy shook her head gently. 'I don't know what you are getting at.'

'Nine months after that, Chloe Korhonnon and another body eight months later. Fast forward to this year and we have Shonda and Kate, just four months apart.'

‘I get it,’ Suzy said. ‘So the accidents are getting more frequent. But what does that mean?’

‘Well, remember that I’m not trying to say that we have a serial killer just yet, but it’s a classic trait of what’s known as a sequence killer, that as time progresses and a murderer remains at large, the frequency of the killings increase.’

‘Fuck.’

‘I watched an Ed Kemper interview once.’

‘Who was he?’

‘He was known as the Co-Ed Killer. He murdered eight young students in California in the early seventies. Towards the end of his reign of terror, his killings got more frequent. He described his first couple of murders as satisfying him for a while, but as time passed, the need to kill only intensified and towards the end, he was killing at the rate of one every couple of months. In what would be his last killings, he killed his mother and her best friend on the same day.’

‘But fuck,’ Suzy said. ‘Why did he kill all of those poor girls?’

‘Well, he’s clearly a psycho, but in his interview, he said it was essentially about control and sex. He found that murdering girls was sexually arousing and stimulating. He was a necrophiliac, he had sex with some of the dead girls, it was the only way he could get off.’

Suzy stuck her fingers into her mouth, pretended to retch. 'How gross. Yeah, I've heard of that. Why would anyone want to have sex with a corpse?'

'It gets worse. Kemper decapitated some of the girls and had oral sex with their heads.'

Suzy wasn't play acting this time. She really did look like she was about to be sick.

'I think I read something like that before,' she said. 'Some fucking nut who kept heads in his fridge.'

'Jeffrey Dahmer,' Saxon replied, 'the Milwaukee Monster, fifteen or sixteen murders I think. He was a necrophiliac and a cannibal. He ate his victims. And Denis Nilsen, the London homosexual killer. He kept his dead victims for sex, sometimes for months afterwards until the smell was too much for him and he chopped them up and put them in plastic bags under the floorboards.'

Suzy held up her hand. 'Enough, I don't want to hear anymore. I was out for a couple of pleasant days on the mountain.'

'I'm sorry,' Saxon smiled. 'But you did ask.'

'Can we change the subject please,' said Suzy. 'I think I've had enough.'

'Of course.' Saxon started to pack away the camping stove, washed out the small kettle in the lake. 'We'll need to get going if we're going to get to Les Haudères before dark.'

Chapter 22

They made it to Les Haudères after a tough and demanding day. It had been an easy stroll along the lake at first, in pleasant sunshine and although a steep ascent had taken its toll on Saxon's knees, they had climbed through the mist and onto a rocky section and a big climb before spotting Les Haudères, through the low clouds in the valley. It had been difficult to navigate, with sometimes no trail at all visible for many kilometres. With no mobile phone coverage, Saxon had resorted to the good old map and compass.

The picturesque small hamlet was overlooked by the imposing Roc Vieux. Saxon had no idea where Kate had stayed the night in Les Haudères, or indeed if she'd even made it there. James said that the town had been in her plans, but she was also the type of girl who could change her mind at the last minute. There was a decent sized camp site at Molignon and two hotels, the main Hotel des Haudères and a smaller one called Dents de Veisivi.

The decision of whether to camp or hotel for the night was a fairly simple one, as Suzy had no tent or sleeping bag.

He tried to explain the importance of carrying shelter in the mountains, particularly at this time of year, but Suzy had smiled flirtatiously and said she had planned to cosy up in his tent, sharing a sleeping bag together.

'Impossible,' Saxon had replied. 'It's a two-man tent but my sleeping bag is light and compact. There's barely enough room for me and once I'm in, you'd be lucky to slip a sheet of paper in there.'

'Shit,' Suzy said mischievously. 'We'll just have to put up with a big double bed and a warm duvet then.'

Saxon thought back to the previous evening and their illicit night of passion.

Suddenly, a damp canvas tent didn't sound so attractive.

They managed to book a double room at the Dents de Veisivi for less than a hundred Swiss Francs. A traditional wooden built hotel, the red geranium window boxes were in late bloom, giving a spectacular display against the background of pine trees clinging onto the sheer rock face which towered over the hotel. The receptionist pointed to the lift. They were on the top floor. 'The best views of the Dents de Veisivi Massif,' she said.

She wasn't wrong. Saxon opened the door with the key card. A beautiful smell of pine from the old wooden walls, the bed, made of solid wood too. Like stepping back in time but with soft, expensive looking furnishings and an ensuite bathroom. The shower was the obvious first port of call. They were both filthy from the effort of a long hard day.

Saxon opened the door to the ensuite. 'Could have done with a good bath, but the shower looks good.'

Suzy moved behind him. 'Big enough for two, I'd say.'

Saxon was already starting to get stripped. 'If that's what you have in mind, we'll have to be quick,' he said. 'I want to check out the campsite if possible.'

'Ever the romantic, aren't you?'

Saxon wanted to say that he'd never asked for romance, that she'd invited herself to the party. He decided to let it lie.

Camping Molignon was situated by a river and surprisingly full for the time of year.

'We still get a lot of campers in the winter. It's a big macho thing,' Suzy said. 'Some of them wouldn't be seen dead in a hotel. They walk and climb, but most of them stick to the lower slopes. Some don't even leave the town centre. For them, it's more about the camping. They love it.'

Saxon could relate to that. There was nothing like a night under canvas in a good tent and sleeping bag. Ever since his father took him camping over to the Lake District as a kid, he'd loved it. Even in the military, when his mates were complaining about their canvas accommodation, he'd never minded too much, except when coming under attack in Iraq. The thin walls of a tent didn't give so much protection to a mortar shell, but thankfully, he'd been lucky. Not so a few of his best pals.

There was a small café bar on site which doubled up as a reception area. It looked like it was about close for the night, a young girl pushing some paperwork into the desk drawers. A small handbag on the desk and a mobile phone, a thick coat also on the corner of the desk.

A student. Research and study books in a large open bag on one of the seats, a pencil case sitting neatly on the top.

'Can I help you?' she asked.

'Yes,' Saxon answered. He pulled his wallet from his pocket, opened it, held it up towards her and said, 'I'm from the British police, investigating the disappearance of Kate Henshaw, a couple of months back.' He quickly returned his wallet to his pocket. 'Do you remember her?'

The young girl looked a little nervous. 'I had heard someone had disappeared. Was that her name?'

'Yes, I was just wondering if she had stayed here. We believe one of her destinations was Les Haudères.' Saxon slipped a piece of paper onto the desk. 'We believe that was the date she would have stayed.'

'Err… I'm not sure. Perhaps I should call my boss. He's not here, he's in Zermatt.'

‘No need. Do you have a guest book? It will only take a minute.’

‘We have a register for anyone that camps. We take some ID, a passport, that sort of thing.’

Saxon put on his best smile. ‘Do you mind if I take a look?’

The girl hesitated. ‘I’m not sure—’

Saxon jumped in. ‘Look, I can have a quick look to see if she stayed or I’ll get the local police to get your boss over here tonight. That’s about a two-hour drive just to get here.’

The girl frowned.

‘It’s up to you, two minutes now or we can all hang around for the rest of the night until your pissed off boss arrives.’

The girl didn’t really have any choice. Reluctantly, she opened the desk, pulled out a large register and started to flick through the pages. She opened it at the specified date and slid the book across the desk. Saxon checked the date, the day before and the day after.

Nothing.

He closed the register, looked up and smiled. ‘Thanks for your help, you can get off home now.’

A puzzled look.

‘And here,’ he slipped twenty francs onto the desk, ‘I was a student too, get a couple of drinks at the weekend.’

As they walked outside Suzy tugged at his sleeve. ‘You didn’t tell me you were with Interpol?’

‘I’m not,’ he smiled.

‘But the gold badge you showed her, what was that?’

‘An AMEX gold card with my thumb over the AMEX logo. It works every time.’

Suzy froze, stood still as Saxon kept on walking. She shook her head from side to side. ‘For fuck’s sake.’

Chapter 23

He'd been incensed when he found her note. It had been quiet. Too quiet, and while at first he thought she was catching up on a few hours' sleep, as it approached midday, he knew something wasn't quite right. He'd crept into the darkened room and switched on the light. It was empty and his eyes focussed immediately on the envelope on the pine dresser. He knew. He knew fucking straight away what it was going to say.

He bounded across the room and ripped it open. He seethed. She'd had enough. The relationship wasn't going anywhere. It was over.

The fucking bitch. She was like all the rest. Mother had been right. Mother was always right.

She hadn't said where she was going, but he had a good idea she would try to catch up with the Brit. 'Les Haudères,' he'd said. The bitch wanted his cock again. She'd been starved for so long and the little taste she'd had the night before made her want more. He'd heard them. They thought they'd been so clever; thought he'd been asleep when she'd fucked and sucked him until the early hours of the morning. He'd heard everything. The bitch. The British bastard. They'd both pay.

He'd packed up his things and set off just after one. He left the cabin unsecure. Fuck the two guests that were booked in that evening, but at least they'd be able to get in. He'd left a note, apologising, a family crisis he'd written and said that they could help themselves to the food in the fridge, the wine in the cellar and that their beds were made up in room three.

Hopefully, they wouldn't contact the authorities and they'd still renew his contract next year, and he'd be back doing what he did best.

He'd picked up a few supplies and packed them onto the quad.

He chuckled to himself as his binoculars focussed in on the couple as they left Camping Molignon, heading back south into the main village of les Haudères. A ten-minute walk to their hotel.

A shiver ran up his spine and he cursed as Suzy reached for Saxon's hand. *Fucking holding hands*, he said to himself. *Fucking bastards.*

They'd be heading for one of the local restaurants or perhaps even back to the hotel they had checked into earlier. He'd be patient. He wouldn't bother them just yet. He'd wait until they were on the mountain and then he'd strike. After all, that was his domain. He'd stalk them.

That was where the real pleasure lay, in the chase. He'd hunted these hills and mountains since he was a child, he'd hunted with mother. Father had long since gone.

She'd taught him well, taught him patience and how hunting was an art form, a battle of wits, of patience. And he'd remembered those days in the hide. The hide that mother had built, a hide so good that nobody had even spotted it in the five years it had been built.

Two days and two nights they'd spent in there. They'd ate, slept, pissed and shit in a bucket and mother had refused to let him step one foot outside the crudely constructed doorway, camouflaged with branches, moss and leaves.

She'd dozed off for a few minutes here and there, but he was convinced she'd never slept more than an hour or two during the whole period. And then she'd poked him in the ribs as he was fast asleep. It was early morning. A blanket of mist seeped eerily into their dwelling. She'd said nothing, just pointed to something in the trees, no more than thirty metres from where they were. A big buck stag, head in the air, nostrils twitching, sensing something but not quite sure what. She'd quietly handed him the rifle.

It was time to come of age.

He could hardly hold the rifle, his hands trembling like the leaves in the breeze.

She'd put her finger over her lips and pointed to the stag again. He raised the rifle, his finger found the trigger and as his mother had taught him he took a long breath and held it. One, two, three, four seconds.

A crack.

The beast fell to the forest floor.

The kill was the climax of the two days.

Or so he thought.

Mother told him that the kill wasn't important. The real thrill was the animal falling into the trap, outwitting him with nothing more than a little cunning and patience. It was about knowing the wind direction, being quiet above all else, about knowing the feeding patterns and the trails.

He'd wanted to sprint over to the dead buck. He could hardly contain his excitement. But not mother. She made him walk over slowly. Respect. Paul had caught the buck in the neck. It was bleeding profusely and breathing heavily, not quite dead. A tiny whine coming from his mouth. He hadn't managed the clean head shot his mother had demanded. She slapped him hard across the face. Told him he had made the animal suffer.

She held out the knife. 'Finish him off,' she'd said.

'How?'

'His throat. Cut his throat, not from side to side but from the bottom of the neck just above the chest, right up to the base of the chin.'

He hadn't wanted to, but his mother wouldn't take no for an answer. She back handed him several times across the head and punched him hard in the chest.

‘Do it, you little fucking wimp,’ she commanded, and thrust the knife into his hand.

As he plunged the knife into the carotid artery, a rush of air escaped from the animal’s throat and it gurgled as a spray of blood hit young Paul in the face. He turned away and vomited.

Mother laughed out loud.

The knife quivered in the beast’s body. Mother demanded he return to the task at hand. She made him grip the sharp knife and slice right up to the animal’s chin.

More blood. More vomit. More laughter.

They gutted the beast there and then, throwing the waste deep into the forest. Mother said that the insides of the deer would feed a menagerie. Nothing would go to waste. The rats and mice would move in under cover of darkness and finally the insects.

The first kill was always the worst. Then it gets easier. In fact, it gets pleasurable. Control. Playing God.

It becomes addictive. Sensual.

Later that night, the deer skinned, sectioned up and wrapped in plastic bags in the freezer, Mother came to him.

He’d become a man that day. That’s what she had said. Not the fucking useless article that his father had been.

She climbed into his bed.

Chapter 24

'I don't think she stayed in the town,' Saxon said.

'No?'

'No, I doubt it. If she didn't stay at the camp site she would have been at our hotel.'

'How do you know she didn't?'

'I checked it out when you were making yourself pretty after our shower.'

Suzy asked how he had possibly managed to do that.

'There was only one person at reception and I created a diversion outside. Her car alarm. When she went outside to check, she was already logged on to the computer and I nipped behind the desk and checked out the dates.'

Suzy stopped. 'Hang on a second. How did you know which car was hers?'

'Easy peasy,' said Saxon. 'There was a little keyring on a handbag behind reception, a mini. There was only one receptionist and only one mini in the carpark.'

Suzy let out a gasp. 'I never would have believed it. Eat your heart out, Sherlock Holmes. You really are the master of observation, aren't you?'

'Elementary, my dear Suzy.'

'But she could have stayed in the other hotel.'

Saxon shook his head. 'Too expensive. She wouldn't have paid that much money for a bed. The cheapest room was nearly two hundred Francs.'

'Ouch.'

'My guess is that she wild camped somewhere up there.' Saxon pointed up into the mountains. 'But there's no guest books up there and no fellow guests either.'

'So that's what you have been wanting to do, trace the other guests who may have stayed with her in the cabanes, the refuges and the hotels?'

'Yes, and the official campsites. I have an acquaintance who is good with computers. I wanted to see if he came up with anyone with a dodgy background.'

'What does a dodgy background mean?'

Saxon laughed, 'I'm sorry, I suppose that's a north of England expression. It means we are looking for someone with a criminal record, a history of violence, domestic abuse against women, that sort of thing.'

'I see. And your friend can check that out?'

'Yes.'

Saxon pondered for a moment. The Flying Pig hadn't come back to him yet. 'Give me a few days,' he'd said. He'd dig what he could on Heinz Frei, the Haute Route specialist, with a playboy lifestyle.

He'd call him first thing tomorrow.

Chapter 25

Suter climbed the hill in the darkness. He had nothing more to pick out his route than the light of the full moon. The moon was useful, but he also knew he was in for a cold night, but hopefully dry.

The hill was steep, there was no track as such, but he wasn't going too far. He picked his way through the dense forest. After no more than twenty minutes, he stopped, turned around and looked out over the village. The lights of Les Haudères twinkled seven hundred metres below him, and he grinned. It really was a picture postcard. What a beautiful place to spend the evening. And then the grin was replaced with a scowl and a realisation of what would be going on in a hotel bedroom not far away.

They'd fucking pay.

He looked around and found a spot. Relatively flat, a slight slope. Perfect. A few rocks and boulders that he quickly removed. But good cover nevertheless, even a fire or a light wouldn't be seen from the town below.

He stamped down the grass, threw a few more loose stones away, and opened his rucksack. It was called a fishing shelter; in reality, it was half a tent with an open front. But it was one of the most expensive on the market. Tough as old boots, strong, sturdy and waterproof.

He checked the wind direction and assembled the poles, pitched the tent and pegged it out, hammering in the steel spikes with a rock. He placed the rucksack in the entrance and located his Maglite.

He needed to eat, hadn't eaten anything since breakfast time. But he'd left in a rush and intended to travel light. He'd make do with the ham and eggs he'd taken from the fridge in the cabane. Perhaps he'd drop down to the village early next morning, find a café that was cooking hot breakfast.

He sat in the entrance of the tent; belly full and binoculars trained on the hotel below.

The binoculars weren't cheap either: Russian made, 12 x 50 with a FMC zoom lens and a tripod for added stability.

The binoculars took him right into the restaurant where the couple dined on steak and vegetables washed down with a red wine. Hell, the field glasses even read the wine label. An expensive Burgundy.

They looked so happy together. And warm. Suter was envious of the roaring log fire towards the back of the dining room. He pulled up his collar, blew warm air into his hands and wondered what he wouldn't give for a hot coffee.

He watched for over an hour until eventually he saw the waiter deliver the bill. Saxon reached for his wallet and placed a credit card on the small silver tray. The waiter brought a card machine to the table. Saxon punched in his pin numbers and the waiter nodded and walked away.

A few minutes later, they stood and made their way out of the dining room and disappeared into the darkness of a corridor.

Suter altered the focus of the glasses. The picture opened up. He trained them in on the whole of the front of the hotel now, not just one table in the dining room. By moving the glasses slightly to the left, he could also see the west side of the hotel. He had established that most of the bedrooms were on the west side and front of the building. Nine bedrooms on the front, a further six on the west side. He prayed that he would be lucky.

He waited, seven bedrooms on the front in darkness, all six on the west side, pitch black.

Less than three minutes later, his prayers were answered when a top floor bedroom window burst into light.

'Hallelujah.'

A change of focus, the whole of the bedroom window filled his viewfinder. Suzy, then the Englishman wandered into the bedroom without a care in the world.

'Bastards, utter bastards.'

Suzy pushed Saxon playfully onto the bed and leapt on top of him.

'Like a fucking dog on heat.'

She straddled him, leaned forward, and kissed him passionately on the lips. Saxon slid two hands around into the small of her back and Suter felt himself surprisingly growing erect.

He reached into his rucksack for the box, lifted it out, and placed it gently onto the grass. The Ruger Ranch Rifle was his pride and joy. A little on the heavy side at four kilos, but well worth the effort. It never let him down. He paired the coated chassis and aluminium hand guard then clicked the pistol grip into place. The buttstock and the barrel next. The rifle was modelled on the classic Ruger Mini-14 a .223 calibre semi-automatic rifle, particularly popular with hunters and target shooters. He connected the Leupold optics.

He was ready.

The binoculars were safely packed away. He wouldn't need them anymore. He focussed in on the bedroom once again. The scope was almost as good as the binoculars, and his excitement grew as he noticed Saxon's hands in the back of Suzy's jeans. Suzy reached around and grabbed his hands as she slowly rose from the bed and stood just a few feet from the window. Fiddling with a belt and the zip, she let her jeans fall to the floor and then her hands were in her panties as they dropped to her ankles.

Suter cursed. He wished he didn't need two hands to hold the rifle.

He took a deep breath and held it.

Suzy was back on the bed, her beautiful ass pointing into the air. What a stunning view he had. Little did she know that high up on the mountain, just over a kilometre away in the darkness, the man she had walked out on was taking in the spectacular night show. They'd left the curtains open, and why not? They were on the top floor. It wasn't as if someone would be looking in and there was no building in the near vicinity that was higher than the Dents de Veisivi Hotel.

A full erection now. It poked uncomfortably into the buttons of his crotch.

Giving him head now. What a dirty fucking whore she truly was.

The focus blurred a little. He needed it sharp. Precise. He raised the barrel a fraction of a millimetre and Suzy's head centered in the cross wire.

He held his breath again and his finger slipped around the trigger.

Saxon reaching behind his head, his face a contortion of ecstasy, as the room plunged into darkness.

Chapter 26

Suzy was still sleeping as Saxon made his way down into the small lounge reception area and collected that day's internet login details. He booted up the tablet and spent twenty minutes collating some more facts and figures and eventually logged into his email account. The first mail he noticed was from the Flying Pig. In the heading, it read *Heinz Beanz Badz!*

As he clicked onto the body of the mail, there was nothing, just two words, *call me.*

Saxon reached for his phone. The Flying Pig answered after half a dozen ring tones.

'You bastard, Sax, you woke me up. Do you know what time it is?'

'Yeah, eights bells.'

'We're an hour behind you in the UK mate, it's only 7 am.'

Saxon hadn't forgotten. 'Sorry buddy, I've just seen your mail about Heinz Frei. How bad has he been?'

'Just a minute.'

The connection went quiet. Saxon heard footsteps slapping across what sounded like a wooden floor. Echoes in an almost empty apartment. Minimalistic. That's how he viewed the Flying Pig's lifestyle. Ornaments and trinkets zero. Limited furnishings, an odd cubist print on a bare white wall, ultra-modern art, nothing more. A cat perhaps. A fat lazy cat.

The sound of the Pig easing himself into a chair.

'Right Sax,' he said. 'This fucker is a strange one, not an awful lot on him to be honest and you're right, a lot of articles about him have mysteriously disappeared into cyberspace. My guess is that they've been taken down with the threat of a lawsuit or even the right money into the right pocket. This dude is absolutely minted. Personal wealth at over twenty million dollars, and not only that, when his padres pop their clogs, he inherits the best part of two hundred million.'

'Jesus Christ. What else have you got?'

'Well, Sax, as you can imagine, he holds a lot of sway in Zermatt. He's a bit of a poster boy for the town, a rich, local celebrity, mixes with the right people, the mayor, the chief of police, that sort of thing. He's in the local Free Masons and we all know what those fuckers are like.'

'Married… kids?' Saxon asked.

'No. He's had a few relationships but they don't seem to last over long and I can't find any girls that have registered at any of his addresses over the years.'

‘So you say he’s been bad.’

‘Yes. There was a court case when he was eighteen. He was accused of serious sexual assault. One of his ex-girlfriends had accused him of a fairly brutal rape. It was a plea bargain, if he admitted to a serious sexual assault, they’d drop the rape charge.’

‘So what happened?’

‘He pleaded guilty. Mummy and Daddy paid the girl off on the proviso she wouldn’t talk to the media. A non-disclosure clause. I read a report that it was as much as a quarter of a million Swiss Francs.’

Saxon let out a low whistle.

‘He escaped jail, Sax, a two-year suspended sentence. A get out of jail free card and then he called upon his pals in the Lodge.’

‘The police?’

‘No, the local newspapers and the TV stations. He sat in front of everyone he could, protesting his innocence, saying that the sex had been consensual and that she wanted nothing more than to blackmail him. Within a few months, the lies he was telling were beginning to hit home. Joseph Goebbels, the Nazi propaganda minister once said, “If you tell a lie over and over again and keep repeating it, people will eventually come to believe it.”’

‘And that’s what happened?’

‘Yes, and the press hounded the poor girl. She was berated in the street and even attacked in a Zermatt bar. The poor bitch only lasted a year before she topped herself. Her parents found her hanging in their garage one morning.'

Saxon was shaking his head. 'And what was Frei's reaction?'

'Another press conference. He spent a few minutes saying how much he cared for her and how much he would miss her. And then when he had them all where he wanted them, he dropped a little bombshell, he quoted from some book. 'Guilt is a weight that will crush you whether you deserve it or not.'

'He implied that she took her own life because of her actions in accusing an innocent man.'

'Precisely.'

'So not a nice fellow.'

'If you look into it, no. But very much the man to be seen with in Zermatt. His reputation is second to none. He can't be touched.'

Saxon knew the Flying Pig too well. He was building up to something.

'Tell me.'

Saxon could hear the movement of papers on the desk.

'I had to go back to his childhood, into his old school records, and I found out that it didn't look as if he'd attended school for nearly a year. He was thirteen at the time. In the register it said that he attended a school in England to improve his English. They even quoted the school. A ridiculously priced public school in Epsom, Surrey, not far from London.'

‘And?’

‘So I hacked the school and went into the records and it’s complete bullshit. No record of any pupil called Heinz Frei at all.’

‘But you found him?’

‘Absofuckinglutely I found him. The little twat was sent to a children’s loony bin.’

‘No way.’

‘Yes, he was in there for twelve months.’

‘What did he do? Did you find out?’

‘Course I did. That’s what you pay me for. He strangled the family cat.’

‘Is that it?’

‘That’s pretty bad, mate. Apparently, the Frei family went through rather a lot of pets over the years. The local vets have nearly twenty animals registered to the family in just over a decade. I found a Facebook post from one of his old schoolmates. They were calling him Mad Manson.’

Saxon felt his blood turn to ice as the Flying Pig continued.

‘I hacked the Vets. The Freis’ had said that their pets had died suddenly or simply disappeared, but it was a next-door neighbour who caught young Heinz throttling Tiddles. By the time the neighbour got there, kitty was brown bread. She called the police, and the boy was taken away, eventually examined by a doctor. He was diagnosed with ADHD and schizophrenia, but there were no charges and the police didn't bother looking into the Veterinary records.'

Saxon was taking notes, scribbling in his notebook. This changed everything.

'I'll send everything over once I get it typed up. It's around three thousand words. The usual rates apply and the usual bank account please, Sax.'

'Before you go, Pig, just one last thing.'

'Shoot.'

'What was the name of the Chief of Police in Zermatt, the one Frei is friendly with?'

A rustle of paper and then. 'Oscar Nuessle, a detective. Quite a low rank normally for the chief of a station, but remember, Zermatt is a small place.'

'Will you run a check on him for me?'

'Sure. I've already got a few details on him, to be honest.'

'That's great buddy, catch up soon.'

Before Saxon logged off, he opened up the Gmail window and sent a two-page update to Blacklock.

Suzy was in the shower by the time Saxon arrived back in the room. He strolled into the ensuite.

'Want to scrub my back?' she asked as she noticed him looking on.

'There's nothing I'd rather do, but there's been a couple of developments and we need to get moving.'

She rinsed the last of the shampoo from her hair and turned off the shower.

Saxon reached for a towel as she opened the glass cubicle door. He couldn't take his eyes off her beautiful, slender shape. She made no attempt to cover herself up. Saxon felt the blood rushing to his groin.

'Changed your mind, Sax?'

She wrapped the towel loosely around her hips. 'I think I could make you change your mind, Sax,' she said, teasing him.

'I'm sure you could, but we've got things to do.'

She smiled seductively, reached for the corner knot of the towel. She pulled. The towel fell to the floor.

Saxon felt for his belt buckle. 'You're a terrible girl,' he said.

He stood to one side and reached for her wrist, spun her round and bent her over the ceramic sink as her face pressed against the steamed-up mirror. He dropped his trousers and boxers to his ankles.

She kicked her legs apart, and he thrust into her roughly as she let out a little squeal. He gripped her slender hips, dug his nails in hard, and thrust deeper and faster. This wasn't going to last long. He didn't care. He felt an uncontrollable, animalistic urge to climax hard and fast, and sensed Suzy was feeling exactly the same way.

'I want to stay here forever,' Suzy said, as her hand rested on his thigh at the breakfast table.

Saxon said nothing. He liked her company, but it wasn't going to work and who knows what her boyfriend was thinking or doing at this very moment?

Her boyfriend was a strange one. He had figured that out almost from the moment he'd set eyes on him. Different altogether from Suzy, he'd never have believed they were an item, as different as chalk and cheese.

'Tell me about Paul,' he said.

Suzy waved a hand in his direction as she crammed a piece of toast into her mouth. 'No, no,' she said. 'You first, you said there had been a development. What did you mean by that?'

Saxon drained his coffee cup. Wiped his mouth with a paper serviette. 'Fair enough. I think you should know.'

The waiter walked over to the table and refilled their cups with coffee. Saxon waited until he was out of earshot, then spoke quietly. 'Well, do you remember when I said that I wasn't suggesting there was a serial killer on the loose on the Haute Route?'

'Yes.'

'Well, I'm leaning more to think that there's something sinister going on. I looked at all of those dates again and it's classic serial killer timing, the pattern fits perfectly and what's more, I think we have at least one person who fits the perfect serial killer profile.'

Saxon paused, took a drink from his cup. Suzy beckoned for him to continue with a swift, circular motion of her hand.

'Remember I told you about Heinz Frei?'

'Yes, everybody knows Heinz Frei.'

'Well… my buddy, the one who's handy with computers, he's been doing some digging on Frei and he's not the clean-cut celebrity hiker you all think he is.'

'In what way?'

'A serious sexual assault charge.'

'No way!'

'Yes. But there's more. When he was around fifteen, he spent time in a mental hospital, quite a lot of time, over a year.'

'My God, that's shocking.'

'It appears that Heinz the horrible strangled his cat, the Frei family's pets were living on borrowed time, killing them was a bit of a hobby to young Frei.'

'That's terrible, I agree, but what has that got to do with girls going missing in the mountains?'

Saxon took out his notepad and flipped a few pages. 'Remember, I told you about the profile of serial killers, how I'd spent some time studying it with the FBI?'

'Yes.'

'Well, it's an accepted fact that all serial killers share some very common traits, a history, behavioural patterns.' He pointed to a list in the notepad. 'Look here, lack of empathy, alcohol or drug dependency, psychological or sexual abuse as a child, a loner and here, look, at the bottom of the page.'

Suzy looked to where he was pointing. *90% of all serial killers admitted to acting out their violent fantasies on animals.*

'Wow!'

'It's believed that serial killers aren't born. That is to say nobody is born to kill. It's all about early development, or rather the lack of it. Most serial killers have been badly abused as a child, sometimes physically, more often than not, sexually. And it's quite common for the mother to be the perpetrator sometimes.'

Suzy remained silent. Saxon detected something in her demeanour. 'Penny for your thoughts?'

'What?'

'An English phrase. You're thinking about something. Tell me what it is.'

'You're a strange one,' she replied. 'I'm surprised you can't tell me what it is I'm thinking about. It's like you have a sixth sense.'

'I can take a guess.'

'Go on then.'

He flicked to another page in his notebook. It was full of scribbles. At the top of the page, underlined, it read, ***Paul Suter.***

'Your boyfriend.'

'Ex-boyfriend,' she snapped. 'And yes, you've guessed right. That's exactly what I'm thinking about. He's an alcoholic to start with. I nearly hit him with a cup the other morning when he had a go at me about the Gluhwein. His drinking sessions are the stuff of legends. And he is a loner for sure. I'm the first girlfriend he's ever had and if I'm honest, I only dated him because I felt sorry for him.'

A tear rolled down Suzy's cheek. 'What sort of warped individual does that make me, sharing a fucking bed with someone like that?'

Saxon moved in closer. Wiped the tear from her cheek.

'Only I didn't really share a bed with him, not in a sexual way anyway. We slept together a few times in the early days, but—'

She hesitated.

'Go on,' Saxon said.

'Are you sure you want to hear this?'

'Yes.'

She sighed deeply. Another tear or two. 'I initiated everything; it was as if he wasn't interested in sex.'

There was more to come. Saxon waited patiently.

It took her a while and then, 'He preferred to jerk off. Can you believe that? How do you think that made me feel?'

Saxon returned to his notepad, halfway down the page. He pointed. *Compulsive and excessive masturbation, a serial killer will often prefer self-pleasure to the physical act of sex with another individual.*

'Holy shit,' Suzy said.

And still there was more.

'His mother,' Suzy said. 'She was a first-class bitch by all accounts. Not that Paul ever told me that. He worshipped the ground she walked on. There were rumours at school about Paul and his mother.'

'You went to school with him?'

'Yes, for more than ten years, apart from the time he went away.'

'Went away?' Saxon queried.

'Yes, he had a bit of a breakdown. He was away in some sort of treatment centre for nearly a year.'

'But he came back to your school?'

'Yes, and he seemed much better. I always thought he needed a break. That's why I couldn't say no when he asked me to go out with him. He was cute enough in his own way, quite handsome. I think I brought him out of his shell a little, and when the job came up at the cabane, I thought it was a good idea.'

'But?'

'A couple of weeks in, I knew I had made a serious mistake.'

'But you wanted to see it through.'

'Yes. For him, more than me. I guessed that it was the perfect place to meet people, to socialise him. After all, getting thrown together in a hut three thousand metres up a mountain with a group of strangers is just about the perfect environment for that sort of thing.'

'But it didn't work out that way?'

'No. Like I've said, there was nothing happening in the bedroom and yet there he was, chasing after other girls and masturbating constantly.'

Saxon couldn't help but grin. 'You caught him?'

'Yes, a couple of times, but more often than not, he'd take off into the bathroom and lock the door. I'd hear him. By the time you arrived at the cabane, I was at the end of my wits.' She smiled. 'You were the perfect excuse to get the hell out of there.'

'It's nice to know I've served a purpose.'

She frowned. 'You know what I mean.'

Saxon flipped another page in his notebook. 'It's probably no more than a coincidence, but we need to look closer at Paul and Heinz. I've also asked my buddy to look into the police chief in Zermatt. There's something strange about him, and of course Kate's boyfriend too. Above all else, I must see the photographs of the dead girls. Their bodies at the scene. That will tell me for sure whether they were accidents or whether—'

'There's a killer on the loose.'

'I think so, yes.'

Saxon starting scribbling more notes. Suzy leaned over and watched.

After a couple of minutes, he closed the book. 'Time to pack up,' he said.

'Where are we going?'

'Well, I'm heading back up the mountain and then I'm going to drop down into Zermatt to try and meet up with the police again. I think I have enough to show them to at least open up an investigation.'

A tinge of sadness in Suzy's eyes. 'You don't want me to come with you?'

An awkward moment.

'The thing is Suzy—'

'It's okay, you don't need to explain. I get the picture.'

She had already stood; she was gathering her things together. 'I'll be out of your hair just as soon—'

'No, no, he interrupted, you've got it wrong, I meant—'

'You meant you didn't want me to come with you.'

'No, I didn't say that. I'm thinking of you. It seems the last thing you need at the minute is another bloody relationship.'

'Who wants a fucking relationship? Don't flatter yourself, soldier boy. I wanted a little fun and some fresh air, nothing more.'

Before Saxon could reply, Suzy had stormed off through the dining room.

'Fuck,' he mumbled to himself. 'It wasn't supposed to be like that.'

By the time he got back to the bedroom, she was fully packed and pulling her coat around her shoulders.

He flopped down onto the bed. 'Suzy, I'm not the sort of bloke who hangs around long. After I've got to the bottom of this little mystery, I plan to cycle around the world. I'm sorry, I should have told you.'

She strode purposefully over to the door and nearly pulled it off the hinges. She turned in the doorway. 'You're too fucking old for me, anyway. You can't keep up with me on the mountain.'

Such venom.

‘It’s you who’s too bloody slow. I was taking it easy. I was waiting for you.’

‘Bullshit.’

‘I’ll race you to Gruben then,’ Saxon said, and then wondered why he had said it.

‘What?’

‘You heard me. If you want another day on the mountain, I’m heading to Gruben. It was one of Kate’s planned pit stops. She was going to stay in a mountain inn, relative luxury for her, a lovely place. Loser pays.’

Chapter 27

Suter focused his binoculars. He watched them walk through the small car park at the front of the hotel. It was late, nearly midday, and he knew what they'd been up to. There'd been a row. He'd watched. Suzy had worn her angry face for some time. He knew her angry face only too well. And then the angry face had been replaced by a mellow look and then another look that boiled the blood in his veins.

They'd fucked again.

Animals.

They turned towards the mountain and headed through the village. Saxon had said he was heading for Chamonix, so he figured they wouldn't get any further than Gruben or possibly St Niklaus by nightfall. That was perfect. He'd drive into Grimentz again and then over to Wildhorn, outflank them just south of Gruben and take the quad up onto the trail. It was a long, tough run, perhaps a couple of hours, but he'd be in plenty of time. He just needed to wrap up well. The quad was a summer toy. No doubt about it.

On the quad, he was already planning his little hide. He'd head up from Gruben and leave the quad in a forest hidden from view. He'd stride out for half an hour, get his juices flowing, his body heated up.

He'd pick the perfect spot, remember exactly what mother had taught him and spend a couple of hours on the construction. Tree branches, a little moss. He'd construct a seating area out of rocks, make a small window with a ledge where he could rest the rifle. He had some snacks and a few bottles of beer in his rucksack. What a perfect way to spend an afternoon in the mountains.

Hunting.

Hunting and stalking animals.

It had rained most of the day. An odd break in the clouds and swirls of mist and then remarkable views, but then more cloud, more mist and heavy, heavy rain. Saxon was a competitive soul at the best of time and from the outset he had increased the pace, determined to win their little wager. But Suzy had surprised him, matched him every step of the way and at times even taunted him to go faster. If the truth be told, they had started too late and just as well they hadn't hung around.

'We should make it an hour or so, an hour and a half at the most,' Saxon said. 'I've telephoned ahead, we have a room and they serve dinner until eight. We should just about make it, a quick shower and then a little nose bag.'

She squinted at him, ‘A what.’

‘Nose bag.’ He laughed. ‘It’s another—’

‘Northern saying.’

‘Yes. A northern saying.’

They walked on another thirty minutes, crested the brow of a hill as the sun dipped below the mountain and darkness crept in within minutes, as if someone had drawn a huge big curtain.

Saxon stopped suddenly. ‘What was that?’

‘I heard it too.’ Suzy said. ‘It sounded like a—’ ‘A rifle. Undoubtedly a rifle.’

He looked at her. ‘Hunters?’

Suzy shook her head. ‘Not at this time of year, not at this time of the day. They usually hunt early mornings. By this time of day, they’re down in the valley, celebrating the kill with beer and brandy.’

Another shot. The sound echoed around the valley. Suzy reached for his hand.

‘Hunters,’ Saxon said. ‘It’s the only explanation.’

Suter had seen the couple approaching him. He’d picked them out with his binoculars and knew immediately that it wasn’t the prey he was looking for. A young couple. Heading for Gruben after a pleasant day in the mountains. Hand in hand. In love. Bastards.

She was pretty. Him, clearly punching above his weight. Short, slightly overweight, a ridiculous goaty beard with long hair. Far too old for the girl he was walking with.

He had to die.

Suter couldn't put a finger on what it was that made him take the decision that he was going to be the main participant of a mass shooting. But without even thinking about the consequences, he knew, at that precise moment, that was what he was going to do. He'd long since admired the planning and precision of the mass school shootings in the US, and in particular, the Norwegian Nazi, Anders Breivik. Seventy-seven young people killed.

'Fucking commies,' he mumbled to himself.

The man's head was in the cross wire and he was already thinking about escape and evasion. If he could get to the Brit and his ex-girlfriend, kill them, there would be nobody to point the finger.

He wasn't like the other killers, bastards like Breivik who knew that their actions would lead to arrest, perhaps even death. No. he didn't want to be caught and there was only Suzy who knew about the rifle. A present from his mother on his 15th birthday. One hundred percent illegal, a US black-market import. Untraceable.

He'd kill them and then make his way back to the cabane. He'd stay up in the mountains for the winter if necessary. The police would come calling, of course, when they eventually found the bodies or they were reported missing. But they'd have nothing on him, the rifle safely hidden away in the forest where nobody would find it.

He'd claim that they'd separated many months ago, that they were nothing more than co-workers.

The couple, the man with the beard. Even closer now. The cross wire on his left eye. Suter took a deep breath. Held it. Pulled the trigger.

He watched through the scope as the stranger's head exploded into a burst of red mist and he fell to the ground.

Screams from the young girl as realisation set in. Suter's hand slipped down to his groin. He squeezed hard. So much control. So much power.

He watched through the scope for a minute. No more. He readjusted the scope. Such a pretty face, a contorted, twisted, wailing face.

Pathetic.

Nevertheless, he didn't want to be the one to spoil the pretty canvas. He lowered the scope slightly. Her left breast. Breath held. Squeezed. Lights out.

He stood. It was time to tidy up. As he walked from the hide, a fine mist settled on the roof.

It wasn't like he could hide the bodies permanently. He knew he couldn't do that; Not enough time to bury them. The dogs would sniff them out, eventually. But he'd buy himself some time. Maybe a month or two. Perhaps even longer. The snow was on its way and he had shot the couple just a few yards from a 500 metre drop, a drop that fell into the valley, into a forest where nobody trekked. A forest that would be a metre deep in snow in less than a week.

He heaved both bodies over the ridge and watched as they tumbled and bounced over the rocks and boulders like two puppets with a demented puppeteer controlling the strings. Broken limbs, cracked skulls, smashed eye sockets, sharp rocks ripping and tearing.

He smiled as he watched them settle in a dense ravine. They were barely visible to the naked eye.

The blood was a problem.

Or was it? Just a matter of time. A curious ibex, a fox or perhaps a wolf with the smell of blood in its nostrils. He'd kill Saxon and Suzy at the same spot, tip their bodies over the same cliff edge and he'd wait. He'd wait and execute the first animal on the same spot, and a day or two later, a curious hiker would stumble across the scene. A dead animal, a lot of blood. They'd think nothing of it. A lazy, trigger-happy hunter.

Missing persons reports in a few days. Four people failed to reach their destination. He laughed inwardly. Those fucking useless Zermatt police. Oscar Nuessle would come out with his usual shit, that the helicopter had found nothing, that the winter conditions were hampering the search. Four more missing persons, nothing in the grand scale of things.

According to the app, it was all downhill.

Fifty-five minutes and they'd arrive at their destination.

The rifle shots had concerned him, but he tried to push it to the back of his mind. He was tired. He looked at Suzy. Breathing hard. She was tired too. He dared to think that he might even win their little bet.

He felt the impact before he heard the crack of the rifle. It thudded into the top of his rucksack and a split second later, the unmistakable sound of a gunshot.

At least half a mile away.

He made a grab for Suzy, threw her onto the ground.

Hysterical at first, 'Fuck Sax, what's going on?'

Saxon was thinking the unthinkable.

'Surely this can't be Paul,' he said.

'It's possible. There's a quad at the cabane.'

'For fuck's sake, and does he have a rifle?'

She didn't answer immediately. She stalled. She was trying to make sense of what was happening. Her eyes were teared up.

'Does he have a fucking rifle?' Saxon repeated, slightly louder than she wanted to hear.

'Yes, a rifle he uses to hunt, something his mum gave him as a birthday present when he was a kid.'

Fuck, Saxon thought to himself. *He's good, plenty years' of practice under his belt.*

Saxon looked around. Out in the open. Exposed.

Another shot. It ricocheted off a rock just behind Saxon's left temple.

'He's playing with us,' Saxon announced. 'We're in the middle of nowhere, stranded. A decent shooter with a decent rifle could have finished us off by now.' He reached for Suzy's hand. 'Now! Run.'

Saxon and Suzy sprinted away.

Another shot.

'Zig zag, follow me,' he screamed.

Saxon ran from left to right, dragged Suzy along with him, two metres left, switch, two metres right. He pulled her harder and faster. She quickly got the message.

Another shot and Suzy went down in a heap. Saxon fell to his knees beside her. She lay on her stomach and he flipped her over. Her face was drenched in blood. She was dazed. He located the wound on the side of her temple, wiped away the blood, and breathed a sigh of relief. A small hole. He pulled out a shard of granite and threw it away.

He lifted her to her knees, 'C'mon, you're okay. Breathe hard, we have to run. It's just a piece of rock, nothing more.'

Suzy looked around, looking confused, felt the side of her head.

'Up, come on, up on your feet.'

Saxon had no time to spare. Instead, he lifted her up, made her stand, and then threw her over his shoulders like a fireman. Sixty metres, no more.

The gunman looked on and cackled like a hyena. The fools. He could pick them off anytime he wanted. But he'd wait. This was a whole lot more fun.

'Damn.' The mist was clouding up his scope.

He lowered his rifle, reached into his rucksack for a tissue. He slit the cellophane packet and pulled one out, turned the rifle and wiped both the front and back of the scope. He repositioned the rifle and lowered his head to the scope. Chin up, closed his right eye and peered through the scope. Out of focus. Twisted the lens.

Where were they? He lowered the rifle and strained to see in the gloom.

'Shit!' In desperation, he grabbed for the rucksack, pulled out his binoculars.

'We're safe. Take deep breaths.' Saxon said calmly.

'Safe, how?' Suzy wheezed.

'We're in low cloud. Whoever is shooting at us won't be able to see us.' He pushed her gently in the back. 'But a little higher, we need to get higher.'

Suzy knew it made sense and had recovered a little from the initial injury. She had a headache and a small cut that might need a few stitches but was otherwise fine. They walked on slowly, the cloud getting thicker every few metres. Saxon was already formulating a plan.

They walked on for another hour before he eventually allowed them to rest.

'That's it,' he said. 'Now we can try and phone the police. I just hope the fuck we get a signal.'

Chapter 28

Suter had sprinted out of the hide, had run as quickly as he could and covered the half mile to where his prey had been in just a few minutes. He found the blood.

He spat and cursed. He was annoyed with himself. How could he have been so stupid? Why hadn't he noticed the low cloud?

Bad hunting. The animals had won. Mother wouldn't be happy.

'Fuck, shit!'

He paced. Walked around a few times in pointless circles and wondered what to do.

'Think… think.'

What would they be doing now? Where would they have gone? It was getting dark. Unlikely they'd be heading for Gruben. Not when they knew the hunter was still on the loose. But he'd never find them now.

He made his decision. He'd wait a few hours and then head back to the cabane. Suzy would have a good idea it had been him shooting at them and that's what she'd tell the police. But as long as he could hide the rifle, they'd have nothing to go on.

He'd be patient. Wait for an animal and clean up. He'd take it slowly, he'd be back at the cabane by first light. No one would know he'd been anywhere near the scene.

The hide. He'd need to clean it up too, raze it to the ground and leave it as he'd found it.

The police helicopter landed just after midnight. They'd tracked the signal on Saxon's phone and he'd guided them in with a Maglite. They'd flown into Zermatt. It took no more than ten minutes and their first port of call had been the hospital where Suzy had several stitches inserted into her head.

It had been Detective Nuessle who'd interviewed them in one of the nursing sub offices.

From the outset, Saxon knew he had a mountain to climb, persuading Nuessle to take their claims seriously.

They explained about Paul Suter. Suzy said that he had a hunting rifle, but Nuessle had checked the police computer and there was nothing registered to him.

'I hear what you are saying, Monsieur Saxon, but this isn't the Bronx. You can't just pick up a rifle in a back street bar in Grimentz.'

'He's had it for years, detective. His mother gave him it when he was young.' Suzy said.

'And he uses it to hunt, you say?'

'Yes.'

Nuessle reached for his mobile phone. 'Give me a few minutes.' He left the room.

Suzy spoke. 'I don't think he is taking us seriously.'

'He sent a helicopter up to get us, so someone believes us.'

Nuessle returned thirty minutes later. He leaned back and rested on the corner of the desk. 'I've run a few searches. The local gun group, the hunting groups from Zermatt, Gruben, Grachen and Grimentz. We have details on all of the members. He's not registered with any of them.'

'He was a loner,' Suzy said. 'He hunted on his own.'

'That may be the case, but he'd need equipment, bullets, cleaning kits, that sort of thing. We'll check the local hunting shops when they open.'

'It was a specialist rifle, American I think,' Suzy said. 'I don't remember him ordering bullets from any shop in town.'

'You've seen the rifle?'

'Errm, not exactly.'

'What do you mean by that?'

'It was in a box, a small case.'

Nuessle frowned. 'But you lived with this man?'

'Yes, for a little while.'

'Where did he keep it, in a secure cabinet?'

'Under the bed.'

Nuessle shook his head. 'Well, if we find it, he's in big trouble.'

'I should hope so,' Saxon interjected. 'He tried to kill us.'

'You don't know that for sure,' Nuessle said, 'unless you saw him or he called you and threatened you.' He turned to Suzy. 'Has he called you since you left the cabane?'

'No.'

'Okay.' Nuessle eased himself from the desk. Walked towards the door. 'You try and get yourself some sleep. I'll deploy an armed response team to the cabane just as soon as I can.'

Chapter 29

They had agreed that it wasn't safe for Suzy to return to her apartment, at least until the police had caught up with Suter. He checked her into the hotel.

The receptionist handed him the key to the room and then reached under the counter.

'This came for you, Monsieur Saxon.' She handed him an envelope.

Saxon took it from her. Not posted, no stamp, no return address. 'Who is it from?'

The receptionist shrugged her shoulders. 'I don't know. It was handed to the concierge on night duty a few days ago.'

'Okay. Thanks.'

Saxon picked up the two rucksacks, and they headed for the lifts.

It was 3.15 am when Saxon looked at the clock. He'd dozed a little, but there was too much on his mind to sleep. Reluctantly, he pulled himself from the bed and walked over to the unopened envelope.

He reached for a ballpoint pen and slid it into the flap, pushed gently, and it peeled back. He opened the envelope and looked inside. Photographs. At least a dozen. He slipped his hand in and pulled them out.

'Jesus fucking Christ,' he whispered. 'Jesus H Fucking Christ.'

It was after 9 am when Suzy woke. Saxon was at the small desk in the corner of the room with his notepad.

'Morning.' She called over.

He turned. 'Morning.'

'How long have you been awake?'

'Six hours,' he replied.

'What? You're kidding me?'

He shook his head. 'How's your head?'

'I've felt better. But then again, I've felt worse.'

'Well, you don't look too bad to me.' He walked over and sat on the bed. He brushed her hair from her face. 'A little bump on the head. Nothing more, still as beautiful as ever.'

'Flattery will get you everywhere.' She pulled the duvet to one side. She was naked. An obvious invitation.

'No time,' he said. 'Get yourself ready and we'll have some breakfast. I'll tell you what was in that envelope.'

Over a cooked breakfast of spicy Swiss sausage and eggs, Saxon explained about the photographs that a mystery man had handed in to the hotel.

'Thirteen of them altogether. Thirteen photographs in which eight represent a crime scene. Five accidents and eight girls who were murdered.'

‘You can tell?’

‘Yes.’

Chapter 30

Detective Nuessle was furious.

Saxon had laid the photographs on his desk. It appeared that the photographs had not been sanctioned by the Chief.

'I'll have his fucking balls on a stick, whoever it is, and I will find him.'

'Or her,' Suzie interjected. 'You do have female police, don't you?'

Nuessle ignored her.

'I'm sorry, detective, I thought you must have sanctioned it.' Saxon said.

Nuessle was still ranting, cursing and muttering to himself. He'd hardly even glanced at the photographs.

Saxon bided his time. There was no use saying what it was he was going to say until the detective had calmed down.

Nuessle glanced at the photographs on the desk. 'And what about them anyway?' he asked. 'I thought you were here to ask about the raid on the cabane, not to try and dig up more dirt from the archives.'

Saxon split the photographs into two piles. Five photographs in pile one. He pushed them to one side, picked up the other eight. He spread them out on the desk, fanned, like a pack of cards. 'I believe these girls were all murdered.'

'Pah!' he mocked. 'You can tell that from a photograph.'

'Yes I can, and so should any good detective.'

'You hold your tongue, monsieur, coming into my station and insulting me and my policemen.'

Saxon wasn't going to hold back any longer. He let the detective have it with both barrels. 'Insult you! I'm not insulting you; I'm trying to bloody help you, but you're too stubborn to realise that. I came to see you twice, I—'

'Now, just a minute, I was—'

'Stop fucking interrupting and listen to me,' Saxon snapped. 'On two separate occasions I fed you information. I told you something didn't add up and you should have looked into it. But no, you sat on your lazy arse and did nothing.' He held up the photographs in front of the detective's face. 'And now these, evidence of a killer, a fucking serial killer in your jurisdiction and all you care about is who gave them to me. Well, I can tell you whoever it was did you a fucking big favour because we might just be able to catch him and stop more young girls getting slaughtered on your fucking mountains.'

Nuessle leaned back in his seat. He tapped a pencil on his teeth, looked as if he was going to say something, and then looked at the photographs again.

Saxon picked up the first one. 'Morgan Murphy. This is the police photograph of the crime scene.'

'You don't know that for sure,' the policeman said, almost in a whisper.

'Oh, I know, I'm one hundred percent sure.' He dived into his rucksack, pulled out another envelope, and reached inside. He slid a photograph across the desk. Nuessle glanced down.

'This is a photograph taken from Morgan's Facebook the day before she went missing. Take a look around her neck, a small locket.' He pointed to the photograph. 'And here, the poor girl's corpse, no locket.'

The detective crashed forward and slapped the desk as he erupted into laughter. 'And that's your evidence, a missing necklace.' The detective stood. 'Get out of here. Don't waste my time. The necklace has become detached in the fall. Logical.'

'Was it found at the scene?'

'No, but it could be anywhere.'

'No, it couldn't. It's a sheer drop detective, a vertical drop. The girl didn't bounce down the mountain off boulders and rocks. She was thrown off and hit nothing else until she hit the bottom five hundred metres below. If the locket had snapped off, it would have snapped off at the very spot where she landed.'

'Nonsense.'

He pushed another photo over to the policeman. 'Selena Garcia, a missing glove. Explain how a glove can fall off during a fall.' Another. 'Nicholle Palmer, a watch, Bridget Smith, missing right boot. Explain to me how a fucking boot can untie its own laces and come off during a fall.'

'The laces could have snapped. It's not impossible,' the detective said.

'Did you find the boot at the scene?'

'I'm not sure, it's possible.'

'You're not sure, detective! It's your job to be sure.'

'It's possible.'

'Then find out. Find out now!' Saxon barked.

Nuessle picked up the phone. Said something in German. Within two minutes, Fassnacht stood in the room.

Nuessle addressed him in English. 'Eggen, the scene of death report for Bridgett Smith. Date of death 12 August 2015.'

'Yes sir.'

'Can you get it for me? The list of the items recovered from the scene.'

'Of course, sir, I'll print it off. It will be with you in less than ten minutes.'

Nuessle puffed out his chest as Eggen Fassnacht walked towards the door. 'We run an efficient office here, Monsieur Saxon.'

Fassnacht was as good as his word. He walked in exactly eight minutes later. He handed Nuessle just one sheet of A4 paper. Nuessle took it. His face fell. He looked up at the civilian. 'Nothing else Eggen?'

'No, sir, a baseball cap, sunglasses and a rucksack containing—' he leaned over the desk. Pointed at the paper. 'A few items of food, two water bottles, a mobile phone and a set of waterproofs.'

'No boots found near the scene?' Saxon enquired.

'No,' the civilian stated, looking rather puzzled.

Saxon pointed to the photograph. 'Look. She is only wearing one boot.'

'Is that so unusual?'

'Well, yes,' Saxon said. 'Unless she had been having a solo hopping competition before she fell to her death.'

'There's no need to be facetious,' Nuessle said. 'Let's have a little respect for the dead.'

'I respect the dead detective,' Saxon said. 'I also believe that people who have been murdered deserve justice.'

'Murdered?' Fassnacht said.

'Susan Muller,' Saxon said, 'missing sunglasses, a photograph taken on the same day she was reported missing. She failed to show up at the hotel she had booked the day before. The day she went missing was a beautiful, sunny day. No sunglasses on this photo.' He looked at Eggen Fassnacht. 'Could you get us the list of items found at the scene?'

Fassnacht turned to Nuessle. Nuessle nodded, gave a weak thumbs up.

As Fassnacht walked towards the door, Saxon stopped him.

And the reports for Nadene Hanses, bandana missing, Emica Chan, a watch, Chloe Korhonnon also a necklace and Taiya de Jong a waterproof gaiter.'

Eggen Fassnacht stopped dead in his tracks. He said just one word. It was more of a statement than a question. 'Trophies.'

Chapter 31

'That's exactly what I'm saying, detective,' Saxon said. 'You have a killer in the mountains and he's collecting trophies from his victims. And look,' Saxon said. Another sheet of paper slid across the desk. 'This is the frequency of the murders, the exact dates.'

Nuessle took the paper and studied it for some time.

Saxon bit his lip. The policeman had to work it out for himself.

'Sequence killings,' Saxon said eventually. 'More frequent. The killer started very slowly. His first kill was almost fifteen years ago, but is now attacking at least every year. Classic serial killer plot and he won't stop until he's caught.'

Nuessle buried his head in his hands.

'And as you know, I've been looking into my friend's disappearance. It's not a secret. There are a handful of people who know that and yesterday someone tried to kill me.'

Nuessle eventually looked up as his hands slid down his face and he rested them on the desk. He looked over at Suzy. 'You think it's connected? You seriously think it could be your boyfriend, that he could be a murderer?'

'I don't know,' Suzy replied. 'I thought I knew him, but a lot of things Sax said made sense. There are a lot of things that need explaining, but given his age, he would have had to be very young when he first started.'

The policeman shook his head. 'It doesn't make any sense.' He picked up a sheet of paper. 'He'd need to have been around fifteen when he started. People don't start killing that early, do they?'

Saxon spoke in a sombre tone. 'I'm afraid they do, detective, the Jamie Bulger baby killing in Liverpool in England. The murderers were aged just ten, the youngest ever convicted killers.'

Nuessle bowed his head, 'It's unimaginable, simply unimaginable.'

'And Ed Kemper, just fifteen when he started his murderous spree, and Jesse Pomeroy, just fourteen. I could go on, detective.'

'Don't, I get the picture. I need a coffee. It's time to get some air.'

As they walked towards the office door, Saxon stopped. 'One final question, detective, those personal items, the clothing listed in the Scene of Death reports. Where are they? Were they returned to the deceased's parents?'

‘Some were. things like jewellery, necklaces, rings and bracelets. Yes, the families request the personal effects.’

‘The clothing,’ Saxon said. ‘What happens to that?’

‘We keep it. A blood-stained sweater or a jacket isn’t the kind of keepsake the families are looking for.’

‘You keep it forever?’

‘Not usually. Even if the coroner has made a ruling, or a conviction has been secured, a case is never ever technically closed. With the recent advancement of DNA, many a case has been reopened, a murderer put behind bars or, in rare cases, an innocent man is released on forensic evidence that wasn’t available a few decades ago.’

‘I’m glad to hear it.’

Nuessle laughed. ‘We have a whole room in the basement where sealed boxes are filed away. Now and again we have a clear out, but we have some dating back to the 1950s.’

Suzy let out a long whistle.

Nuessle looked at his watch. ‘We’ll know soon whether my team has caught up with Suter. The chopper left twenty minutes ago.’

They left the station. Nuessle took them to a coffee shop nearby. He was anxious about the phone call from the Cabane Moiry.

Nuessle and Suzy walked through the door. Just as Saxon did the same, his mobile rang.

Important. It registered on the display as the *Flying Pig*. 'Just a minute,' Saxon called through the doorway. 'I have to take this.'

He turned around and walked back outside. Pressed answer. 'Speak to me, mate.'

'Hi Sax, how you doing?'

'Felt better. Somebody has been taking potshots at us on the mountain, but we got lucky.'

'Jeez, mate. You think someone knows you are onto them?'

'I'm not sure yet. Not the same MO to be fair. The nut who is killing the hikers is throwing them off mountains. This fucker was hunting us like animals with a rifle. He was playing with us. Maybe he had no intention of killing us, maybe just trying to frighten us off.'

'But you thought the killer was a hunter when we last spoke.'

'True. Anyway, I'm just about to have coffee with the chief. Tell me what you've got.'

'Oscar Nuessle?'

'Yes.'

The Flying Pig started talking. 'He's got a back story Sax, I'm not a hundred percent sure what it is yet, but there's defo a back story.'

'Go on.'

'Well, ten years ago, he was in Zurich. He was flying high, a Deputy Chief Constable, the second highest position in the police hierarchy and the youngest man in that position for over fifty years.

'Really?'

'I've found a piece on him in the Zurich Post from eleven years ago. They described him as one of the most talented police officers that the Swiss Police had ever produced. His department had a clear up rate second to none. And then a couple of years later, something happened. He was demoted to a lowly Detective Sergeant. They dropped him about half a dozen ranks, moved him out to Zermatt where crime is about as rare as rocking horse shit. They still call him the Chief, of course, which is true in a way, because he is the man in charge of the Zermatt Station. But the Zermatt Station is more or less just a small sub station to Montreux and Lausanne. There's an odd burglary or someone dealing soft drugs, but robbery and shootings and murder are not everyday occurrences. It's not even a city, it's just classed as a small town.'

Saxon focused through the window of the café. Suzy sat with Nuessle. The waitress was already at the table. Suzy gave a little wave when their eyes met. He waved back.

'It's like a New Scotland Yard Chief getting moved to the Isle of Mull,' the Flying Pig continued. 'It's not uncommon for a copper to get busted a rank or two, but five or six is absolutely unheard of.'

'So you reckon it was something quite big?'

'Massive. mate.'

'But you don't know what?'

‘No, not yet. My guess is that it was completely covered up.’

A thousand thoughts flying through Saxon’s mind.

‘And one other thing, mate.’

‘Tell me,’ Saxon said.

‘Heinz Frei ain’t Kate’s killer. That’s assuming she’s been killed.’

‘No?’

‘Absolutely not,’ he was booked on a Qantas flight to Oz three days before Kate went missing.’

Saxon sighed. Frei had fitted the profile perfectly. Was it back to the drawing board? Kate dead? An accident, murder, taken against her will?

He thanked the Flying Pig and pressed end. As he walked through the door and his eyes settled on Nuessle, he wondered what the hell he had done all those years ago. Something told him that coming straight out and asking the detective what he’d been up to wouldn’t go down well. He’d wait. The Flying Pig would come good.

It was Nuessle’s turn to apologise and rush outside. The phone call from the chief of ops of the armed response team at Cabane Moiry.

‘Excuse me. I can’t take this in here, too many ears.’

They watched Nuessle carefully. An odd word Saxon could lip read. As if Nuessle realised, he turned his back towards the glass window. The conversation was a long one. Saxon checked his watch. Twelve minutes. Nuessle was back at the table. He called the waitress, settled the bill. He said that they'd have to head back to the station. Couldn't talk where they were.

'There was no rifle,' Nuessle said. 'No evidence of any sort that he has ever possessed one. My men even checked the freezer for wild meat, nothing but a few sausages and some packs of bacon.'

'He's cleaned up,' said Saxon. 'He had time.'

Nuessle's head tilted to the side. 'Perhaps, or perhaps you've just been caught up in a hunter's arc of fire.'

'Impossible,' Saxon said. 'There were four or five rounds within inches of us. Whoever did the shooting was shooting at us.'

Suzy leaned forward. 'Did they ask him about a rifle?'

'Yes.'

'And?'

'He said he didn't know what you were talking about.'

'But he definitely had—'

'But you never saw it?' Nuessle interrupted. 'We've checked the hunting and outdoor shops from here to Grimentz. Suter never had an account, never purchased any bullets, not even a hunting knife, not even a bloody Swiss army knife. He wasn't a hunter.'

'I saw him butcher an ibex in the kitchen,' Suzy said. 'It was a couple of months back.'

'No evidence,' Nuessle said. 'I'm sorry.'

‘So you aren’t bringing him in for questioning then?’

‘No. He’s still up at Cabane Moiry. It appears that he’s going to stay there over the winter. He says he has nowhere else to stay,’ He turned to Suzy. ‘Claimed that you kicked him out of the apartment you shared together.’ He pointed at Saxon. ‘That you took off with this one and that you are just bitter, that you wanted to get him into trouble.’

Suzy’s jaw dropped open. ‘But that’s ridiculous. If anything, it’s him that should be the bitter one. I just feel a little sorry for him.’

Nuessle said nothing.

Saxon felt it slipping away. He had really hit a sensitive spot with the policemen when he’d pointed out the missing items in the photographs and when he’d detailed the dates.

Nuessle would have said if they had found anything.

‘My team are still up there,’ Nuessle said as if reading his mind. ‘They are looking for trophies, as you put it, but so far, just blanks. Suzy,’ he said, ‘was there any other house or building he laid claim to or was it just your apartment?’

Suzy paused to think. ‘He said he was homeless when I took him in, but to be honest, I’m not sure. I guess his mother must have lived somewhere before she died. When we were at school, there was a cabin in the mountains. I think that’s where they lived, but nobody at school ever visited. Nobody knew where it was, but he always complained about the long walk to school.'

'And there's another thing,' Nuessle said. He got up and walked to where the large map was pinned to the wall. He pointed to a thin red line. He traced it. 'I think we have located the exact position where the bullets were flying over your head. His finger moved to the right a couple of centimetres. 'Here, on the main trail, on this downward section, about an hour's walking time from Gruben. This is where it was.' He looked around, his finger still on the map. 'Would this have been about right?'

Saxon stood. Moved closer, and studied the contour lines of the map. 'Yes, I think that's about right, just before the hill we ran up to get into the low cloud.'

Nuessle nodded. Took his finger from the map and sat back down at the desk. 'The helicopter pilot spotted it when they flew over about an hour ago.'

'What?' Suzy asked. 'What did he spot?'

'A dead ibex. He took the chopper right in. There was a lot of blood, it looks like it had been shot through the head. There was also a pair of black sunglasses, female we think, expensive, Gucci.'

'They're mine,' Suzy said. 'They must have fallen out of my pocket.'

The policeman cleared his throat.

'I'm fairly sure you two were caught up in an innocuous hunting accident. I don't think you've anything to worry about.'

Chapter 32

'The bastard didn't believe us,' Suzy said.

They sat in the hotel lounge. A TV played in the foreground. The sound was turned down. A news channel. Subtitles in French or Italian, Saxon wasn't sure which.

Saxon noticed an aerial shot of the Matterhorn taken from a helicopter. A picture of a couple. Late twenties, early thirties and then a map.

Suzy was about to speak when Saxon held up a hand. 'Look,' he pointed at the TV. 'A map. That's Gruben. What are they saying?'

Suzy jumped to her feet and walked over to the TV. Turned up the volume. Another picture. A hospital.

'They were two young doctors from the same hospital in Geneva. They were walking into Gruben yesterday, just like us.'

'And?'

'They never arrived. They've gone missing.'

'For fuck's sake,' Saxon said. 'You sure?'

‘Of course, I’m sure. It’s my language.’ She listened again. ‘They were on the same path as us.’

‘What time?’

‘It doesn’t say, just that they’d set off from early that morning from the village of Bagnes, checked into a hotel in Gruben around lunchtime. They phoned from the mountains and stated their estimated time of arrival was 18.00 hours.’

Saxon could feel his heart beating heavy in his chest. *Those two shots.*

Suter enjoyed the feeling of taking life.

The signal wasn’t over good in the Cabane du Moiry, the picture on the TV a little grainy but the sound quality perfect. He’d murdered two doctors. How about that?

It had been an eventful couple of days, and he couldn’t be happier. He’d even duped the police, been the model of cooperation, and had made them all coffee, fed them organic chocolate biscuits.

The armed response team had stormed in like a fucking Texas SWAT team, waved a search warrant in front of his face, but he had told them it wasn’t necessary. He had invited them in. He hadn’t been fazed at all.

By the end of the interrogation, he had won hands down and they were treating him like a long-lost friend, asking for more biscuits.

It wasn’t the first time he had killed.

Hans had been like him, a loner, a boy from a broken home, and he'd ran away countless times. It was important to think about murder carefully. The best serial killers in history killed and killed and killed again. Some were on the loose for twenty, thirty years, some were never caught at all. They chose their victims carefully. Lots of hitchhikers, runaways and prostitutes. Victims who wouldn't be missed.

He was a little annoyed at the nature of the attack on the two doctors. No planning whatsoever.

It was sporadic. Something had snapped as he recalled it was something as innocuous as the way the male doctor dressed. A stupid multi coloured ski hat.

But no worries. He'd taken care of it. More snow forecast that night and the only thing that could link him to the scene was hidden in a place that they would never find.

The two doctors were a mistake.

Or were they?

He'd taken more from those two rifle shots than when he'd strangled young Hans. Instant death exploding in the rifle's scope. Beautiful. Satisfying.

Something inside of him had been rekindled. He hadn't slaked his thirst for death. He needed more.

But he'd need to plan well. Those doctor's bodies would eventually be found. Most of the animals would be hibernating for the winter, too sleepy to help him dispose of the evidence.

A smug grin pulled across his face. He wanted them to be found. Yes, of course he did.

That was part of the appeal. The fame, the notoriety, press conferences, instilling fear in the community.

He wouldn't stop. No way.

Chapter 33

'He couldn't have buried the bodies,' Saxon said. 'The ground up there was more or less frozen. He'd have to have hidden them somewhere.'

'But why would he kill them?' Suzy said. 'Do you think he may have mistaken them for us?'

Saxon shook his head. 'Unlikely. Remember the pictures on the TV? They didn't resemble us at all. And anyway, all rifles have telescopic sites. It would be like looking at them with binoculars.'

'Then why?'

'Because he's unbalanced. Because he enjoys it.'

'But—'

How much do you know about him, Suzy? Has he killed before? Were there any incidents as a youngster?'

Saxon looked on as the blood drained from Suzy's face. 'What is it?' he asked.

'Oh my God—'

'Tell me Suzy.'

'When he was fourteen, one of his mates went missing, a young boy called Hans. Paul and Hans were inseparable, but then one day, Hans disappeared. He had a history of running away, so the police weren't unduly concerned and anyway, there were no parents or family to speak of. Nobody missed him. Nobody bothered to chase the police up and eventually he was forgotten about. They interviewed Paul.'

'He was the last person to see him alive?'

'Yes. Paul and Hans had been hiking a few days before.'

'Was his body ever found?'

'No.'

She turned to Saxon. 'You don't think he killed Hans, do you?'

'Difficult to say without finding a body.' Saxon walked over to the window. Looked out and gazed up at the mountains. 'All I know is that up there,' he pointed, 'is the perfect killing ground, the perfect place to hide bodies. Seventy-five thousand square miles, population practically zero. A killer could go to work up there and the chances of catching him in the act are almost nil. Not like in a city where if you take a shot at somebody, the chances are that someone will see you, or at the least you'll be caught on camera.' He turned around and faced Suzy. 'And if he wanted to hide a body or two, what are the chances of finding them? And yet—' Saxon stalled. He was gathering his thoughts.

'What is it, Sax?'

‘Well… you recall that I’ve studied the make-up of serial killers?

‘Yes.’

‘Well, the thing is that most of them don’t hide the bodies.’

‘No?’

‘Perhaps half-heartedly, but at the end of the day, most of the buzz out of doing what they are doing is the thrill of the discovery of a corpse. That way, they can create the terror that they are craving for. Most never bothered to even hide the bodies, but even those who did buried them in shallow graves, or threw them in ditches or light undergrowth. Killers like Jeffrey Dahmer and Dennis Nilsen kept the corpses at home.’

‘My God, that’s gross,’ Suzy said. ‘The bodies would be stinking.’

‘They were. That’s how Nilsen was caught. His neighbours reported the smell.’ Saxon was pacing the room now. ‘Even as far back as Jack the Ripper, he slaughtered those poor women and just left the bodies where they fell. Every woman in London was petrified, and that’s exactly what he wanted at the end of the day.’

Suzy stared into space.

‘Penny for your thoughts,’ Saxon said.

‘No, I’ll throw it back to you,’ she said. ‘Penny for yours.’

Saxon raked his fingers through his thick hair. ‘You sure?’ he asked.

Suzy nodded.

He walked over and settled on the sofa beside her.

'I know we were shot at; I know it was no hunting accident. I am also well aware of those two shots we heard before we were targeted and now,' he pointed to the TV, 'two people are missing. Paul Suter fits the bill. I believe you when you say he had a rifle, that he hunted and butchered up an ibex in the kitchen while you looked on. Why would you possibly make that up?'

She squeezed his hand. 'Thanks. Nuessle made me feel a bit shitty to be honest.'

'I believe you, Suzy. I'm also guessing that you know there's something not right with Paul, that his childhood wasn't easy, that he spent some time locked up as a teenager and I also believe he had a spell in prison in his early twenties.'

'What?'

'Yes, I have that information. It was nothing too serious… GBH. He got into quite a few scraps in his younger years and unfortunately didn't know when to stop, ended up putting a couple of guys in hospital.'

A tear escaped from the corner of her eye. 'It makes sense. I recall that he was away a few times over the years.'

'If he has got something to do with Hans' disappearance, then he's quite capable of killing again.'

'I can't believe what's going through my head. It's all starting to add up,' Suzy said. 'And the missing girls… you think—'

‘No, I don’t,’ Saxon said without hesitation. ‘It’s a different modus operandi altogether. I’m sure if any of those girls had been shot, the coroner would have picked up on a few bullet holes. This is different. This is a crazed gunman on the loose, a gunman who may have killed before. Perhaps when you walked out on him, something snapped.’

‘Oh my God—’ Suzy shook her head, pulled a tissue from her pocket and wiped her eyes. ‘It’s not possible Sax, we weren’t even that close. It was a relationship of convenience. We weren’t even sharing the same bed. I won’t have it.’

Saxon reached for her hand. ‘It’s not your fault, Suzy. Anything could have happened to tip him over the edge. We were talking about girls going missing at Cabane Moiry, possible murder. It could have stirred up some emotions from way back. That’s all it takes sometimes.’

Saxon could see that Suzy was beginning to lose it. She was trembling, beads of sweat appearing on her forehead. What on earth was going through her mind, sensing, believing that the man she’d had a relationship was possibly responsible for murder?

‘Okay,’ Saxon said. ‘We’ll have a little dinner, perhaps some wine. It’ll help us sleep. If those two doctors haven’t turned up by tomorrow morning, we’ll take it from there.’

‘And what does that mean. What can we do?’

‘We’ll go and find them.’

Chapter 34

They'd left it until lunchtime and the local midday news had confirmed that the doctors still hadn't been found. Nuessle was on the TV news station. A press conference. He'd been in touch with the doctor's families and promised a search by the weekend.

'Too fucking late,' Saxon had snapped at the TV screen. 'Is he for fucking real? It's below freezing up there and if they are still alive, they'll be frozen to death by the weekend.'

'You think they might have had an accident?' Suzy asked.

'It's a possibility. But you heard the report, they were only equipped for a day hike. No tent, no food, just a small pack each and some waterproofs.'

Inside Saxon was seething. He couldn't believe the lackadaisical attitude of Nuessle and his department. The same old story. And yet it didn't make sense. Nuessle had been a high flyer at one point. This wasn't the response from a man who had risen so rapidly through the ranks of the Swiss police.

They had taken the bus to Gruben and checked in at one of the small hotels. They were on the mountain by 7 am the following day. It was only an hour's walk to where they had been shot at and they found it quite easily. The dead ibex marked the spot.

Saxon hunkered down. He spent some time looking at the scene. Suzy sensed he was concentrating and said nothing. He stood. Walked around in circles, crouched again and fingered the surrounding grass.

'What is it?' Suzy asked.

'Too much blood, he replied.'

'It's a dead animal,' Suzy said. 'Of course there's going to be blood.'

'Not this much,' he said. 'The ibex has been shot through the heart. The killer is a good shot, which means the animal would have died instantly and the blood from the heart would have stopped pumping almost immediately. This is where you suffered your head wound, but most of that blood ended up on your clothing. But look here.' He pulled at a tuft of grass. 'A big stain, I'd say a pint or two at least, more becoming of a head wound. A head wound produces a huge pool of blood, and look, it's several feet from where the ibex is lying anyway.'

'And how do you know all this?'

'Because I was a soldier, I've seen it more times than I'd care to remember. That's a head wound, blood consistent with a human head wound. I'm guessing that this is exactly the spot where the doctors were murdered.'

Saxon stood and looked around. He dug the heel of his boot into the ground. It barely made an indentation.

'Come, follow me.'

Saxon was already walking away from the corpse of the animal, Suzy skipped along behind him.

'Where are we going?' she asked.

'Over here, towards the edge of the mountain. If he'd killed those doctors and wanted to hide the bodies, he wouldn't have had time to bury them. The ground is too hard.' He stopped and pointed over Suzy's shoulder. 'And look, the nearest forest is nearly a kilometre away. There's no way would he have had time to carry both bodies deep into the forest. It would be too risky and anyway, if it was Paul, he'd have known we were close behind them and he wouldn't want to be out in the open too long.' He turned 180 degrees and started walking again. He called over his shoulder, 'His only option would be to drag the bodies thirty metres this way and chuck them over.'

They both stood on the edge and looked into the precipice.

Saxon pulled his rucksack from his back and placed it on the ground. He opened it, took out his binoculars.

It was almost a vertical drop, save for a few small outcrops. He lifted the binoculars to his eyes and fingered the focus wheel.

After a minute, he spoke. 'There's a covering of snow down there, which is a bit of a bugger if it's fallen through the night.'

'It would cover the bodies?'

'Yes, and there's a fair bit of forest down there too. I don't think it's the sort of terrain that attracts too many hikers. They prefer to be up here.'

Saxon lowered the glasses, walked a little further along the cliff edge. 'Stay back,' he called to Suzy. 'It's a little icy.'

Suzy didn't like heights. She didn't need to be told twice.

Saxon edged closer. Looked over and then back at his rucksack. 'There's a length of rope in the rucksack Suzy, will you get it for me please.'

'Sax,' she said. 'For God's sake, what are you doing?'

'I'm going over. There's a little ledge about twenty metres down. It juts out. I'll be able to get a better look.'

'No, please Sax, it's dangerous. You've said it's icy.'

'Give me the rope.'

She knew Saxon was the determined type and wouldn't listen to her. Reluctantly, she located the rope and walked over to him. 'Be careful.'

'As always.'

Saxon secured the rope around a big boulder the size of a car, five metres from the edge. He reached into the rucksack pocket and pulled out an abseiling harness, two leg loops, and a belay loop. Attached to the harness was a belay device. He climbed into the harness and made a few adjustments before feeding the rope through the belay device.

Suzy looked on nervously as he disappeared over the edge. 'Be careful,' she shouted as the rope pulled taut.

Saxon lowered himself onto the ledge and sat with his legs dangling over the edge. He made himself comfortable and pulled the binoculars to his eyes. It was a direct drop. He figured that if they had been shot, the shooter wouldn't have wanted to make it difficult for himself. This was the nearest possible place to drop two bodies.

He'd figured right. It was only a few minutes before he spotted a hand sticking out of the snow.

He shouted up to Suzy, 'I'm coming up now. Just pull the rope in as I climb.'

Saxon called Nuessle in Zermatt as soon as he'd detached the rope and coiled it into his rucksack.

'A hand,' he said to Suzie. 'Nothing else that I can see, but definitely a hand. I'd bet my life that it's those two poor doctors.'

Chapter 35

Saxon and Suzy were at the police station before Nuessle reported for duty. They sat in the small reception area and he arrived at five minutes to eight.

'Come through to my office,' he said as he walked through the door.

'We'll need to wait until the bodies are examined.'

'They've been shot. I'll lay my life on it.'

Nuessle had sent up the helicopter as soon as he'd received Saxon's phone call. Saxon and Suzy had waited until it arrived. Saxon pointed out the exact location and the chopper had flown in low. The crew had also confirmed that they had seen what looked like a hand sticking out of the snow but it was impossible to land and they had photographed the scene and the mountain rescue team had been called and were due to leave at first light the following day.

Twenty-four hours later and the two doctors' bodies were on the marble slab at the coroner's office in Sion. Although Nuessle had to wait for the official cause of death, there was no doubt in the eyes of the police and mountain rescue team who dug the broken, frozen bodies out of the snow.

The gunshot wounds to both bodies were clearly visible, and the detective had been sent the photographs within just a few minutes of the team's arrival on the scene.

Nuessle had assembled his team and briefed them before the press conference, which was about to take place.

There were many emotions running around the policeman's head. He was angry for sure and frustrated that the ex-military man from England had opened up wounds that he'd thought had long healed, exposed his vulnerability and his inability as a detective. Jesus fucking Christ, the press, they'd eat him for breakfast, he wasn't sure he'd be able to cope.

Get a grip, man! he told himself. It was hardly his fault that there was a killer up there. It wasn't as if he had killed them with his own hands. Not exactly.

Chapter 36

Suter was cooking an early lunch at Cabane Moiry, when he heard the thac, thac, thac of the rotor blades. He looked out of the kitchen window. A mechanically induced blizzard made it difficult to see, but he could just about decipher the *police* logo on the tail as it hovered below him, the pilot seeking out a suitable landing spot.

Nuessle had been flown in by helicopter to interview him.

When they'd first interviewed him about the shooting, it had been nothing more than a little gentle questioning. This time, it was different. They had two dead bodies to talk about.

Nuessle had two policemen with him. The helicopter pilot walked in too. He made straight for the kitchen and started to make some coffee. The policemen conducted a full search of the cabin. They found nothing.

Nuessle spoke with Suter for over two hours. He told Suter that he was still a suspect in the murders of the two doctors. He'd been in the right place at the wrong time. There hadn't been that many people on the mountain at the time they had been shot.

The relationship with Suzy. Suter had said that he didn't give a fuck about her, that their relationship was purely platonic, and they had agreed to go their separate ways months ago.

'The thing is,' Nuessle said, 'I have no reason to doubt what Suzy said. Your ex-bed mate said you hunted, said she'd seen you butchering animals, that she'd even enjoyed some of the barbecued meat.'

'She's lying.'

'But why would she lie? She seems like a nice kid.' Nuessle pointed a finger directly in his face. 'But you, however, Suter, I know all about you, about your past and your little trip to prison as a teenager. You spent more time in the prison hospital than your cell. Did they chain you to a radiator?'

Nuessle pushed harder. Interviewing criminals was his speciality, there was no one better in the force.

Suter clammed up. He answered no more of Nuessle's questions, refused to rise to the provocation.

He had to admit, the young man gave nothing away and despite Nuessle setting a few traps, he never fell into any of them. But Nuessle still had an ace up his sleeve.

As they were about to leave, Nuessle stood up. 'Okay Suter, before we go, I'd like to take away the two ski coats for analysis, the ones that are hanging on the hook by the door.'

It was the first time that Suter had shown any signs of anxiousness.

'But you can't. It's minus five out there. I'll freeze to death. I need supplies and—'

'Relax,' Nuessle said. He pointed to one of the policemen. 'Officer Macron will give you his. We'll have them back to you in a few days if they're clean.'

'Clean… wh… what do you mean?'

'You told me you don't possess a gun, Herr Suter. In which case if we test these coats for gunshot residue, they'll be clean. Gunshot residue hangs around on items of clothing for about a week, so by my calculations we still have a couple of days.'

'But I—'

'I'm not stupid and neither are you. I reckon that gun is well hidden, deep in a forest somewhere, maybe a secret hunting cabin in the mountains and you've cleaned this cabin from top to bottom, it fucking stinks of disinfectant.'

'It's my job, Herr Nuessle. I'm quite obsessive about cleanliness.'

'I bet you fucking are. But be aware, all killers make mistakes. Suter, even the cleverest criminal, will make at least three mistakes relating to the crime they have committed. They will make at least one fuck up, before, during and after the crime. I call it the three-stage meltdown. I'll find those mistakes and those mistakes will lead me right to the killer's door.'

Suter steepled his hands, stared into space, and waited patiently for the policemen to leave.

Nuessle walked towards the door. Lifted the coats from the hooks. 'In the meantime, don't be getting any ideas about wandering off into the mountains. Officer Macron will be staying with you until we get the results.' Nuessle smiled. 'He can't go anywhere anyway. He hasn't got a coat.'

Officer Macron nodded and Nuessle and the other policeman and the pilot walked towards the door.

Nuessle opened it, and then he turned. 'By the way Suter, have you seen anything of Heinz Frei this summer?'

'Heinz Frei?'

'Yes, surely you know of Heinz Frei?'

'Yes… yes, I know of him. He was here a couple of times early in the season.'

'I see.'

Nuessle zipped up his jacket as a gust of wind blew into the cabane. He pulled up his coat collar and walked towards the helicopter situated on a large, flat piece of terrain, fifty metres below the cabane terrace. The wind was picking up, flakes of snow danced in the early evening air.

Macron and Suter watched until the helicopter disappeared into the clouds.

Chapter 37

It was just after two in the morning and Saxon was wide awake. Again. Suzy lay beside him, the delicate shape of her features just about visible in the moonlight, that peeked through a small gap in the curtains.

He didn't want to be here, hadn't asked to be here, and he certainly hadn't planned any sort of a relationship.

Too soon.

But who was he kidding? This girl had awakened feelings inside him that he hadn't experienced for many years.

Why the fuck had Blacklock even called him?

He pulled the duvet back and climbed out of bed. Much against his better judgement, he opened the drawer to the desk and pulled out the half bottle of Glenfiddich. He poured a large measure and walked over to the minibar, opened the freezer compartment and prised an ice cube out of the small plastic tray. He dropped it into the glass, swirled it around for a few seconds, and then took a decent mouthful. He held the single malt in his mouth. A creamy, butterscotch with a subtle oak flavour. Magnificent. It had been a long time since he'd been acquainted with his old foe. He tipped his head back and allowed the liquid to slip down his throat.

It was the exact eureka moment he was looking for.

It was a mess and it had nothing to do with him. He'd come here to find out what happened to Kate, nothing else. He didn't need to get involved and he certainly didn't need to try and convince a third-rate policeman to take his own enquiry more seriously. He had no concept that those girls' deaths were even suspicious. *Or had he?*

And that bloody press conference.

Saxon had crept into the back room of the hotel just as Nuessle had started to read out his prepared statement.

The two doctors' identities had been confirmed. Their families notified. They had died from gunshot wounds, and it appeared that their bodies had been thrown into a forested area from a great height.

A Zermatt reporter had asked if there was a psychopath on the loose, or could the two doctors have been specifically targeted.

Nuessle said it was too early to tell.

'Did they have any enemies?' Another journalist asked.

Not that the police knew of. They were in a relationship. There were no known ex-partners on the radar.

‘So it was a random attack?’ a female journalist asked.

Nuessle pulled at his shirt collar. Clearly uncomfortable. ‘Too early to say,’ he answered.

Nuessle was sticking to the script. A total waste of time.

The news of the two assassinations had filtered into a few publications around Europe. The headliners sprang into action. One headline read, Massacre on the Matterhorn. Not strictly true, of course. It was neither a massacre, nor was it on the Matterhorn, but when did the truth stand in the way of a good story?

A good story? That wasn’t a good story. Saxon was about to ask a question of the detective that would hit the newspapers and online Internet publications around the globe.

He stood up. ‘Detective Nuessle—’

The policeman’s face turned to stone.

‘Do you have any more information on the other murdered girls?’

Chapter 38

It was seven in the morning when Saxon walked out of the bedroom and made his way down into the foyer of the hotel. He found a quiet corner and took out his phone.

'Jesus fucking Christ, Sax,' Blacklock said. 'It's six in the morning. This better be important.'

'Sorry, sir, I forgot about the time difference.'

He hadn't.

'Have you seen the headlines?'

'No,' Blacklock replied.

'Tell me.'

'The two doctors, the coroner confirmed they had been shot, thrown from the mountain like the others.'

'But not like the others, Sax. The others were all single females, weren't they?'

'Yes, and they hadn't been shot.'

'No.'

'So what are you telling me? There are two killers out there?'

Saxon took a deep breath. 'The thing is, Neil, I think we are losing focus of why I'm actually here. I came here to find out what happened to Kate. Nothing more.'

'But Sax—'

'Listen mate, I checked a few things out yesterday and through the night. It's more complicated than I thought because Paul Suter was away in prison when one of those murders was committed.'

'I see, so it's pointing towards the other fellow, the mountaineer?'

'No. His Facebook page threw a spanner in the works. He's off the hook too, because when two of those murders took place, he was in Australia. It couldn't have been him either.'

'You sure?'

'I'm positive. I've had someone check out the register of the hotel he was staying in.'

'How the hell did you manage that?''Best you don't know. Furthermore, he was in Australia when Kate went missing.'

'He was?'

'Yeah, flew out on a Qantas flight a few days before.'

'So what are you going to do then?'

'I don't know to be honest. If I could have worked with the police, there may have been a chance, but Nuessle clearly doesn't want me involved. I think it's over to the police now. I've laid it on a plate for them on more than one occasion and they've thrown it back in my face. They wouldn't have it that we had been shot at, and now they have two dead doctors on their doorstep and eight unsolved murders.'

'What about the girls? Are they taking it seriously? Doesn't he get it?'

'Oh, he gets it all right, but whether he does anything about it is another matter. I am really tired of their incompetence. They're like a set of Dixon of Dock Greens, totally out of their depth. His face was like thunder at the press conference when I asked him about the murdered girls. But get this, there's barely a mention of it in the press. It doesn't make sense. Why wouldn't they report something as dramatic as that?'

'I don't know. If that had been in a press conference in London, it would have filtered into every major daily in Europe and around the world.'

'It's the closed Zermatt circle, the Heinz Frei and Nuessle boys, the press conference received no publicity, just a few Zermatt journalists casually notified that something was taking place.'

Saxon was thinking. Nobody could bury their heads in the sand so deep. There was something more. The words *cover up,* filtered through his mind.

'So what are you going to do, mate?' Blacklock asked. 'Are you throwing the towel in?'

That's exactly what Saxon wanted to do. He wished he'd never set foot in Zermatt, never set eyes on Nuessle. And he was in a relationship of sorts, or at least he had feelings for Suzy, and that was the last thing he wanted. He'd planned a cycle trip around the world and he couldn't have been happier than when he'd got those first few hundred miles under his belt, when he'd cycled through Holland and crossed into Belgium. He'd been sleeping under the stars without a care in the world. Then a phone call from Blacklock that changed everything.

'My hands are tied, Neil. I've even given the police two names, two suspects who at the very least, should have been arrested. One of them is up in a cabin nine thousand feet up the bloody mountain enjoying the peace and the tranquillity and the views, they haven't even questioned him properly and the other is nowhere to be seen, poncing around Australia somewhere, without a care in the world.'

That's where Saxon wanted to be, in a world where he didn't want to have to care, to plan. He wanted to climb on his bike and just go. Go anywhere. It didn't matter.

'I was hired to find Kate.'

'You were hired to find out what happened to Kate, or at least to find some proof that she'd died up there.'

'And I haven't done that, and quite frankly, Neil, I don't know what else I can do. Winter is setting in now. We've just a week or two of milder weather left and then a big white blanket will be pulled over the mountain and then you can forget about any sort of search for months.'

There was a prolonged silence on the other end of the phone before Blacklock spoke. 'I get it Sax, I do. You've been great, you've uncovered so much shit and ruffled a few feathers at the same time. I couldn't really ask any more.'

'The snow is the boss now mate, so what's the point of covering my expenses for the next six months when I can guarantee I won't find a dickie bird?'

'You're right. I think she's dead, Sax. If she'd met with any sort of accident, we've run out of time.'

'I have to agree. A few weeks back, there was a little hope. She was well trained. She could survive for a period of time, but not this long. And given the incompetence of the Keystone Kops, I can quite easily understand why they haven't found her body.'

Blacklock told Saxon to wind the operation up, to compile a final report for Kate's family, put it in writing what he believed had happened to her. Perhaps when they read the report it might bring on some sort of closure.

Chapter 39

At breakfast, Saxon explained the brick walls he'd walked into relating to the possibility of Frei and Suter being the killer. The timings didn't add up. Neither Frei nor Suter could have been responsible unless they had been working together. But that was a no go. Frei and Suter were from different sides of the fence. They didn't know each other, had never been seen together.

Suzy was genuinely relieved. They even dared to discuss the possibility that the gunman may not be Suter after all.

'He lied to the police, though,' Suzy said. 'Claimed he didn't have a gun and wasn't a hunter. That concerns me. Why would he do that?'

'An illegal firearm?' Saxon offered.

'It's possible.'

'And if he'd only shot at us, I could quite believe that he was trying to scare us, but those two doctors, why would Paul do that?'

'I don't know, Suzy. I really don't know.'

Saxon explained his phone call to his old RSM. He said that he was going to wind the operation up. There was little hope that they'd find her alive now.

'It's due to snow again soon, Lenny.'

'I know. That's why it's going to be impossible to find anything. It's pointless staying here. I've told Blacklock I'll be checking out at the weekend.'

Suzy's face fell. She didn't say anything.

'I'm going to continue my cycle trip; you'll need to get back home soon too.'

Suzy nodded.

'We can still stay in touch,' he said.

'Of course, that would be nice.'

'We both need to get on with our lives.'

'There's no other way.'

Saxon reached for her hand. 'If you're a little worried, rent your apartment out, find a new town or village and keep your head low until this has all blown over.'

He offered her a few practical solutions, even offered to help her financially.

'I've got money,' she said. 'Enough to last me a year or two and I've never found any difficulty getting work.'

They finished their coffee and left the dining room. They were walking past the reception area when the girl stopped them.

Saxon froze on the spot. It could have been a ghost.

'Good morning, Mr Saxon,' she said. 'I wonder if we could have a little chat?'

'Sure,' Saxon said. 'What's it about? Who are you?'

She pointed to a corner, a small, empty table with four chairs. 'It's quiet over there. We won't be disturbed. I'm Kate's sister.'

Suzy kissed him on the cheek, made her excuses to leave them in private. 'Just make sure you give me a shout when you're finished.'

'I will.' Saxon watched as she walked towards the stairwell.

Becky Henshaw was in her early thirties and very attractive. She said that she'd driven from her home in Vevey, Switzerland, checked into the hotel late last night. Despite the obvious similarity to her sister, Saxon felt that there was something else. He recognised her from somewhere.

As they got talking, Becky explained who she was, a fiction writer who had gained worldwide acclaim and success from her debut novel and subsequent books in the series about a female detective from Clydebank.

'I lived in Glasgow for more than seven years, so it was only natural to set my first novel there. They do say that you should write about what you know, so I wrote about Glasgow. It was more of a hobby at the time, but the book was picked up by a small publisher and it went crazy, sold over a million copies in the first year. Before I knew it, they'd offered me a six-figure advance for book two and three and the rest, as they say, is history. I'm making a bloody good living writing books. How cool is that?'

'What was your book called?'

'More Dead Than Alive, the detective was Alice Chamberlain.'

The penny dropped.

'That's where I've seen you,' Saxon said. 'I've read your book. There's a photo of you on the inside back cover. You're B J Henshaw.'

Becky smiled. 'I hate that photo.'

'I don't know why.'

'Well, I do. I'd always wanted to blend into the background. I never wanted any of the limelight, but unfortunately the six-figure sum came with some strings attached.'

'I can imagine.'

'Press conferences, radio and TV, as many as three or four podcasts a week.'

'My heart bleeds.'

Becky stretched back in her seat. 'I know, I shouldn't complain. It's a great way to make a living. I just wish they'd let me lock myself away in my little mountain retreat. I'd give them more books and that way and we'd all make more money. It seems as though I just get stuck into a chapter when they call and want a piece of me.'

'You live in Vevey, you said.'

'Nearby, I live a kilometre outside, a small village in the mountains called Palézieux, but nobody has ever heard of Palézieux so it's easier to say Vevey.'

'It sounds beautiful.'

'It is. Sometimes in winter, the snow cuts the village off for weeks. It's the best time of the year for me. That's when my words really flow.'

'You like the mountains then. You're just like Kate.'

'Yes, when Mum and Dad were alive, when we were small, every holiday we took was in the lake district, climbing the hills and the fells around Keswick, Borrowdale and Buttermere.'

'Wait a minute, your mum and dad are dead?'

'Yes, a car crash five years back.'

'But the man who hired me, he said Kate's family had—'

'That would be me, Mr Saxon. I'm Kate's family, some aunts and uncles and cousins back in England but not really that close. It was me who made contact with the RSM, so in effect I pay the bills. You are working for me.'

Saxon wondered if it was time to tell her what he had discussed with Blacklock, that there was nothing more they could do. Not just yet. 'Now I know,' he said. 'So what brings you to Zermatt?'

Becky explained that she'd received the reports from Blacklock, based on the things Saxon had discovered. 'And when I'd read that there was going to be a press conference, it seemed like a good idea to kill two birds with one stone. It's only a two-hour drive after all. I wanted to meet you, of course, but I also wanted to see the whites of Nuessle's eyes.'

'You don't like him then?'

'Not at all.'

'And what about Kate's boyfriend?'

That question changed Becky's face. It told Saxon a lot.

She hesitated slightly. 'I suppose he's a nice enough kid, if not a little boring.'

'You've met him then?'

'Yes. Just the once, before they set off on their grand adventure. I'd never seen Kate so happy so I guessed that their relationship must have been okay.'

'There's a but isn't there?'

'Yes,' Becky nodded. 'There are a few buts, actually. There's a big but about him, he could hardly look me in the eye when we met and there's a big but about why Kate went out with that sort of fellow in the first place, he just wasn't her usual type. If you were to twist my arm, I'd say it was more a relationship of convenience. They'd pooled their finances, bought the motor home, and he would be a good companion for her. But I'm not sure that my little sis was head over heels in love with boring James. That's why she used to take off solo most of the time.'

'Are you going to see him?'

'I guess I should. I expected him to be at the press conference, but he didn't show.'

‘He’s down at a campsite in—’

‘Yes, I know, you told Blacklock in your email.’

‘I spoke with the RSM this morning, Becky.’

‘Yes?’

‘The thing is, we both agreed that this investigation isn’t going anywhere.’

Becky lifted her coffee cup to her lips.

‘And winter is coming. The snow will have the mountains buried in just a week or two.’

She placed the cup back on the table.

‘You must realise we’re not going to find anything now.’

Becky stood. ‘You’ll have to excuse me for a second. I have to nip to the little girl’s room.’

They took more coffee at midday. Saxon called Suzy, and she came down to where they were sitting.

He briefed Becky on everything that had happened up the mountain, how they’d been shot at and nearly killed. She sat in silence as he told her about Paul Suter, how he’d lied about his gun and hunting ibex on the mountain.

‘The plot thickens,’ Becky said. ‘If I wrote this in one of my books, they’d tell me it was too far fetched.’

They had lunch in the hotel restaurant. The conversation lightened a little and then Suzy disappeared into town, to the supermarket for some provisions.

The inevitable question had to be asked. Saxon had put it off too long. ‘Do you think she’s still alive?’

There was no hesitation. 'I do. We were very close, almost like twins. Things happened in our childhood years.'

'What sort of things?'

'Kate broke her ankle when she was thirteen. She jumped down from a tree and it snapped just below the shin bone. I was four miles away, on the other side of town, and at that exact moment when she lay on the ground screaming for help, I felt a strange sensation in the same leg. It wasn't exactly painful, but it was very unpleasant and when I got the phone call from Mum, and they told me about the break, I knew immediately that it had been her right ankle. I was at the hospital within a couple of hours and it was no surprise to me when they wheeled her out in a wheelchair with her right leg in a cast. Of course the scientists will tell you that's impossible, but believe me, it wasn't the only time things like that happened.'

'And you felt nothing like that when Kate went missing?'

'Nothing at all. I would have expected to have felt something, especially if she'd had a fall. I'm convinced she's still alive, she's out there somewhere, she hasn't had an accident and she certainly hasn't been murdered. I want you to continue, Lenny. I don't care what it costs.'

Saxon explained that it wasn't about the cost, it was about wasting money. 'Once the winter snow arrives, we won't even be able to make it up the mountain, Becky. It's a pointless exercise. Kate was a high hill hiker. As you know, she wasn't one for strolling around the low valleys. I've checked all the forecasts, all the previous winter's stats and within a couple of weeks at the latest, it will be a white out from two thousand metres up.'

Saxon reached into his pocket and pulled out his phone. He opened the notebook app and turned it to face Becky. 'This was her proposed route during those last few days.' He pointed to the screen. 'And here, her last locations. Both the Europahütte and Cabane de Moiry are well above the two thousand metre mark and the last mountain she scaled, Col de Valpelline, ridiculously high at over three thousand five hundred metres. We have to assume she disappeared somewhere up there, because that's what she loved, that's where she belonged, Becky.'

'She's not dead,' Becky said in defiance.

Saxon sighed. 'Becky, we have to face facts. Even if she's up there and alive at this very moment, then why hasn't she made an appearance? Why hasn't she contacted anyone? If she was holed up in a refuge but was immobile, then no refuge has enough food stored to last a few weeks, let alone a few months.'

She shook her head. 'I know what you are saying, Lenny, and none of this makes sense. But just do me a favour, will you?'

'Anything, of course.'

'Just hang around another couple of weeks, go and see James, talk to him, talk to Nuessle again too.'

Saxon nodded. 'If that's what you really want.'

‘I do. Please, just stay. Have a couple of weeks with your girlfriend here in the hotel.’

How could he refuse?

He gave in. ‘Two weeks, no more.’

Becky stood and shook his hand. ‘Thanks, Lenny, I really appreciate it.’

Saxon leaned forward and kissed her on the cheek. ‘It isn’t easy, Becky, I know, but all the signs point to an—’

‘Accident, yes, I know. But I won’t accept that outcome until we find a body.’

Saxon thought about telling Becky how many years the mountains could hide a body. Some bodies were never given up by the mountains.

Perhaps it wasn’t the right time.

Becky walked away, towards the lift. Halfway across the reception area, she stopped. Turned.

‘Lenny,’ she called over. ‘You don’t think she’s been kidnapped do you?’

Chapter 40

The Flying Pig called around 3 pm. Saxon was in his room, Suzy in the shower. They'd planned the rest of the day out, and she wanted to freshen up.

He got straight to the point. 'The thing is, Sax, although Heinz Frei had a seat booked on that Qantas flight, he never arrived in Sydney. He never took the flight.'

'You're kidding.'

'I'm not. I checked the hotel too, just in case he rescheduled another flight. He hasn't checked in like he normally does. It looks like he never made it to Oz.'

'My God! That changes things a bit.'

'And I've something else.'

'Tell me.'

'Nuessle, I've found out why he was demoted.'

'Go on.'

'You're gonna love this one.'

'C'mon then.'

'A bit of a scandal, really. Remember those eight girls who we think were murdered?'

'Yes.'

'Well, one of them, the second one, Selena Garcia, way back when Nuessle was in Zurich, was found at the bottom of Gran Combin. At first they treated it just like an accident, solo climber, numerous broken bones, no witnesses, blah, blah, blah. However, her husband refused to believe that she'd go anywhere near where there was a danger of falling. She didn't like heights and sheer drops, she got vertigo. He insisted on another coroner and a second opinion. He was quite a wealthy fellow and paid for a private investigation.'

Saxon listened intently.

'The second coroner found evidence of sexual assault, a possible rape and lo and behold recovered an unknown pubic hair. At that point, they called in the big boys from Zurich.'

'Nuessle,' Saxon said.

'Bingo! Nuessle and his men and the only evidence, the pubic hair, were handed over to the Zurich team for analysis. The hair was to be sent away for DNA checking.'

There were a hundred things running around Saxon's head.

The Flying Pig continued. 'And here's where it gets interesting. The evidence went missing, mate. It never reached the DNA lab.'

'You're kidding me.'

'I wish I was. Nuessle, or someone on his team, should have either personally delivered the bagged item or it should have been delivered by special courier. Someone claimed they sent it by ordinary post, not even a recorded delivery, no record of where the hell it went.'

'For fuck's sake, that's scandalous.'

'Yep, and Garcia's husband went mental. He rattled more cages than a troop of monkeys in a zoo and there was a major enquiry. The original coroner had recorded an accidental death, but the second coroner disagreed with him. He labelled it *suspicious*, but for some reason the official verdict stood and is the one that appears on record even to this day.'

'So what happened in the enquiry?'

'They blamed Nuessle and a civilian who handled the postage.'

Saxon knew who the civilian was before his name left the Flying Pig's mouth.

'Nuessle was labelled incompetent, Eggen Fassnacht was said to have made a grave error of judgement and Nuessle's investigation was, and I quote, "Not up to the standards expected of such an experienced policeman." After the enquiry, Nuessle was moved to Zermatt and at first the civvy was sacked.'

'But he got his job back?'

'Yes. His union stepped in, said his treatment was harsh. He was later reinstated.'

'I know,' said Saxon. 'I've met him, he's on the front desk at Nuessle's nick.'

Chapter 41

It was late evening by the time Suzy and Saxon returned to the hotel. They'd spent the day and the evening chilling out in Sion, just an hour away by bus. They'd explored the two hilltop fortifications, a 13th century ruined castle and a basilica. They'd dined in the town square and caught the last bus back to Zermatt at nine o'clock.

'I'm absolutely wrecked,' Suzy said as they walked through the doors of the hotel. 'I'm going straight to bed.'

Saxon felt the same way. Sleep had been hard to come by these last few days. There were a hundred thoughts and scenarios flying round his head and they didn't necessarily stop when his head hit the pillow.

Saxon's eyes scanned the area immediately in front of him. Old habits die hard. Becky sat over in the lounge area by reception, reading a book. He pointed. 'Are you sure you don't want a nightcap?'

'Absolutely not.'

'I think it's only polite that we say hello.'

‘You go,’ Suzy said. ‘Really, I need to sleep. I think I got no more than a couple of hours last night.’

Suzy kissed him on the lips and walked away.

Saxon wandered over. ‘Good book?’

Becky looked up. ‘Oh hi. How you doing? Where have you been all day?’

Saxon explained about their cultural trip out. ‘Would you like a drink? I’m just having the one and then I’m heading to my room.’

‘Why not? A Baileys with ice will go down nicely.’

‘You got it.’ Saxon walked towards the bar and caught the waiter’s eye. It was quiet. The man strolled over straight away.

‘A Baileys with ice and a small beer.’

‘Right away, sir,’ the waiter said.

Saxon walked over to Becky’s table and sat down. ‘The book,’ he repeated. ‘Any good?’

‘It’s hard to say, I’ve just started it and I’m only a few chapters in. It’s hard to get into it to be honest. I haven’t been reading much lately.’

She turned the book cover to face him.

‘You’ve read it, Lenny?’

Saxon nodded. ‘Yes, Neil Gordon’s book. I read it last year. I think you’ll enjoy it, though I didn’t think it would be up your street.’

‘And why not?’

‘Well, it’s a million miles away from your Scottish detective. American spies and undercover agents, a bit too Hollywood, even for me if I recall.’

Becky closed the book and laid it on the table. 'You're very shrewd, Mr Saxon, observation like Sherlock Holmes, which I suppose is a good trait for a detective.'

'I'm hardly that.'

'Nevertheless, you're spot on. I'd never buy anything like this. It was sent to me by a fan about a month back.'

'That's nice.'

'I get a couple of dozen books a year, generally at Christmas time or around my birthday. This one is unusual because it's not Christmas time and it's not my birthday. It came from a fan who forgot to even send a name or an email so I can thank them.'

She picked up the book and opened the inside cover. She prised a card out. 'Sent from a small bookshop in Montpelier, Vermont, in the States. I like to thank those sorts of fans personally. These people are the ones who spread the word and tell the world about your books. She even took the time out to wish me well for the future.'

'She, you say the fan is a she? What makes you think that?'

'No specific reason. The writing looks smooth and soft, neat and tidy. Not from a heavy male hand, very similar to my own writing, I suppose.'

'But it's not familiar to you?'

'No, I don't think so.'

The waiter placed the drinks on the table. Saxon reached into his pocket for his wallet, pulled out a note, and placed it on the table. Now he knew who was paying his expenses, he wasn't going to put it on the room bill.

'Thank you very much,' Becky said, as she raised the glass to her lips.

'I owe you at least one drink,' he said. 'You've covered my bar bill for the last few weeks.'

Saxon wasn't a natural speed reader, but for the purpose of Neil Gordon's book, he had already read it anyway and he just wanted to clarify a few things. He located the book in his Kindle library and opened it and started to read.

Jim Grant had disappeared, been in hiding from the FBI for over thirty years. He had established a new life, a new identity.

It was all Saxon needed to know. There was something not right about a fan sending a book, taking the time to write a few lines and not even mention who they were. *Montpelier, where exactly was Montpelier?* He finished the book at exactly 02.11 on the hotel bedroom clock display. He took out his notebook and made an itinerary for the next few days. It was at least another two hours before he fell asleep.

Chapter 42

It wasn't easy getting a meeting with Heinz Frei's parents. It wasn't even easy getting to talk to them by telephone. Half an hour on an Internet search and Saxon had established that they were office based in the Grand Hotel, in the centre of Zermatt, one of their hotels. They had owned it for over twenty years and had an office on the top floor. To the south, a view over the most elegant part of town, to the west, a spectacular view of the Matterhorn.

A call through to reception had been deflected to no less than three people and Eventually Mrs Frei came to the phone.

'Herr Saxon,' she said, 'but I don't know of anybody of that name and you haven't told any of my staff the nature of your enquiry.'

'I'm sorry,' Saxon said, 'but it's rather sensitive. Could I come along and see you in person? I'm here in the city on business.'

'What sort of business?'

'I'd rather not say.'

'Then I choose not to meet with you.'

Before Saxon could offer more, she'd ended the call.

Saxon was happy enough that he had established that at least Mrs Frei was in situ in the Grand Hotel and within ten minutes he was sitting in the foyer of reception nursing a hot coffee. He had pulled a photograph from Google, a newspaper article from a few years back. Mr and Mrs Frei with their son Heinz and a large cheque made payable to a local charity. Nice. Good people.

Or so it seemed.

Shortly before 2 pm, the double lift doors opened and Mr and Mrs Frei stepped out. Mr Frei looked much older than his photograph in the newspaper. He was frail and slightly stooped, with thinning grey hair, a cigarette dangling from his lip. He was fast approaching seventy years of age or so it appeared in the cold light of day. Saxon knew how old Mrs Frei was, fifty-nine.

She held her years well, she could have passed for a lady ten years younger, very attractive.

They walked towards the dining room; Saxon deliberately cut them off before they reached the large oak doors. Mrs Frei in particular looked a little alarmed.

'Mrs Frei,' Saxon said. 'We spoke on the phone. I'm Leonard Saxon. We need to talk.'

Mrs Frei took a step back, snarled, 'I told you on the phone, we have nothing to talk about. Now if you don't get out of my hotel this minute, I'm calling security.'

Time to play the trump card, Saxon thought to himself. He took out his wallet and reached for the AMEX gold card. He held it out with his thumb strategically placed. 'I'm with Interpol. It's about your son Heinz.'

Mrs Frei fumed. Mr Frei was altogether cooler and more relaxed. 'What's the bloody rascal done now?' he said.

'He's in Australia,' Mrs Frei said. 'We've nothing to say.'

She called over to reception, 'Get me security, get security here now.'

There was a burst of activity behind reception. Someone picked up a telephone. Saxon took a deep breath, turned to Mrs Frei. 'Your son isn't in Australia. He never got on the plane.'

'Security, security,' Mrs Frei shouted. A burly man in uniform rushed over towards them. Saxon noticed that Mr Frei wore a puzzled expression. Why had his wife acted that way? Saxon had hardly been threatening.

The security man gripped Saxon by the arm. 'You're coming with me, sir.'

Saxon turned his head to the right, whispered, 'You have two seconds to take your hand off me.'

'And what if I don't?'

'Distal, proximal and middle phalange. You have fourteen of them in your hand. I promise I'll break every single one before you can say Mr and Mrs Frei.'

The security guard's arm fell to his side. He glanced at Mrs Frei, then back to Saxon.

Saxon leaned in and whispered to Mrs Frei, 'Now, send your gorilla back to his cage and you can tell me about your son's encounter with Selena Garcia.'

The security guard was quickly dispatched back to where he came from. Mrs Frei led Saxon to the office on the top floor and Mr Frei shuffled slowly behind. The meeting didn't last long, as Mrs Frei took on the persona of a concerned mother.

Frei was clearly missing. Saxon showed her the passenger flight list, the blank check in page from the hotel in Sydney on the date Heinz had been due there, and nearly a month of non existent Facebook activity.

'He posted on Facebook and Instagram regularly. It was his business after all, that's where he got most of the hiker clients from.'

'Pah,' Mr Frei exclaimed. 'The boy has no business, he has no work ethic, he has been living on the back of our dividends for decades. Oh, he plays the game well, of that there's no doubt.'

'Shut up, Rutger, you never give him any credit.'

'Pah, running around hills and chasing women, he'll never bloody change.'

'Quiet, Rutger!'

Mrs Frei was scrolling through her phone, checking Heinz's Facebook for herself. The colour was rapidly draining from her face as the reality set in.

'When did you last speak to Heinz, Mrs Frei?'

A look of despair, of shock. 'I… I don't recall, probably the day before he left for Australia.'

'He didn't arrive, Mrs Frei. He never made the flight.'

'But—'

'Who took him to the airport?'

She didn't answer. She took a handkerchief from her pocket. Dabbed at the corner of her eyes. Genuine shock. There was no doubt about it.

'Then where is he, Rosie?' Mr Frei said. 'The boy is missing. Is this what the cop is saying?'

Mrs Frei held up a hand, waved it in her husband's direction, said something to him in Swiss. He reached for a bottle of water and let out a long sigh as he flopped into a big easy chair by the window.

'He was arrested when Selena Garcia was found dead, wasn't he?' Saxon asked. 'Tell me about that.'

Mrs Frei regained her composure. 'It was an accident. That's what the coroner said. 'Heinz was simply helping the police with their enquiries.'

'But there was a second coroner, wasn't there?'

'A charlatan. He didn't know what he was doing.'

'He was a professional with over thirty years' experience.'

'Nonsense, they were raking up dirt, nothing more than that.'

Another brief conversation with her husband in Swiss, and then, 'It's time for you to go Herr Saxon. I've heard enough of your bullshit.'

'Tell me about Oscar Nuessle?

'What about him? What's he got to do with anything?'

'A fine boy,' Mr Frei said. 'One of the best, he's been like— '

'Shut up, Rutger.'

But the old man didn't hear and he mumbled on, singing Oscar Nuessle's praises, saying how much he had been a part of the boy's life, how he had introduced him to the hills and hunting and how to read maps and use a compass.

Eventually Mrs Frei blew her top, leaned into her husband's face and screamed blue murder at him, threatening all sorts of repercussions.

Saxon studied the old man. A door mat, a cash cow. Nothing left in the sham of a marriage.

The meeting was over; Mrs Frei had had enough. She stood and walked towards the door.

Saxon didn't object. The meeting had served its purpose. Now he just had to wait. It was only a matter of time.

He took the lift to the ground floor and walked into the bar just by reception. He ordered water and took it to a table by the door. It had a perfect view of reception and the glass revolving door to the street.

It was fifteen minutes before Nuessle arrived.

He hovered around reception for a minute and then took his mobile phone from his pocket and made a call. Like a good, observant detective, he scanned the area around him. As the policeman's eyes settled on the entrance to the bar, Saxon raised his right hand and gave a little wave.

Nuessle wasn't happy. 'You're in trouble now, Herr Saxon. Impersonating a police officer is a serious offence.'

'I don't know what you are talking about.'

'Mr Nuessle said that you were from Interpol. You had an Interpol ID card.'

'She must have been mistaken.'

'In your wallet, you showed her ID.'

'Not me.'

Nuessle didn't arrest him but instead asked Saxon to accompany him to the station to clear things up.

Saxon volunteered to a search, gave the Zermatt Police his wallet in which they found his driving licence, two HSBC bank cards and an AMEX Gold Card. Nuessle oversaw the search and then told Saxon he was free to go.

Saxon bid him goodbye, offered his hand, which Nuessle refused. 'You and Mrs Frei go back a long way, don't you?' Saxon asked.

'I know of her,' Nuessle said lamely, without any conviction.

'I think you know her very well,' Saxon said. 'Very well indeed.'

Nuessle clenched his fists by his side, took a step towards Saxon. ‘Get out of my fucking sight, Herr Saxon, before I lock you in one of my cells and throw away the fucking key.’

Chapter 43

There were several good reasons why Saxon was trekking up to the Col de Valpelline. For a start, the weather had turned milder and after three days of below freezing temperatures and light snow flurries, the temperature had crept above freezing and the snow had turned to rain. It wasn't the best weather for hiking, but it was the best he was going to get for at least four months.

In addition, he felt it was wise to get out of Zermatt. It was only a matter of time before Nuessle and the Zermatt police came calling. He knew how close he was to being arrested, or at the very least, they would place an exclusion order on him and run him out of town.

It was a good idea to get out of Nuessle's space. Calling him out about Rosalie Frei had touched a raw nerve. That was exactly why he had said it and now Nuessle knew that he knew and that could be fraught with danger.

The weather forecast told him that he had no more than seventy-two hours to find the dead body, otherwise it would be buried for months. If the winter was a severe one and there was above average snow, it could be hidden for years.

He'd left a note for Suzy and Becky. It was straight to the point. He said there had been a development and that he'd be back by the weekend.

Saxon had earmarked twenty-nine, potentially dangerous spots between the track that led out of Zermatt to the likely route Kate would have taken as she returned to the valley from the summit of Col de Valpelline. Unfortunately, as they now knew, she never made it to Zermatt.

It took Saxon nearly six hours to reach the Charles Kuonen Suspension Bridge, which spanned the Zermatt valley. It had rained most of the time, on and off, but at times torrential. He thought about his sleeping bag tucked away in the bottom of his rucksack. It was in a sealed plastic bag, but Saxon knew the rain better than that. It often found a way in and there was a good chance he'd be spending a wet, miserable night with little sleep.

The bridge was almost five hundred metres long, eighty-five metres above the valley at its highest point. As he reached the bridge, he removed his rucksack and reached inside for his binoculars. As he set foot on the grating of the bridge, he knew it was unlikely that Kate had met with any sort of accident here. She certainly hadn't fallen, the two main steel cables were at shoulder height and head height, impossible to fall over and although it may have been possible to slip through the gap between the two cables, or indeed launch yourself over the top on a suicide mission, Kate was scared of heights so wouldn't have gone anywhere near the gaps and to the best of his knowledge, she wasn't suicidal.

Could two people have fought on the bridge? Yes. Could a body be pushed between the steel cables? Yes. That's why he needed to check it out.

Saxon spent more than an hour walking back and forth across the bridge, focussing his binoculars on the densely wooded pine forests directly below certain sections of the bridge.

Only when he was satisfied that he'd covered every single tree branch, did he leave and contemplate setting up camp for the night.

Saxon hiked a little further, he encountered more danger points, several routes which involved rope climbing and ladders. Sheer drops. Another long section, a narrow, well-trodden path but the mountain fell away to the right leaving him feeling exposed and vulnerable. An encounter with an aggressor at this point would be fraught with danger, but again, the valley floor was barren, no trees, nowhere for a body to be hidden from view. He spent another couple of hours with the binoculars, hiked across a long flat section and while most of the terrain was grey rock, ice and boulders, he found a grass section relatively frost free and pitched up his tent for the night.

It was getting dark, the mist and clouds descending into the valley below. Thankfully no snow, four or five degrees above freezing, but at least the rain had stopped.

His sleeping bag was dry. He breathed a sigh of relief and crawled into the tent. He set up the stove, boiled up some water and threw a handful of pasta bows into the pan. He let it cook and drained the water, mixed in a tin of tuna and settled down to his evening meal.

He slept well, the half hip flask of Glenfiddich helped.

Saxon was up at first light and packed his kit into his rucksack after a hot coffee with plenty of sugar.

He was now climbing at two thousand four hundred metres with stunning views south to the Matterhorn and in the north, Wandfluehorn and Schonbielhorn. He had checked out another half dozen danger points, but with no signs of anything. It was fair to say that it was the slowest mountain trek he had ever embarked on.

The rain and the snow held off until lunchtime and then a fine sleet began to fall from the low-lying cloud. At times visibility was poor, other times a gap would appear in the clouds and to the west, Col de Valpelline, way in the distance. The mountain stood at three thousand, eight hundred metres and Saxon's plan was to climb the summit and stand at the very spot where Kate had taken her final photographs. If he hadn't found anything, he'd try alternative routes on the off chance Kate had taken a detour to a viewpoint or a place of interest. And if that yielded nothing and the weather was still kind to him, he'd climb back up to Col de Valpelline and start all over again.

However, as his binoculars scanned the valley floor at another point where the recognised path fell away into a five hundred-foot rock face, he noticed a flash of red which stopped his breathing for a second. He steadied the glasses, aware that he was trembling a little, focussed the glasses in on the same spot. There again. His eyes hadn't been playing tricks on him. The white of the snow and probably no more than an inch or two of red material. Easily missed.

Had the incident happened here?

Saxon lowered the binoculars and tucked them into his rucksack pocket. He walked a dozen yards. He was now directly above where he had spotted the red material. He scuffed a line in the dirt path, the central point. If a body had been pushed or had fallen, it would have to be no more than twenty metres in either direction of the line. He lowered his rucksack to the ground and looked up at the sky. He didn't have long; darkness was creeping in and he'd have to make camp for the night. He checked his mobile phone. No reception. 'Shit!'

He switched his phone onto torch mode and crouched down as he meticulously started to creep forward, scanning the dirt path for any clues. He'd gone no more than ten metres when he found it. A rock. About the size of a large fist, a sharp jagged edge with a trace of blood. No doubt about it.

And where the rock lay, more signs, signs of a struggle. The rough ground was a series of short scrapes, grooves and gouges in the hard earth. A struggle, a fight. Kate could handle herself, there was no doubt about that, her attacker wouldn't have had it easy. And then, higher up on a sharp rock that jutted out of the face, a strip of denim, two inches long, a third of an inch wide, blood soaked into one of the corners.

Was this the exact point where Kate had encountered the man who wanted to kill her, the serial killer who got off throwing young girls off mountains?

Saxon built up a small rock stack on the line. A foot high. He'd have to return first thing in the morning. Hopefully it wouldn't snow through the night and he'd find a manageable route down to where he'd seen the red material. There was a body under there. He had no doubt whatsoever.

He walked half a mile and found a suitable spot. His actions were slow and laboured. It took him longer than it usually did to throw his tent up. Again, the rain held off, and he slipped into the tent. Saxon boiled up a little white rice with some cured Swiss sausage and an onion. He had no appetite but convinced himself he had to eat. He needed to maintain his energy levels if he was going to make it down the cliff face. He forced his food down and then checked his ropes. It was only around 9 pm when he climbed into his sleeping bag. He drained the last of the whisky from his hip flask, but this time, sleep would not come to him.

The wind picked up in the early hours of the morning, but his tent held firm. He thought about the good times and the tough times Kate and he had shared together. The girl was a monster. Whatever they threw at her, they couldn't break her.

He'd first met her at the Commando Training Centre Royal Marines (CTCRM) in Lympstone. The tests were gender neutral. Whatever the men had to endure, the females had to do exactly the same and the training course was widely recognised as the toughest in the world. Nearly half of all recruits failed. The endurance course was the worst: two miles of water filled tunnels, pools and streams, filth ridden bogs akin to open cesspits, not to mention the thirty-mile march across Dartmoor.

Each recruit carried their own equipment and rifle. It had to be done in less than eight hours. Saxon completed it in seven and a half. That rifle felt as heavy as a Sherman Tank at the end, he'd crawled over the finishing spot.

Kate completed it five minutes later. They both hugged on the line. Kate burst into tears, the only emotion he had ever seen from her, but they both knew that they were in and nothing was going to stop them.

It was still pitch black at 7 am. The sun had yet to make an appearance, and Saxon shivered in his tent as he brewed up a pot of coffee.

He wondered if it might be a good idea to walk into the valley and raise the alarm. But no, he had to be one hundred percent sure.

Saxon stood by the stack of rocks that he'd laid the previous day. The binoculars once again trained in on the small piece of red material and Saxon breathed a sigh of relief that a covering of snow hadn't obscured it during the night.

It was going to be a tricky descent, of that there was no doubt. Patches of ice and snow wouldn't make it any easier and he only had a fifty-metre rope.

He secured the rope and equipment, then attached the harness and began a slow and controlled descent down the cliff edge.

He was using a retrievable anchor on a doubled rope, with a maillon on both ends. His first descent was only five minutes and, as he settled on a wide outcrop, pulled the rope through the anchor and broke the loop. He pulled on the remaining single rope and the whole rig fell down.

Then he started all over again. He wasn't taking any chances. Abseiling all the way down was the safest way to reach the spot where he'd seen the flash of red material.

He had arrived where he wanted to be in just over thirty minutes and, for some reason, hesitated. He knew there was a body under there, he just didn't want to see it.

The red material was poking through a covering of fresh snow. Once again he cursed the incompetence of the Zermatt Police search. At the height of the search and rescue operation, this area would have been almost clear of snow, the material of the clothing was red. There were no excuses.

He packed away his ropes and equipment, took a deep breath and started talking to himself. 'Don't put it off, do it now.'

He'd seen enough dead and broken bodies in his time. But this was different.

He sank to his knees, edged forward towards what looked like the collar of a jacket, the snow had settled just above it. The unmistakable shape of a head. He removed his glove and started scraping the snow away. A few strands of hair and then the forehead and a nose, broken and bloody. He carefully scraped away the snow and finally revealed the entire face of the corpse. Barely recognisable, just about smashed beyond all recognition and a little decomposition too, though the cold weather had preserved the body quite well.

A dozen emotions coursing through his body now, anger, regret, sadness but above all an overwhelming feeling he had to finish the job.

He stood. For a fleeting moment he wished he had a semblance of faith. A prayer or a poem at least seemed to be the right thing to do.

Instead, he cut down a branch from a nearby tree and made a makeshift flagpole with a spare yellow t-shirt he had in his rucksack.

He pushed it into the snow and loose earth underneath and then checked his mobile phone. Still no signal.

He took a photo of the flag and then his bearings. He set off for the village of Les Haudères.

This time he wasn't hanging around, wasn't looking for anything, and he made it to the village in just a few hours. He picked up a hot sandwich from a local café, a large coffee in a plastic cup, and took a taxi from the rank outside the bus station. It was less than a hundred kilometres to Zermatt, but the journey took nearly two hours. It gave him time to think and plan, and he filled half an exercise book with his notes. His mobile phone reconnected with civilisation just after they left Les Haudères and he booked his airline ticket.

He messaged ahead to Becky.

He'd meet with her and then tell Suzy where he was going.

Nuessle was more of a problem and wondered how he was going to tell him. Once again, he had done the policeman's job for him. But it wasn't going to be easy, Nuessle was going to take this badly.

Becky was waiting at the entrance to the hotel when the taxi pulled up outside. He told the taxi driver to wait. He'd pack a few things and then the man would drive him to Geneva Airport. They'd already agreed the fare, the taxi driver was more than happy.

Becky took the news badly. Her little sister. Why?

He had spared her a few of the details, but it hadn't made it any easier. Saxon was glad to get away up to his room to pack. He explained to Suzy that he didn't know when he'd be back. He'd take the flight and then it was in the lap of the gods. It might take a day; it could take a month.

She understood.

It was time to leave the hotel. They both agreed and he told her that Becky was going to help her find an apartment in Zermatt for the time being. Saxon didn't want her going anywhere near Grimentz. Not yet anyway.

'But where are you going?' she asked.

'Burlington International Airport in the States. My flight leaves from Geneva in seven hours.'

He emailed Nuessle at the police station, from his phone in the taxi. The message was brief and to the point. He gave the coordinates and a photograph of the yellow flag, and then,

Body found here, suggest a search and recovery team.

Make appointment with coroner. Sorry for your loss.

Len Saxon

Nuessle organised a team the next morning. He headed up the operation himself. He was one of the first on the scene. They recovered the body by midday. Nuessle signed himself off sick when he arrived back at the station. Compassionate leave.

Chapter 44

Burlington International Airport was a joint-use, civil-military airport ninety minutes south of Montreal in Canada and a hundred and fifty minutes north of Boston, Massachusetts.

Saxon was surprised to see a couple of military planes as he landed and would later find out on the taxi run to his hotel that the First Burlington Air National Guard and the 158th Fighter Wing were based there.

It was a forty-minute run to Montpelier and his accommodation at Artful.

He had booked it online, not a hotel, but a number of self-catering lodges with small kitchens equipped with an oven, microwave, toaster, fridge and coffee machine, as well as a private bathroom. He could be in Montpelier a month or more, and the thought of being cooped up in another small hotel room did not appeal.

The reviewers for Artful had written about spacious and tranquil accommodation, with spectacular mountain views from the backyard. It was thirty-five kilometres from Camel's Hump Trailhead and located in Montpelier.

They had offered him the flexibility he had been looking for. The admin email had asked how many nights he wanted. Saxon had replied, 'Haven't a clue.'

He was wrecked by the time the taxi rolled up. He'd spent most of the eight-hour flight writing up notes and researching online, using the planes onboard WIFI in a desperate attempt not to fall asleep. He also sent another report to Blacklock and an update to the Flying Pig.

The six-hour time difference meant that he arrived around midnight Montpelier time and the place was closed up and in darkness. It was biting cold, several degrees below freezing, with a white frosty rind on the grass.

As arranged, he found the key to his lodge under a stone beside a dog kennel at the side of the main building. He made himself a quick cup of tea and crashed onto the large double bed. He was asleep in seconds.

It was 11 am, Montpelier time, when he made it out of the lodge and decided to introduce himself and find some breakfast.

The receptionist and owner, Bethany, her name tag read, welcomed him cheerfully, and he handed over his passport and credit card. 'We don't do breakfast,' she said. 'All the lodges have their own facilities but there's a couple of nice spots in town.'

‘Where’s the nearest one?’ Saxon asked.

‘Kismet is nice,’ she said. ‘They do wonderful scrambled eggs and as much coffee as you can drink. Just follow the road down to the river, it’s about ten minutes’ walk.’

‘Great, I will.’

Bethany photocopied his passport and handed it back to him. ‘You don’t know how long you’re staying then?’

‘Not really.’

‘That’s different.’ She grinned. ‘What are you doing here then, you a professional hitman or something?’

He laughed. ‘You have a vivid imagination.’

‘I read a lot of books,’ she retorted.

Saxon decided now was as good a place as any to start his enquiries. He reached for his phone and opened the gallery. It was the first photograph in the line. He clicked on it and it opened on full screen. ‘I’m looking for someone,’ he said, turned the phone around to show Bethany the photo. ‘Don’t suppose you’ve seen her around?’

Her reply took Saxon by surprise.

‘Yeah, she’s kind of familiar.’

‘You’re joking?’

‘No. I noticed her in town a couple of months back. Bit of a loner, kept herself to herself, always walked around with a small rucksack. It’s a small town we live in. If a stranger breezes into town, they tend to get noticed.’

That's what Saxon had thought, Montpelier, the least populous state capital in the United States, a population of under eight thousand according to Wikipedia. An unusual place to settle if you wanted to blend into the background, but then again just the sort of town where Kate could live out her dream. At least for a year or so. It was too close to the Appalachian Trail to be a coincidence, the mysterious book sent from a bookstore in town about a man who wanted to disappear but was very much still alive. The dots were joining up. Now he just needed to find her.

Bethany poured him a black coffee from the cafetière in reception and they sat and chatted for a while. Saxon showed her the photograph of the two of them in service in the Marines together, convinced her that he didn't mean Kate any harm. He ran her through the story that the Swiss Police had thought she'd met with an accident but how he didn't buy it and that she'd always wanted to hike the Appalachian Trail

'She's a hiker. She was always nomadic. Every new day was a new horizon.'

Bethany topped up his coffee. 'But you realise the traditional route of the AT starts in Georgia, don't you?'

'Yes, I'd read that, and it's clearly not the time of year to hike the high ground anyway, especially this far north. I'm guessing Kate is just lying low and planning a trip in the spring when the weather breaks.'

'That makes perfect sense.'

Saxon drained his coffee cup and stood. 'I need breakfast badly. Have you eaten?'

'Yes, as it happens, but perhaps another time.'

Saxon found Kismet easily, and Bethany had been right. A truly American size portion of scrambled eggs, six strips of bacon and four slices of toast. More coffee, the waitress told him that fill ups were free. He thanked her and looked out over the Winooski River. There were worse places for an office. He lifted his notebook from the pocket of his rucksack and started to make notes.

If Kate was holing up in or around Montpelier, she'd need cheap accommodation. He took out his Kindle and logged onto the Kismet WIFI.

An economy lodge right here in town. 'Unfussy', it read, 'with free breakfast.' A possibility, but when he clicked on the photograph, it somehow didn't suit Kate at all. Another two-star motel, The Inn. If Kate was here, then she'd have been here nearly three months. Somehow, he couldn't see her staying in either of those places. Doyles Guest House and a little farther out of town, other possibilities in Worcester, Woodbury and Calais. There was any amount of accommodation within a fifty-mile radius. The Artful lodges where he was staying would have been a perfect choice, but he knew Kate's budget and it was a little expensive. A three-month charge would have wiped out her savings for sure. James had said as much and although they had their separate accounts, Kate's Marine pension was a pittance, and there was no realistic possibility of saving any money.

Kate loved camping, but that was never a possibility either because of the weather and the duration of her stay. Wild camping was all well and good too, and as cheap as it comes, but washing in a lake and crapping in the woods wasn't something anyone would like to do on a permanent basis.

Something in-between, he scribbled on the page. The curser hovered over Country Camper. What was it? He clicked. The Country Camper store sold new and used RVs, motor homes and caravans. He scrolled down. Nothing about rentals, but if there were any rentals available, surely they would know at the store. He thought about calling them. No, he'd take a trip up there, speak to them in person, probably first thing tomorrow.

He decided on some fresh air. He hadn't stretched his legs in over forty-eight hours. The walk would do him good, give him time to think a few things through.

It was nearly a five-mile walk to Country Camper. He walked up through the town and took a detour. No hurry. It would be good to get his bearings.

He walked along Towne Hill Road and found a small track that headed back towards the Winooski River. He crossed a bridge at the end of Codling

Road, turned right, and the store loomed up in front of him.

It was quiet. The end of November. Saxon glanced over towards a glass fronted office. A salesman sat with his face in a desktop computer. He looked up and then back to the screen. Junior, not much experience and by the book he guessed. Saxon would have to tread carefully; this youngster would tell him very little.

Saxon strolled between a couple of RVs. The salesman appeared after a couple of minutes.

'Good morning, sir. May I help you?'

'Possibly. I love these things, my idea of a fun time.'

'A British accent if I'm not mistaken?' the salesman said with a big grin.

'Yes, I flew in a few days ago.'

'And what brings you here at this time of year?'

Saxon had to think quick. 'Well, I'm planning a trip on the Trail in spring, something I've been dreaming of for a long time. There would be around six of us, my old military buddies and me, and we were considering one of these things as a kind of support vehicle. We'd take it in turns to drive, meet up with the rest of the gang each night and it would cut out the hassle of trying to find accommodation.'

'I see.'

'We like camping, but we're getting on a bit. We've had our fill of sleeping on grass and I suppose this is the next best thing. You are at one with nature, but with a mattress and a roof that doesn't leak. We'd be looking to rent one for around three months.'

'Well, sir, we don't advertise rentals. To be honest, it's more trouble than it's worth sometimes. The clients bring them back in a terrible state and we've stepped out of the short-term rental market completely. We also used to have a problem with theft, but that's been sorted now. But if you are looking at a three-month rental, I'm sure the owner would be able to accommodate you.'

Now we are getting somewhere, Saxon thought to himself.

He prised a few prices out of the salesman, established that spring and summer were very pricey, but anyone wanting a rental in winter would get a real bargain because nobody wanted to sleep in a tin box in the snow.

'Do you get many winter rentals round these parts?'

'Not really, sir. While I love these vehicles, I'm sure we'd all agree we'd rather be in a nice hotel or a guest house when the snow starts to fall.'

The hook, line and sinker had been set. Now for the bite. Saxon pointed outside to the snow flurries that had just been brought in on the easterly wind. 'Exactly. Who would want to sleep out in this type of weather?'

'Well, sir, only you Brits, it would seem.'

He followed his sentence up with a long guffaw. 'We had one such lunatic who rented one only last month. A chic. Damn sexy piece of ass if you don't mind me saying.'

Saxon pulled out his phone. Clicked on the gallery. 'Would this be her?'

Saxon didn't look at the phone. He looked directly into the salesman's eyes.

'I'm not at liberty to say, sir, I'm sorry. Client confidentiality and all that.'

Saxon patted him on the shoulder. 'Don't worry, you've told me what I want to know.'

'Look, sir, I'll get into trouble if the boss thinks I've been talking about our clients, and I … '

'Don't worry,' Saxon interrupted. 'My lips are sealed. She's one of our advance party, she's sussing the Trail out for us.'

'… I see.'

A little happier now. The strange Brit was a friend.

'Well yes, sir, that was her.'

Saxon was on a roll; he couldn't have hoped to have achieved more in a few short hours in his wildest dreams. Not one, but two people had clarified that Kate had been in town.

Another question to the salesman. 'My friend is called Kate.' The salesman's eyes gave the game away again. 'Now… if she was wanting to park the camper somewhere around here and hook up to an electric point, say… where would she likely be?'

The salesman threw a huge spanner in the works when he answered the question. 'In Vermont, sir, literally hundreds of places, this state is a camping paradise. And if your friend has travelled into New Hampshire or Maine, then you're talking thousands of pitches. And as you probably know, she took the RV on an open-ended deal, so I guess she is heading somewhere and not hanging around town.'

Shit!

Saxon set off back to his lodge via a different route along the Winooski River. The river was iced up in some places. He wondered if it was ever cold enough to freeze up completely. The town was well kept and clean. It had a nice feel about it with beautiful views of the pine forests and the mountains and the air was crisp and fresh. He could see why Kate would choose somewhere like this but also felt that because of the climate she had possibly headed south to warmer climes. There was nothing to stop her now she had her own transport.

He called into the Hunger Mountain Supermarket and stocked up on a few days of groceries, and against his better judgement, a twelve pack of beer.

As he walked up the long grass verge to the entrance of the lodge, his mobile rang. The display read Becky.

'Hi Becky, how are you?'

'Oh my God, Sax, you were right, they've just announced who the dead man was. It was Heinz Frei all right, the whole of Zermatt is talking about it.'

Saxon had known immediately. Despite the injuries, he still recognised him from the photos he had seen and, of course, there was that red snood that he seemed to wear all the time, his trademark.

'They held another press conference,' Becky continued, 'but Nuessle wasn't there. He's had some sort of mini breakdown, took a few weeks off work.'

'I'm not surprised,' Saxon said.

'But he's a police officer, Lenny, he should be able to cope with a dead body.'

'Not when it's your own flesh and blood, Becky.'

'What? I don't understand.'

'Heinz was his son, Becky.'

Silence.

'I had noticed a familiarity in their features some time ago and I did a little digging. I found photographs of Heinz's mother and Oscar Nuessle from way back, as teenagers, more photos of them in their 20s. I found a photo of Nuessle at about eleven years old and a photo of Heinz at the same age. They were like two peas in a pod. No doubt about it.'

'But for some reason Rosalie married the millionaire hotel magnet, Mr Frei.'

'Yes, and I'm guessing that at some point early in the marriage she rekindled the sexual side of her relationship with Nuessle, and bingo! Five years into the marriage, along came baby Heinz.'

He heard Becky let out a loud, long whistle.

'I guessed they were still close, and I tested the water at the Frei's hotel, the Grand. I made a bit of a nuisance of myself and wondered how Rosalie would react.'

'And?'

'Nuessle came running to her within a quarter of an hour, threatened to have me arrested and thrown out of the country. I confronted him about his relationship with Mrs Frei and he didn't deny it. I could see it in his eyes. That's when I decided to make myself scarce for a few days and the weather was good so I decided to hike up to Col de Valpelline because now I was fairly certain that Kate met with Heinz soon after she took her final photo on the Col.'

'But what were you searching for?'

'I wasn't completely sure, not necessarily a body, but some sign of a fight or a struggle. Kate could handle herself. When we were in the Marines, she was one of the best in the unit when it came to unarmed combat. Even in the boxing ring she could get the better of some of the lads. Heinz was a slip of a bloke, I found a weird shaped rock with blood on it, I suspect he hit her with it from behind. But he didn't hit her hard enough. I've seen Kate absolutely battered in the ring but she never hit the canvas once. She would have put up a hell of a fight and I dared to dream that it would have been Kate who came out on top. Before I even got to the body, I knew there was a good chance that it would be Heinz Frei.'

'Jesus Christ, Lenny, so if they had a fight up there and Kate came out on top, there's a chance she's still alive.' Before Saxon had a chance to reply, Becky was asking more questions. 'But if she's still alive, then where is she? Was she injured too? Is it possible that her body could be buried down there too? I don't understand, why hasn't she—'

'She's still alive, Becky.'

'What?'

'I found two reliable sources who have both seen her.'

It was a shock to Becky. The initial silence gave way to sobbing and then a gut-wrenching wail of appreciation. It was a full minute before she could utter her first words. 'You sure, Sax.'

'One hundred percent.'

'Oh my God!'

He'd have preferred a face to face, a long hug afterwards and an even longer explanation.

'So where is she?' Becky asked.

'That's the million-dollar question,' he replied.

Chapter 45

Where to start?

Saxon had spent most of the next day researching the various camping spots in Vermont, Main and New Hampshire and while the salesman had exaggerated when he had said thousands, Saxon had still managed to find over eight hundred.

It was a non-starter trying to find her if she'd taken to the road, and he didn't even want to think about the possibility that she'd headed even further south.

The Nomad. She was well named.

He walked into town again, this time choosing a small café on Ridge Street. Café Ana gave him a view of the book shop less than fifty yards down the street. He didn't feel much like breakfast. Just coffee. Plenty of it.

He took out the phone and scrolled to the Flying Pig's number.

It rang out just twice.

'Hey, Sax, how are you?'

'Great mate, I'm in the States.'

‘Yes, I’ve just read your update. You reckon Kate is out there somewhere in Vermont?’

‘For sure, but I’ve got a little problem and you might be able to help.’

‘Shoot.’

‘Well, I found out that she rented a small motor home from a place in town, but I don’t know where she went. I’m guessing at this time of year she wouldn’t be hiking the Trail, but she may have headed a bit further south, perhaps scaled a few summits.’

‘Gotcha.’

‘Yeah, but the problem is that there’re an awful lot of mountains on the Trail, well over fifty, so chasing after her blind is a no go. Now, I know she has to get back to town at some point, because she has to bring the RV back, but that could be another month or more.’

Saxon explained about the salesman, that he said there was no specific date to return the vehicle and that while he had managed to prise a little information out of him, he genuinely didn’t know where she would be and he certainly wasn’t going to give any details about the RV. As Saxon was about to speak, a waitress walked over to his table. She carried a large pot of coffee. ‘Top up, sir?’ she asked.

Saxon nodded.

She walked back behind the counter.

‘But there was something he said during our conversation.’ Saxon said.

'Go on.'

'He said that they'd had a problem with RVs being stolen in the past, but they'd fixed that problem now.'

'Okay, so if I'm thinking what you're thinking, you're guessing that they might have been fitted with trackers?'

'Great minds and all that.'

'And you want me to hack the system in this RV spot and see if we can find her?'

'Flying Pig. You're a fucking genius.'

'I know. Send me the details and give me a couple of days.'

The waitress was a short but not unattractive girl who had lived in Montpelier all her life. Not so much a loner, but she chose her friends carefully and, after a particularly nasty sexual assault in her early teens, was naturally suspicious of all men. She liked the look of the stranger who had called in for coffee, a tough but beneath the manly features, a kind look.

But there was something very serious about the phone call he was engaging in. When she'd walked over to top his cup up with fresh coffee, he'd stopped the conversation dead and waited until she was out of earshot before resuming.

She looked around the café, another half dozen tables occupied but all taken care of with full plates and cups. Although she was on her own, she had a few minutes to spare.

She lifted her mobile phone from the small leather satchel that hung from her hip and punched in the number. Waited.

No niceties or small talk. 'He's here, your man has arrived in town.'

'You sure?'

'I've taken a photo; I'll send it now.'

The waitress placed the call on hold and sent the photograph through on WhatsApp. She reconnected. 'You should have it any second.'

She heard the ping instantly. 'Got it?'

A few seconds' pause. 'Yeah.'

'And?'

'That's him. You've done me proud.'

'No worries, glad to have helped.'

'I'll see you tomorrow, Eva, I owe you.'

Chapter 46

The Flying Pig had hacked into the computer when all of Montpelier was asleep. He had infiltrated their email account with a new remote spy management software system and then rebooted their three desktop PCs. He'd remove it once he had the information he required and when the RV store switched on their system the next morning, they'd never know he'd been there, the system as clean as a whistle.

It was quite a sophisticated system, but after ninety minutes running the software, he was in. He had opened up his own computer and the screen and every icon that would normally be on display to anyone who booted up the computer system in the Country Camper store in Montpelier, was on display on a screen in front of him in his box room office in his small but tidy apartment in York.

He located a file with the registrations of all new and used sales stocks and the dozen RVs reserved for long-term rental. He found Kate's details. She had registered under her own name, paid a month's rental up front and signed an agreement that Country

Camper would debit her £$200 for each additional week she held onto the vehicle. There was no return date listed.

Saxon had been right; Country Camper had installed trackers in all of their hire vehicles in the spring of 2019.

He found the word document file in a folder called security and cursed the owner of the store for his lackadaisical approach to such an important issue. The registration of the vehicle, the tracker ID.

It was 03.39 when he removed the software from the Country Camper computer system. It was 08.39 in the UK.

The Flying Pig wandered through to the kitchen. He'd cook a little breakfast and then nip into town for some groceries. He'd call Saxon later that day.

Chapter 47

A few hours later, the Flying Pig called. He had managed to get in and locate the security folder from the RV company. He'd said that their firewalls were poor, almost non-existent, and he'd confirmed that all of the rental RVs had been fitted with trackers. Saxon had dared to get a little excited. Kate was tantalisingly close.

But then the Pig had delivered the bad news. Despite the company having one of the poorest computer security systems he'd ever breached, the satellite tracking system that they'd attached to the RVs was one of the most sophisticated on the market and after more than twenty-four hours of research, telephone calls to experts and online forums and chat rooms, he hadn't been able to breach the system.

Saxon had taken the phone call in Café Ana, which was effectively his new office. The food was good, the coffee strong and the WIFI connection solid.

The waitress, Eva, was part owner. They'd talked at length on several occasions. At times, Saxon felt she was too attentive.

When he'd taken the phone call from the Flying Pig, it was almost as if she'd had a second sense, as if she had known the person on the other end of the phone had delivered a hammer blow.

'More coffee,' she'd said, 'or would you like something stronger?'

Saxon looked at his watch. It was past six. Why not? 'Give me a beer please, Eva.'

'For sure, Lenny, you're gonna need one.'

She walked away towards the counter.

What had she meant by that?

When she returned with the beer, he felt compelled to ask her. 'What do you mean… I'm going to need one? Are you a mind reader or something?'

She didn't answer at first. She sat down at the table and poured the beer from the bottle into his glass. He lifted it up and took a drink, replaced it on the table.

'Empty the glass,' she said.

Without knowing why, he drained the last dregs from the glass. The beer was strong, he felt light headed. She stood. 'I'll get you another.'

She returned with two bottles.

'Are you joining me?'

Eva shook her head. 'No. But she is.' She pointed towards the door.

Saxon's world stood still.

She walked over. 'Hi Sax,' she said. 'I knew you'd find me.'

Chapter 48

It wasn't the biggest shock of Saxon's life; he knew he'd been close to finding her, but the fact she'd found him had taken him completely by surprise. Talk about the highs and lows of life. He'd been on a rollercoaster in the space of five minutes.

That initial euphoria when the Pig had said he'd breached the computer system and then the big let down when he had said the tracking system had been impregnable.

It was a so near yet so far moment and the next few months flashed before his eyes. He liked Montpelier, in fact he liked it a lot, but the thought of hanging around for another month or two on the off chance that Kate would deliver the RV back to its original pick up point was something he hadn't wanted to contemplate. Country Camper had other stores in America and in Canada too. What was to stop Kate dropping the RV off at their outlets in Baltimore, Maryland or Greensboro?

And as he'd wondered about picking up the phone and looking for flights back to Geneva, he'd looked at

Eva and wondered why she was acting so strange; the door had opened and Kate stood there in the doorway.

She walked over and sat down. ‘I guess I have a lot of explaining to do,’ she said.

Saxon reached across the table for her hand. He squeezed hard, lifted his backside from the seat, and leaned over to kiss her on the lips. ‘I’ve never been so pleased to see anyone in my life.’

‘But you are pretty pissed off with me, eh?’

Saxon shrugged his shoulders. ‘Yep, if you were a bloke you might have just got a slap or two.’

She smiled. ‘I’m so sorry, Sax, I owe you so much and I’ve led you on a wild goose chase for months, but I will explain.’

‘You don’t owe me anything and I think I know most of the story anyway.’

‘You do?’

‘Yes. I can guess why you ran.’

‘Go on then, tell me.’

He took a deep breath. ‘You were attacked on your way back from the summit of Col de Valpelline. Your attacker clouted you with a rock, but you didn’t go down. You fought back, you gave him as good as he got and you were tougher than him because you are a little hard bastard. I’m guessing that at one point your Seoi-nage Judo move came in useful as you threw him off the mountain.’

Kate’s jaw had slowly fallen open as Saxon continued.

‘I found his body Kate, he was a man called Heinz Frei.’

Kate was nodding slowly. ‘I read it online. The bastard had been following me for most of the morning, always a few hundred metres back, but when I stopped to let him catch up, he stopped too. I knew that I was in trouble, but I swear I didn’t mean to kill him. You were right. I threw him over my shoulder, a simple Hane Goshi, but we were fighting on the edge of a cliff. He’d picked the spot deliberately. There was hardly room for two people to pass.’

‘His bad judgement, Kate.’

Tears welled in her eyes. ‘And he went over and I watched him bounce down the mountain. It was awful, Sax. I didn’t mean to kill him, I didn’t.’

She burst into tears. Saxon stood up, walked around the table, and sat beside her. She fell into his arms.

Eva sat down, too. Saxon wondered how much she knew.

‘Bad news?’ Eva asked.

‘Not really,’ Saxon said. ‘Tears of relief, I’d say.’

Eva poured the remains of the beer into a glass. ‘I picked up on a troubled soul as soon as she walked in here.’

Kate wiped at her eyes with a tissue. ‘Troubled soul doesn’t cover the half of it.’

'Eva, I'm sure Kate could do with some food, me too. Do you think you could rustle up a plate of sandwiches, a couple more beers?'

'Sure. Coming right up.'

Saxon watched as she walked away, out of earshot. He looked back at Kate. 'Okay, tell me how much she knows… quickly.'

'I knew it,' Kate responded. 'I'm in trouble, aren't I? They know I killed him. They're looking for me.'

'Tell me now,' Saxon said abruptly. 'Does she know? Does Eva know anything?'

'No, of course not, just you and the Swiss police.'

Saxon shook his head. 'They don't know. They believe Frei had an accident. There's just me and you know what happened and that's the way it's going to stay for the time being.'

'Okay.'

How badly were you hurt, Kate? I guess you didn't need to go to hospital.'

'No. He hit me here.' She pointed just above her right ear. 'It hurt like hell and I felt a pop, like the sound you hear when you crack an eggshell, but there weren't the pints of blood I thought you'd get from a head wound. Anyway, my hair absorbed most of it and it dried up after a little while. I managed to dive into a small outside toilet in Zermatt and clean myself up. I guess it probably should have had a few stitches, but honestly, it's no big deal and it's left me with a little dent in my head, no more than that.'

He looked on behind the counter as a plate of sandwiches grew bigger by the second. American portions. Eva opened some bottles of beer and placed them on a tray.

'Look, we haven't got long,' he said. 'Eva will be here any second. I want you to calm down because nothing is going to happen to you. But once we've had something to eat and a few drinks, we're going somewhere quiet and then you're going to call your sister.'

Chapter 49

Kate's phone call to Becky was as emotional as it gets. Saxon had put the phone on loudspeaker. He'd been the first to talk, and he found himself welling up at those first few words.

Becky answered on the third ring. 'Hi, Sax… I was heading to bed.'

A slight pause. 'She's here, Becky.'

'What?'

'She's with me now, Becky, she's safe.'

'Kate? Kate is with you?'

'Right next to me.'

The two sisters burst into tears at the same time. There were no meaningful words for a while. Saxon did most of the talking. Becky questioned the hows and the whys, where she'd been for the last few months. Kate kept apologising, but didn't give any real answers.

Saxon suggested the obvious solution. 'Get the next available flight into Burlington Airport. We'll meet you there and you can stay as long as you want.'

Before they even finished the call, Becky announced that she was checking the flights online.

There were more tears. Becky told Kate she loved her at least half a dozen times and even told Saxon that she loved him too. During the phone call, Becky announced that there was a flight out of Geneva at lunchtime the next day. It flew directly to Burlington.

'Get some sleep and we'll see you soon,' Kate said.

'Not much chance of that,' she replied.

Five minutes later, she'd said goodbye. She had to pack a case or two. She'd bought a one-way ticket. There was no hurry to get back to Switzerland.

Chapter 50

Kate hadn't wanted to travel to Burlington International Airport, convinced that she would show up on the airport security cameras and that she'd be arrested by gun wielding cops as soon as she set foot in the vicinity.

Saxon had tried to reassure her that she was under no suspicion at all, that nobody knew that she had ever met Frei. Furthermore, the coroner had delivered his verdict of accidental death and Frei would be buried in a private ceremony in Zermatt within the next week or so.

Yes, she was a missing person who had gone AWOL voluntarily, but it was hardly an offence that was going to send her to the electric chair. If she was unlucky, she could be charged with wasting police time, but unless she volunteered the information that she'd fought with Frei, no more than that.

He was convinced there was something Kate wasn't telling him. Why be so paranoid? During the journey to the airport, he made a few mental notes.

Becky was disappointed that her younger sister wasn't there to meet her, delaying a long overdue meeting. Still, she was excited, like a little kid on Christmas Eve, when Saxon told her that the journey was less than an hour. As they climbed into the hire car Saxon had rented, he explained that she had changed from the confident, outgoing person he once knew and she needed time to adjust.

'She'll tell you all about it when we get back, I hope,' Saxon said. 'I think she'll open up more when she sees you. But heaven knows where her head has been these last few months. She had been convinced that she was a murderer on the run, that the authorities had found Frei's body and somehow some evidence to connect her with a crime.'

'But she's right, Sax. You said that there was a fight up there and there's a dead body, so the police will want some answers.'

'The police don't know, only me you and Kate know, and that's the way it's going to stay for now. As far as I'm concerned, Frei attacked her and got what he deserved.'

They pulled in front of the Artful Lodges. Kate was outside, wrapped up in a big red ski jacket and white bobble hat. Becky almost took the car door off the hinges in her eagerness to get to her. Saxon sat still. They needed a few minutes on their own.

They hugged and kissed and hugged some more. The tears flowed. After a few minutes, Saxon climbed out and opened the boot. He lifted Becky's bags out and carried them towards the main entrance.

The two sisters hadn't made it inside. They stood on the sun terrace. Pleasant in the summer, Saxon thought. Far too cold this time of year.

'There's a little lounge area in the conservatory at the back,' Saxon said. 'I'll ask if they'll bring us some coffee.'

'That would be great,' Becky said.

Kate led her sister towards the conservatory and Saxon took the bags into Lodge Eight, where the sisters were sharing a large studio.

He found Bethany chopping wood out at the back of the lodges in a small outbuilding and she agreed to his request.

Ten minutes later, Bethany reappeared with a tray of coffee and a plate full of chocolate biscuits.

The conversation ambled along slowly. Questions were tricky and although both Saxon and Kate were no strangers to death and violence, he sensed that Becky was having a tough time accepting that her sister had killed a man.

Kate talked about coming clean, about handing herself in and explaining what happened.

'But you ran away, Kate,' Becky said. 'It wouldn't look good.'

Kate nodded and then shook her head. She looked pale and worried. Saxon reminded her that an autopsy had already been concluded and the inquest recorded accidental death.

‘Why did you run, Kate?’ Becky asked out of the blue. ‘You’ve no idea what you put me through. What if Sax hadn’t found you? Was that it? Would you have let me think you had died on that mountain?’

No words.

Kate shook her head. She tried to speak, but Becky beat her to it.

‘I mean, I hardly deserved that. You did nothing wrong. Surely the police would have realised that in their investigations, he hit you with a rock for fuck’s sake.’

The initial euphoria and relief had given way to anger. Becky had endured weeks of torment and grief.

‘The book Becky, I sent you the book. I thought you would have realised.

‘The book? The book was goddamned awful and I couldn’t concentrate at all. I dare say if Sax hadn’t put two and two together, we might not be here and I’d still be crying into my cocoa every night.’ Becky lifted the coffee cup to her lips. ‘I think I need an explanation at the very least. Tell me what you were going to do for the rest of your life.’

‘James,’ Saxon said. ‘It was James, Wasn’t it? You wanted to leave him; you’ve wanted to leave him for some time haven’t you? You panicked. Disappearing seemed like the perfect solution.’

Tears welled up in her eyes. A nod of the head, barely visible, and then words.

‘James wouldn’t have taken it well if I’d told him it was over. He was very jealous and controlling. Not at first. In the beginning he was nice enough, the perfect companion and as the months ticked by, I began to realise that he was just that… a companion. I never loved him. I never told him that I loved him, yet he told me over and over again. There was a time when I wondered if it could work. He treated me well. He seemed to like the mountains as much as me, but I began to realise that my best days in the hills were the days I spent without him. And I had no intention of leaving the hills. I wanted to hike higher and longer. James wanted to go back to civvy street, and I suggested one evening that we should go our separate ways.'

'He didn't take it well?' Saxon asked.

'No. He made all sorts of threats. Not violent ones, because I can look after myself and he knew that. If it ever got violent, he knew, and I knew that I would have eaten him for breakfast. He couldn't fight sleep. He wasn't a violent man.'

'Then what did he threaten you with?'

'It was psychological mind games. He played on my guilt, said that he couldn't live without me, that life wouldn't be worth living.'

'He threatened suicide?'

'He did, and there was a half-hearted attempt to kill himself. He drank a half bottle of whisky and said he'd swallowed a bottle of pills, but he did it when he knew I was heading back from a hike. I found him slumped over the table. I thought he was drunk but when he told me what he'd done, I called an ambulance and he was blue lighted to hospital.'

'How long ago was that?'

'About six months. He begged me not to leave him, and I agreed. It was the stupidest thing I could have done because he changed from that day. Suddenly, the mountains were no longer his thing. He wanted to go back to normal land, talked about settling down and buying a house.'

That was the last straw for me. I told him it was over. I said that he could threaten whatever he wanted, but I wasn't going back to the UK, not for all the money in the world.'

Saxon didn't interrupt. He knew there was more to come.

'He was clever when it came to computers and unknown to me, he had hacked into my emails, my personal files. He told me that he would never accept me walking out on him. If that happened, he would send the file to every contact in my email box.'

'The file?'

Kate was shaking her head. She looked at her sister, who nodded, 'Tell us Kate, we are here to help you. We need to know.'

Her head in her hands now. 'My God I was so stupid.'

'A sex tape?' Saxon said.

'Yes, a fucking pornographic sex tape. I was just twenty-four, home on leave, and you know what that was like, Sax. We let our hair down, we drank away the horrors of what we had been through. It was the easiest way to forget.'

'You were drunk?'

'Yes, but that was no excuse. I knew what I was doing.'

Becky spoke. 'Look, we get the picture and I don't want you to go into graphic detail, but how bad was it?'

The first smile, then a brief laugh. 'Hah! Not that bad, not that bad at all compared to what's out there on the porno sites nowadays. I agreed to a threesome, another girl, and my boyfriend at the time. What I didn't know was that he had his mate hiding in a wardrobe filming it all.'

'The bastard,' Becky exclaimed.

'We separated soon afterwards and not long after we split up, he sent me the file. I was devastated, as you can imagine.'

'And he blackmailed you?'

'Not exactly. He said he wanted sex, said if I didn't agree to one last sexual liaison, he would send it to all of his mates. There was one little problem though: I was in Germany at the time and he was in London. I laughed it off, I said, "Sure, get yourself on a flight and I'll bang you as much as you want." It was all a bit of a joke and he sent the video to me a few more times, generally when he was pissed up. In the end, he never bothered contacting me. I deleted all the files and confined them to the computer recycle bin. I don't know how James ever found them, but he did.'

'I don't think it's too difficult,' Becky said. 'Even deleted items are still on the hard drive.'

'I guess so, and the bastard has them and he also has my emails, all three hundred and fifty-seven of them, my friends in the Marines, you two, friends from school, aunties, uncles, cousins. My God, if that ever got sent, I'm sure I will disappear for real. I'd never show my face to anyone again.

Chapter 51

As the day progressed, Kate confessed that she was feeling a whole lot better. She had actually been relieved that she'd got the sex tape scandal off her chest.

It was a complicated business. Saxon needed to think it all through.

After a few hours, he left the two sisters and returned to Eva's café with his tablet and ordered a beer.

Kate's Jim Grant type disappearance was really quite ingenious and he couldn't argue with the fact that as far as James was concerned, he was history and there was little point in sending the sex tapes to anyone now that Kate was presumed dead.

It was time to make the call to the RSM.

Four in on the secret. He'd also need to contact the Flying Pig too. He'd been great as usual. He deserved to know. Five. No more.

In the end, he settled for an email to the RSM. It was brief and to the point.

I have her. She's safe and well, but I can't say where. I'll tell you the details in due course. She isn't in a good place mentally, and I'll stay with her for the next few weeks. Her sister is here too. We'll take good care of her and perhaps we can meet up at the end of my cycle trip.

So many details to fill you in on, but the time isn't right, so please accept my apologies.

The RSM fired a mail straight back.

Result, I knew you could do it. Pass on my regards and take good care of her. No apologies needed.

He ordered a second beer. As Eva delivered it to the table, his mobile rang. The Flying Pig. Strange.

'Hi Sax, have you seen the news from Zermatt?'

'No, why? What's happened?'

It's Frei's mother. She'd put a couple of private detectives on the case and they've found something.'

'What?'

'Yes, some blood and fibres, right at the point where Frei went over the cliff. They have said it looks like a fight has taken place and Frei's mother is paying for another autopsy, some forensic professor from Annecy in France, the best in the business apparently, a bloke called Josep Falcoz.

It wasn't right to break the bad news just yet. Kate and her sister had been through enough. They booked dinner at a restaurant in town, sat at a corner near the back, and proceeded to get a little drunk. It was just what the two sisters needed.

But Saxon was worried. The phone call from the Flying Pig had changed everything, because if the expert from Annecy found just a trace of Kate's DNA on Frei's body, it would set the cat among the pigeons for sure.

He made the decision to keep it to himself for the time being. He'd tell her soon enough if the Annecy man came up trumps on the DNA.

Chapter 52

Frei's body had been in the morgue cold store for two weeks and was remarkably well preserved. It had lain in almost freezing temperatures ever since he'd been thrown to his death. There was a lot of dried blood and Professor Josep Falcoz had taken twenty-one swabs which had been bagged and sent to the lab. The injuries were so bad, it could never be ascertained that an altercation had taken place prior to the fall. Frei's skull had been fractured in four places, another forty-seven broken bones, including three vertebrae, all consistent with a fall from a great height. Falcoz examined the body with a powerful magnifying glass for more than four hours.

With a pair of tweezers, he was able to dig out a miniscule fragment of hard matter from a deep bruise on Frei's neck. A fingernail, he thought to himself, a fragment of fingernail for sure.

His final two bags of the day were the sample of blood and fibres recovered from the point where the private detectives said that Frei tumbled to his death.

It was now just a matter of time. The lab results would be back in twenty-four hours. Mrs Frei had paid the technicians to prioritise the case.

Saxon watched the press conference on a live link beamed back from Zermatt. He half expected that Nuessle would be holding it, but he was nowhere to be seen. Still on sick leave. There were two policemen that he hadn't seen before, sitting at a long table with an array of cameras pointing at them, and Mrs Frei sat in between, sipping from a glass of water. At the end was a dour-looking man, grey hair thinning on top. His cardboard place name read *Professor Falcoz.*

Saxon felt a sickening feeling building up in his stomach.

The more senior looking detective on the right didn't hang around and got straight to the point. He introduced himself and his colleague, the professor and Mrs Frei and said the Zermatt Police had made a request that the case into the death of Heinz Frei should be reopened given the discovery of significant DNA on Herr Frei's body, which did not match that of the deceased.

He opened the press conference to questions and there was a flurry of activity from journalists all keen to get in on the act.

It was the third question in, that caused Saxon's heart to skip a beat.

The journalist was an elderly, stout man. He spoke perfect English. ‘And do you have a match from the other DNA on poor Herr Frei’s body?’

The detective shot a slight glance at his colleague. A faint nod.

‘Yes we do. We recovered an identical match on an item of clothing found in a motor home on a campsite near Randa. We are now trying to trace the person who we believe disappeared around the same time Herr Frei was killed.’

‘The girl,’ another journalist called out. ‘Is it the girl who went missing, the English girl?’

Another exchange of looks between the two detectives. ‘Yes, we believe that Mademoiselle Henshaw may still be alive.’

Chapter 53

Kate took the news badly. The euphoria of the past few days was wiped out the second Saxon told her. He wasn't going to lie, this changed everything and he openly admitted, for once, he didn't have the answers.

'I have to go back. I have to hand myself in,' she said.

Becky sat at the table of the apartment sobbing gently.

'I booked the flight in my own name,' Kate continued. 'Hired the motor home in my own name using my card and passport as ID. It's only a matter of time before they find my flight and where I am.'

'America's a big place,' Becky said.

Kate stared at her. 'So you prefer if I become a fugitive, is that it?'

'No, I didn't mean, it's just—'

Saxon interrupted before it developed into a full-scale argument. 'Girls, can we just think this through, please?'

And yet it was difficult to think through. There was no easy solution to the problem, too many loose ends. Kate had fled a crime scene, no matter that it was clearly obvious to him that it had been a case of Kate defending herself.

'We need a good lawyer, I think,' he said.

'So you think I should go back?' Kate ventured.

Saxon shook his head. 'Not yet. I'll go back there. I'll find a lawyer, do some more investigating. I think we have a good chance of proving it was self-defence, especially if I can prove that Frei was responsible for multiple murders.'

'What the fuck are you on about?' Kate said.

Saxon took a deep breath. He looked at both of them. 'I think there's something I should tell you, so why don't you sit down and make yourself comfortable? This could take a while.'

The two sisters did just as Saxon asked, though after just a few sentences were on the edge of their seats. Saxon told them about his investigation, which started out as a search and rescue mission but which uncovered some unsettling statistics.

'It was as clear as day that something was seriously amiss, and what made it worse was the police's attitude to it all.'

Kate was stunned into silence, it was Becky who was throwing the questions. 'But why didn't you tell me, Sax? That would have made all the difference.'

'It wouldn't, and besides, I haven't been able to prove it yet. I need to do a lot more before I can take it any further because right now it's only the Zermatt Police who can reopen the cases and as far as they are concerned, the girl's deaths are accidental deaths and that's the way it's going to stay.'

Saxon told them about the photographs and the trophies and then threw the big spanner in the works, saying that Heinz Frei couldn't have been responsible for all of the deaths. There was something missing.

He turned to Kate. 'And to cloud issues even further, I believe we have another killer up there, someone with a fairly powerful rifle, a good shot, someone who took shots at Suzy and I and killed two innocent hikers.'

'What the fuck, Sax? Why would anyone want to do that?'

'Why would anyone want to throw all of those girls off a mountain?'

Kate had turned a pasty shade of pale. Despite the mess she was in, she now knew just how close she was to becoming the next victim. It was not just a random act of violence, Frei had set out to kill her.

Becky got to her feet and began to pace. 'But surely if the police know this then they'll understand. They'll realise that Kate was attacked and it's a cast iron case of self-defence?'

'I agree,' Sax said. 'Kate has given those families of the girls a justice that the police never did, but therein lies the problem. Despite all the evidence I've given them, they still refuse to reopen the cases.'

‘The bastards.’

‘My sentiments exactly.’

Chapter 54

It was the following morning when Saxon called a meeting. He told Kate and Becky that they were to head south and enjoy a holiday for as long as they could. They objected at first until Saxon explained the reality of the situation. He told them about the relationship between Nuessle and Heinz Frei, how the Frei family owned half of Zermatt, that the Chief of Police was in their pocket.

'My guess is that as soon as they get their hooks into you, you'll be charged with murder, manslaughter at the very least. You'll be remanded in custody until the trial. There's no chance of bail because you are a flight risk. You've already done it once.'

'But it'll look better if I go back now.'

'Yes, but it will be at least six months to the trial, so tell me, would you rather spend six months on the Appalachian Trail or six months in a women's high security unit in Geneva?'

'It's a no brainer,' Becky said. 'She'd go mad.'

‘It sounds corny,’ Saxon said, ‘but head for the hills, Kate. Becky has the money. Hand the camper van back and stay in cheap motels and lodges. Get to know each other again, do some hiking. Every day out there is a day less you’ll spend behind bars.’

‘It’s settled,’ Becky said. ‘I’ll contact my publisher and agent, tell them I’m having a bit of a breakdown and need time off.’

‘And you,’ Kate said at last. ‘What will you do, Sax?’

‘I’ll need to get back.’

‘And?’

‘I’ll need to prepare the case for the defence.’

Things started to move relatively fast the following morning. Kate notified Country Camper that she was on her way back to the UK, paid the outstanding fees and returned the vehicle to the store.

Despite Becky’s objections, Saxon insisted on driving up over the border into Canada. They found an outdoor store in Sherbrooke and kitted Becky out in winter outdoor clothing and a good pair of boots. They purchased a forty-litre backpack and paid for everything in cash.

During the two-hour drive back to Montpelier, Saxon told Becky that she would be dumping her expensive range of matching Tumi luggage in the nearest charity store.

‘Have you any idea how much that cost?’ she said.

‘Don’t care,’ he said, ‘and your designer clothes, and those heels, they have to go too. From now on you are two hippy punk sisters on the backpacking trip of a lifetime.'

'For fuck's sake,' she muttered.

'And that hair, I want it cut. I want you to get a new look.'

Becky's mouth fell open as Kate burst out laughing in the back.

Saxon looked into the rear-view mirror. 'I don't know what you are laughing at. I want your head shaved!'

Kate thought he was joking when he said he was shaving her head. He wasn't. It was the punk look, he said, shaved to the wood a couple of inches above the ear with the hair long and tied up on the top.

Even Kate had to admit after she had got used to it, the look wasn't all that bad.

Saxon insisted on a couple of photos, and then it was time for Becky to visit the local hair salon.

After they had settled the account at the Artful apartments, they climbed into the car and drove through the night, south, to North Carolina. They filled the car using Kate's credit card, rested up and then drove the remaining six hours to Fannin County in Georgia, the start of the Appalachian Trail.

Saxon made them fill the car again, using Kate's credit card.

The weather was a balmy twelve degrees, pleasant walking, and Saxon noticed a buzz of excitement from Kate. Even Becky had admitted she was looking forward to a few hiking days, as long as they took it easy.

They found the tourist offices of the Appalachian Trail in town, and while Kate and Becky stepped inside to get their AT passports, Saxon waited in the car park. The AT passports offered discounts at hotels and motels along the way as well as a section for stamps at various locations, to prove that the hiker had indeed trekked every mile of the Trail.

Saxon looked at the passports, once again purchased with Kate's credit card.

'Great,' he said. 'I think we are ready to go.'

'Just one thing,' Kate said.

'Speak to me.'

'If the Swiss authorities are mad keen on bringing me back to Switzerland, won't this make it fairly obvious where I am and what I'm doing?'

'Yes. That's why we are heading to Canada.'

They had left the car in a rough-looking Project estate on the outskirts of town and walked back to the main railway station. They'd paid for the tickets in cash. It involved five train changes. The first overnight leg of the journey took them through Chicago and on to Minneapolis for the first change at 11.01 am the next morning. They were booked into a four-bed sleeper carriage, luckily bed four was unoccupied, which meant they could talk quite freely.

'We're going up to fucking Calgary,' Becky exclaimed. 'It'll be bloody freezing.'

‘Minus eleven,’ Saxon said with a grin. ‘Aren’t you glad we bought decent winter gear?’

‘Three days of my life bloody wasted,’ Becky complained. ‘Three bloody days. I’ll never get back.’

‘Four days actually,’ Saxon said. ‘It will be four days all told by the time you get to Calgary, but I reckon that will buy Kate three or four months of freedom, so it’s worth every minute.’

Kate said nothing. Saxon guessed there was a little guilt creeping in, and yet he’d noticed something between the two sisters. It was an expectation, a feeling of adventure, the simple pleasure of travelling, something they hadn’t experienced together since they were teenagers. There was also an element of inevitable excitement, the danger of getting caught, and although Becky complained bitterly, he sensed she hadn’t had so much fun in years.

The train stopped in Chicago for fifteen minutes and they picked up some beers from the station. Before all the beers had been consumed, they’d all fallen into a deep sleep as the train rumbled through Wisconsin.

Chapter 55

Nuessle was back at his desk and now he had a bone between his teeth, a mission to find the missing girl. It was now a murder enquiry. That's what he'd written on the file. And for once, he was happy to work with others. Not the former Marine, no, he didn't care for him at all. But the two private detectives that Rosie had employed, well, they were different, they were on the payroll and therefore they were on team Frei and at last Nuessle could see a way out of this mess.

Chapter 56

Saxon had left the sisters in Minnesota. He'd spent a week being a tourist and planned in the evenings. He'd hiked a little around Lake Superior and Michigan before retracing his steps, heading back to Burlington International Airport.

He knew the police would be watching his every move, no need to give anything away.

Eighteen hours after his flight took off from Burlington, he was back in Zermatt, digging around, ruffling a few feathers. After all, that was another of his specialities.

James Bonnier was easy to track down. The Flying Pig had been able to lock on to his mobile phone tracker and the camper van was parked up at the edge of a lake inside the Italian border at a place called Stresa. It appeared that Bonnier wanted to make himself scarce, but didn't want to stray too far from the action.

That suited Saxon just fine.

He cycled there, a hundred and twenty-six kilometres, and it was good to get back on the bike again. He set off at first light and pulled into the small car park just before six in the evening.

He wasn't going to hang around, no point in delaying what it was he was about to do.

Saxon spotted the familiar van and walked over.

The lights inside the van were on, dusk pulling in over the blackness that was Lake Maggiore. Saxon imagined it would be quite spectacular in the light of day. He'd find out tomorrow morning.

Bonnier was sitting at the small table staring into the luminated screen of a computer.

He knocked on the door.

Bonnier didn't open it, instead a call from inside. 'Who is it?'

Nervous. On edge.

Saxon wanted to say it was his worst nightmare, but instead, 'It's me, Lenny Saxon.'

A key in the lock on the other side of the door and then the door swung open. A puzzled look, 'Lenny, how are you? How are you doing? How did you find me?'

Saxon stepped up to the threshold of the door, pushed past him. 'I find people. That's what I do. A beer would be good, James.'

'Sure, of course.'

As Bonnier walked over to glass fronted fridge in the corner of the van, Saxon scanned the interior.

'Here you go, mate.' He handed Saxon a can of Carlsberg.

Saxon eased into the small seat by the laptop and spun the screen around. 'What are you working on, James, or are you just surfing a little porn?'

Uncomfortable with the last remark. 'Hah, I wish, the signal's shit out here, man.'

Saxon eased back in the seat. Waited.

Bonnier cracked first. 'So she's alive then. The police reckon she's alive.'

'Oh, she's alive James, I've been with her this last week.'

Saxon studied his face closely. Genuine surprise.

'She passes on her regards.'

'She does?'

Saxon shook his head, 'Nah… not really. You see, you were one of the reasons she decided to disappear.'

'She did?'

This time an act.

'But why? I love her. I worship the ground she walks on.'

A big act.

Bonnier reached for a tissue from the table and blew his nose, wiped at the corner of his right eye.

'I love the girl, Lenny. Why would I have anything to do with her disappearing? Whatever it was, we could have worked it out.'

'I doubt it,' Saxon said. 'You see, James, you wanted different things from life. Your relationship had come to a crossroads and while you wanted to turn left, Kate wanted to walk straight on.'

'But I—'

'Shut up, James, and let me finish. The sooner we clear this up, the better.'

Saxon leaned across the table, made sure James could smell his breath as he spoke.

'You were boring, James. You bored Kate, and you tried to manipulate her and control her. You wanted her to want the same things as you and that was never going to happen.'

'But surely I—'

'Didn't you hear me, James? Shut the fuck up and let me finish.'

Saxon stood. He leaned onto the table and edged a little closer.

'You found the sex video James, you went through her private mails and hacked into her hard drive and you found a harmless little video from years back and you thought it was the way to sink your claws into Kate for good.'

Saxon pointed to the laptop. 'Is that yours?'

'Yes.'

'And Kate's laptop?'

'In the kitchen cupboard.'

Saxon slammed his fist on the table. 'Then get it, get it now and bring it here!'

Bonnier jumped to attention and darted over to the workbenches, opened a drawer and lifted out a small Medion laptop.

Bonnier placed it on the table, Saxon moved it to the side and noticed he was trembling. This was going to be easier than he thought. Saxon reached into his pocket and pulled out an eight-inch ball pein hammer.

Bonnier sank back into the seat and burst into tears. 'No please, I apologise, I didn't mean to and I—'

'Shut up snivelling, you little fuck.'

Saxon brought the hammer crashing down onto the keyboard of Bonnier's computer. Again and again, another half dozen blows until the internal works of the computer spilled out onto the table. He located the hard drive and pounded the hammer into it another ten times. 'Okay, now your mobile phone.'

Please, Lenny, no, all my contacts, all my work, my—'

'Your mobile phone or your face? Your choice.'

Bonnier reached into his pocket and slid the mobile phone across the table and one hard blow into the centre of the screen did the trick. He took out the sim card, reached for the lighter on the table and set it on fire. As the tiny flame took hold, he cast it into the small sink and watched it burn away to nothing.

He returned to the table. 'Get me a pen, you worthless piece of shit.'

Meek as a lamb, Bonnier stretched across the table and grabbed a pen. He handed it to Saxon.

Saxon reached into his pocket and put an envelope on the table.

'What? What's that?' Bonnier asked.

'That's the ownership log book for the mobile home. Open it.'

Bonnier lifted the flap and reached inside. 'Where did you get that?'

'From Kate, obviously you dummy. She kept it with her passport.'

Bonnier held the three-page document in his hand. 'So what about it?'

'If you look at the last page, at the bottom, you'll see a transfer of ownership slip. I've filled it in for you, you no longer have a fifty percent share in the vehicle. You've given it voluntarily to Kate.'

Bonnier glared at Saxon.

'You just need to sign on the bottom.'

'No way, I won't do it?'

Saxon let out a sigh. 'Look mate, we can do this the easy way or the hard way.'

Bonnier shot to his feet. 'I won't do it, I won't. I'm going to the police. I'm telling them everything.' He pointed to his mobile phone and the broken laptop. 'I have all the evidence I need. Now get out, get the fuck out of here.'

Saxon stood. 'Fair enough. I gave you the choice.'

He walked towards the door, placed his hand on the door handle and with the other hand turned the key and locked the door. 'Did I ever tell you? I fight dirty.'

Before Bonnier could react, Saxon had leapt across the table and grabbed him by the throat. He punched him just once in the face. It was enough to render him helpless, and he fell to the floor. There wasn't an ounce of fight in him, and Saxon dragged him to his feet and threw him back onto the seat. 'Right-handed or left?'

Dazed, still, 'What?'

'Right or left-handed, tell me now.'

Bonnier sensed there was a period of unpleasantness unfolding. He thought it wise to comply. 'Right, I'm right-handed.'

'Left hand on the table,' Saxon said softly.

'No man, please, no, I'm sorry.'

'Left hand on the table. You had your chance to take the easy route.'

'No, man, please.'

Saxon smacked him on the forehead with the hammer. He squealed like a baby as a purple, black ring appeared in the centre of his head and a trickle of blood ran into the corner of his eye.

'Left hand on the table. I won't tell you again.'

Crying quite freely now, Bonnier slid his left hand into the middle of the table and Saxon grabbed his wrist firmly. In quick succession, he brought the hammer down just four times, aiming for the middle phalange of each finger.

He gave Bonnier a couple of minutes. He had thrown himself on the floor of the van, writhing and squealing in agony.

He stepped over him and grabbed his hair. 'I'm not finished with you yet; you just sit at the table like a good lad.' He hauled him up and threw him into the seat. 'Now, you said you were right-handed, so I need your signature here and then you can go.' He slid the form across to him. 'Careful with the blood, we don't want to mess it up.'

'You won't get away with this.'

'Oh I will, there's no doubt about it because as I've already told you, I'm good at finding people and if you ever raise your ugly little head above the parapet again, I'll hunt you down like an animal and I'll take you away somewhere quiet and I'll torture you for a week and then I'll break your scrawny fucking neck.'

Bonnier didn't find the need to reply, instead he reached for the pen and scribbled his signature on the bottom of the page.

'Date it.'

He complied with the instruction.

Saxon reached for a large rucksack lying on the sofa bed. He threw it at Bonnier. 'You have five minutes to fill that with whatever you want and then you have a ten kilometre walk to the nearest hospital where they'll reset your fingers. Take a taxi or a bus to Malpensa Airport. It's about two hours away and then you can fuck off back to the UK.'

Bonnier was whimpering like a dog, nodding his head repeatedly.

Saxon knew he'd have no more trouble from the blackmailer.

Saxon had enjoyed a few weeks in the motor home on the shores of Lake Maggiore. It was peaceful. Nobody bothered him and he spent a lot of time getting his head around the case and laying it out in a format that was simple and easy to understand. He made a call to Becky's burner phone. He told her he had secured the mobile home and intended to drive it up to her house in Palézieux.

Becky gave him the exact directions and said that the house was unalarmed, the crime figures were some of the lowest in Europe and a key to the house lay under a yellow flower pot in the greenhouse. He could stay there as long as he liked.

'Thanks, I'll take you up on that, it's an ideal base.'

'Great, it should save me a little on the hotel bills I've been paying,' she joked.

Saxon didn't want to burden the two sisters with unnecessary information, especially when he was just at the beginning of his preparation for the case. However, he had secured the services of the barrister Becky had recommended in Geneva and was due to visit him as early as next week. Palézieux was only eighty kilometres away. He might even consider cycling it and have a few nights under canvas on the shores of Lake Geneva.

'Good idea. It's a beautiful setting.'

'Talking of which, how's your camping trip going?'

'Well, Lenny, I never thought I'd say this, but I'm absolutely loving the whole experience. Kate and I have reconnected again, and we feel like teenagers. I can understand how she loves hiking so much. She was always the outdoor one. I was the bookworm, but once we've got out of this mess, we've decided to meet up at least once a year and do a big trip. We stayed in hotels in January and February. It was too bloody cold even though we'd bought the best sleeping bags money could buy, but once the weather warmed up, we went for it and I rather surprised myself.'

'Tell Kate she'll never see Bonnier again. At least that's one problem out of the way.'

'You sure?'

'Yes, the sex tape is history and I have her personal laptop for her when—'

'I hear you, Sax, it's not going to be easy, but I hear you. If there's a way out of this, then I'm sure you will find it.'

They talked some more and then Saxon pressed end. He'd leave for Palézieux first thing in the morning. He'd be there early afternoon.

Chapter 57

Palézieux was a convenient place to stay, only eighty kilometres from Geneva, which was another forty kilometres away from his target, the man who truly held the key.

He crossed the Italian-Swiss border just north of Vargo, the summit of Punta de Terrarossa just to the west, a flurry of fine snow making it difficult to see at times.

Just before Martigny, he passed through a small village called Saxon and a powerful notion to stop and spend some time there and explore.

Another time, perhaps. Yes, he'd definitely come back here one day, do a little digging. He'd always wondered the origins of the first named Saxon family. Right now, he had too many other things on his mind.

It was slow going with the mobile home, poor acceleration, top speed around a hundred and ten kilometres per hour but because of the gradient and the twisty roads, the average speed, poor. Nevertheless, someone once told him that the way to see the world was slowly, ideally at bicycle speed.

Makes sense. He tried to forget his frustration and just enjoy the trip. There was absolutely no hurry to get there. It could be another month or two before they caught Kate.

They would catch her. That was for sure and even if they didn't, there'd be a time where Kate would want to get caught or even hand herself in. Six months maximum, he figured. Then the reality would set in and she'd get a little bored or deliberately careless because she knew that she couldn't live like that forever.

Chapter 58

Nuessle had every bit of evidence he needed and the fact that the girl had been on the run for nearly seven months was frustrating, but then again, played right into his hands. Once they got her and put her on trial, the months on the run would be their trump card. Along with a few others. The Chief Prosecutor agreed it was a cast iron case. First degree murder, minimum sentence twenty-five years.

The telephone call from Interpol came in at lunchtime.

Eggen Fassnacht put the call through, Nuessle clicked on the video icon and the screen filled with the image of a large black man in a dark suit.

In a deep French, Canadian accent, he said, 'I think we've found your lady.'

'Port Renfrew?' Nuessle exclaimed. 'Where the hell is that?'

'It's in British Columbia buddy. You said she was a hiker, and it all makes sense, because that area is an absolute haven for hikers and at this time of year it's the perfect temperature for walking. Maybe a little chilly in the evenings. I wouldn't like to camp out at night, but hell, those types of people just love that kinda shit.'

'It's nowhere near the Appalachian Trail, then?'

'Three thousand miles away.' He laughed. 'No wonder we couldn't find her. We were looking in the wrong place.'

Nuessle was fuming. They'd spent months trying to track her down. Hundreds of thousands of Swiss Francs on air fares and private detectives, as well as a considerable chunk of the annual Zermatt police budget which he'd authorised personally. At one point, they'd had three vehicles and six detectives combing the AT, from Fanning County to Maryland.

'You've been duped buddy; my guess is that all of those credit card transactions were deliberate, a red herring and you guys fell for it. I reckon she took a train and pissed off as far as she could go.'

'But Canada?'

'Yes, a beautiful part of the world. Why not?'

'But she's been away in the winter months.'

'Absolutely. Who would have thought to look for her up there?'

The Interpol policeman's laugh annoyed Nuessle, but he was right. She'd completely conned them.

'She's travelling with another girl. I'm going to send you a photograph over. We caught them on CCTV at a local camping store.'

Nuessle waited. Exactly ten seconds later, his phone pinged. He clicked on the WhatsApp icon and opened the photograph.

Nuessle grinned 'That's her, that's the murdering bitch.'

Chapter 59

Nuessle wanted the glory himself and, along with another two police officers, flew out to Vancouver on the next available flight. They crossed onto Vancouver Island after the Canadian policeman had told them that he was fairly certain the two girls would be trekking the Strathcona and Pacific Rim National Park. Every policeman on the island had been notified.

Nuessle had his own idea. Camp sites. Henshaw loved the wild outdoors and there were more than a dozen camp sites on the south of the island, several which looked out onto the Gulf of Alaska.

Nuessle and his team had settled in a small hotel in Courteney, within easy reach of all the campsites, and thirty-six hours after they'd checked in, the call came. Two girls matching the description of the fugitive and her companion had just booked into a beach front camp site called Walbran Creek.

It took three hours to reach a point just before Port Renfrew and then the three policemen hiked to the camp site no more than five miles away.

It was early evening, Nuessle saw no point in hanging around. There were six small tents spread out on the beach that led down to the water's edge. A quite beautiful spot, Nuessle thought to himself.

The first two tents were empty, the third tent contained the treasure he had been looking for.

'Kate Henshaw,' he said. 'I am placing you under arrest for the murder of Heinz Frei. You do not have to say anything, but it may harm your defence if you do not mention when questioned something that you later rely on in Court. Anything you do say may be given in evidence.'

Kate peered through the flap of the tent. 'Ah… Detective Nuessle, I've been expecting you.'

Nuessle couldn't help feeling a little uncomfortable at the cool demeanour of his fugitive. He watched her closely for the duration of the flight from Vancouver to Geneva. Smiling and laughing with her sister. Not a care in the world, a good appetite, no signs of any worry, even enjoying a couple of drinks somewhere over the North Atlantic Ocean.

Puzzling.

Chapter 60

It had been six weeks since Kate had been brought back to Zermatt in a mass media frenzy and a blaze of publicity.

Nuessle, as expected, had led the parade, giving interviews to any television or media outlet going. He was very careful not to make any accusations, aware that it might jeopardise any potential trial verdict and stuck to the script, saying that it had been hard work and professionalism that had brought the fugitive to trial.

Becky had stayed a few nights acting as a support but then returned home to Palézieux to meet up with Saxon when Kate had been sent to a women's prison in Dielsdorf, close to Zurich. They knew there had been no chance of bail. They hadn't even asked the judge. Dielsdorf was just over two hundred kilometres from Palézieux and they had been granted two visits per month.

Becky had received the latest update from the barrister. The trial had been scheduled for three months. The prosecution was happy with that timescale, which worried Saxon a little. Zermatt court authorities were also able to accommodate what was being billed as the biggest trial in Zermatt for decades. In reality, serious crime was almost non-existent, most crimes heard by deputy federal judges, the equivalent of a British magistrate.

Their first visit to Kate in prison would be a tough one, not least because they had bad news to deliver.

The prison was not what Saxon expected at all. It was not high security; it was small, a brilliant, white washed one storey building with bars at every window. If the bars hadn't been there, it could have masqueraded as a holiday camp. There were a total of fifty-seven cells for female prisoners awaiting pre-trial and preventive detention.

There was a separate block for women who had been convicted, but generally for women who had been sentenced to terms of less than a year or as a consequence of unpaid fines or financial penalties.

It didn't make any sense other than geographically; it was about as far away from Zermatt as you could get.

Kate was looking well. The hiking and camping adventure had hit the spot, there was colour in her cheeks and a smile on her face.

'You don't look too happy,' she said. 'What's wrong?'

Becky looked at Saxon and then back through the Perspex glass to her sister. 'It's the jury, the barrister didn't like it, six men and six women.'

'So what's wrong with that?'

'All from Zermatt.'

'Oh!'

'Yes, and you know what a legend Heinz Frei was in his home town.'

'So they'll need some convincing?'

'That's what he said. He asked for a complete change of jury. Perhaps the trial moved somewhere else, but the judge kicked it out and we are stuck with it.'

'And the judge?'

'From Zermatt.'

Saxon eased back in his seat. There was nothing he could really say to ease the pressure. It was bad news. There was no way to dress it up. Positives, he'd need to find positives.

'Your barrister is a good guy; I have supplied him with the details and he has every confidence that he can present a good case.'

'So what are my chances?'

'He wouldn't commit. He is waiting on more DNA results.'

Kate let out a long sigh. 'Wow, I don't even want to think about a guilty verdict, because there's no way will I last in a place like this.'

'Try not to think about that,' Becky chipped in. 'I'm sure between the barrister and Sax, they'll work it out.'

It was a two-hour visit and despite their time apart over recent weeks, they struggled to find anything meaningful to say in the last thirty minutes or so.

As they walked away from the white building and into the garden area, Saxon took a look around. He wondered how easy it would be to break a prisoner out.

Chapter 61

Saxon had decided to cycle to Annecy. It was good to get back into the saddle and explore the road that skirted Lake Geneva for nearly eighty kilometres. It was a hundred and twenty-five kilometres in total and he had decided to do it all in one day, leaving early morning, booking into a hotel in Annecy, that evening.

It had to be one of the most pleasurable days he had ever been on a bike and thanked his lucky stars that the weather had been kind to him, too.

It was a fast road, very little in the way of climbing, and the traffic was light and on his left-hand side most of the way, the beautiful blue waters of the huge lake, the largest body of water in Switzerland, with views of the Chablais Alps towards the south and the Bernese Alps to the east. A few hours into the journey, Saxon thought that some of the mountain peaks looked familiar, and sure enough, when he stopped and checked the map, he confirmed that the high summits of Grand Combin and Mont Blanc were clearly visible at times.

Cycling was great thinking time and Saxon planned out exactly what he was going to say at the meeting with Professor Josep Falcoz, at 9 am sharp, the next morning.

Saxon stopped in Geneva just before one and enjoyed a light lunch. He filled half a dozen pages in his notebook and felt quietly confident that he could persuade the professor to help their cause.

Money talked, and Becky had plenty of it. Professor Josep Falcoz had been well paid by the Frei's. The Flying Pig had been able to track down his invoice, and Saxon knew exactly where to pitch his offer.

The fact that Annecy to Geneva was only forty minutes by car should swing the professor's decision to take the case on. He wasn't a Zermatt man and didn't think he held any allegiance to the Frei family. He was an industrial gypsy, a mercenary, no more, and with what Saxon was going to disclose to him, it would be the biggest thing he had worked on for at least a decade.

Saxon stood outside the wrought iron double gates of Josep Falcoz's house at 8.50 am. He checked his watch… again.

The house stood in its own well-manicured grounds, on a small but select urbanisation, each house facing Lake Annecy with views across to a large chateau on the north side of the lake. A millionaire's paradise.

He was a little apprehensive, nervous even. He had promised Kate that everything would be fine, that she would be walking free soon and although he had convinced her, he wasn't sure he had convinced himself. *Little by little,* he whispered under his breath. Step *by step.*

The house was monstrously huge, the two marble pillars that flanked the double gates were topped with two statues of golden eagles, wings spread, looking to the right. *Opulence at its best,* Saxon thought. *A statement of wealth.*

The professor answered the door himself and greeted him with a limp, cold handshake.

'I see you like my eagles, Monsieur Saxon. I noticed you studying them.'

Saxon nodded his head. 'They're a little different, I must say.'

'You have half an hour,' Falcoz stated sharply, 'not a minute more.'

'Thank you, professor, that will be more than enough.'

'Good, I'm glad to hear it.'

Saxon had at first tried to contact the professor by email, but three emails had gone unanswered.

His initial telephone call had been intercepted by a secretary who had told him that the professor did not want to take on any more cases and was winding down towards retirement. Only when Saxon had mentioned the Frei case and that his representatives were prepared to pay whatever it took had the professor agreed to see him, and only after an upfront consultation fee of 1,000 euros had been credited to his account.

'So,' the professor said, 'talk to me. You say this is about the Frei case?'

'Yes, my friend is the accused, Kate Henshaw. I served in the military with her.'

'Go on.'

Saxon spoke uninterrupted for nearly forty minutes. The half hour deadline came and went and Falcoz showed no sign of interrupting. He laid the case bare, showed him the photographs of the dead girls, detailed the dates and his theory that Frei was a serial killer. He was amazed at just how attentive Falcoz was.

Falcoz second guessed exactly what it was that Saxon wanted him to do. 'And you want a DNA link to the dead girls?'

'Yes, sir, we probably can't prove that they were murdered, but if we can link Frei to just a few of those girls, we can sow the seeds of doubts into the jury's mind.'

'And your friend will get a not guilty verdict.'

'That's right. I spoke with Kate a lot, she told me exactly what happened and I believe her one hundred percent. Kate had never even met Heinz. Why on earth would she want to kill him?'

Falcoz nodded ever so slightly. 'I've often wondered that myself, but of course she fled the scene and that wasn't a good move. Ninety-nine times out of a hundred, it's the one who flees the scene who is the guilty party. My job was to find the DNA, I'm afraid it was the police who took it from there.'

'I accept that,' said Saxon, 'but I'm convinced that Frei stalked her and attacked her at the point where he fell from the mountain. Kate was more than a match for him, unlike those other poor girls.'

'And you're sure they were all murdered.'

'Absolutely, but I don't need to prove that. I just need to prove that Frei was there, at least at a few of the scenes.'

The professor stood. He stretched and arched backwards, let out a long groan, and then leaned forward and touched his toes. He looked at Saxon and smiled. 'The old bones and joints aren't what they were. I need to do a little yoga just to keep mobile.'

Saxon kept quiet.

Falcoz continued.

'I'm not sure I can help you. In suspicious deaths, sudden deaths, unexplained accidents and open verdicts, the files are always there, always ready to be revisited just in case something new crops up. But in Frei's case, I had a body to work with and that's where I found the DNA. These girls' cases are years old, there are no bodies.'

'But there are evidence bags,' Saxon said, 'clothing and various articles recovered from the scene.'

The professor grinned. 'Yes, Monsieur Saxon, it's possible that there are indeed evidence bags in the pits of a police station somewhere.'

Saxon sensed there was a *but* coming.

'But not often. It's normally left to an individual policeman to dispose of any unclaimed property, generally the first policeman on the scene is assigned to the case. And if for example, a bloodstained rucksack or a sweater is labelled as unclaimed property, it's the policeman's responsibility to tidy up his paperwork and dispose of unclaimed property in due course.'

'And what sort of time frame are we talking about?'

'There is none, but a good policeman should have cleared his case within a twelve-month period. However, I've known some police stations hang on to items for five years.'

Saxon explained how he had seen the evidence bags at Zermatt. One evidence bag was a lot older than five years.'

'Sloppy police work, Monsieur Saxon, sloppy police work, or they have a big basement.' Falcoz laughed. 'The more space they have in the basement, the more likely they will hang on to stuff that nobody will ever look at.'

'But there are a lot of dead girls. Can we try?'

Falcoz stretched up to the ceiling again, controlled his breathing, and let out a long sigh. He looked down at the table, at Saxon's list. 'You have a note of all of the individual police stations in relation to each girl?'

'Yes, sir.' Saxon slid another piece of A4 across the desk.

'Good,' said the professor. 'I can email the relevant magistrates and judges first thing in the morning. My fee will be 10,000 euros whether we find anything or not.'

Saxon decided to stay another night at the hotel in Annecy. He called Becky later that evening. It was a bittersweet exchange. While it was good news that they had secured the professor, Saxon also explained what the professor had said, that they weren't guaranteed to find any evidence bags, how the police system worked and how it was generally up to individual stations and individual policemen to perform the task of disposal.

'I gave the professor a list of each girl in chronological order and he said we have to hope that they might just be some evidence bags from the girls who have been killed more recently. As long as we find something, a rucksack, a cap or an item of clothing there's a chance that he can perform his magic and lift off some of Heinz Frei's DNA.'

Becky wasn't over talkative. It was a bit of a blow to her because they had both naturally assumed that there would be an evidence bag in some sort of storeroom for every girl.

'The professor reckons we only need a couple of DNA matches, so let's just keep our fingers crossed.

He said if we get two, there is no jury in the world that would convict Kate when they know Heinz Frei has been involved, or at least at the scene of another suspicious death.'

'I wish I shared your optimism, Sax,' she said. 'All I know is that my poor sister is rotting in jail and the best-case scenario is that we have a fifty-fifty chance of getting her out. When we were in America and Canada, we promised her better odds than that.'

It was a painful thing to hear, but Saxon couldn't argue. His mind drifted back to when he left them in America and Kate had been a free girl, albeit a fugitive. She was a lot happier than when he first arrived. He'd had a little time to work on her, to convince her to trust him. He had everything sorted. He'd find a way, that the truth always won through in the end. She did nothing wrong, other than defend herself, and she had to believe in the judicial system. But she'd run, she told him time and time again, and he'd sat her down and went through the names of every girl who had gone missing or met with an accident and he told her that she had ended the killing spree and that had to count for something.

And in the end she had believed him. He saw it in her eyes. She trusted him.

Towards the end of the discussion he'd asked the professor's opinion on how many of Frei's DNA samples he'd need to come up with to throw doubt in the jurors mind. The professor hadn't wanted to be drawn into any guessing games but Saxon had pressed him. One would be sufficient, he eventually said, two would be like hitting the jackpot.

Chapter 62

It was six weeks later when the professor had called him. It was late on a Saturday evening and he'd been having dinner out in Vevey, with Becky. The name Falcoz had appeared in the call screen and Saxon nearly choked on a piece of steak.

The professor's call was short but ever so sweet. He said they'd hit the jackpot. His very words.

Saxon listened quietly and Becky somehow sensed that something dramatic was taking place. The professor had located three evidence bags in total, two from the more recent sudden deaths and one from more than ten years ago in an obscure Swiss police station in a village called Tancua. The policeman who had been assigned to the case had been on long-term sick and when he'd returned to work he'd assumed that the case had been allocated to someone else. Falcoz had recovered and taken thirty-five different dried blood samples and a black hair from one bobble hat, knowing that the girl who had died had long blond hair.

And he'd struck gold. The DNA from the hair sample had matched that of Heinz Frei and although thirty-four samples had all matched the DNA of the deceased girls, on a rucksack belonging to Morgan Murphy, a blood sample match to Heinz Frei had been found.

Saxon wanted to jump for joy. He couldn't wait to end the call and give Becky the news.

'But there's one other thing,' the professor said. 'We had another alien blood sample on victim number three, but it wasn't a strong enough comparison to categorically say that it matched Frei. It was all rather strange.'

'I'm not with you, was it or wasn't it Frei's blood and what do you mean, not strong enough?'

'Well, the blood certainly didn't belong to the victim and there was no match on the data base so we don't know whose it is.'

'But—'

'But it was a ninety percent match up to Frei's.'

'Which means.'

'Which means it was probably Frei's, but the lab just couldn't get enough of the sample to take it to the required level that it was beyond doubt, and the labs are very particular. They are very protective of their reputation.'

'But it doesn't matter, right? We have two matches, which is one more than we dared to hope for.'

'Absolutely, monsieur, it's everything that we wanted, more than enough. We have established that Heinz Frei was at three separate locations where sudden deaths occurred, one of which was his own. I'd say that your friend is as good as free. You must notify her lawyer immediately.'

Saxon pressed end and smiled across the table.

'What is it?' Becky asked.

Poker face.

He caught the waiter's eye and the young, smartly dressed man walked over. 'Yes, sir,' can I help?'

'Yes, I'd like a bottle of champagne please, a Bollinger if you have one.'

'Certainly, sir.'

Becky twisted her face. 'What the… what's happening, Sax? Who was that?'

'That, Becky, was the professor you paid ten grand to.'

'And?'

'And he's only gone and hit the fucking jackpot.'

It was 1.30 am when they arrived back at Becky's house. The motorhome, Saxon's humble abode, parked at the bottom of the long approach road, where it had been for the last eleven weeks. It was more than three hundred yards from the house, but Becky sped past it in her Mercedes E Class four-wheel drive.

'Whoa,' Saxon said. 'Where are you going? It's raining. I'll get soaked on the way back?'

'You're not sleeping there tonight, Sax. We need to get up early and go to see Kate. Get a good night's sleep indoors, the weather forecast is terrible, raining right through the night and you won't sleep a wink.'

The rain was hammering against the Mercedes windscreen, the automatic wipers at their maximum setting, and it suddenly sounded like a good idea.

'I'll make you some breakfast and book a double visit as soon as the prison office opens.'

'Sounds like a plan.'

Becky parked as near as she could to the house but it was still a twenty metre sprint to the front door and they were soaked.

As they burst through the door, they were giggling like school kids, a little drunk and high on the news they had received from the professor.

'I shouldn't have driven back. That was stupid,' she said.

'I did tell you to call a cab.'

'Madness. You shouldn't have ordered that champagne.'

'But it was good, wasn't it?'

Becky nodded. She looked into his eyes and for a second or two, time stood still.

'Want another?' she asked. 'I have at least a hundred bottles in the cellar, presents from publishers and prizes that come with book awards. The thing is, I never drink in the house on my own and, well… this seems like a good excuse.'

Becky returned with a dusty, but ice cold bottle of HENRI GIRAUD champagne 'It's bloody freezing down there, no need to throw this in a bucket of ice.'

After another hour, Saxon sensed it wasn't going to be such an early start after all, but even so, after two large glasses each, he called time. 'We really need to be getting some sleep, Becky. I can feel my eyes closing.'

'Lightweight,' she giggled. 'I thought the Commandos were hardcore.'

'Another time, another day,' he said. 'Just point me to where I'm sleeping.'

Becky stood. 'Follow me, the bed's made up.'

Saxon did as instructed and followed her upstairs to the long corridor with three bedrooms on either side. Becky had given him the grand tour of the house some weeks back. He knew that she slept in the large room at the end, the one on the left with spectacular views of mountain ranges and Lake Geneva. Becky walked right to the end, turned to her left, and then opened the door. 'You're in here, soldier boy.'

'But that's your room, Becky. Where are you sleeping?'

'I'll be sleeping in there too, as long as you've no objections.'

There were no curtains on the window. No need. Becky liked to be woken by the sun or natural light and hadn't used any sort of alarm call for nearly ten years. It was the only way to wake, she'd said.

Saxon couldn't disagree and the gentle rays of the early morning sun tugged at his eyelids and eventually he prized them open.

A few seconds taking in the strange new surroundings and realising where he was and what had happened and for a while regretting everything. Becky was missing, her side of the bed empty. He reached over with his hand. Still warm, she hadn't been away for too long.

He threw his legs over the bed, stood and stretched, located his boxers and walked through into the en-suite bathroom.

He found Becky in the kitchen. A strong aroma of coffee filled the air. She had her back to him, reaching into a high cupboard and pulling out two cups. She wore a white shirt, nothing else, and it just about covered her modesty.

'Morning,' he said.

Becky turned to face him. She smiled. 'Any regrets?'

'Not at all. I was just a little shocked, that's all.'

'Shocked at what? We girls have needs too. I don't know how I lasted so long.'

She poured two coffees and handed him one and they sat at a pine table in a large bay window facing south.

'I thought Suzy was your girlfriend at first, otherwise I'd have made a move on you a lot quicker,' she said. 'I'm not looking for anything serious or long term, but I guess I liked the girl and would have felt a bit guilty.'

'So what changed your mind?'

‘The last couple of months, I can’t recall a single phone call you’ve had with her, so it certainly isn’t anything major. I’d take a stab in the dark that it was a brief affair and you might be looking her up one day, but you’re certainly not rushing back to Zermatt to put a ring on her finger.’

Saxon couldn’t help laughing. He took a long drink from the cup and said, ‘You’ve nailed it. That’s exactly how it is. I like the girl a lot, but I’ve no plans to settle down any time soon.’

‘Good, I’m glad to hear it. You’re quite decent in bed. I might be tempted to drag you in there some more.’

Saxon was genuinely shocked at Becky’s honesty. They shared a cooked breakfast and he couldn’t remember laughing so much in a long time. The relationship had changed overnight. Becky was different, a little cheeky, the odd playful insult, and she seemed a lot more relaxed and at ease.

No doubt yesterday’s news cheered her up. The odds had swung back in Kate’s favour.

Chapter 63

Kate's visit had been booked in for noon, and an appointment with the lawyer, Sven Bernall, in Geneva, early evening.

Becky and Saxon had agreed not to go overboard, not raise Kate's hopes too high, not until they had heard what the lawyer had to say.

But, nevertheless, they couldn't hide the fact that they were in high spirits, far happier than the last time they had both visited and it was naturally infectious.

They left after two hours, and promised Kate a phone call as soon as they came from the lawyer's office.

It had been a long day, just three or four hours of sleep had not helped, but at least the lawyer hadn't kept them too long.

He was ecstatic, couldn't hide his delight, and made notes of the DNA results and took the professor's details. 'I'll need him in court, of course. Probably won't be needed, but just in case I can call him.' He looked at Becky. 'He'll want a fee, of course, but pay him whatever it takes. He holds the key to your sister's freedom.'

'So we are on a winner, you think?' Saxon enquired.

'Absolutely, beyond reasonable doubt, those jury members can only enter a guilty verdict if they are absolutely certain that Miss Henshaw deliberately attacked Frei with a premeditated intention of killing him. It's a murder charge, not manslaughter. The prosecution is going in with both barrels. They won't contemplate a self-defence manslaughter charge.'

'You've mentioned that to them?'

'It's my job, Mr Saxon. I had to test the water just in case our defence went south.'

'How could that have happened?'

'Anything could have happened to weaken our case, anything at all. A mysterious witness, more evidence, a bad character reference and I've no doubt the prosecution have poked into her military records, her past history and they will have been looking for any misdemeanour to bolster their case.'

'I see.'

'But thankfully that hasn't happened. In fact, the opposite is true. This is fantastic news, truly fantastic, it really is.'

He hesitated for a moment. Saxon picked up on it immediately. 'What is it? You were going to say something.'

'Well—'

'Come on, say it,' Becky interrupted.

‘Well… there’s a chance we could get her freed immediately. This is so good that we could apply to the Supreme Court. The judges in the Supreme Court can have her released in twenty-four hours.’

Becky couldn’t contain her excitement. ‘Oh my God, that’s fantastic.’

A cautionary hand was raised by the lawyer. ‘Hang on a minute, we need to think this through. It’s not guaranteed.’

‘But what’s to think about? At least give it a try. There’s nothing to lose. If the judge says no, then we are in the same position as we are now.’

It was Saxon who spoke next. He took them both by surprise.

‘We have everything to lose, because if the Supreme Court denies the application to free her, then that lot in Zermatt will have been forewarned and it will give them time to plot and scheme again. We’ve seen how they can make evidence disappear in the past. Who knows what might happen?’

The lawyer sank back into his seat. ‘Well, well, Monsieur Saxon, I see you’re a shrewd man and I couldn’t have put it any better. This DNA is gold dust and we can’t give them any chance to scatter it in the wind. We need to hit them with this at the trial. Not a moment sooner.’

Becky was disappointed and protested at first. But the lawyer soon explained the practicalities, the very real danger of alerting both the police and the prosecution team to this new development.

'The trial is a month away,' he said. 'If it was a year or eighteen months, I'd say give it a go.'

'She'll survive, Becky,' Saxon said. 'She's tougher than you think.'

'I guess so. It makes sense.'

They were in and out of the lawyer's office within an hour and as soon as they got outside, they delivered the news to Kate when they rang the prison. They never mentioned the Supreme Court to her. There was little point.

Coincidently, little over forty kilometres as the crow flies, there was another phone call taking place.

'Madame Frei, how are you? It's me, Josep?'

'Josep, I'm good. What's up? Is there a problem? We've settled your account as far as I'm aware.'

'Yes, of course you have. It was paid last month. No, that's not why I'm calling. I'm afraid there has been a development that I think you should be aware of.'

Chapter 64

Kate was brought in just prior to the judge, and after the public gallery had quietened down. It was packed full, the small courtroom which seated no more than two hundred was packed to the gunnels, and the press benches packed in like sardines.

Kate sat, scanned the courtroom and when her eyes settled on her sister and Saxon on the opposite side of the courtroom, she gave what can only be described as a grimace. She was not comfortable with where she was. It was alien to her and being under lock and key was beginning to take its toll. She had lost weight, her hair hadn't been cut for some time, her normal near olive toned, glowing skin had taken on a pale pallor. Day by day, Saxon noticed that his former comrade was deteriorating slowly.

It was painful to watch at times. Bernall had been spot on. The prosecution was playing dirty. At one point, they had mentioned Kate's service in the military and pointed out that she had fought in two armed conflicts and was no stranger to killing. Bernall had objected in the strongest possible terms and the judge had admonished the prosecution lawyer, but the damage was done. The jury wasn't going to forget it.

Bernall held the ace card and was determined not to play it until the last possible moment.

That moment came on the last day of the trial, day ten, when the judge had asked the relevant parties to sum up their cases.

The prosecution lawyer was good, unsurprisingly the best that money could buy. Courtesy of Madame Frei.

Saxon looked over at Falcoz, who had been patiently waiting for his moment. He looked relaxed and no wonder; he had demanded another €10,000 just to attend the trial with additional expenses of €250 per day.

And the lead for the prosecution, a hotshot young man in his mid-thirties. Saxon had read up on him. Ignacio Saladin Fontaine the III came from a long line of family lawyers and judges and had been groomed and destined for the top from a young age. He had studied at Harvard Law School and returned to his home in Paris aged twenty-six. He spoke seven languages fluently, including Mandarin, and had established an enviable strike rate with the courts.

His closing speech lasted twenty-seven minutes. It had been well prepared and rehearsed and even though Saxon hated to admit, he was a league above Bernall. Concise. Perfect breathing and timing, placing emphasis on the points he needed to emphasise.

Saxon studied the jury every few minutes. Like attentive students, taking everything in. Even a few slight nods. The body language wasn't good.

Bernall stood. He'd been recommended. He was part of a network, all highly paid consultants and lawyers. They were high-flyers, ridiculously expensive, with many years' experience, and perhaps that was the problem. As Saxon stared at him, he took his place. Approaching retirement age, perhaps not so hungry as he was in the old days, perhaps not as hungry as Ignacio Saladin Fontaine III.

He began.

A nice start, pleasant smiles in the direction of the jury, summing up the case, telling them that it was as clear a case of self-defence they would ever see. Ten minutes in, he delivered a brief slideshow, the photograph of the rock that had been found on the mountain with the blood that matched Kate's DNA and then the photograph that Saxon had taken in America of Kate's shaved head with the scar tissue clearly visible. With a clever software program, Bernall brought them together in slow motion, showing that the head wound and the edge of the rock were an exact match.

Saxon had wanted to bring this evidence into the trial much earlier, but the defence lawyer had wanted to play a late hand. He had said that he wanted the real powerful evidence to be fresh in the mind of each juror as they retired to consider their verdicts. This was also one of the reasons why he hadn't introduced the DNA evidence earlier in the trial.

During the morning recess, Bernall openly admitted that the prosecution team was probably slightly ahead on points, but he was going for a final round knockout and put them down on the canvas with a blow that they would never recover from.

Saxon studied the jury yet again. He had hardly taken his eyes off them since the trial had begun. Sure enough, the general demeanour had changed a little after Bernall's slides. A few looks of confusion on their faces. One woman had edged forward in her seat a little, clearly taking an interest.

Good signs at last. That was exactly the look that Saxon was looking for.

Beyond Reasonable Doubt, those were the words Bernall had used throughout the trial and Saxon couldn't disagree with him. The prosecution had gone all out to secure a premeditated murder conviction and therefore all Bernall had to do was sow doubt in their minds, a little confusion. No one had ever tried to claim that a struggle hadn't taken place, no one had ever tried to claim that Frei had lost the battle in that struggle and had fallen to his death.

Needless to say, from the very beginning, the prosecution had alleged that because Kate had run away and disappeared off the face of the Earth for several months, it was an admission that she had something to hide and that she had run because of the guilt factor.

During the previous days of the trial, not once had Bernall been able to deliver a constructive reason why Kate had left the scene.

Ignacio Saladin Fontaine III had said that Kate had the perfect lifestyle, hiking in the mountains she adored, a boyfriend who loved her and a highly successful author sister who happened to be a millionaire. He painted Kate's life as one of the most idyllic that anybody could ever imagine. She had a long and distinguished career in the military and no money worries of any sorts.

Ignacio Saladin Fontaine III had turned to Bernall at one point and said that if he could provide a valid reason why Kate had fled the scene, he would be happy to concede the case there and then.

Bernall had remained silent and in his seat.

Bernall was wrapping up, moving towards the climax of the trial.

'Ladies and gentlemen, as we come to the end of proceedings I would like to remind you just one more time that it is up to the prosecution to deliver to you, categorical proof, beyond reasonable doubt, that my client set out to deliberately inflict harm on Monsieur Heinz Frei. Perhaps it comes as no surprise that they have been unable to do that for the simple reason that there are only two people who can possibly know that. One,' he pointed to Kate in the dock, 'is my client Kate Henshaw, and the other, unfortunately, the deceased Monsieur Frei. I can give you no reason why Mademoiselle Henshaw fled the scene, other than she was traumatised and she panicked. I hope I have demonstrated that she was indeed struck by a rock with some force, though my learned friend,' he pointed to Ignacio Saladin Fontaine III, 'would have you believe that she fell and came into contact with it during the struggle. We must ladies and gentlemen, give the benefit of the doubt to this young lady sitting with us here today, a young lady who has already been held in our penal system for some time and the reason is that my learned friend has not proven the case for the prosecution, beyond reasonable doubt.'

Saxon felt an elbow in his ribs. 'Here it comes,' Kate whispered.

'But there is something else,' Bernall said, pausing for dramatic effect. 'There is something I feel I must share with you, something that will show you fine ladies and gentlemen from Zermatt, that perhaps Heinz Frei wasn't the fine upstanding citizen that you believed he was.'

The young lawyer leapt to his feet. 'Objection Your Honour, Heinz Frei is not on trial here.'

The judge looked towards Bernall. 'He is right, monsieur, the deceased is not on trial. Where is this going? Please explain.'

'Well, Your Honour, I intend to introduce new evidence that—'

'Objection, Your Honour, my learned friend cannot introduce new evidence at such a late stage in the proceedings. This is a summing up, nothing more.'

'The evidence has just come to light, Your Honour. It must be disclosed to the jury, it proves categorically that Heinz Frei was—'

'Objection, Sir. Heinz Frei is not on trial.'

For the next sixty seconds the exchange between the two lawyers developed into a full scale argument and Saxon had the feeling that the young lawyer from Paris claimed the upper hand though Bernall did have the last word, almost screaming at the young lawyer, telling him that the only reason he didn't want the evidence to be heard, was because it would prove Kate Henshaw didn't attack Heinz Frei and that it was in fact, the exact opposite, that Frei had been the aggressor from the outset.

Eventually, the judge called for a thirty-minute recess and ordered the two counsels into his back office.

The court was cleared and Saxon and Becky gave a little wave to Kate who was taken downstairs into the bowels of the court building, to be placed in a cell.

'I don't like it,' Becky said as they stood by a coffee machine on the first floor.

'Probably nothing to worry about,' Saxon said. 'I would think that the judge is just giving them both a bit of a bollocking.'

‘I’m not so sure, that lawyer of theirs knows his stuff and as soon as Bernall mentioned introducing new evidence he was objecting.’

Saxon couldn’t lie. That had worried him too, Bernall had jumped to his feet immediately, almost sensing what was about to happen and then he’d fought tooth-and-nail in a stand up battle with Bernall, determined that he wasn’t going to allow him to breathe a word about the new evidence, or bad mouth Frei in any way.

They stood around the corridor for nearly an hour and with every second that passed Saxon grew ever worried. This wasn’t a simple telling off, there had been a development.

They were about to find out.

A court official called them all into the court and it was reconvened, the public, officials and the press took their places, and Kate was brought in as soon as everybody was seated.

The two lawyers also walked in from a back office and a minute later the judge appeared and took his place

The two lawyers were sitting alongside their representatives, and Falcoz, for some reason, had taken his seat at the end of one of the rows in the public gallery.

The judge spoke.

‘Ladies and gentlemen of the jury, may I offer my apologies for the confusion at the end of our last session? I have met with the two relevant parties to clarify and clear up a few points. As you are aware, Monsieur Bernall made an attempt to introduce new evidence at this late stage. As you may or may not know, this is not normal practice, particularly at the point of summing up the case where all evidence should have been previously submitted and discussed.

The prosecution quite rightly objected in the strongest possible terms, and my initial thoughts were that they had a valid point. Monsieur Bernall had indicated to me that his team was not in possession of the new evidence until only recently, but this was disputed by Ignacio Saladin Fontaine III, who advised that a Professor Falcoz had telephoned Madame Frei over a month ago. As Professor Falcoz is in court today, I asked him to confirm or deny that fact. I am sorry to say that Professor Falcoz confirmed that the evidence came to light nearly five weeks ago and that the defence knew all about it.'

Saxon and Becky couldn't believe what was happening. This was their worst nightmare. It was worse than a nightmare, as it was all they had.

Saxon looked over towards Kate. She listened intently to the judge, but she looked confused. She didn't know anything about the way Bernall was going to handle the case; they thought it best not to tell her that he was relying on the impact of the new evidence on the final day.

The judge continued, saying that the defence lawyer was in contempt of court. He had deliberately chosen to falsify a claim and had lied in open court.

He said that he had committed a process crime and that he would consider a fine or possibly a short jail sentence.

And then the lifeline that Saxon didn't think was coming.

'I have consulted with several colleagues during the recess and my clerk has researched defence lawyers submitting late evidence under recent Swiss and French jurisdiction. Apparently, it is not an unusual occurrence, though,' the judge glared at Bernall. 'It's a rarity when the defence lawyer lies to me deliberately.'

Bernall bowed his head towards the floor like a castigated schoolboy, no doubt wondering if he was heading to the cells anytime soon.

The judge continued. 'There are several cases within the last ten years where a defence lawyer has submitted late evidence and withheld it from the prosecution prior to doing so. In each case, the prosecution has quite rightly objected, requested that the trial be extended and in one particular case, after a not guilty verdict was brought in, requested a retrial.' Another glaring look in the direction of Bernall. 'So, Monsieur Bernall, I will allow you to disclose your evidence but I hope you realise that it could have dire consequences and it may result in a possible retrial for your client.'

Bernall nodded meekly and stood slowly. Every movement was an effort. 'Thank you Sir, and I do wish to apologise to the court and, in particular, the jury. It was not my intention to mislead anyone.'

'What a fucking mess,' Saxon whispered under his breath.

Bernall cleared his throat, coughed once into his hand. 'Your honour, ladies and gentlemen of the jury.'

'Objection.'

It was Fontaine III. 'I cannot permit this evidence to be heard, as the evidence which we understand to be new DNA is not directly connected to the case.'

Bernall looked around in apparent bewilderment, as did the judge. Murmurs were coming from the direction of the jury benches.

Before the judge could say anything, Fontaine III continued and spoke confidently as he referred to his notes. 'Your Honour, in all of the cases that you have referred to, those of Lefort vs Smit 2011, Raiders vs Stefan 2013, Kohler vs Kuhn 2014, Noser vs Bachmann 2017 and Hess vs Zaugg 2020, the evidence was connected directly to the accused person. I can categorically assure the court that the evidence Monsieur Bernall wishes to present to the court has nothing to do with Mademoiselle Henshaw, but refers to separate, historical, sudden deaths, all of which were recorded as accidental. Therefore, it is not allowed to be heard in open court.'

'I see,' the judge said. He called an official to the bench and they spoke for some time. She handed him some papers and he studied the text.

Saxon had to admit, the simplicity and delivery of those two or three sentences from the young lawyer were brilliant.

The judge turned to Bernall. 'Well, counsel, it appears your opponent is correct. I cannot allow this evidence to be heard. It has nothing to do with this case or Mademoiselle Henshaw directly.'

Bernall had nowhere to go. Or so they thought.

Bernall threw an accusing pointed finger in the direction of his opponent. 'He doesn't want the jury to hear the evidence because he knows exactly what that evidence is.'

'Objection.'

'Sustained! Monsieur Bernall, you are testing my patience. I've made my decision and I've heard enough.'

When the judge called an end to proceedings, Bernall hadn't even completed his closing statement, saying that the jurors had heard more than enough to arrive at a decision.

The court was adjourned, the jury sent to a hotel for the weekend. They were not allowed any communication with their families or any newspapers and their mobile phones were confiscated. The judge said he was determined that the verdict should not be influenced by outside forces.

Saxon, Becky, and Bernall retired to a small bistro adjacent to the courtroom. There were a few reporters asking questions. 'No comment.'

By the time they entered the establishment, they had got the message and drifted away.

'I think I need something strong,' Bernall said with a smile. 'He was good, damned good. That was one of the hardest cases I've ever had to deal with.'

'It didn't go too well at the end,' Becky offered.

'In what way?' Bernall replied.

'Isn't it obvious? The judge wouldn't allow you to submit the DNA results from the sudden death victims.'

Bernall twisted his face. 'No matter. It would have been nice but I've got what I wanted, I've sowed the seed of doubt in the jury's mind and they'll be sitting in their little hotel bar now, as we speak, and all they'll be talking about is the evidence that they were not allowed to hear about.'

Saxon sank back in his chair. *Well, well,* he thought, *perhaps I have misjudged this man. Beyond reasonable doubt, he had said again and again and again.*

Becky didn't seem so convinced.

'He's right,' Saxon said. 'We would have liked to have made the DNA results public, but this is the next best thing because the jury at least knows about it, knows there is something the prosecution wanted to suppress.'

'Beyond reasonable doubt,' Bernall said. 'The three greatest words in the legal language.'

They sat with Bernall for the next few hours and all three proceeded to get a little drunk. They enjoyed some dinner in the classy bistro and Bernall insisted on champagne, the best the Bistro had to offer. He picked up the tab.

Saxon thought he was jumping the gun just a tad early.

Becky and Saxon checked into a local hotel for the evening. In a suite with a king-size double room and a hot tub on the terrace. Bernall summoned a driver from somewhere and headed in the direction of Geneva.

Saxon and Becky decided to stay in Zermatt all weekend. As he had left, Bernall predicted that the jury would deliver the verdict on Monday morning. It was as clear as day. There was little to discuss.

Chapter 65

Bernall had been just a few hours out.

The verdict was delivered early afternoon.

Saxon and Becky had stayed in bed until after 10 am and then took coffee and breakfast on the terrace.

Just after noon, the message from Bernall pinged through on Saxon's WhatsApp.

Court reconvening at 2 pm. Verdict in.

'Well,' Saxon said to Becky. 'This is it. This is what we've been waiting for.'

Nobody felt like any lunch. They returned to the same Bistro that they had been in the previous Friday evening.

Bernall threw a copy of the local Zermatt newspaper across the table.

'I think we have a leak,' he said. 'This is today's newspaper printed around 6 am this morning. It says that they have exclusive information that the verdict will be given today.'

'Are they speculating what the verdict is?' Becky asked.

Bernall's face dropped. 'They are,' he said, 'but don't forget this is Zermatt paper, I prefer to look at the nationals to get a more accurate picture.'

'It's a guilty then, I take it?'

Bernall nodded. But he was quick off the mark, pulling up a webpage on his mobile phone of the Geneva-based Swiss Daily. 'These are the sort of newspapers that we should be listening to. This reporter was at court and gives an in-depth account into the reasons why the new evidence was never heard in court. He speculates quite accurately that the new evidence must relate to old unsolved cases, and that it is inevitable that Heinz Frei must have been at the scene of some of them. He goes on to say that the jury must bring in a not-guilty verdict or at the very least, fail to arrive at a unanimous verdict in which case there may be a retrial or the judge can order that Kate walks free.'

'A retrial, Becky said. 'That's the last fucking thing we want. She wouldn't take that at all well.'

Saxon reached across for her hand. 'Don't worry. I don't think it will come to that. Let's keep positive.'

It was a mob that stood outside the court. There was no other word to describe it. It reminded Saxon of an old-style execution where the crowds lined up for blood. Most of them would be disappointed, as the public gallery in the courtroom that day was by invitation only.

Much to Saxon's surprise, the public gallery was only half full, although the press benches were standing room only.

As had been the procedure of the previous days in court, Kate was led in by two uniformed officers and within minutes of taking her seat, the door on the far side of the room opened and the judge walked through.

He gave a nod of acknowledgement to the jury members and took his seat.

He went through the normal formalities and the foreman of the jury stood.

'Have you reached a unanimous decision?' he asked the foreman of the jury.

'Yes, Your Honour.'

And do you find the defendant guilty, or not guilty?'

'Guilty, Your Honour.'

Chapter 66

It was amazing, the power of those three words. She'd heard a few cheers from the public gallery. One woman sneered at her, a clenched fist raised high into the air with hatred in her eyes and at that moment, Kate's knees buckled and she dropped to the floor.

This wasn't supposed to happen. This wasn't what she'd been told would happen. She had placed her trust in Saxon and the Swiss legal system, and it had failed.

She felt two pairs of hands lifting her from the floor. She was unable to focus, and tears filled her eyes.

Why?

A stranger's voice. 'Come on lady, on your feet, we need to take you downstairs now.' The next few minutes were a blur as the accompanying officers pushed through the crowd of reporters wanting a final few words from the convicted woman.

The cell was bleak, four whitewashed walls, yellowed with cigarette smoke, a stench of desperation, of hopelessness.

She wondered what her permanent cell would be like, the cell she would spend countless years. And then a thought. She hadn't been sentenced. Why?

Bernall answered her question thirty minutes later when the policeman opened the cell door and let him in.

'The judge will sentence you tomorrow. He said he wanted a little time to think.'

'Is that a good thing or a bad thing?' she asked.

'I don't really know. I can't remember it happening before. I think the jury's verdict took him by surprise, as did us all.'

'You weren't expecting that verdict?'

'Not at all, nobody was.'

'Saxon said in the beginning that it was bad news that the trial was being held in Zermatt.'

'I can't argue with that,' the lawyer said. 'I can't believe they brought that verdict in, but don't worry, we'll lodge an appeal immediately.'

'Don't waste your breath. I have no faith whatsoever in this fucking system. I didn't do this. He attacked me and yet they still convicted me.'

Kate buried her face in her hands and wept as Bernall tried to comfort her.

He told her that there was a press conference to be held in an hour. They would probably speculate on the length of the sentence. He said that it would likely be a life term, but under Swiss criminal law, a conditional release was possible after ten years.

Kate looked up, and between the tears. ‘That gives me great comfort.’

The sarcasm was not lost on the lawyer as he shrugged his shoulders. ‘I’m sorry,’ he said. ‘I did everything I could and, of course, I will handle your appeal.’

‘There will be no appeal,’ she said. ‘I don’t want you to appeal. I want to be left alone. I have no intention of spending the next ten years in prison. In fact, I have no intention of spending the next ten days in prison.’

‘What do you mean?’ said Bernall.

‘Take a guess. I’m an outdoor girl. These last few months have been hell on earth.’

‘But—’

‘You really have no idea, do you? You can’t begin to imagine what it’s like being told what time you go to the toilet, being told what time you can eat, when you can exercise. Not that I call walking thirty minutes around a backyard the size of a postage stamp exercise. It’s an insult to call it exercise. It’s ridiculous. I can walk the hills for three hours without breaking into a sweat, four or five hours in, I start to feel alive and only then does my breathing labour a little and only then if I keep pushing myself. I’m dying in that cell, the life is being choked out of me. I did my best to survive, but only because I sincerely believed I would be walking free. Now my life has come tumbling down around me and I don’t want to go on. I won’t live with nothing more than the hope of an appeal, and from what I've read that could take a couple of years anyway and I don't plan to hang around that long.'

The lawyer didn't correct her. He knew the system well enough.

Towards the end of the conversation, she asked if she could see Saxon. He told her that Saxon wasn't available, that he had taken a front row seat in the press conference which, he glanced at his watch, was due to start shortly.

'Why the fuck would he want to do that? They'll only be sitting there gloating.'

'My thoughts exactly,' said Bernall. 'I haven't got a clue why he wants to be there.'

Chapter 67

Rosalie Frei had once again taken centre stage. She had a seat alongside Nuessle who had, at last, made an appearance. He had been absent throughout the trial.

It was exactly the same setup as the previous press conference, other than Falcoz, who was conspicuous by his absence. *Unfinished business.*

Saxon took a seat at the back of the room. Nuessle gave him a glance, a smiling sneer followed. He had won. Or so he thought.

Unusually, Mrs Frei kicked proceedings off, commending the police for their splendid police work and waxed lyrical about her dead son for eleven and a half minutes. She talked about a memorial for him, one that she had already talked about to the Mayor of Zermatt and concluded by saying that she hoped the judge would hand down a sentence that befitted the crime.

The police were next. A spokeswoman said that they were pleased with the outcome and praised her team of hardworking and diligent officers.

The press were last. A fifteen-minute question and answer session. All the usual questions. Not one member of the press mentioned the evidence that had been withheld. It was as if they hadn't been at the trial.

And lastly, as planned, the young reporter from the London Times, the young woman Saxon had convinced that it would be worth her while for an exclusive, a once in a lifetime scoop.

She stood. She addressed nobody in particular. 'Gemma Stalane of the London based Times. I'd like to ask a question of the police, and that is, are they aware of the exact nature of DNA evidence that was not heard in court?'

Nuessle wriggled in his seat. He looked at the police spokeswoman and she looked the other way.

'A simple yes or no would suffice,' the Times girl said.

Nuessle. 'No we are not, we just know it is related to another case. That's why the judge would not allow it.'

'I see,' Stalane said, 'and will there be any police action relating to that err… other case?'

'No there will not,' Nuessle stated.

'And why is that, sir?' Stalane pulled out a piece of A4 paper. 'Because I've been given something quite extraordinary.'

Nuessle turned grey.

'Detective Nuessle, do the names Morgan Murphy and Selene Garcia mean anything to you?

Nuessle knew those girl's names only too well. 'Not that I can recall.'

'Well, that's very strange, because I believe that those are the names Mr Leonard Saxon gave you some months back. He asked you to specifically reopen those cases and you have failed to do so. Those are the two girls whose sudden deaths remain unexplained, the same two girls whose possessions have yielded the DNA of Heinz Frei as confirmed in a forensic report carried out by Professor Josep Falcoz.'

It started as a light murmur reverberating around the room. Silence from the assembled police panel sitting at the front. Saxon looked at the journalists from Zermatt, journalists that he now knew by name, Moosberg, Tarile and Waller. They were cemented into their seats.

Stalane sat down. She had opened the can of worms. Job done.

Another journalist stood, another Saxon invitee, Alain Merchant from Le Monde. 'And Susan Muller, Nadene Hanses and Taiya Jong, further forensic reports have been carried out on items of their clothing recently. They were still held in the police stations where their disappearance had first been reported. These reports were carried out independently, not by Professor Falcoz but by…' He read from a message on his mobile phone. 'TRATIC, the leading DNA recovery forensic laboratory in France. They have confirmed that Heinz Frei's DNA has been found on items connected with all three girls.'

Nuessle had nowhere to run, nowhere to hide. Rosalie Frei stood, signalled to a man at the back of the room, who walked up towards her and escorted her from the raised platform.

More journalists stood and started firing questions at the police. A representative from Reuters, the BBC, Huff Post and CNN, all Saxon invitees. He had even managed to persuade a representative of the Drudge Report to attend, with the promise of an all expenses paid two weeks fact finding mission, courtesy of the famous author B J Henshaw. The Drudge Report was co-created in 1995 with the help of the media mogul Andrew Breitbart and he had produced what was known as the biggest news aggregator on the web, with monthly hits estimated in excess of more than a billion.

As the journalist from Drudge, fired in a question about serial killers, he dropped the bomb shell that Saxon had fed him in a prior meeting. 'Is it also true, Detective Nuessle, that your DNA was found on a baseball cap relating to Antoinette da Silva?'

Saxon stood. He had seen enough. The pain etched on Nuessle's face was more than he could stand.

Plan B, he thought to himself. *Always have a Plan B.*

As he reached the door at the back of the conference room, he couldn't resist, turned and gave

Nuessle a wave. Then, with the same hand, he drew his finger across his throat.

Bernall had launched Kate Henshaw's case to the Supreme Court within four hours of Death on the Haute Route story breaking to an astonished world.

Three judges met seven days later and within twenty-four hours an order had been sanctioned for Kate's immediate release. The lead judge said at a press conference, 'The Swiss legal system had let Mademoiselle Henshaw down, Detective Nuessle's department in particular, had not performed their duties in a way that was expected of the Zermatt and Swiss Police.'

An arrest warrant had also been issued for Oscar Nuessle who had been missing for three days.

Chapter 68

It had taken Saxon little under two weeks to compile the report. It was two hundred and thirty-four pages long and just over sixty thousand words. Saxon detailed the DNA found on the possessions of the six murdered girls, Saxon used the term *murdered* on more than twenty occasions within the report.

He gave his theory that Nuessle had been the initial perpetrator of the murders and in a bizarre and sickening twist, passed on those skills to his son. The evidence against Nuesle had come to light when Professor Falcoz had found DNA which was not conclusive to Heinz Frei, but at nearly a 90% match, Falcoz had said that it was undoubtedly somebody very close to Frei, possibly a brother or sister. Falcoz didn't think for one moment that a parent could have been involved, nor did he know at the time that Nuessle was Heinz Frei's biological father.

While Saxon did not have any of the DNA evidence relating to the other sudden death girls, he laid out his logic and his reasoning as to why he suspected that nearly twenty girls had been murdered on the Haute Route over the last decade. He also supplied the photographs of the before and after bodies and the missing items, which he suggested Frei and Nuessle had taken as trophies.

Saxon had personally delivered the report to each judge, three days before they met in the Supreme Court.

Their decision had been unanimous. All three judges arrived at the conclusion that Kate was to be set free. There would be no retrial or no repercussions and they had set aside a considerable sum of compensation for the British girl.

Saxon and Becky were waiting for her in the car park as she walked from the large gateway of Gefängnis, Dielsdorf, a municipality in the Canton of Zurich.

Kate embraced her sister and then turned to Saxon. 'I can't thank you enough.' Tears. 'I doubted you a few weeks back when the trial wasn't going well. But then I knew you'd always have—'

'A Plan B.'

'Yes.'

The drive from Dielsdorf to Palézieux took two hours and when they arrived Becky had a little surprise arranged. She had paid someone to decorate the garden and the house and two young waitresses stood with glasses of pink champagne on a silver tray.

Becky announced that a private chef was inside preparing the evening meal. She turned to her sister.

‘I wanted to give you the exact opposite to the shit they have been serving you behind bars.’

As they walked towards the waitresses, Kate reached for Saxon’s hand. ‘Will you stay with us a while, Sax? I really owe you for this.’

‘A few days,’ he said. ‘No more.’

‘Where will you go?’

‘Cycling,’ he said. ‘Where do you think? You interrupted my world tour, or have you forgotten?’

Chapter 69

Saxon pitched his tent in the dark, five hundred metres below the peak of Pigne de la Le. He covered the entire tent with loose branches and foliage. His binoculars gave a perfect view of the Cabane de Moiry.

It was hunting season for ibex. It was only a matter of time. He just had to be patient.

He had to wait four days before Suter left the Cabane de Moiry. He left on the quad and headed down the mountain. Saxon tracked him most of the way into Grimentz. It wasn't difficult. The tracker he had fitted to the quad was well secured and hidden beneath the rear axle. He followed the tiny yellow dot on his mobile phone and as it came to a stop outside the main supermarket in Grimentz, he was satisfied that it was nothing more than Sutar stocking up on supplies.

It was day eleven when Sutar set off from the cabane on foot. He had a large rucksack on his back.

This had to be it.

Saxon followed him with the binoculars in the direction of the Zinal Glacier and when he felt it was safe to do so he broke cover and followed on behind.

They'd walked for no more than an hour when Sutar left the path and headed through thick grass towards a forest. As he disappeared into the trees Saxon hunkered down and waited.

Sutar reappeared fifteen minutes later with a fully assembled rifle strapped to his back.

Click.

As he headed westwards, a side shot. *Click.* And as he walked away. *Click.* A shot from behind. Saxon zoomed in closely on the rifle. *Click.*

It was three hours before Sutar returned to the forest. Saxon registered a little blood on the cuffs of his waterproof jacket. *Click.*

An hour later, the quad started to move and Saxon decided it was time to head back to the tent, carefully checking the route the quad was taking and giving it a wide berth.

He'd been at the tent for fifteen minutes, tracking the quad on his phone, when it made a U turn. Sutar was heading back to Cabane de Moiry.

Sure enough, a little later he heard the quad and once again picked up the camera and zoomed in on the neat structure perched high on the mountainside.

Click. The perfect picture as Sutar roared into the frame, a young, dead ibex strapped to the back of the quad.

Saxon dismantled the tent and packed everything away. He looked at his watch.

More than enough hours of daylight, he thought to himself.

Sutar had been sloppy and Saxon's military training in tracking skills led him to the rifle within five minutes of entering the forest. He followed a clear trail of broken branches, snapped twigs and footprints that stopped beside a large tree and started to climb.

Three metres up he located the rifle together with four boxes of ammunition and a ski jacket.

Chapter 70

He delivered the rifle and the ski jacket personally to the main police station in Bern. He felt that it was far enough away from Zermatt so that the enquiry would be taken seriously and investigated thoroughly.

He explained to the chief of police and three of his officers about the shooting of the two doctors and that he and a female friend had also been targeted.

'You'll find that the ballistics match those of the dead doctors,' he explained. 'And furthermore, Sutars's fingerprints are all over the rifle. I'm guessing you might get a little gunshot residue off the jacket, but then again, possibly not. It's been a long time and gunshot residue doesn't hang around forever, as you know.'

The chief of police had the case file up on a computer screen on the desk. 'And Sutar denied that he ever owned a rifle or hunted on the mountain.'

Saxon opened up his phone. 'What's your email?'

The policeman gave his email address.

'Okay, I've sent you some photos. Sutar carrying the rifle and a couple with an Ibex strapped to the back of his quad. Sutar is a liar and a killer. You'll find him in the Cabane de Moiry and he needs to be arrested and charged.'

'He doesn't know you have his rifle?'

'No.'

'But what if he finds out it's gone? He'll disappear for certain.'

'He won't.'

The Chief stood. Picked up the phone and dialled a number, spoke to someone for a couple of minutes before replacing the receiver. 'We are on it straight away,' he said. 'There's an armed response team being assembled right now, vehicles leaving within the hour. We have placed the Zermatt helicopter on standby.'

The police station was a hive of activity for the next fifteen minutes, by which time Saxon had disappeared out of the back entrance.

Chief Yann Henchoz of the Bern Police had decided to take on the responsibility himself as he walked towards the Cabane de Moiry terrace, lined with wooden picnic benches. They had been trying to communicate with Sutar for nearly two hours by loudspeaker. They didn't know what other weaponry he had in the cabane and had urged him to come out peacefully, unarmed, with his hands in the air but he hadn't complied, in fact they'd heard nothing other than a series of grunts and wails.

It was time.

Henchoz had his police issue revolver drawn. He was flanked by two police officers with assault rifles as they approached the main door.

Cautiously, he fingered the handle of the door… gripped… pushed. The door swung open without resistance.

'Sutar,' the policeman shouted. 'Armed police, we know you are in there. Come out with your hands in the air.'

It was clearer this time. Just one word. *Help.*

'Did you hear that?' he asked the two armed policemen.

They nodded.

He beckoned them through the door, and they proceeded cautiously.

They found Suter in the kitchen area of the cabane. He was naked, padlocked and chained to an iron radiator, and claimed he had been there for two days and nights without food and water. He posed no threat at all, and Henchoz slipped his revolver into his underarm holster.

He lay in a pool of congealed, dried blood and required hospital treatment. A pair of bloodied bolt cutters lay just out of arm's length on the kitchen floor. His right index finger had been removed and was nowhere to be seen. He babbled about never being able to fire a gun again.

'Who did this to you?' Henchoz asked.

Sutar shook his head from side to side. Tears rolled down his cheek.

The policeman used the bolt cutters to release him and allowed him to dress before handcuffing him, reading him his rights before leading him to the helicopter. Within the hour, the helicopter had landed at Sion hospital where a medical team were waiting for them. Sutar was in a bad way, dehydrated and undernourished. The early stages of hyperthermia had set in.

'He'll survive,' Henchoz told one of his police colleagues, who stood guard at the ICU entrance. 'It's that fucking military man, he has to behind it, but Sutar won't have it, he's absolutely terrified and won't say a word.'

'Who's worried?' the guard said. 'That crazy bastard's shot those two doctors and we have him. That's all I'm worried about. If he'd cut off another six fingers, it wouldn't bother me in the slightest.'

Henchoz exhaled. 'Well, it worries me. I won't have people taking the law into their own hands.'

The guard shook his head in defiance. 'He has delivered Sutar's head on a plate. For me he deserves a medal.'

Twenty-four hours later, there was more drama in the mountains above Zermatt. It was reported to Zermatt police and later to Henchoz and his department in Bern. A climber on the Gornergrat had stumbled upon the scene.

The Gornergrat was one of Nuessle's favourite excursions. He'd take the cog railway up to the rocky ridge, which opened up to give breathtaking views of the Matterhorn and the Gorner Glacier. He'd always felt alive up there, a place where his worries would melt away like the spring snow.

Not that particular day, though. Nuessle had issues, major issues and it was only a matter of time before his own men would ask the questions that he had no answers to.

His rucksack was light. A bottle of water, a windbreaker jacket and some gloves, his police issue P210-2 revolver.

He managed around ten kilometres give or take and sat down by a small lake, where he took a drink of water and sat down on a patch of dry grass. He reached into the pocket of his rucksack and pulled out the revolver. He checked the chamber and flicked off the safety catch. He pressed the barrel under his chin and four seconds later pulled the trigger.

Chapter 71

Josep Falcoz had finished his daily yoga session with his young instructor, a twenty-two-year-old student desperate to pay her way through college.

He always finished with a cool down, a swim in the basement pool, and then a massage.

They all had a price.

In the case of Dominique, it was €300.

When he'd first made the proposal two years ago now, the poor girl had run from the room crying.

But she'd soon returned. Falcoz apologised, paid for a three-month sports massage course and qualification and after he'd given her a wage rise, she returned to resume her yoga duties, supplementing her meagre income with a massage and then… the happy ending that she eventually agreed to.

She was a good girl, he'd told her it was a professional service, nothing more than that and he was an old man and couldn't have sex anyway, but this was the next best thing. His therapy, she was his therapist. For God's sake, she didn't even need to take her clothes off. But sometimes he insisted on that too.

'Thank you. Dominique, that was splendid,' he said. 'Your money is in the usual place.'

'Thank you, Monsieur Falcoz, I'll see you tomorrow.'

He watched out of the window as Dominique walked down the long gravel drive towards the gates. She was no more than ten metres from the gate when she stopped. Her hand covered her mouth and then she turned. Falcoz noticed that the colour had drained from her face.

He met her in the doorway. 'What is it Dominique? Tell me.'

'Why Monsieur Falcoz, it looks like someone has shot the heads off your eagles.'

Falcoz was livid. He dressed and walked out towards the gates. He had already contacted the police and they'd promised they'd be there as soon as they could.

He looked at his watch. 'What the fuck was keeping those useless bastards?'

He opened the gates and swung them wide open as they clicked against the magnetised locking system.

He looked up. 'Fucking bastards.'

The statues had been hand made from black opal and overlaid with gold leaf. If the vandals who had done this knew how much they were worth, they would have stolen them, not destroyed them.

‘Fucking idiots, fucking imbeciles,’ he muttered as he bent down and picked up a section of broken wing.

It was the noise that alarmed him at first, a whistling sound and then a dull thwack and then the shock as he lost the power of his legs and his knees buckled. It was a few seconds before the pain registered in his right knee and he looked down to see that his trousers were stained with blood. A small, perfectly round, polished pebble lay a foot away.

He was under attack. What was going on?

He tried to stand. Hopeless… his kneecap was shattered like a broken eggshell and he started to cry and whimper as he realised just how vulnerable he was. He rolled over onto his back. ‘Where the hell are those police?’ he sniffed.

He reached into his pocket and pulled out his mobile as he located the police number and pressed, *call.*

Chapter 72

The Bootneck Reunion wasn't something that he regularly attended, but this time was different. It had been five years since he had met up with some of the lads in 40 Commando and there was one man in particular who he couldn't wait to see.

There were about fifty ex-servicemen in the large open bar area of the Courtyard Hotel, situated in Oxford City Centre. He spotted a few familiar faces from 40 Commando and made a vow that he wouldn't leave the party until he had caught up with every single one of them, but right now there was only one man he was looking for.

He cast his eyes around the room and spotted him standing on his own at the bar. He was drinking water. Their eyes met and he raised his hand in the air.

Saxon walked over. They shook hands and the man wrapped his huge arms around him in a bear hug before planting a kiss on his cheek.

'For fuck's sake, Davey, there's no need for that,' Saxon said.

'Yes there is, I owe you everything, Sax. What's a little man kiss between friends?'

'You're getting soft in your old age. I swear I'll knock you out if you try that again.'

'I love you too, captain.'

Saxon shook his hand again, 'And I love you too, Davey Valentine, you're looking great.' He pointed at the glass. 'Still off the beer, I see.'

'Yes. I have it under control. I'm not teetotal, a few beers a few times a year, but never too much. It's been more than three years since I was drunk.'

'Glad to hear it, buddy. Are you having a beer with me tonight?'

'Absolutely, but not yet. Maybe a couple towards the end of the night.'

Saxon ordered a beer, and they retired to a quiet corner of the bar, as previously arranged. They had some business to talk about.

'Quite a decent result,' Valentine said, 'but you were sailing close to the wind at times.'

'I was convinced she was dead, Davey, but that book, it was that book that she sent to her sister that started the alarm bells ringing.'

'America, who would have thought that?'

'Not me. And then there was the trial. She didn't deserve to be put through all that shit.'

'But all's well that ends well.'

'Yep, and she asked me to pass on her thanks. I told her all about you.'

'I hope you didn't tell her my real name.'

‘Of course not. Don’t worry.’

‘Good, that’s good, Sax. My income depends on my anonymity. You’re the only bloke I work for who knows the real me.’

Saxon took a drink of beer, wiped a little froth from his lips. ‘Business good?’

‘Decent. I don’t need to earn a boat load of money. My pension just about pays the bills, but there’s a little work that comes in most months.’

Saxon reached into his pocket. He pulled out an envelope. ‘That reminds me, Becky sent you a little bonus.’ He handed it across to Valentine.

‘No need for that, mate.’

‘It’s not from me, Davey, it’s from the multi-millionaire, best-selling author B J Henshaw and she can well afford it.’

Valentine opened the envelope and peeked inside at the notes. ‘Fuck me, Sax, there must be five grand in there.’

‘She pays well, I know that.’

‘And there’s a note in there too.’

‘Read it. She might be after your number after all the good things I said about you.’

Valentine grinned. He pulled out the note.

Dear Flying Pig

Thanks for all of your help, this little bonus is my way of saying thank you. Sax said he couldn’t have found Kate without you, and your research is the best around. He says it’s unlikely that we will ever meet up as your work is very secretive in nature. I fully understand, but I do a few book signings in England and if you ever want to reveal yourself, you are more than welcome.

'Sounds like a nice girl,' Valentine said.

'She's adorable. mate.'

Saxon stood. 'C'mon Davey, let's join the party.'

'I'm right behind you. mate.'

As they walked towards the main function room where the party was now in full swing, Saxon stopped and tugged at Valentine's sleeve.

'What is it. mate?'

'Davey,' Saxon said. 'You used to love a scrap back in the day, didn't you?'

'I did mate, you've seen my file. I was nearly bounced out of the regiment at one point.'

'Well, I'm not one to encourage violence, but I have a little unfinished business in Newcastle. I might need someone to watch my back.'

Valentine grinned. 'I'm in the gang, mate. I'll have your back.'

Saxon smiled. 'There's no one I'd rather have behind me, mate.'

The End

Ken Scott has also written or collaborated on the following books.

Race Against Me
This Heart Within Me Burns
Do The Birds Still Sing In Hell?
The Girl in the Pink Shoes
The Monster I Loved
Twenty Years a Stranger
Ghost of a Stranger
The World's my Oyster
Who The Hell is Alice?
A Million Would Be Nice
Jack of Hearts
Revenge is Sweeter than Flowing Honey
The Blue Door
Sherlock's Squadron
Fitted up but Fighting Back
Call Me Mistress
The Genesis Chamber
In Violet Sleep
The Gate That Cried Blood
The Devil Couldn't Break Me
The Survivor
The Girl With the Flower
Undercover in a Jihad Training Camp
And then the Penny Dropped
Not all Robbers Wear a Mask
Two Cops and a Robber
My Journey Through Hell
Soldier, Prisoner, Hunter Gatherer
The Five Amigos
The Psychiatrist
Heroes of Lamsdorf
Simply Fate

The War Within
Cycling the Camino de Santiago
Under a Spanish Sun
Don’t Die Yet Dad
The Undesirables

Printed by Amazon Italia Logistica S.r.l.
Torrazza Piemonte (TO), Italy

71515690R00254